Meet Me At
RAINBOW CORNER

BY THE SAME AUTHOR

The Happy Hoofer
Not Quite Nice
Nice Work (If You Can Get It)
Sail Away
A Nice Cup of Tea
Orphans of the Storm

CELIA IMRIE

Meet Me At RAINBOW CORNER

WITH HISTORICAL RESEARCH BY
FIDELIS MORGAN

B L O O M S B U R Y   P U B L I S H I N G
LONDON • OXFORD • NEW YORK • NEW DELHI • SYDNEY

BLOOMSBURY PUBLISHING
Bloomsbury Publishing Plc
50 Bedford Square, London, WC1B 3DP, UK
29 Earlsfort Terrace, Dublin 2, Ireland

BLOOMSBURY, BLOOMSBURY PUBLISHING and the Diana logo
are trademarks of Bloomsbury Publishing Plc

First published in Great Britain 2024

A catalogue record for this book is available from the British Library

ISBN: HB: 978-1-5266-1635-7; TPB: 978-1-5266-1636-4;
EBOOK: 978-1-5266-1638-8; EPDF: 978-1-5266-7672-6

2 4 6 8 10 9 7 5 3 1

Typeset by Integra Software Services Pvt. Ltd.
Printed and bound in Great Britain by CPI Group (UK) Ltd, Croydon CR0 4YY

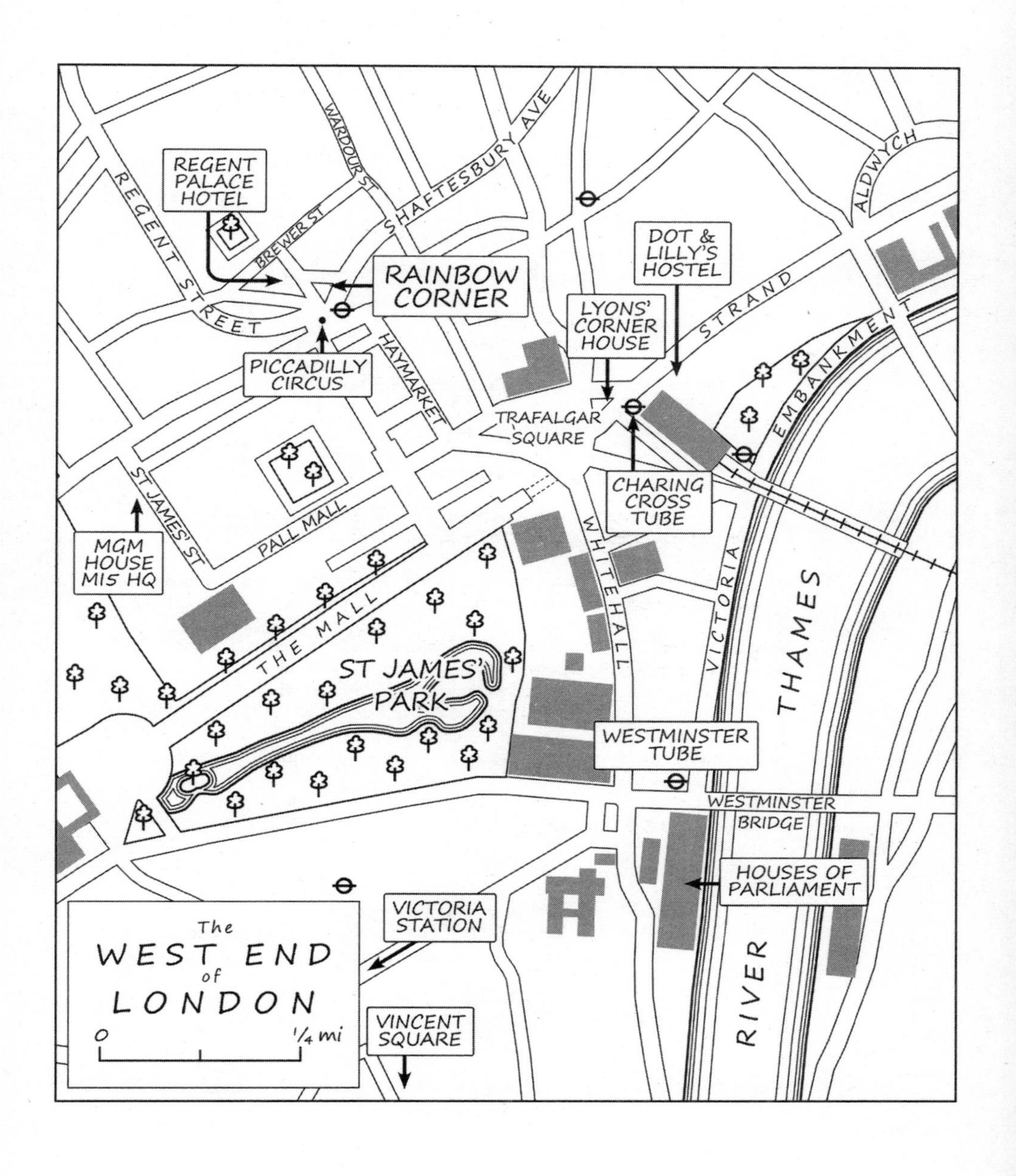

The WEST END of LONDON
0
1/4 mi
REGENT PALACE HOTEL
RAINBOW CORNER
PICCADILLY CIRCUS
DOT & LILLY'S HOSTEL
LYONS' CORNER HOUSE
TRAFALGAR SQUARE
CHARING CROSS TUBE
MGM HOUSE MI5 HQ
ST JAMES' PARK
WESTMINSTER TUBE
WESTMINSTER BRIDGE
HOUSES OF PARLIAMENT
VICTORIA STATION
VINCENT SQUARE
REGENT STREET
BREWER ST
WARDOUR ST
SHAFTESBURY AVE
HAYMARKET
ALDWYCH
STRAND
EMBANKMENT
PALL MALL
ST JAMES' ST
THE MALL
WHITEHALL
VICTORIA
THAMES
RIVER

CAST

PEOPLE AT RAINBOW CORNER

Dot Gallagher – Royal Navy VAD Red Cross nurse from Liverpool

Lilly Deane – ATS corporal from Haywards Heath

Nancy Newton – WAAF sergeant by day, hostess by night

June Worth – WVS by day, hostess by night

Liz Webb – Art teacher at Rainbow Corner's Dabbler's Den, hostess by night

Violet Beckton – WVS volunteer, on sewing corner, also works at the British Restaurant

Thelma – Young WVS girl, RC canteen by day, Lyons' Corner House nippy by night

Peggy Hunter – In charge of the canteen at Rainbow Corner

Gloria Fergusson – Controller, head of the Rainbow Corner office

Barbara Caruso – Married to GI Tony Caruso

Pearl Heaton – Pilot Air Transport Auxiliary. Drummer in all-woman band

Paul Rigby – Waiter at Rainbow Corner, also from Liverpool

General Andrew Smith – Retired US Army, works in Rainbow Corner office

THE GIS

Otis Oakewood – lieutenant, formerly billeted with Dot's parents

Jack Kirk – Chief warrant officer

Howard Hopkins – captain

Art Pemberton – sergeant, and layman of the church

Sydney Olsen – farmer from Kansas

Tony Caruso – Bronx Italian American

Marty Joyce – military policeman, former all-in wrestler

Virgil King – military policeman

Edward Cornell – Legendary American flying ace, first with the RAF then with the USAAF

Earl Young – From New Orleans, double bass in Pearl's previous band

Elan – Part of Jack's team

OTHER CHARACTERS

George Widmer – Baronet, British Army colonel, neighbour and family friend of Lilly

Billy O'Brien – Dot's childhood friend

Jean-Claude Toussaint – Frenchman who answered de Gaulle's call, previously guitarist in Pearl's band

Sister Sullivan – Ward sister at Vincent Square Hospital

Dolores – Donut Dolly

Clarice Titchmarsh – School friend of Dot and Billy

Norah – War bride, enters the story at Tidworth Camp

Maisie Froncek – Nurse and war bride, enters the story on board RMS *Queen Mary*

PART ONE

1944

Prologue

As she came out of South Kensington tube station, scurrying along the street, head down, the woman clutched her handbag tight. It would be unthinkable if some ne'er-do-well jumped her now and stole it. She didn't worry about the money inside. There wasn't that much cash there anyway. A few coppers and a ten-bob note. She'd deliberately slipped her ID card and ration book into her inside coat pocket as she left work. But this evening she was carrying something far more valuable.

It was just after teatime, but already dark and very cold. Everyone she passed left a trail of breath, coming out in clouds, hanging in the air like cigarette smoke.

Suddenly she could hear the thrum of scores of aircraft overhead, as she knew she would tonight. She glanced up. One searchlight caught the wings flying eastward through the narrow moving strips of light.

British planes – mosquitos, Spitfires – bearing the familiar RAF roundel on their wings. Some Yank planes were in the mix too, with their familiar star.

So she knew she could go on walking, secure in the thought that a warning siren wouldn't divert her from her route or some officious ARP warden direct her down into a shelter.

She turned off the main Old Brompton Road into the quieter Sumner Place, striding briskly past all the white stuccoed houses with their pillared porticos. Her heels clacked on the paving stones and the sound reverberated from the tall buildings.

Wait! Were those male footsteps behind her?

She paused and turned.

Silence.

She walked on, footsteps again. She glanced over her shoulder.

Just a lone GI, pushing open the door of the pub on the corner.

She walked on.

Once in Onslow Square she crossed to the garden side and turned the corner, edging along the railings. Only when she was opposite the house did she stop. Lights were on inside, upstairs at least. She could see the pale yellow streaks radiating around the edges of the blackout curtains.

Looking left and right, she crossed. She stopped and brushed down the front of her coat, then she tripped lightly up the five front steps and pressed the button for the doorbell.

She had expected a servant to open, but the man himself stood there, tall, elegant and good-looking. He wore a beautifully tailored pin-striped suit and a smart grey tie. Always the perfect gent.

He smiled.

'Good evening, my dear. I was beginning to think you had stood me up.'

'Of course not,' said the woman, clicking open her handbag and pulling out a roll of papers which she hastily thrust at him. 'I'm only late because the train got stuck in a tunnel.'

'Typical! They can't get anything working properly.' Glancing down at the roll, he nodded almost imperceptibly, then asked: 'Any more coming?'

'Give me time, sir. I'll be back in a few days. Either me or my friend. Things are hotting up, you know.'

'Oh, your friend. Doing OK?'

'Just fine. Hanging on, you know.'

'Where is this stuff from, by the way?' the man asked, pulling the elastic band from the papers and letting them gently unfold.

'I'd better be off now or they'll miss me.'

He raised an eyebrow. 'Are you not going to give me your source?'

'Rainbow Corner.'

'Rainbow Corner! Ah, yes. Memory not what it was. Anyway … wonderful!' He beamed, peering down now at the detail on the pages. 'Thank you so much, my dear. You're invaluable to us.'

'I do my best.'

'Excellent work. Thanks once more,' he said, pocketing the papers. 'Oh … and let's not forget.' He clicked his heels together. 'Heil Hitler!'

'Heil Hitler!' she replied.

ONE

JANUARY 1944

When the sirens started up, Dot Gallagher was sitting on her bed in the women's Red Cross hostel writing a letter home. 'Dear Mammy and Pop...'

She knew the drill. She'd been in Liverpool throughout the May Blitz. Air-raid siren – take cover, head for a shelter.

Putting the letter away and grabbing her shoulder bag, she threw her uniform cape over her shoulders, and ran down the stairs and out into the street.

It was cold, even for January. People were rushing towards the Charing Cross tube station.

Dot knew that London hadn't seen any air raids for months, and the real Blitz had fizzled out two years ago. What luck, to have arrived down here this afternoon, hours before the first air raid in months. What was the likelihood of that?

She prayed that German bombers weren't doing the same thing up north. With her not there to help, she prayed her mother would make it to safety. At this time of night, her father would be on ARP duty in the city centre.

Pulling her uniform scarf tight against her black hair and pinning it with kirby grips, Dot joined the crush pressing down into the shelter, carried along by the surging crowd.

After the loneliness of her room at the hostel, it was rather comforting to be amid so many people.

Grabbing tight to the handrail, Dot ran down the final flight of steps.

Somewhere up above she felt the dull thud of an exploding bomb.

She hoped that wasn't her digs collapsing. If all her possessions blew up, she'd have no photos to calm her when she felt lonely. No snap of Mammy and Pop leaning against the back door, blinking into the evening sun, in the yard of their house in Walton. No grinning Billy (wherever he was now), cap tilted jauntily to one side, standing proudly on the deck of his merchant navy ship.

'Could you give me a hand, love?' An old woman touched Dot's elbow.

'Of course, dear.' Dot supported the woman's arm, and they slowly took the last few steps.

'Get on with it,' yelled some young man behind them.

'I'd ask you to be patient, please, sir.' Dot shot him a look. 'There are people less able-bodied than you.'

'You tell 'im, love.' The old girl snorted. 'God bless you.'

Dot walked the lady along the station platform, until they found a place for her to sit.

She felt better for having helped. Though she knew it was only a pleasantry, being told 'God bless you' was a comfort too.

At the far end of the platform, Dot could hear a gang of men laughing. Then, suddenly, music started playing. Drumbeats. A dance band. Benny Goodman! One of her favourites.

'Sing, Sing, Sing'. A real uplifting song to blow the blues away.

You could stick your Vera Lynn and Jack Payne. For Dot, it was swing and jive all the way.

Picking up the rhythm, she politely stepped over the legs of people stretched out on the platform, their backs resting against the curved wall. She had to get nearer to the wonderful music, drown out her loneliness and fear.

Walking in time with the beat, clapping her hands, clicking her fingers. How could anyone resist the urge to dance to this? She swirled her Red Cross cape in time with the rhythm.

When she reached the end of the platform, she found the source of the music – a group of American servicemen operating a wind-up gramophone.

She quickly scanned the faces to be sure *he* wasn't here.

Then she continued dancing, as if she was in the mess room up in Liverpool after work. She and the other nurses always danced together to wind down. She'd have to write to Billy and tell him about it. She and Billy both loved music, bought all the latest records.

Suddenly one of the American boys jumped up and grabbed her hands.

'Come on, baby, you've really started something here! Let's go!'

She wanted to tell this man that she shouldn't really dance with him, she was engaged. Though that wasn't strictly true. She and Billy weren't *actually* engaged. But they'd talked about it in letters. Now she was waiting for him to come home and *then* they would really get engaged, like they'd always planned, ever since they were little children walking home from school.

As they jived, Dot tried to imagine this American boy's life. He moved so easily, smiling all the while, yet he must be thousands of miles away from home. She was only two hundred miles away and felt miserable. Dot knew that if she was really desperate, she could hop on a train and be home in a few hours. These poor fellows maybe hadn't seen their loved ones for years.

She grinned at him. He grinned back.

He had kind eyes.

'What's your name?' she asked as he pulled her close, ready to fling her out again.

'Howard,' he replied. 'What's yours, babe?'

'Dorothy,' she cried. 'And before you ask, no, I don't know any wizards and I don't possess red shoes, and if I did, I'd be too embarrassed to wear them.'

'A red-lined cape, though,' he grinned. 'Like Superman.'

When the record ended, another man came forward for a dance.

'Could I be next?'

'Watch out,' Howard whispered into Dot's ear as he moved away. 'Clodhopper alert...'

As Howard strolled back into the corner and sank down on his haunches by the gramophone, the new soldier introduced himself.

'I'm Sydney,' he said.

'Dorothy.' Dot smiled kindly. This poor gangly man was obviously nervous. Not only that, but a very awkward dancer. It was lucky she didn't have red shoes, as he repeatedly stepped on her uniform lace-ups.

'Where do you come from, Sydney?' Dot tried to make polite conversation. 'Is it very far away?'

'Oh no, up the road. We're stationed out of town. A place called Richmond, Surrey. Though to me the real Richmond is the capital of Virginia.'

'No ... sorry! I meant where do you come from in America?'

'You'll not have heard of it. A little place called Cottonwood Falls.'

'Sounds lovely. Pretty name. Is there a waterfall there?'

Sydney laughed. 'Kinda the opposite. It's in Kansas. Have you heard of Kansas?'

'My name's Dorothy. Since that darned picture came out, every time I say my name I hear of little else!'

'That must be perplexing, it's true.' Sydney didn't laugh. He just nodded sagely as though Dot had said something profound. 'Luckily, when you're called Sydney there are no such allusions.'

'Sydney Greenstreet?'

'No. My name's Sydney Olsen.'

Dorothy continued dancing, trying to keep her feet out of the way of Sydney's clodhoppers, embarrassed that her attempted joke had misfired.

When a slow song came on next, Dot decided to sit down and get her breath back.

'You jive well, kid,' said Howard, making a space for her on the concrete floor beside him. 'Like an American. Where did you learn your moves?'

'Working in a hospital with lots of your boys. Liverpool. We had a loads of your airmen and sailors stationed nearby.'

'I was up there for a while myself.' After a silence, Howard leaned towards her and said quietly: 'You're a very good dancer. I wondered if you ever considered doing it for the war effort?'

'What, you mean dance Hitler to death? How does that work?'

'You're Red Cross so…' He pulled out a notepad and scribbled some words in pencil. 'We have a social club, bottom of Shaftesbury Avenue, Piccadilly end. The dance hostesses they provided for us would be all very well for the troops under Abraham Lincoln – that's to say, for anyone who wanted to partner up for the foxtrot and waltz. But red-blooded Americans want to jitterbug…'

'I love the jitterbug!'

'… Well then, Dorothy, when you have a moment free, please drop by. Go up to the office on the fourth floor and speak to a crotchety old biddy called Controller Fergusson.'

Dot took the slip of paper.

It bore two words – Rainbow Corner.

'She'll give you the evil eye and tell you to scram. Then you smile your bright Liverpool smile and tell her Howard sent you. OK?'

'Yes, sir!' Dot gave Howard a mock salute, then glanced at his epaulette. 'I mean, yes, Captain!'

Someone put on Bing Crosby singing 'I'll Be Seeing You'.

'Come on!' Howard took Dot's hand, pulled her to her feet, then put his arm around her waist. 'It might be slow, but I love this one, don't you?'

As they danced in close circles, shuffling together on the crowded platform, he crooned into her ear: '"I'll be seeing you in every lovely summer's day, in everything that's light and gay, I'll always think of you that way..."'

Dot let herself relax. In Howard's arms it was warm, lovely.

She was fearful at first that he would try something on, his hands go wandering, but he danced so smoothly, singing along quietly. '"I'll be looking at the moon, but I'll be seeing you."'

A large woman with an umbrella came up, pointed to the gramophone and told him bluntly to turn it off. 'People are trying to sleep,' she shouted. 'You're barmy, you Americans! Go home. Or at least go to bed.'

'Ah, well,' said Howard. 'Just when the music was floating our cares away.'

Once the gramophone was turned off, it felt strange sitting with a bunch of strangers, so Dot excused herself, then picked her way slowly back along the platform.

She found somewhere to sit on a not too draughty landing halfway up the steps. Closing her eyes, she rested her head against the glazed wall tiles.

She wondered how everyone was doing at home. Would they be tucked cosily in bed? Would Trixy be curled up on the rug, so near the dying embers in the grate that his fur started to singe? Would Mrs Carey, next door, have the radio blaring full blast because once again she'd lost her hearing aid? Perhaps the St Vincent de Paul people had been round and her parents would have a new foreign airman to shelter – a Pole or a Canadian, perhaps, and he'd be creaking around in the spare room.

But that reminded her of the GI who had stayed...

Dot blushed at the memory.

She moved on to think of the nurses she'd been working with. They'd be walking the wards now, a tiny, dim nightlight on the desk, listening for a soft cry of pain. Perhaps they'd be chatting in the supply room, rolling bandages ready for tomorrow.

Dot felt like crying. It wasn't the first time she'd been away from home but this time it felt different. Mainly because all the other postings were a kind of promotion while this one was definitely not. Her first was a hospital at Barrow Gurney, outside Bristol. She finished her training at Oxford, staying at a very posh place called the Manor House, Stratton Audley, where everyone stared at her because she said 'bath' with a short A. Then, with her full uniform, including the swishy cloak, red waistcoat and shiny Red Cross badge, she'd been posted back to Liverpool.

It was all going so well.

But the matron at Crosby had treated Dot like dirt. Accused her of being some kind of temptress, stalking the wards to pick up men. But surely being kind to the patients, having a laugh with them, was all part of healing, wasn't it? These poor men were never going to recover if they only saw scowling, taciturn nurses growling at them in gruff voices. The poor lads were in hospital so far away from their loved ones. It would make you feel very homesick indeed if you never saw a smiling face.

But the final straw came when she agreed to go for a walk on the beach in the moonlight with that damned lodger. Always a smile with him. A smile and a quip. His tongue ran so fast you'd have thought he came from Liverpool, not Hollywood. He was scared he'd get lost without her to show him the way, he'd said. How on earth had she fallen for that corny old line?

Next day Matron went for her again, saying that she didn't take her work seriously enough and recommended her immediate transfer to London.

Because of the events of the night before, Dot had agreed.

The all-clear siren howling through the darkness above roused Dot from slumber in the early hours. Time to go home. Or what was going to pass for home for the months to come.

Slowly Dot trudged up the steps to the street. The Strand was in chaos. There were fires burning everywhere and many buildings were now reduced to smoking rubble.

'Scotland Yard's a direct hit!' she heard someone yell as he ran past. 'And Big Ben's on fire.'

Back in her room Dot went back to writing home. 'Arrived safely in London, just before an air raid. I danced with some GIs. They were very nice, especially a man called Howard.' She would finish it tomorrow, when she could talk about the new hospital.

She undressed, took the photos from under her pillow. She kissed her parents goodnight.

Then she looked at the snap of Billy. Poor Billy. When she'd last heard from him his ship was leaving Port Said, wherever that was. Billy himself never knew where the ship was bound until they arrived. 'Careless talk' and all that. She wondered if he would be heading into the Med, which would mean into the heat of the war action, and danger.

Please God, she prayed, don't let any harm come to Billy.

She put the photo down, scared that Billy would see some guilt on her face.

But she'd not really done anything wrong on that beach in Crosby, had she? That stupid boy who'd told her he came from the Golden State, where the oranges came from, and that he was an actor, and one day soon he was going to be a movie star and if she wanted to marry him she could be a movie star's wife.

It was all ribbing, she knew that. He obviously didn't mean any of it. Probably made it all up.

He was lonely, far, far away from home, looking for a bit of comfort.

And it was around Christmas, time of goodwill to all men. If there had been mistletoe hanging above them, no one would have batted an eye.

And, anyway, it was only a kiss.

TWO

THE TRAIN JOURNEY FELT endless. Nothing to look at outside, as it was too dark. Inside the lights were low, the blinds down. Blackout precautions.

Nonetheless, Corporal Lilly Deane was glad she was sitting next to the window.

The carriage was full. Opposite Lilly sat an elderly matron, squashed in beside a fat old man clutching a bowler hat tightly on his lap. Either side, two glum-looking soldiers in khaki battledress, rotating their caps between nervous fingers. Bulging precariously in the luggage rack, their huge sack-like bags made the sense of claustrophobia more intense.

At least Lilly only had one person pressing against her, a snazzily dressed man who reeked of pomade and bay rum. She couldn't see who sat beyond him and she wasn't going to lean forward and peek in case it gave Mr Snazzy the wrong idea.

As a child, Lilly had always found coming up to London from her parents' home exciting. Now, having reached the age of eighteen in time for the restrictions that wartime brought, it *should still* be fun. It *could* still be fun.

But not today.

She had been really enjoying her job in the ATS, driving vans, ferrying soldiers around or sitting behind the steering wheel of an ambulance, hurtling through the Surrey countryside, carrying some poor soul to hospital. So Lilly found it very aggravating to be forced to relinquish all that. Especially when the reason was so stupid – a totally avoidable tumble from her bicycle in the driveway of her childhood home. She had been larking about. Now she had to wear a splint around her ankle and walk with the aid of a stick. Doctors had warned her that this hideous state of affairs would continue for a few weeks, if not months. She had pressed her commanding officer not to send her home to convalesce. She told the formidable woman that she needed to go on working, to support the war effort in any way possible, recklessly adding she would do *anything*.

That was a big mistake. Some clever clogs in head office had hit on the horrible idea that Lilly should be posted to London, where she would work in an office.

An office!

She had always loved the outdoor life, adored staying on the move, the hustle and bustle, never knowing what would happen next. But now her horizon was predictable and bleak. She would spend eight hours a day sitting behind a desk in some grim room on the fourth floor, where no doubt even the windows were going to be grey, impenetrable with dust.

Her vinegar-mouthed colonel had even suggested that, if a successful replacement was found, Lilly might never get her old job back. She would stay in that office forever. Or at least until this beastly war came to an end.

The only office Lilly had ever been inside was the purser's office at school, and only then because she was in trouble. If the place she was working in was anything like *that*, she knew what to expect. No doubt some ancient dragon would be in command, an expert in shorthand typing, criticising every move she made, pointing out her mistakes with a gnarled finger.

When Lilly had asked the colonel for another role she secretly hoped to be asked to go on the training course to work on the anti-aircraft searchlights or even better, the ack-ack guns. But she was roundly informed that those jobs demanded even more physical fitness than that needed for driving a truck.

The American Red Cross building in Piccadilly, she was assured, was currently working at peak levels, though things were about to get worse as more and more GIs arrived to swell the Allied forces.

That stupid gravel! Why had she braked so sharply? She knew biking on gravel was lethal, and that it could only lead to a skid and a subsequent fall.

Lilly sighed.

'Sigh no more, lady.' An American-accented voice came from a man seated on the other side of Mr Snazzy. 'And that's a quotation from your old friend Shakespeare, so you can't ignore it. It's as good as an order from the high commander. You see, lady, you should pay attention to him.'

Lilly took in the body belonging to the voice – a uniformed Yank, mid-twenties, all white teeth and bulging muscle. She'd heard all the tales, but so far hadn't actually seen a GI, not in the flesh.

In a minute no doubt the jovial American would dig into his pockets and offer everyone in the carriage some chewing gum.

Even before she'd finished the thought, he piped up.

'Now that we've broken the ice, ladies and gentlemen, may I ask: some gum, chums?' The GI's hand shot out, proffering a pack of chewing gum. The fat man opposite took a piece as did both the British soldiers. Lilly could sense their resentment at having to be grateful to these grinning boys, ingratiating themselves with their presents: nylons, gum and good cheer.

The carriage relapsed into silence, broken only by the opening of the gum wrappers. Within seconds the carriage was imbued with the scent of spearmint.

'Clapham Junction, next stop.' The train conductor's voice boomed. 'Clapham Junction. Change for Vauxhall, Waterloo, and all services to the south-west. Also for Arding and Hobbs, or is it Harding and Obbs? Anyway, you'll find the place closed at this hour of night. Clapham Junction.'

A slight girl with short fair hair, sitting next to the GI, rose and timidly slid open the compartment door.

'Here, sweetie – let me get that for you.' The GI leapt to his feet. 'Hey, gal, you can't leave without accepting some gum.' He thrust a piece into her hand. 'You're a cutie – have two.' He gave her a huge wink. 'And another – take some home to your mom and pa.'

The girl accepted the pieces of gum and, blushing, left the carriage.

Rather than get the inevitable comment from the GI, Lilly disguised another sigh with a cough.

She wondered what the Red Cross hostel would be like. The girls who were billeted around Haywards Heath all slept in Nissen huts. Surely London wouldn't have those. Having only left boarding school a few months before the outbreak of war, four and a bit years ago, Lilly was used to communal living and dormitories.

'Victoria Station. Change here for London Underground and buses, trains to Kent. And, as they say in the news cinema – platform nineteen to all of you who want a quick visit to the flicks while you await your connection – "That's all folks!"' The speaker crackled a little, then the conductor's voice came through again. 'May I remind you to take your belongings. I don't want to be lumbered with forgotten kitbags, as clocking them in adds twenty minutes to my working day. Don't forget – I'm sure you won't – that, though Jerry hasn't been around the place for a couple of years now, there is still a blackout. God bless you all – and a particular thanks to all those in the services. Where would we be without you? Have a good and peaceful night. Victoria Station, next stop, terminus ... Oh and by the way, for all the Yanks on board, that means the end of the line.'

Grabbing her stick, Lilly got up and reached up above the seats for her suitcase, but it was already on its way down, in the hands of the GI.

'Here you go, ma'am.' The GI took a step back to allow her to pass. 'I'll carry this on to wherever you're heading.'

Lilly was torn. It would be an enormous help. She hadn't got used to this stick business. On the other hand she didn't want to feel indebted to this relentlessly cheerful puppy dog.

'I'm sure I can manage, Lieutenant.' Slinging the strap of her canvas bag over her shoulder, Lilly lost grip of her walking stick, which tumbled to the carriage floor, banging the legs of the elderly matron, who let out a yelp.

'Look where you're flinging things, my girl. I don't want to be wearing a splint. Not at my age.'

The GI grimaced in Lilly's direction then turned to the old lady with a smirk. 'Perhaps I could help you too, ma'am. Can I aid you? Might I perhaps take your purse?'

'My purse! Certainly not!' The old lady shot him a dirty look and flounced out of the compartment. From the corridor they heard her exclaim, 'Americans! Dreadful types.'

'I'm sorry about that.' Lilly was embarrassed. They might be brash, these young men, but they were guests here, volunteers to get them out of a hole. 'Most of us feel pretty glad that you all came over to help fight this vile war.'

'The old dame didn't have to be quite so snappy.' The GI pulled a hangdog face. 'Especially after I was only offering to help.' He winked. 'You know, I think she may have been jealous cos I was paying so much attention to you.'

'No, no. She thought you wanted to steal her money. Over here, a purse isn't a handbag. It's where you keep your readies!'

'Your what?'

'Cash.'

'Oh, that old English language of yours! Pity we don't all speak like my friend Shakespeare. "If music be the food of love" and all that.'

'Yes, it would be easier if we all spoke the same lingo.'

'So tell me, Corporal, whither are we bound?' Swinging her case, the GI led the way down the train corridor, leapt down onto the platform and held out his hand to help Lilly off the train.

In the main station concourse, Lilly glanced up at the clock.

'Eight thirty! No wonder the journey felt so long. It was thirty minutes late.'

'Sounds pretty normal to me.' The GI shrugged. 'Even in the US trains rarely run to time.'

Without saying anything, they walked briskly into Victoria Street. Lilly now felt strangely uneasy at the silence. She was about to ask him what he was doing over here, then remembered the 'Careless Talk Costs Lives' campaign and decided that the fewer questions about his military service the better; who knows who might be lurking in a doorway listening. Instead she asked: 'Is it your day off?'

'Doing a favour for a friend. Taking a birthday gift down for her sister, cos she couldn't get the time off or the travel permit. I wanted a stroll on the beach. But it was forbidden, lumbered up with barbed wire.'

'Listen, Lieutenant. You've been very kind. But I'm sure I can manage. I'm only heading up to Charing Cross. It's a twenty-minute walk. If that.'

'Aw, come on, gal. You gotta let me have some sense of purpose. I'm beginning to think you lot got us over here on false pretences.'

'How do you mean?'

'Well, I've been in this cold, bleak country almost two years. Stationed here, there and everywhere, north, south, east and west, and ... well ... nothing. Just boring drills and stuff we could as easily have done back home. I'm starting to think y'all made up those stories about bombing raids. Haven't heard one single explosion.'

'Oh, it happened. Believe me.' Lilly laughed. 'And it was terrible. Thank your lucky stars you missed it.'

The GI shifted Lilly's case from one hand to the other, then, focussing his torch on the pavement, he flicked the beam a little to the side.

'Nice legs, ma'am,' he said, passing her the torch. 'As a resident, perhaps you should be the leader.'

Lilly didn't want to admit that she'd only ever visited London to go to the theatre or the shops and didn't know the city at all well. She had checked her route from the station to the hostel on a map. So she went along this street till she reached the Houses of Parliament, then turned sharp left up Whitehall and she'd be near Charing Cross Station. The hostel was beside it, that was all she knew.

They trudged along silently, chasing the circular beam bouncing on the grey paving stones. Other people, shadows in the dark, office workers on their way home, soldiers on their night off, passed them.

At the corner of Westminster Square, the GI pointed.

'Here's the thing. I travelled all the way from California to London, England, and I can't even get a glimpse of that famous edifice called Big Ben, cos they wrapped it all up like a parcel. And you know what? I know they did it to spite me.'

As the GI finished speaking, the air was filled with the waxing and waning moan of an air-raid siren.

Above them a pale criss-cross of searchlights started to scan the black sky.

'What's that weird music?'

'That's not music.' Lilly could barely speak for fear. 'That's an air-raid warning.'

'An air raid? Seriously! Not a practice, or drill or something?'

'Afraid not. This is the real thing.'

'Oh, shucks. Opening my big mouth.'

Lilly had not heard a siren for ages – and that one was only a false alarm.

'We have to get inside.' She failed to disguise the tremor in her voice. 'A tube station, or…'

'I hear planes. Uh-oh!' The GI looked skyward. 'Lots and lots of planes.'

Lilly looked around for anything indicating a bomb shelter. Her parents had an Anderson shelter at the bottom of the garden. During the Blitz, they simply went down there. But here Lilly had no idea where to go.

'You know, I thought it would be exciting. But it's scary. Those are real Nazi planes above us, aren't they?'

‘I see them too!’ Lilly’s mouth was dry. She limped along as fast as she could. ‘We have to get to a shelter! Now!’

‘Agreed, kiddo. Heebie-jeebies. Get me outta here, you’ve gotta show me the way. This calls for drastic action. Prepare for lift-off.’ The GI lifted Lilly off her feet and slung her over his shoulder like a kitbag. ‘Hold on tight, and don’t let go of that flashlight. Direct me. I’m going to start running.’

‘Straight ahead, straight ahead!’

As the GI moved into action, the first bomb fell, exploding with a shuddering blast about 800 yards behind them.

‘Head for any blue light. That’ll be a shelter.’ Lilly lifted her head to see a building behind them burst into flames.

‘I see a subway on the other side of the square.’ The GI cut right across the road and onto the grass.

‘There! There!’

Bouncing against his back, Lilly grabbed hold of his belt to keep from sliding off.

‘These planes are right above us,’ he shouted. ‘Hundreds of ’em. Goddamned Nazi scum!’ He stumbled, wobbled for an instant, then walked steadily forward, speaking quietly. ‘Hey, peg-leg, point that flashlight in front, would you, not behind. I need to see where I’m going.’

Another bomb exploded nearby, throwing them both forward. Lilly felt herself falling as the GI ran forward, trying to maintain his balance. She hit the grass and curled into a little ball.

The GI scrambled to his feet. ‘Stupid statue in the way. Come on. We’re going to make it. Give me your hand.’

He hauled Lilly up and stooped to get her over his shoulder once more.

‘Don’t know about you, gal, but I don’t have an appointment in Samarra tonight.’

‘What are you talking about?’

‘Tell you later.’ He galloped ahead, crossing another road. As they lumbered into the Underground station, another explosion, only yards away, blew them right inside and threw them forward, tumbling down the concrete steps.

THREE

As a result of last night's escapade, it was no longer just her ankle which ached. Both Lilly's legs were now very badly bruised, as was her elbow and a large swathe of her back and buttocks. Rolling down concrete steps tends to have that effect. She and the friendly GI, whose name she had learned was Otis, had taken a bad fall.

In the early hours they heard the 'all-clear', but when they started the trudge up the steps of the shelter, an ARP warden was at the top, shouting to everyone to go back down and allow the emergency services space to work.

They had settled down for the night in a long, curving corridor, Lilly resting her head on her suitcase. Otis had tried to be a little touchy-feely, but she had warned him that if he got fresh with her she would knee him in the groin.

When she awoke, he was gone. She took a cab to her new workplace, and sat inside wondering how the other girls in Haywards Heath were doing, and whether the raid had affected them. Probably not.

At the Red Cross Club she gave her name to the smiling American lady at the front desk, who tried to prevent her entering as she was wearing a British not American uniform. Lilly rooted in her case and brought out the official letter with the details of her new job. After that the American lady was all smiles.

'The controller will give you a badge. That will be enough to ensure you don't get stopped again. Good luck.' The lady leaned over the counter. 'It's four storeys up. You'll never do it with a stick and a case. Might I keep the case back here?'

Lilly agreed and shunted the case around the counter. Beside the front desk, under the banner 'Is There Someone Here From Your Home

Town?', an enormous map of the USA covered in small red flag pins hung on the wall.

'That's so the boys can see if there's anyone here they might know from back home.'

Lilly was moved to see how many tiny red flags were posted. So many men leaving their homes to help fight the Nazis.

As she limped to the staircase she glanced around. She had never been anywhere like it. The mess rooms and service clubs in Haywards Heath seemed busy, but were little more than scout huts. This place, crammed with people hurtling this way and that, gave a real ring to the term 'like Piccadilly Circus'.

The depressive and burdened atmosphere which had seized England for the last two years was absent. The very corridors seemed to ring with joyous laughter. The support columns were decorated with coloured cardboard signs reading 'Washroom', 'Rainbow Ballroom', 'Cafeteria', 'Mending', 'Penny Arcade', 'Dining Room' and 'Dunker's Den'.

As she hobbled up the stairs to the office she wondered what exactly happened in the 'Dunker's Den'.

Lilly had been correct in her predictions about the office. Her boss was a dragon who went by the name of Controller Gloria Fergusson. The grim-faced lady, in her mid-sixties, spoke in brisk, short sentences and seemed incapable of smiling. Lilly had yet to see her breathing fire, and hoped never to do so.

However, although Fergusson was in charge of Lilly, she was not the real boss, for she reported to retired US General Andrew Smith, a ruddy-faced old gent with a shock of white hair not only on his head, but curling round the top of his collar, and on the backs of his hands. He seemed to have no formal duties apart from sitting in an easy chair, rattling newspapers and laughing at the strip cartoons.

The office was there to organise everything from visits to Parliament with Nancy Astor, to pinball machine tournaments and complimentary tickets to West End shows, catering for everything GIs might need while away from home.

'You can't type?'

'No.'

'What can you do?'

'Drive.'

'Not with that leg. Sort those...' Fergusson pointed to the corner, where two large mail sacks balanced precariously against the wall next to a large cardboard box. '... into that.'

Lilly emptied the bags onto a table. The red-, white- and blue-edged envelopes were carefully sealed with 'Examined by Censor' stickers and the familiar red triangle. Lilly felt uncomfortable that these young men's letters from home were being read by total strangers, but everyone was aware that if the smallest piece of evidence, the name of a platoon, ship or aircraft, fell into the wrong hands, it could be used against them all.

Once the mail was sorted, Lilly took the box, heading for the mailroom. But on the landing she saw it would be impossible to grip the handrail and carry the box at the same time. She thought of sailing the box down, but was scared that it would bang into someone, and that all her sorting would be a waste of effort.

A burly young man galloped down from the fifth floor. 'Hey, lady! 'Ow you doin'?' He stopped and cocked his head. He reminded Lilly of Popeye. 'Here. Let me carry that for you.'

Lilly accepted, hoping that Fergusson didn't hear.

'Mailroom, I presume?' The man started down the steps. Stick in hand, Lilly gingerly followed.

'It's what keeps us goin'. Hearin' from the folks back home. I'm a New Yorker, me. Run a famous eatery on Broadway. It's called San Remo, being as my family came from a pretty town in Italy called San Remo. I'm Italian. But you knew that.' He pronounced this as 'eye-talian'.

'I'm Tony, by the way. Tony Caruso, like the singer.'

'Lilly Deane.'

'I'd shake your hand but I'm holding this box and you need both hands to move,' he continued as he stepped down. 'The country boys suffer more than us city rats. They're more apron-bound, if you get my meaning. They live and breathe for those letters from home.'

At the second floor Tony swung through an open door into the mailroom. Several young men were anxiously waiting.

'There they are – the desperados!' Tony whispered, putting down the box on the table in front of the pigeonholes. 'See you round the place, Lilly Deane.'

And he was gone.

Lilly opened the box and looked with dismay at the rows and rows of pigeonholes. She had seen similar walls behind the welcome desk in hotels, usually with keys dangling from each compartment. Here, each letter of the alphabet was broken down further – so for instance, she had separate holes to fill for Ma, Mc, Me, Mi, Mo and Mu.

The soldiers pressed in on her.

She could see why it had been a good idea to presort.

'Hey, hey, hey, guys. Give the little lady a chance, won't you. Back off.' A gangly sergeant with steel-rimmed spectacles held up his hands and the men moved back. 'I'll help you, ma'am. I know some of these guys so I can pass them on directly.'

'OK, Art.' The soldiers backed away, forming a small semicircle around her. 'Whatever you say, Art.'

Art grabbed a large handful of letters and helped her. Aa-Ag, Ah-Ap.

Lilly had been told when she finished to take thirty minutes for lunch.

She didn't need to read the signs to the cafeteria, you simply had to follow the hullabaloo. Inside the swing doors, the cacophony was even worse. Lilly joined the end of the queue of uniformed soldiers.

Lilly wondered whether Otis might be somewhere in the building, but among so many American uniforms it would be like looking for a needle in a haystack.

She glanced at the plates on the trays the GIs were carrying off to their tables.

The servers seemed to be piling the food high. Hamburgers, chips, even steaks. What had happened to rationing?

When her own plate was also crammed with food, Lilly felt obliged to lean across to the server, a plump middle-aged lady bearing a name badge which read Peggy Hunter.

'I'm sorry but there might be some mistake, Peggy. I've more food on this plate than I usually get in a month.'

'You new here?' said Peggy. 'This is America, love. Once you enter here, there is no rationing. You're in the US of A.'

After the delicious lunch Lilly felt like a bloated whale. Her stomach wasn't really used to digesting that much food. She hoped she wouldn't fall asleep.

As she entered the office she got the feeling she was interrupting something. The raised voices she had overheard from the landing were replaced by a thorny silence.

She sat at her desk, wondering what to do next.

'I know you were up all night, girl. We all were. That's no excuse for just lounging around.' Fergusson slammed a filing cabinet shut and spiked across the room before spinning round to face Lilly. 'We do everything here but wipe their noses. How well do you know London?'

'I don't really.' Lilly decided to be honest. 'I know what the famous sights are, but I wouldn't know how to get from one to another.'

'So that's tour-guiding out of the way.' Fergusson pursed her lips. 'I've no idea why they sent you. Is there anything you *can* do?'

Fergusson had a point.

'Your predecessor, Sergeant Nancy Newton, was excellent. Well-turned-out. Exceptionally bright. Always so quick to pick things up. Knew London like the back of her hand. Great way with the GIs. But she had to...'

The general coughed in an unnatural way.

'... move on to other duties.'

Lilly felt humiliated. If only she could get back into a truck and drive away.

'Nancy is walking out with the distinguished American airman Lieutenant Colonel Edward Cornell. You may have read about him. No doubt you'll bump into her in the club. Him too. She now works in Whitehall by day, but at night she is still a hostess here. Many of the young men who come to this club are engaged or married to English girls.'

Lilly wondered how they would cope, these English brides of American servicemen, then realised that, while war raged, it would be much the same as dating British soldiers. Only when war ended would their marital status become an issue.

Fergusson rustled about on her desk and picked up a pile of airmail letters which she slammed on Lilly's desk. 'At least you can read English and know your alphabet. They're enquiries from families who want to contact their boys. Deal with them.'

Lilly started pulling the letters out of their envelopes. Some were written in shaky hands by mothers who hadn't heard from their sons for weeks, asking if there had been any news; others from wives telling of the birth of a baby, hoping that the American Red Cross might be able to pass on the details.

Lilly feared that some of these men, mainly the aircrew and pilots, were probably dead.

She decided to prioritise Air Force men, as they had seen much action, and suffered many losses. Then she thought it would be better to start with the letters which might have a happy ending.

General Smith whispered something to Fergusson, who whispered something back.

Lilly wondered whether her presence was causing this edgy atmosphere.

'I have a phone call to make.' Fergusson picked up the telephone receiver and her finger rolled the number barrel. She started flicking her hand in Lilly's direction, indicating with her head that Lilly should get out of the room. She cupped the receiver and hissed: 'Get us some coffee, girl. Two cups. No milk, one with sugar.' She returned to the call.

Lilly left the room so quickly that it was only when she was on the landing she realised she had left her stick resting against her desk.

She wasn't going to go back in to retrieve it.

*

Dot took notes while she was shown around by Ward Sister Sullivan. After an afternoon dealing with a couple of blanket baths and a few cases of first aid, she went to Rainbow Corner and climbed the stairs to the fourth floor.

On the third landing she crossed a girl, obviously in pain, slowly descending the stairs.

'Is this the way to the controller's office?' Dot looked at Lilly's ankle splint. 'Shouldn't you be using a stick?'

'The office is round the corner one flight up. The controller appears to be in a bad mood. Is it something important?'

'I'm looking to volunteer as a hostess.'

'I'd wait a bit if I were you.'

'Okey-doke. Meanwhile, let me help you down.' Dot flapped back her cape and held out an elbow. 'My name's Dot, by the way. Dorothy, really, but … I'm from Liverpool, if you hadn't guessed from the accent. Today's my first day in the big smoke. I'm trying to keep myself useful so I don't get homesick. I'm no good at sitting on my own in a hostel. The girl I'm to share with never turned up.'

'Not the hostel in the Strand?'

Dot nodded. 'Some run-down hotel they've commandeered, by the look of it.'

'What's your roommate called, do you know?'

'Nice name. Lilly Deane.'

'That's me! What a coincidence. Unfortunately I got caught in the raid and spent the night at Westminster tube.'

'I was in the Strand tube. But I did get out in time to catch a couple of hours' kip before work.'

'Because Big Ben went up in flames they wouldn't let us out, even after the all-clear.'

They took a table together. Dot got them both a coffee.

'What exactly…' Lilly spoke hesitantly, 'is a hostess?'

'You dance with the boys.' She laughed. Lilly had clearly got quite the wrong idea. 'Women wouldn't need them. But men aren't like us, they won't dance with one another. They think it would make them look like cissies. You should apply to be one.' Dot glanced down at Lilly's ankle splint. 'Oh dear. Wasn't thinking. I'd better get those coffees you need for them upstairs. Perhaps it'll put her in a better mood. Make it tasty,' Dot said to the woman behind the counter. 'It's for the general and the controller.'

'I think you'll find that's no milk, one sugar,' said the server.

When Dot glanced back to double-check, Lilly was facing the other way, waving into the corner. The room was starting to get crowded.

'I'm Peggy Hunter, by the way. Not seen you around before.'

'I'm Dot. Came down from Liverpool yesterday.' She smiled at the plump middle-aged woman. 'I'm a Royal Navy VAD. Hoping to be a hostess.'

'You wouldn't think there'd be a lot of call for Royal Navy nurses in London.'

'There are a few hospitals here. I'm at the one in Vincent Square.'

'Busy?'

'I haven't been here long enough to know.'

Peggy pushed the tray across, then pushed a stray hair back under her headband.

'Get it up to the office quickly before it cools down. Fergusson doesn't like her coffee lukewarm.' Peggy cocked her head. 'If you don't work here, how come you are taking up her coffee?'

'Oh, it's for Lilly. She's working up there, but she hurt her leg.'

'Doesn't do to get things wrong for Controller Fergusson. Does it, Thelma?'

Behind the counter a pale girl with wispy platinum blonde hair nodded meekly.

As she picked up the tray, Dot looked at Thelma, so frail and thin. Together she and Peggy reminded her of a female Laurel and Hardy. 'I suppose you don't have any special treats that the powers upstairs might fancy? I'd like them to be in a good mood.'

Thelma lifted a tray of biscuits from her end of the counter, from which Peggy took a pair and plonked them on the tray. 'That should get you the job.'

'Chocolate biscuits! I've not seen them in years. Thanks.'

'They're lovely,' said Thelma. 'Best reason for working here. Apart from the donuts.'

'By the way,' Peggy grinned, 'in here, biscuits are called "cookies". Don't forget! These Americans have a whole different vocabulary.'

'You're great, Peggy. Thanks.'

'The place would fall apart without me!'

Dot thought how nice it was to have such a motherly woman running the canteen, someone who must make the poor GIs feel at least someone was there for them as she dished out their grub.

'Come on, kid.' Dot turned back to face Lilly. 'We need to be getting you up those stairs.' Balancing the tray on the side of the table, Dot put out her hand to help Lilly.

'Hello, Skipper!' A GI behind her grabbed the tray from Dot's grasp. 'Fancy seeing you here!'

'Oh God! Otis!' Dot was so shocked she could barely get the name out.

'Don't tell me you two are friends!' Lilly slowly rose to her feet. 'I don't believe it. He saved my life last night.'

'We're not friends, exactly.' Dot knew she was gabbling. 'We hardly know each other. He was billeted with my parents for a fortnight.'

'And Dot is a cracker of a nurse.' Otis gave a knowing wink. 'Comes complete with aftercare.'

Dot was mortified. She knew her cheeks were redder than the lining of her cape. What was he trying to imply? The episode on the beach was nothing more than a little kiss.

'Miss?' Thelma, the pale girl behind the counter, called out. 'Dot?'

Dot turned.

Pushing in front of Thelma, Peggy held up a hand. 'Sorry. Mistake. Off you go, Thelma, and get some more milk from the storeroom.'

'Come along now, Lilly.' Dot took the tray back from Otis. 'We have to get this coffee upstairs while it's hot!'

Otis turned and waved at Peggy. He patted the end of his nose. 'Tell Thelma, Emily Bowe got her gift. Some old guy opened the door and took the packet, didn't ask me in for a cuppa, or even say thank you. Thought you Brits were supposed to have good manners.'

Dot wondered why Peggy glared at Otis as though he had done something wrong. But, oblivious, Otis turned back to Dot. 'So, Dotty, when you gonna take me for another walk?'

Dot offered Lilly her arm to balance. She wanted out of the man's presence.

'Nice to see you again, Otis. But I'm busy at the moment.'

Otis pulled the familiar hangdog face of disappointment.

'I really can't chat now. See you around.'

As Dot steered Lilly out and up the stairs, Lilly murmured in her ear: 'What was *that* all about?'

'A lot of hot air,' said Dot.

*

Back in the office Lilly could sense Fergusson's antipathy. She decided to ignore it and get on with her work. While she continued filing and sorting papers, she wondered why Dot had not come inside to ask for the hostess role, but instead thrust the coffee tray into her hands, pushed open the door and fled down the stairs without a word.

'As it's your first day here, I suppose someone should give you a tour of the building.' Pulling across the blackout curtain, Fergusson glanced out of the window at the darkening sky, then looked pointedly at her wristwatch. 'I'll buzz down and see if I can get one of the girls up before they go off.'

But before she got through to anyone, the dismal drawl of the air-raid sirens started wailing.

'That's decided it.' Fergusson opened the door, ushering the general out. 'Follow me, Corporal Deane. And this time, please do remember to take your walking stick. I don't like you wasting another girl's time because you feel coy.'

Fergusson flicked off the light and walked briskly down the steep steps, Lilly limping behind her. Office doors opened on each side, and more women filed out, heading downwards. Quizzical GIs poured from rooms, joining the flood of people, asking, 'Is this for real or just a practice?'

'Do we go to the Underground station?' asked Lilly.

'Don't be silly. There is a vast basement. An old ballroom, in fact. "Dunker's Den".'

As they took the final twist in the stairs, they could hear voices. The noise from below swelled as they got nearer. It sounded more like a party than a group sheltering from an air raid.

Fergusson stood at the balustrade and waved down to a large red-headed girl seated at a long table on the side of the room, under a sign 'Get Your Stripes Sewn Here!', with smaller signs along the edge of the table: 'Sew It Up!', 'Knit for Victory', 'Mending, Darning, Patches Sewn' and 'Make Do and Mend'.

'Violet, would you take this fledgling under your wing? Then, once the hullabaloo has passed, perhaps you'd show her round. I'm off to the officers' quarters.'

Fergusson left Lilly alone to make her way down the last three steps. There was a heady scent of food. It was sweet. Lilly felt as though she was in a dream.

Suddenly music started. An American tune. Glenn Miller's 'In the Mood'.

'It's nice that they have the jukebox, dear, ain't it?' Violet, the tall redhead, said loudly as she patted the empty chair beside her, indicating that Lilly should join her. 'Got one last set of stripes to sew on, then I'm all yours.' Violet had the dress jacket of a GI sergeant on her knee. The sergeant in question was standing nearby, waiting for her to finish. On the table before her, there were rolls of thread, pincushions and a stack of farthing coins. Violet took a coin and slipped it under the triple chevrons. 'I always put one in, for luck. You never know, it might be the farthing which stops a bullet and saves their life.'

While Violet stitched, Lilly surveyed the room. Hundreds of men huddled around tables covered with gaily checked cloths. Others stood in groups around the edges of the room, casually chatting, swigging from bottles of Coca-Cola.

'It's a novelty to them, these raids.' Violet lowered her voice. 'Till last night, most of them never saw one. But we've all gone through it for years, so...'

Another waft of sugary scent. Lilly could bear it no longer. She had to ask. 'What is that wonderful smell? I'm almost fainting from it.'

'Donut machine. Apparently Yanks can't go anywhere without them, so they've installed the thing over there, past the jukebox. It goes day and night.' Violet suddenly raised her voice and yelled into the crowd, making Lilly jump. 'Oi! Sydney! Grab a donut for my friend Lilly, would you?'

The man who responded was head and shoulders higher than the others in his gang.

'I'm a big girl,' said Violet conspiratorially. 'I usually tower over men, so it's good to find one taller than me. Sydney's from Kansas. He has a farm.' A dull thud reverberated through the wall behind their backs. 'Ooh!' she shouted. 'That one was near. Don't fancy going outside.'

'Don't be dippy, Violet,' grinned the waiting GI. 'That was the door slamming at the bottom of the stairs.'

'I always fear the worst.' Needle still in hand, Violet gave a short mock sign of the cross. 'Funny, isn't it? But this war thing doesn't get any easier.' She raised a fist and punched it into the air above her head. 'God 'elp us all and send those narsties to hell. Don't mind me, love, I go on talking, talking, talking. Anything to take away the fright. Did you lose anyone in the Blitz, dear?'

Lilly shook her head. She felt bad. The area around Haywards Heath had been rather quiet. She'd read terrible things about London, Liverpool and Coventry. Violet carried on speaking.

'I lost my neighbours in Newington Butts. I was out at the time, working down at Waterloo – the British Restaurant, you know. I was standing out in the open during the raid, and they were in their shelter. It should have been me, really. But that's the way luck goes, ain't it? After that, I moved. Couldn't bear looking in the garden, thinking about them...'

'Here you go, doll!' Sydney loomed before Violet's counter bearing a plate with two donuts.

'Go on, Lilly. Feast yourself. Who's the other one for, Sydney? You got another girlfriend on the side?'

'I wouldn't have the energy for two, Vi. You're enough of a handful for me.'

He handed Violet the remaining donut.

'You trying to make me fat? He's a horror. Eat it yourself, Syd. You need fattening up, lanky-legs.'

Lilly sank her teeth into the cushion of sweet dough. She chewed slowly, taking in the texture and flavour. After all these years of rationing and her mother's rather grim cooking, picked from their kitchen garden, it was like ecstasy.

Violet elbowed her. 'You don't need to treasure it like that, love. No ration books in here, no limits. Donuts galore. Dig in.'

Lilly was about to ask Violet how it felt, knowing that after the war if she was going to carry on with Sydney, she'd probably have to move to America, but was interrupted by Peggy arriving at the table with Thelma.

'Here you go, Vi. Give us a pair of needles and some thread and we'll help you out.' They both squeezed past Lilly to sit behind the sewing table. 'We're off duty really, but nothing doing till we get the all-clear.'

'I should be on my way to the Corner House,' said Thelma nervously. 'At night I'm a nippy.'

Lilly looked at the girl, so thin and pale, with her wispy blonde bob. She could imagine her in the familiar Lyons' waitress uniform.

Peggy picked up a jacket and started to sew a corporal's stripes onto the sleeve. 'My luck that the warning came as I was putting on my coat to go home, whereas, for Thelma, it's a lucky break.'

Just then a woman's loud voice made everyone look up.

'Good God! I had to run through fire and brimstone to get here tonight. Under no circumstances was I going to rough it with the plebs in Piccadilly tube.'

The woman in a WAAF uniform shouting down into the room from the balustrade was one of the most elegant people Lilly had ever seen.

'Oh, here we go!' Violet groaned. 'Her Majesty arrives just late enough to command the attention of the room.'

'Who is she?' asked Lilly. 'She looks like a movie star.' The woman's carefully made-up face matched the bravado of her stance – narrow, curved eyebrows, pale complexion and blood-red-painted lips. To top the image, a beauty spot on her right cheek was shadowed by her uniform hat, poised at a raffish angle on her immaculately cropped black hair.

'If I were you,' said Peggy, 'I'd steer clear of that dame. She's a tricky madam.'

'She's called Nancy Newton,' added Violet.

'Sergeant Newton,' added Peggy.

'A cut above us common slobs … in her own opinion.'

Lilly looked over at the GIs. They were staring at Nancy in subordinate admiration. Some of them looked as though they might start panting. Meanwhile, Nancy accepted the hand of one of the GIs to help her down the last few steps.

'She used to have my job,' said Lilly under her breath. 'How will I ever match her?'

'More to the point,' asked Peggy, 'why did she leave?'

'Just what I was wondering. Did she jump or was she pushed?' Violet grunted. 'I think the gen took a shine to her and Controller Whatsherface didn't like that one little bit.'

Lilly knew that it would be hard enough for her, but if Nancy was the standard of hostess that was expected around here, Lilly worried Dot would be eaten alive.

'Are you a hostess, Vi?'

Violet laughed very loudly.

'How could I be a hostess? I'd tower over so many of them. The hostesses are there to reassure the men, make them feel better in themselves. Anyhow, I'm busy enough as it is, working at the British Restaurant and coming here to help out.'

'Hello, Vi! I don't suppose Earl is back in town, is he?' A blonde woman in her late thirties appeared at the table. 'Have you seen him around the place?'

'Sorry, Pearl. None of his lads are in. Haven't seen them for weeks.'

Recognising the voice and linking it immediately with the name, Lilly looked up from the sugary crumbs on her plate. 'Pearl Heaton?'

'Oh Lord. Lilly, isn't it?' Pearl beamed. 'Fancy you being here.'

Lilly had last seen Pearl six years ago, in Paris, before the war. Lilly remembered Pearl had been wearing a pink sparkly top and slacks. Now her frizzy blonde hair was swept up in a patterned scarf and she wore a navy blue siren suit. She was shorter than Lilly remembered.

'Didn't know you were London-based, Lilly. I thought you lived out in the country. Home Counties. Mind you, since this ruddy war started everyone's everywhere. I've just flown in from Newcastle. Thought I'd pop in in case the old boy was back.'

When Lilly had met Pearl she had been playing in a jazz combo in a café, up in Montmartre. 'Do you still play in that group?'

'No. I'm in an all-girls big band. We play here sometimes, and all the airbases.'

'How's Earl?' Lilly asked.

'Haven't seen him for weeks. Been off on some manoeuvre. I was living in hope by now he might have got leave.'

'Did you hear from him?' asked Violet.

'We write all the time. Last known whereabouts – Sicily.'

'I'm surprised the censors let that through, Pearl.' Peggy looked up from her stitching. 'Don't they black out those locations?'

'Oh, Peggy love, I can read Earl like a book. And despite the censor we always let each other know where we are.'

'How?'

'He told me he'd had a glass of Marsala wine, and loved the taste of local lemons. So that's Sicily. A few days back he talked about eating couscous, so I'd say he was in North Africa. I could always write back to him and tell him yesterday I was eating a stotty cake. But as he's a Yank I doubt he'd get that one!'

'What's a stotty cake, when it's at home?' asked Violet, gnawing through a knot in the thread with her teeth.

'Down here we'd call it a bread roll, pet. But up in Geordieland it's a stotty cake.'

Throughout the conversation Lilly had been wondering how to ask Pearl about the other member of their band, a handsome Frenchman, who, one bright afternoon, had taken her down to walk along the banks of the Seine. Together they had sat in the sun, cradling a bottle of wine, tearing off pieces of baguette and smearing them with creamy French cheese. Jean-Claude had been every sixth-form girl's idea of a dreamy Frenchman. But now Nazis ran Paris. She hoped Jean-Claude had made it south to Nice, where his parents lived. But she feared that, after the German tanks rolled in, he might not even have been able to escape the occupied zone. She tried a less direct tactic.

'I presume you all left Paris before the German tanks rolled in?'

'Earl and me, yeah. We heard many of the French boys we knew were lined up and shot. Someone left a bomb outside Nazi HQ so they randomly picked up fifty men and…' Pearl acted out a firing squad.

Lilly felt as though an electric shock rang through her. Jean-Claude couldn't be dead.

'Luckily Jean-Claude managed to get out,' continued Pearl, as if reading Lilly's mind. 'He came over to London a year or so ago. Answered de Gaulle's call. I've seen him about now and then.'

'He's here?' Lilly's relief was enormous. 'If you do see him, Pearl, could you tell him I'd love to catch up with him.'

'In fact, he asked after *you*. So it's lucky we bumped into one another today.'

'Very lucky,' said Lilly.

FOUR

THE EVENING SIREN WAS a false alarm. But Dot still went to bed fearing that every vehicle horn, every slamming door was going to turn into another air-raid warning. All night long she was ready to leap from her bed, hastily dress and run down to the tube. But it didn't go off again. The next morning, Dot wondered if she'd have got a better night if it had. She roused herself and slouched down Whitehall, aghast once more at the ruins left from the previous raid.

It wasn't as upsetting as the sights she had seen in Liverpool, where not just offices and shops, but rows and rows of homes, people's whole lives, had been reduced to smoking rubble. The hardest thing was seeing bodies lying everywhere.

The ward at Vincent Square was pretty quiet. At the start of her shift, Dot noticed one of the sailors in the corner bed summoning her.

She went over.

'Black Bess! I didn't think I'd see you down here in London.'

'Sorry?'

'Black Bess. That's what we called you up in Liverpool. Your black hair, you know.'

Dot remembered him. Joe. A marine suffering badly from malaria after a stint in North Africa.

'How are you, Joe? What are you doing in here?' He was so thin and yellow-skinned, she realised she shouldn't have asked.

'Another bout of the old shakes,' said Joe. 'Only been transferred to London a few days when the fever started up again. I feel like death and look like a tipsy banana. Anyway, dear Bess, it's good to see a familiar face.'

'It's good to see you too, Joe.'

Dot caught Sister Sullivan's disapproving eye. She excused herself and went to the desk.

'What's going on over there?' Sister Sullivan thrust a dish containing a collection of thermometers into Dot's hands. 'I don't like nursing staff being over-friendly with patients.'

'I was treating him before, up in Liverpool,' she explained. 'He recognised me. It would have been rude to ignore him.'

'Nonetheless, Nurse Gallagher, there is a golden rule.' Sister shot her a look. 'No familiarity with the patients. Now do the daily checks. You know the drill.'

As Dot moved around the ward, filling in the patients' charts for the morning, she wondered why they had this silly rule. It must be nicer for the men to feel cared for, to see a friendly face, rather than be tended by grim-faced battleaxes.

While taking Joe's temperature, Dot tried not to catch his eye, but he pulled a face indicating his collusion. Fastening the cuff around his arm, she heard him whisper, 'Can't wait to get out of this place. It's not like it was up north. And, by the way, you still owe me that dance.'

'Hold still, please, patient,' Dot said rather too loudly while she pumped the rubber balloon to inflate the cuff, for Sister's benefit.

'Aw, you promised me, Bess.'

'My name is Nurse Gallagher,' said Dot firmly. 'And, OK, Joe, once you get yourself fit and well, I'll go dancing with you.' She remembered that as Joe had been in the same division as Otis, they probably knew each other. They'd both be at Rainbow Corner. If she danced with one…

She couldn't risk that.

So she added: 'We will go dancing, Joe, but I'm going to choose where. Somewhere different, a posh London hotel, somewhere like the Adelphi, instead of Rainbow Corner, eh? How about it?'

Joe tried to grab her hand, but Dot extricated herself, and went to take the temperature of the man in the next bed.

After lunch, a hastily devoured sandwich eaten leaning against a pillar in the square, Dot was sent to work on another ward, this one full of men with injuries rather than illness. She spent the afternoon replacing dressings and cleaning up wounds. Finally, at the end of her shift, she noticed Sister striding down the steps towards the exit, so she nipped around the corner into the medical ward to wave goodbye to Joe.

He looked perturbed and was signalling to her. Glancing over her shoulder to make sure the coast was clear, Dot rushed to his bedside.

'It's what you were saying earlier, nurse.'

'I can't chat, Joe. I'll be sacked.'

'There's something worrying me.'

'You don't want to go dancing with me now, is that it?' As Dot looked into his eyes, she could see that he wasn't doing at all well. His skin was bright yellow now. She knew the drug was so strong it killed almost as many as it cured. She smiled, reassuring. 'Well, Joe, I'm going to keep you to it. Fancy cocktails on me.'

'Not that. Rainbow Corner. What do you know of the place?'

'Nothing much. There are people there I…' She didn't want to fill in the name. 'People I…'

'That's what I mean!' Joe grabbed her arm with bony fingers and pulled Dot down till she was sitting on the edge of his bed. 'People who're on the other side?'

Dot didn't understand.

'I'm not joking, nurse. I followed a woman. By accident. She was going the same way as me, down to South Kensington, Onslow Square…'

Joe's hand was gripping her wrist, holding her down, shaking badly. Dot tried to remain standing. It was absolutely forbidden to sit on patients' beds.

'She was acting suspiciously, always looking back, checking. So I pretended to go into a pub, then, very quietly, I followed her. She stopped at some big house and I overheard her talking with this toffy-nosed fellah.' He tightened his grasp on her arm. 'There's at least two traitors inside Rainbow Corner. They're passing on information, working for *them*.'

'Them?'

'The Nazis.'

'Nurse Gallagher!' Sister stood in the centre of the ward, glaring at her. 'Here. At once.'

Dot glanced at Joe.

Was this sudden outburst about traitors a symptom of his illness, some kind of manic delusion?

'Nurse Gallagher!' Sister glanced down at her watch. 'Your shift is over. But while you are wearing uniform and are within my wards, you will obey the rules. I will not brook disobedience, nor disrespect. It's after six o'clock. Go home.'

Dot looked at Joe.

'I won't warn you again.'

As Dot turned out of the ward, she caught one last glimpse of Joe, staring wide-eyed, desperately trying to communicate.

But with Sister staring her down, anything he wanted to say would have to wait till tomorrow.

When Dot came out into the square, it was pouring with rain. She ran up to Victoria Street and jumped onto the first bus heading for Trafalgar Square.

Sitting upstairs, she stared out of the rain-streaked windows. The bus was foggy with condensation. She wiped the glass pane, creating a shiny semicircle which reflected smeary coloured lights from traffic signals. Green, red, amber.

What had Joe been trying to tell her? Or was it simply another symptom of his illness? Malaria came with all kinds of rages, anxiety and delirium. Joe's fever had been high this afternoon. Was he hallucinating?

But what if he was telling the truth? Could he have witnessed a traitor? Was someone in Rainbow Corner working against them all, aiding and abetting that monster, Hitler?

When Dot got back to her room, Lilly was there, sitting on her bed, cradling a cup of tea.

'Oh dear, Dot. You look all in. Get out of those wet things while I get you a cuppa?'

'That would be lovely.'

As Dot took off her cape, headscarf and Red Cross apron, she wondered whether she should confide in Lilly. After all, she did work at Rainbow Corner. And if anything *was* going on, it would be better to know.

Dot wrapped her dressing gown around her and flopped down onto the bed. What if everything Joe had said was simply feverish rambling, nonsense words? There was no point stirring things up if the whole thing was a fantasy. Before saying anything to Lilly, Dot decided to get more sense out of him.

Lilly came back and handed Dot the tea. 'I hope it's strong enough. Sometimes the ration makes you feel you're really only drinking beige hot water.'

Dot blew on the cup, warming her hands.

'So ... I've been waiting all day to ask...' Lilly sat crossways on her bed, resting her back against the wall. 'How on earth do you know Otis?'

Dot was thrown off guard. The only way she could apply the brakes was to reverse the query. 'Well, Lilly, for that matter, how do *you* know Otis?'

'He was on the same train as me, coming up from Sussex. Offered to carry my case, and we were caught in the open during the air raid. I was too slow with my stick. He carried me to safety. You?'

'He was billeted with my parents for a fortnight.' Dot wanted to keep the story as bare as possible. 'That's all.'

'Are all your parents' lodgers so familiar with you?'

'I like to be friendly. I got in trouble about that today.' Dot wanted to make sure that Lilly had no more questions about Otis. 'Otis was rather over-chipper. Cheeky, to be honest. Kept wanting to take me out to tea or for drives in his jeep.'

'Sounds lovely.'

'Not really. You see, I'm engaged.'

Dot caught Lilly's eye glancing down to her empty finger.

'It's not official, yet, but…'

'Haven't you noticed, Dot?' Lilly laughed. 'There's a war on. It changes everything. The rules have changed since we were at school.'

'What do you mean?' Dot imagined that the rules of romance had been the same throughout history.

'Before the war, how many people did you know who died?'

'Just my grandmother.'

'And since the war started?'

Dot thought back on the last three years. Of all the young men she had met and laughed with who never made it back from sorties with the RAF, of neighbours and friends of her parents bombed out during the May Blitz, of sailors whose ships had been blown out of the Atlantic, of shopkeepers and fellow nurses killed when incendiary bombs had burned down their homes. Of battered bodies she had herself helped to pull from collapsed buildings and put onto stretchers to be taken to the morgue.

'And you've probably had a few near misses yourself, Dot. Times when, but for a quirk of fate, you weren't in the wrong place at the wrong time.'

Dot had been blown across the room once, when a bomb had exploded on the road outside her parents' house. Had that Luftwaffe pilot pulled the button two seconds later it would have been them.

'There's a new intensity to life, Dot. We're living on the edge. The other night I fell in Westminster Square and it could so easily have been curtains. And this is true of everyone. We live, but we are surrounded by death, and there's nothing to guarantee that we'll make it. The bomb with our name on it could easily fall tonight … and then … what? Nothing. The end. We have to live now, not put it all aside for a future … which may not happen.'

Dot knew Lilly was right. All her school's religious lessons about eternal life and a hereafter seemed meaningless in this new reality. At school, for instance, she had taken her parents for granted. Now she worried about losing them all the time.

'Anyway, Dot, aren't you very young to tie yourself down?'

'Do you have a boyfriend, Lilly?'

'Yes. My parents want me to get engaged to him. But I'd prefer to wait a bit.'

'Is he nice?'

'I realise I haven't really compared him to anyone else. He's the type of man that a girl like me is supposed to marry. Came out of Sandhurst just before the war, already a commanding officer, a colonel. Father's a baronet.'

Dot laughed.

'It's a bit different up in my neck of the woods. All they want there is to make sure it's not a shotgun wedding, with the bride marching up the aisle with a six-month bump!'

They both laughed.

'How old is he?'

'Four years older than me.'

'My word, he must have seen a lot of action to be a colonel already,' said Dot.

'It's different when they've been through Sandhurst. They jump over all the lower ranks and go straight to the top.' Lilly lay back and gulped her tea. 'Not fair, really. His parents are very posh.'

'To me you sound very posh,' laughed Dot.

'George's father is Sir William Widmer. I mean, if I do marry him, I'll have financial security and eventually be called Lady Widmer. But the war has made me doubt everything, hasn't it you? I realise that I'm not cut out to be one of those nice Home Counties wives, especially a military one. I can't spend my days organising bring-and-buy sales, hosting beetle drives, joining the bridge club. And that's what would be expected. I'd be a twenty-two-year-old acting as though I was forty. All headscarves, handbags and dinner parties. Before the war I thought it was a lovely idea. But, after having such freedom, all the while realising how fragile this life is, I have developed a yearning for the sort of liberty that that safe life wouldn't allow.'

Dot could think of nothing nicer than being married to some handsome, dashing officer and keeping house for him. Even marrying Billy and moving into a little flat with him sounded lovely. But while this war was banging on there was no prospect of that, not for her anyhow.

'Have you ever been out of England, Dot?'

Lilly had a dreamy look in her eyes as she reminisced.

'I've been to Ireland many times, of course, and I was stationed in Wales for a bit.'

'In the summer of 1938, I was just out of school and went touring France with my parents. We went to Paris and the South of France, the French Riviera. That was the most glamorous place. All palm trees, beaches, cafés and sparkling blue sea. Nothing like here. Not the food, the people, the scenery. I'd been abroad before when I was younger, to St Moritz, Monte Carlo and Biarritz, but I was too young to appreciate it then. When this beastly war is over, I'd like to go off again like that, see different kinds of culture, explore.'

'Couldn't you do that with your boyfriend?'

'Not with George. A weekend freezing to death on the Scottish moors, grouse shooting with a lot of titled old bores would be more his idea of an adventure.' Lilly shuddered. 'I want sun, sand, palm trees, horses, music, exotic food. If I do marry George, I hope he'll understand that I will suffer his interests with a smile, but only if he will join me in mine without moaning.'

'The way you talk about him you've nothing in common.'

'We're the same class, live in the same area, know the same people, share the same interests…'

Dot thought of herself and Billy. Wasn't this exactly what she had with him too? Familiarity?

'We used to go riding together. That's how we got to know one another.' Lilly swung her legs over the side of the bed.

'Riding horses, you mean?'

Lilly nodded.

'You own your own horse?' Dot had read novels about girls who went off to boarding school and owned ponies. She tried to imagine cramming a horse into the backyard up in Liverpool and it was her turn to laugh.

'I never had my own pony, but George's family has about ten. A whole stable. Some of them are racehorses.'

Racehorses! Dot knew about those from the family's annual excursion up to Aintree to see the Grand National.

Thinking of Liverpool flooded Dot with gaping misery. Lilly looked at her and paused.

'Are you all right, Dot?' she asked.

'I don't know about you, but I keep going into despair.' Dot sipped her tea, gazing into the cup. 'Will this war ever end? It might go on till we're old and grey. Remember at school, "The Hundred Years War"? I couldn't live like this forever. I miss my parents and my dog so much, a roaring fire in the grate, my own little room. I miss not being frightened or brave or both all day and night. I want to go back to normal life.' She suddenly burst into tears. She was embarrassed to be sobbing like this. She pulled a handkerchief from her pocket and dabbed at her eyes. 'Nursing is a way of trying to help, trying to make it end. But there's no escape. I've already got on the wrong side of Sister Sullivan for being too friendly with the patients. Not a good start. Do you not miss your parents, Lilly?'

Lilly laughed. 'It's not that I ever saw much of them at the best of times. Brought up by a nanny, you see. Only really got them to myself a few times a year, Christmas and going on holiday in the summer. And that was usually some social thing for my parents. Fun for me, though.'

'Aren't you tempted to get a pass and go down to see them next time you get a forty-eight-hour?'

'Father is way too busy running Surrey Defence Volunteers – he's here, there and everywhere, training young men in bomb disposal – while Mums was last heard of in the Highlands of Scotland organising the Lumber Jills.'

'Who?'

'Forestry branch of the Women's Land Army.'

'It's silly but I just feel homesick,' said Dot, sliding between the covers and laying her head on the pillow. Both women grew quiet for a bit.

Lilly broke the silence. 'Perhaps it'll make you feel better, Dot, to know that I'm not coping that well in my office either. My boss, Fergusson, is a nightmare. And I just clapped eyes on her pet girl, Sergeant Nancy. Jeepers, what a dame. I'm not sure why she gave up the office job. I heard that General Smith took a shine to her. I picked up some frisson between Controller Fergusson and the hairy general, but I'm not sure what that's about. It's a strange place, Rainbow Corner. I saw a list today of all these women who are engaged or married to GIs, and realised what a huge step that was. Do you realise if their marriage is to succeed, they're all going to have to give up everything and move to America for good? I can't imagine it.'

'How brave,' said Dot. 'What a huge step to take for love.'

'I know. It gives a whole new meaning to the name Rainbow Corner, doesn't it?'

Once again Dot was tempted to tell Lilly about Joe. How there were people there who were not to be trusted. But she held back. Why stir things up when she only had the vaguest information?

'Oh, and that scary Nancy is also dating everyone's favourite GI.'

'Not Otis?'

'Otis! Good God, no! Why would you think *he* was everyone's favourite GI?'

'What you said before.' Dot realised that the colour had rushed to her cheeks again. 'I thought you had taken a fancy to him.'

'Oh God, no! Otis! Not at all. Otis isn't my type. A bit too up front, you know. Have you taken a fancy to him, then, Dot?'

Dot knew that the only reason she had refrained from applying to spend her evenings dancing at Rainbow Corner was her fear of being ensnared or shown up by Otis. But how could she confess this to anyone?

'No, Lilly,' she said. 'I have not taken a shine to Otis. Quite the reverse.'

FIVE

BEING A SUNDAY, NEXT morning Dot got up early to go to Mass before work. When she arrived on the ward she went straight to talk to Joe. She needed to find out more about his suspicions. Perhaps he could describe the woman. Then she would report the details to Lilly and she could tell her boss.

But Joe's bed was empty, the mattress bare.

Dot prayed that Joe had been moved to another ward.

Sister Sullivan came up behind her.

'I'm afraid he died in the night.' She gently patted Dot's shoulder. 'I know that you were on personal terms. A very sweet man.'

Sister escorted Dot to the staffroom where she made her a cup of sweet tea. 'There is a reason behind our rules, Nurse Gallagher. By keeping a distance, it makes moments like this a little easier to cope with. Not that it's ever painless to lose a patient.'

Dot slowly sipped the hot drink, realising the wisdom behind Sister's warning about getting too emotionally involved with her patients. Even though Dot hardly knew Joe, it was always a shock when a patient died. She felt very sad, but at the same time concerned that now she would never know what Joe had been trying to tell her about Rainbow Corner.

'Matron tells me that you have only recently moved down from living with your parents in Liverpool. And that you're staying in a hostel. Might I ask what you do to wind down after work?'

Dot shrugged. 'There was a raid where I slept in the tube station, and last night I stayed in my room and chatted to my roommate. That's it.'

'What are your hobbies? Or better put – when you were living at home what did you do with your evenings?'

'I used to go dancing, or round to a friend's where we'd play records. But I don't know anyone down here, and I can't really go out on my own.'

The sister looked down at her desk, and pushed aside some paperwork.

'They're looking for hostesses at the American Red Cross Club in Piccadilly…' Sister picked up a letter and read: '"Charming, beautiful English girls who know how to dance needed at Rainbow Corner." I'd say you fit the bill perfectly, nurse. You could enjoy your evenings in cheerful company, while doing a patriotic job.'

The world seemed set on sending her to Rainbow Corner. First Howard, now Sister Sullivan. The place might be huge, but while Otis was hanging around, Dot really couldn't face it.

'My roommate works there. But I don't really think…'

Sister picked up the phone. 'I'll give them a call.'

'I can't go there. I…' As Sister chatted into the receiver, Dot felt desperate. How could she explain her fears?

After exchanging a few pleasantries, Sister replaced the receiver and turned to Dot. 'I've spoken to Controller Fergusson. She's looking forward to welcoming another Red Cross nurse to the ranks of hostess. You'll be given an American Red Cross badge and an ID card at reception. So you're all set.'

How could Dot get out of this? 'But at the end of each day I'm so tired…'

'Spending time with others will give you a little bump up. They have dances about three nights a week.'

'I should be helping out…'

'You *will* be helping out. These poor American boys depend solely on letters from their loved ones, and us. They're here to help us out. The least we can do is cheer them up. A girl like you has much to offer. You're kind and warm, and at Rainbow Corner, your social qualities, while not encouraged on a hospital ward, would be ideal.'

Dot hadn't a clue how to respond to this compliment but how could she explain?

'No more buts, Nurse Gallagher. It's an order. You will report there tonight, or tomorrow I will be very cross.' Sister took away Dot's empty cup. 'Now go back to Ward B and put a cast on the left leg of the boy in the first bed. The bandaging and splint is all done, it's simply a job of applying the plaster. The mixing kit is over there on the table near the sink.'

Dot had done this many times. She rather liked the feel of slopping on the warm plaster, then smoothing it and waiting for it to set.

'Was the poor boy injured on training?'

'Silly thing was looking the wrong way last night in the Strand. Got knocked over by a bus. He's quite a card, this one. Not at all like Joe.'

At the mention of Joe's name, Dot felt sad again. She moved to the table, grateful for something to do. She emptied the white powder into a rubber bowl and added water, stirring all the while. As the mixture started to heat up, Dot hurried through to the ward and pulled back the curtains.

The patient looked up, with a sheepish grin. 'Hey, Skipper! When they brought me in here I was hoping I'd get you.'

'Otis!'

In her bewilderment, Dot started smearing the warm plaster onto his leg. Otis put his hands behind his neck and lay back.

'Now, Dotty dear, can you explain me one thing: why do you limeys feel the need to drive on the wrong side of the road?'

*

Lilly spent the morning and early afternoon painstakingly typing out her replies to the letters from anxious mothers and wives. Mid-afternoon, as she put the last letter into an envelope, the phone on Fergusson's desk rang.

'Controller Fergusson speaking … Yes? … Not again! When was this? … Certainly, sir. I'll have words with the general immediately.' A pause while the person on the other end of the line spoke at length. 'I assure you, we're keeping a keen eye on the situation.' Fergusson cupped her hand over the receiver. 'It's Blenheim.'

The general was on his feet now and standing very close to Fergusson.

'Pass it to me.'

The general took the receiver. Fergusson turned towards Lilly and glared. 'Coffee! Now!'

Lilly grabbed her stick.

'Take your time coming back,' added Fergusson. 'We'll need half an hour. Go to hospitality, would you, and pick up today's requests. Then coffee.'

At the hospitality desk Lilly was given a pile of handwritten notes from GIs.

She flipped through them while she waited in the long canteen queue. 'Where can I go for a long bicycle trip?' 'On my day off are there any castles I could visit?' 'Where can a guy go fishing?' She presumed that she would have to answer these requests later on, so tried to get some of the work done mentally. Hampton Court and Windsor for castles, bicycling and fishing might prove a little harder...

'Anyone seen Tony?' A woman cradling a baby wandered up and down the line, asking the same question, over and over.

'Barbara!' Peggy called out. 'He was in here at lunchtime. His CO hauled him off.'

Barbara smoothed the baby's forehead. 'Tell him I'll be waiting for him back in quarters.' She hoicked the baby on her hip and left the canteen.

'Poor Barbara.'

Lilly turned to find Pearl standing behind her in the queue.

'She worries so about Tony. Always thinking he's cheating on her. One baby down, another on the way, and the man's only been over here eighteen months.'

'Is that Italian Tony?'

'Caruso, like the singer!' Pearl picked up her tray and moved along. 'She's got a good one there but she doesn't believe it.' Pearl looked down at the bunch of papers in Lilly's hand. 'How's it going? She's a prickly old bird, Controller Fergusson, but she means well.'

'She hasn't taken to me.' Lilly waved her stick. 'I yearn to get rid of this thing and get back to active service.'

'Oh, I bumped into Jean-Claude. I told him you were here. He'll try and pop in later. I'm here all day rehearsing and hoping for a message from Earl.'

'Still eating spaghetti?'

'I presume.' Pearl laughed. 'Didn't you see today's headlines? The Allies have almost reached Rome!'

Lilly looked at her watch. Another fifteen minutes before she was due to take up the coffee. She got to the front of the queue where Peggy was busy making beverages.

'Peggy? Please could I order some coffee to take upstairs to be ready in ten minutes? They don't want me back till then.'

'Count on me. Important phone call?' Peggy winked.

'Blenheim! I suppose that's the palace.'

'Looks like you're stealing my job.'

Lilly had no idea what Peggy was talking about.

'I usually take the coffee up to His Lordship. Probably better for me if you do it though, those stairs are killers. Just pop back to the front of the queue in ten and I'll pass it to you. Meanwhile, a cup for yourself?'

'Please.'

Lilly took her coffee and went to a table near the door. Pearl joined her shortly after.

'Are you coming to the dance tonight?' Pearl pulled back the chair and then helped Lilly sit. 'I'm playing. I know you won't be jitterbugging, but you could tap your toes.'

Lilly was in two minds. It would be nice to have a quiet night in.

'And before you put it off, it's one night only. Tomorrow's fight night.'

'Fight night? What on earth is that?'

'Boxing match. The Yanks go quite mad about it. Can't stand all those punches, broken lips and flying sweat myself. If there's a night not to be in here, that's it! The audience gets very excitable.'

Lilly chatted with Pearl about Paris, and how sad it was seeing the photos and newsreels of Nazis goose-stepping up the Champs-Élysées.

By the time she glanced at her watch again, it was five minutes over time.

She waved in Peggy's direction and limped over to pick up the coffees.

'Give me those.' Pearl was right behind her trying to snatch the cups from Lilly.

But a khaki-clad arm reached out and took the cups.

'Corporal Deane, hand those over to me. And that's an order.'

Lilly was amazed to see George. 'What on earth are you doing here?'

'A little birdy let me know you were here, so I thought I'd pop in and catch you before you clocked off.'

'A few hours to go. How did you get in? The girls at the door aren't supposed to allow British uniforms in, unless by private invitation.'

George gave a huge wink. 'I have my ways.'

Lilly gestured towards her friend. 'This is Pearl. You remember, I told you about meeting her in Paris.'

'A lady drummer, if I remember. That would be a rare spectacle to behold.'

'You'll both come to the dance tonight?' Pearl asked as they headed towards the stairs.

George turned back towards Lilly. 'Why else would I turn up unannounced?'

*

When her shift finished, Dot went home, changed into her dress uniform and walked briskly up to Piccadilly Circus. Perfectly safe to try Rainbow Corner while you-know-who was laid up in Vincent Square.

At the front desk she was handed her new badge and directed to the dressing room.

A rather scary babble of women was already gathered there, chatting loudly while making up. Cigarette smoke hung round the ceiling like blue fog.

Dot took the first empty chair.

'I'm June Worth,' the woman beside her announced. 'You're new, aren't you?'

Dot was struck by June's misty blue eyes.

'You'll have to show me the ropes.'

'There are no ropes, petal.' June carefully smoothed her light brown hair back from her high forehead. 'You go out there, the chaps ask you to dance, and you dance with them.'

'Do they get drunk or anything?'

'Only on Coca-Cola! But they talk a lot about home. And to warn you, they have quite a few words with different meanings to us. If someone tells you he wishes he was wearing his best vest and pants, for instance, he'd not be an exhibitionist. That's a waistcoat and trousers.'

Dot started to panic. Maybe this wasn't the job for her. She didn't want to offend anyone by getting some silly word wrong.

June smiled and put out a reassuring hand. 'Don't worry, love, there's never much time for talking. The music's loud and lively.' June leaned back and squinted at Dot. 'You're a pretty young thing. You'll do well.'

Dot thanked her, patting June's arm, and noticed that she flinched. She withdrew her hand quickly, wondering why June had reacted that way. She felt a little awkward, and surveyed the room instead.

Women in matching sparkling jackets and long skirts started moving over to the back door, lining up.

'Do we have to dress up like that? I don't…'

'That's the band, petal. We wear dress uniform. You're lucky. A naval VAD uniform is a lot smarter than our WVS. Those navy jackets and brass buttons are so dashing, while we're stuck in drab green overalls.'

Dot was aware of June's thick make-up. Surely such an attractive woman didn't need to plaster on foundation and powder like that?

'You're new!' A young woman wearing an artist's smock grabbed the seat on the other side of Dot and started neatening her unruly black hair which had been bound up in a makeshift red turban. 'I'm Liz, by the way. I give art classes in Dabbler's Den.'

'You're late, Liz!' June gazed in the mirror, touching up her already ample eyeshadow. 'Been anywhere interesting, petal?'

'Not really. Work.'

'But there aren't any art classes today.'

'Day off today, so I went for a walk in Kent to see some green.'

Dot noticed that Liz's clothes and the backs of her hands were flecked with grey paint.

'I thought you said work? Why go to Kent? How about Hyde Park?'

'Cor blimey, June. I went for a walk in Kent, all right?'

'Whereabouts?' June grinned.

'I don't remember.'

'Don't be silly. You've only just come back.'

Dot watched Liz, who was clearly hating this interrogation.

'Penshurst.' Liz muttered the place name through gritted teeth.

'I know it well. There's a small airbase there.'

Liz spun around. 'How do you know that?'

Now June looked as though she was in the hot seat.

'Someone I knew used to work there. Before the war. Ages before.'

Music struck up, and the hostesses scrambled to their feet.

The ballroom door opened and a glamorous woman in WAAF uniform appeared, clapping her hands for attention. 'Come on, you lot…'

'Watch out,' sighed June. 'There's a Nancy about.'

Nancy shouted to the room: 'I can't hold the fort all alone. What are you waiting for? Armistice Day?'

A gust of 'Button Up Your Overcoat' filled the dressing room. Music! Dot's spirits rose. Sister Sullivan was right. This *was* the way to fill her evenings.

*

Lilly stood at the side of the ballroom chatting with George. The floor was full of dancers jumping and jiving to the lively tunes. She could see Dot, dancing very energetically with Sydney.

'I've missed you, old girl. Stupidly forgot that you were in no position to dance.' George put his arm around Lilly and pulled her close. 'Anyhow, this American music is a bit much, don't you think? Practically jungle drums. Let's go somewhere more civilised.'

Nancy danced past, snuggled up to an American airman with a head of blond curls. George jabbed Lilly in the ribs.

'I say! That's Edward Cornell. I must shake his hand.'

'Now is hardly the moment,' said Lilly. 'He's dancing with his girl.'

'He deserves someone as stunning as that.' Lilly felt George's fingers loosen their grip a little. She wasn't going to tell him that Nancy was something of a bitch.

But George seemed only to have eyes for Lieutenant Colonel Cornell. 'He was one of the first Americans to come over. Before the call-out. Flew in the Battle of Britain. Now he's a squadron leader.'

'How do you know all this?'

'An article in *Picture Post*. Lieutenant Colonel Cornell hangs around with the Lindberghs. He even owns his own plane and flies it over his home doing little displays for the neighbours. Imagine that! His own private plane.'

'Don't think about following suit, George. I don't think driving a tank over the neighbours' front lawn would go down awfully well in Haywards Heath.'

But George wasn't listening.

'Let's sit.'

He found a table by the dance floor. When Nancy and Edward sat nearby, George gave Lilly the nod.

'Keep hold of this table. Don't want you straining your ankle any further. I'm going over.'

Lilly watched bemused as George approached Edward Cornell. They shook hands. Nancy's face lit up at George's words. How Lilly wished she could lip-read. George indicated their own table. Next thing she knew, Edward and Nancy were moving over to join them, while George buzzed about moving chairs.

'I don't think we've met?' said Nancy, sitting in George's seat. 'I'm Nancy.'

'Lilly.' She decided to give no more information than that. 'It's a great dance. The band is wonderful.'

Nancy threw her head back and guffawed. 'Only if you enjoy being entertained by a gaggle of sad old dykes.'

Feeling very uncomfortable, Lilly watched the dancers whirl past. The band was playing a slow waltz.

'We have to pick up drinks at the bar,' said Edward, moving off with George.

'There go Gog and Magog,' said Nancy.

Head and shoulders above all the others, Violet and Sydney twirled slowly.

'So lucky to find one another. You should hear him going on about his place in America. His farm is so big, he says, "everything, as far as the eye can see". I'm always tempted to ask if he's seen a doctor about his short sight.'

George arrived bearing a tray of drinks, led by Edward.

'War damage?' asked Edward, pointing at the splint on Lilly's leg.

'Idiocy,' she replied. 'Riding a bike on gravel. Now I'm grounded. I so much preferred my old job, driving vans and ambulances.'

George spoke over her last words. 'How come you're slumming it in here, Edward? I would have expected you to be at the officers' club in Grosvenor Square.'

Edward inspected the pips on George's epaulettes. 'I could say the same to you, Colonel. I'm here cos of my girl.'

'Me too.' George stretched out and took Lilly's hand.

She prayed he wasn't going to announce that she was the new assistant in Fergusson's office, especially in the presence of the former one. But his voice took on the tone of a BBC announcer as he said: 'In fact, I am here tonight to ask Lilly whether she would make a limey soldier very happy by accepting this…' He reached into his uniform pocket, pulled out a small box and fell to one knee. 'Lilly Deane, will you marry me?'

The whole room took on a strange atmosphere, like a dream sequence in a film. Lilly knew she had no option but to say yes. With hundreds of people watching, how could she say she wanted a long engagement, needed time to enjoy some independent life during peacetime before she could settle down and dwindle into a wife?

But before she could say anything, a shadow fell over the table.

'Lilly? 'Ow are you? Remember me, Jean-Claude? Guitar player with Pearl?' He indicated the stage where the band was now pumping out 'Jumpin' at the Woodside'.

Jean-Claude clearly hadn't noticed he was interrupting something rather important. Shaken out of the moment, Lilly stood up and clasped his hand. 'Jean-Claude! Let me introduce my friends.'

The two men rose and shook hands with Jean-Claude.

But Nancy dragged it back to the engagement.

'Well, girl? Poor George! Aren't you going to give your answer?'

Lilly felt the blush rise. Cornered. Why had George staged this so publicly, without giving her a clue it was about to happen? If only to put an end to it, she said loudly, 'Yes!'

SIX

DOT KICKED OFF HER shoes, sank back onto her bed and reread Billy's letter. Tonight not only had she had an utterly exhilarating evening without a care in her head, but she had come back to find two letters in her cubbyhole. One from her parents, including a snap of Trixy lying in front of the fire, the other from Billy.

Tomorrow she would thank Sister Sullivan. Although she was exhausted, it was a good kind of tiredness.

She'd had a dance with Sydney again, taking care this time that he didn't land his size tens on her best uniform shoes. He had told her again about his farm in Kansas. But it was hard to imagine, as, back home in Liverpool, 'as far as you could see' simply meant the other side of the road. Sydney told her that in Kansas they had 'big skies', which Dot liked the idea of, even though she didn't really know what that meant either.

Then she had danced with a very serious GI called Art who kept pushing his steel-rimmed specs back up his nose while they danced. She remembered him from that night down in the Underground. Short for Arthur, he told her, like the king with the round table, which he felt sure had been modelled on the table at which Jesus took his last supper. Art explained that he was what is called a Baptist and that in his religion grown men have their whole bodies dipped in the holy water. Dot was rather relieved that it had only been her head which had been immersed, and that she had been too young to remember it. Either way, she felt that the dance floor wasn't really a place to be discussing Jesus. He had redeemed himself, however, by giving her a beautiful illustrated magazine all about America (which he referred to as 'God's own country').

Another GI had pointed out two men standing in the corner, whom he described as Snowdrops. That had made Dot laugh out loud, as they looked like great big thugs. But the GI explained that the name came from their white helmets, which they wore at all times, as they were military policemen.

Dot had danced with many men who knew Otis. They all rolled their eyes at the mention of his name.

It turned out that Howard had known Otis from his schooldays. He even called Otis 'incorrigible'. Howard seemed thoughtful and funny, a real gentleman. The army obviously thought so too, as he was a captain.

Dot turned to the back page of her diary and noted all the men's names. Part of the job was to make them feel at home, so she couldn't start calling them by the wrong ones. Sydney, beanpole, farmer. Art, religious, quite boring. Howard, captain, great dancer.

Dot looked up. While dancing with Art she had glimpsed Lilly, sitting at a table with scary Nancy and two men, one a US airman, the other a British officer, who she presumed was her aristo-next-door boyfriend with a string of horses. The officer got down on one knee and everyone started clapping. Dot was dying for Lilly to come back. Had she really got engaged?

She sipped her tea and reread her two letters, starting with the one from Mammy and Pop. The potatoes Pop had grown in a bucket in the yard had made a feast of mashed potato. A Czech airman was now in the spare room. His name was Karel, which had caused hilarity because Mrs Winskill, in the corner shop, had heard that the Gallagher's lodger was a woman called Carol, so when Karel turned up to carry home the groceries, she had refused to hand them over.

While unloading in Sicily, Billy's ship had been under fire. No one thought that the merchant navy ever came under fire, he wrote, but they did. The little cat they had brought on board in Cairo had died. Billy hoped to be ashore, with a forty-eight-hour pass next weekend, and planned to come to London … if by then Dot hadn't run off with some Yank. This was followed by a row of exclamation marks.

She took a deep breath and slipped the letter under her pillow. She flicked through the magazine Art had given her. America was much more than she thought it was. She had imagined a world of sky-scrapers but the photos in this mag were of vast green fields with buffaloes, gigantic waves crashing on rocky coastlines, long boulevards lined with palm trees and wide deserts scattered with gigantic red rock formations. It seemed such a disparate country, no wonder these boys were all so different. She put the mag down and pulled up the covers. She still couldn't sleep, so went down to the common room to see if anyone was there for a chat. But the place was dark and deserted, so she headed back up. Barely had she reached the second step when the front door swung open, and in walked Lilly with a man.

'Dot! Look!' Lilly held out her hand, a ring on her fourth finger. She sounded slightly squiffy. 'This is George, my fiancé.'

So she really *had* done it.

'Congratulations!' Dot shook hands with George. 'I'm so thrilled for you both.'

'We went dancing at the Savoy to celebrate. It was divine. And George did the gallant thing and walked me home.'

'The whole two hundred yards,' said George.

'There's a really famous dance band that plays at the Savoy,' said Dot. 'Carroll Gibbons. Were they good?'

'They were lovely. They played lots of romantic songs.' Lilly placed a hand on George's chest. Dot noticed that she teetered.

'Oops.' Lilly grimaced. 'I might have had one too many. I'll see you upstairs in a few moments, Dot. I'm just going to say goodnight to my … I can't believe I'm using that word … fiancé!'

Dot took the hint and rushed up the stairs as quickly as she could, leaving the lovers to their farewell. But as she turned on the landing she overheard George say: '*That* girl's your roommate? Dear Lord. She's rather common. I hope it doesn't rub off.'

SEVEN

THE FOLLOWING SATURDAY DOT went to meet Billy's train at Euston. She wasn't looking as good as she would have liked, as she had spent another night down in the tube station. On Friday night a storm of incendiary bombs had rained down on London. Curled up on the steps in the tube she hadn't got much sleep.

Dot leaned against one of the marble pillars and watched passengers streaming off trains from the north. So many different uniforms, so many war-weary faces, so many GIs.

Then she saw Billy, radiant among the khaki, the collar of his navy blue coat turned up, his cap at the usual slant.

She ran forward and hugged him.

'Boy, am I glad to see you.' She pressed her face into the rough dark blue wool of his lapels. 'I've been really lonely.'

'Hey, kiddie. Don't worry. I'm here now.' As they came out into Euston Road, he took her hand. 'Know somewhere good for lunch? I'm ravenous.'

'There's a Lyons' Corner House opposite my digs. You can drop your kitbag in my room.'

'Lead me there, kiddie.'

As the sun was shining, after lunch they went to Trafalgar Square and sat on the steps beneath the lions, watching a gaggle of WRNs feeding the pigeons.

They chatted about Liverpool, Billy's escapades on the convoy through the Mediterranean and Dot's new jobs, both as nurse and hostess at Rainbow Corner.

'Matron a dragon?'

'Ward sister. She's strict but fair.'

'What are the patients like? Are they nice to you?'

Dot wasn't going to tell him about Otis, especially as he had now been issued a pair of crutches and released. The only other patient she could think to mention was Joe. She told Billy about the strange things he had whispered so urgently.

'Have you said anything?'

Dot shook her head. 'It all sounds so fantastical.'

Billy fiddled with the fingers of his gloves. 'How well do you know the authorities at Rainbow Corner?'

'Not at all. I go in the evenings straight to the dressing room and onto the dance floor. My roommate works in the office.'

'Tell her, then.'

Dot couldn't bear to explain that since that crushing remark of George's, Dot had been doing her best to avoid Lilly.

'That's the answer,' said Billy, patting her knee. 'Has anyone there caught your eye doing anything suspicious?'

'Just people dancing and having a good time.'

'What about the other girls? Any of them strange?'

'There's one woman there who frightens me. She looks like Margaret Lockwood and has a very sharp tongue.'

'She hang around with any Nazi-looking types?'

'No.' Dot laughed at the thought. 'Only one of the most famous American fighter pilots.'

Billy shrugged. 'Unless she's using him to get information…'

'Everyone at Rainbow Corner seems so lovely. It is hard to believe there's a traitor among them. Sometimes I wonder whether it might have been Joe's fever talking.'

Billy looked up. 'Do you know any other GIs? Someone in Liverpool who might perhaps have known Joe, someone he might have confided in?'

The heat Dot felt on her cheeks must be showing as a deep scarlet blush.

'There were two men in his division. Howard and Otis. Howard goes quite often to Rainbow Corner.'

'And Otis?'

'He broke his leg. He was on one of my wards for a few days but he was discharged.'

'Really, Dot!' Billy threw his hands up. 'While he was captive in your own hospital, didn't you even think of asking him? How can you have flunked that?'

Dot wondered if now was the time to confess the kiss to Billy. Get it over and done with. It might make her feel better to tell him. Like going to confession.

Before she could open her mouth, Billy had seized her arm and was leading her through the narrow streets up to Piccadilly Circus.

'We're going there now.'

'Hey, mate!' A male voice from across the road. 'Too lily-livered to join the services?'

Dot looked up to see a gang of British soldiers staggering out of a pub, pointing at Billy.

'Leave him alone,' she said. 'He's merchant navy. They don't wear uniform.'

Billy shouted back: 'I'll have you know I've stood on the deck with Nazi planes firing at us while we zigzagged through U-boat torpedoes...'

Dot could feel Billy straining forward, eager to fight. She gripped his elbow, holding him back, but he went on yelling at the soldiers.

'And you know what we were doing? Picking up sugar and iron and all kinds of things to bring home for you, you fat, lazy loafers. How much action have you seen? Come on? Sat in some camp in Salisbury doing damn all, I suspect.'

'Don't bother with them, Billy.' Dot tugged at Billy's sleeve and managed to get him away. 'They're drunk.'

'Probably had to get drunk cos they're worried they might be sent where the action is.' Billy brushed himself down as he walked away. 'Nobody seems to understand that without the merchant navy, Britain would be cut off, with hardly any food or raw materials. We're as much a part of the war effort as they are.'

Dot was relieved when they finally reached the doors of Rainbow Corner and they could change the subject.

At the front desk, Billy asked whether Howard or Otis was in.

The girl looked at him, stupefied.

'The place is packed. We have hundreds of men here.'

Billy looked over to the huge wall map.

'Where are they from, kiddie?'

'California. Los Angeles.'

Billy moved to the western side of the map and stared examining the little red flags. While his back was turned, Dot saw Howard entering, Otis at his side. She turned away from them to face the map. But Billy looked around, saw the crutches and lurched forward.

'Hey, you! GI? Are you Otis?'

'Who wants to know?'

'I do,' replied Billy, squaring up to him, blocking his way forward.

'Hey, Skipper,' yelled Otis. 'Ain't you going to say hello?' He pointed over Billy's shoulder. 'That's everybody's favourite nurse over there, she's called Dot.'

Dot turned and faked surprise at seeing him.

'Oh, Otis! This is my fiancé, Billy O'Brien.' She put emphasis on the word fiancé. 'He needs to speak to you both on a serious matter.'

'Fiancé?' Billy turned to her. 'Is that a proposal?'

Dot squirmed. The situation was getting worse by the second.

'What do you need to talk about, sir?' Howard spoke calmly, putting himself slightly between Otis and Billy.

'Outside would be better.' Billy's tone was rather too heavy for Dot's liking. As they moved out of the building and down to the circus, she noticed Howard throw Otis a dirty look. In silence they walked to the steps beneath the boxed-up statue of Eros. They sat.

Billy made Dot tell the story of Joe. Both Howard and Otis were pop-eyed.

'Someone inside our club is feeding info to the Nazis?'

'That's what Joe was implying,' said Billy.

'But he did have a very high fever.' Dot wanted to remove the tension from the situation. 'Delirious people say strange things.'

'Shut up, Dot. You're not helping.' Billy turned his back to her. 'My ship was near blown out of the water last week. I'm merchant navy. If anyone is feeding information against us, I want to know about it.'

'Really, there's no need to get snippy with us.' Howard put up his hands, appeasing. 'Let's face it, sir, if there's a Nazi informant working inside our club, it's likely to affect us Yanks more than you British boys.'

'Get lost!' Billy leapt to his feet. Dot feared he was about to raise his fists. 'Don't patronise me.' Billy stepped forward as Otis clambered to stand. He looked as though he was going to kick away Otis's crutches.

Dot pulled at Billy's coat. 'Let these two men enjoy their day off, Billy. You'll be back in Liverpool tomorrow night. Come away.'

As she led Billy through the traffic, she turned back and mouthed, 'Sorry!'

She saw Howard make a placatory gesture, while Otis was shaking his head, eyebrows raised, indicating that Billy was a mad man.

'Those Americans earn five times our pay. More probably,' Billy grumbled. 'Come over here, grinning like loons, doling out nylons and gum, flashing their sparkling teeth, thinking the world owes them a living…'

Dot didn't like to tell him about all the food in the club or the English girls who had fallen in love with these men and planned to move to America with them as soon as the war was over.

The rest of the day was tense.

Next morning Dot met Billy to go to Sunday Mass at Westminster Cathedral.

As they came out into the milky January sunlight, Dot said to Billy: 'I have an idea. If you find it so difficult in your job during wartime, why not sign up for the Royal Navy?'

'I'm happy where I work. I don't want to start all over again at the bottom.'

'I thought…'

'No, you didn't think, Dot. Always impressed by a fancy uniform with brass buttons, weren't you?'

It might as well have been a punch.

'Now you're down here, you think you're so sophisticated. You've changed. Whatever happened to the little girl I was at school with?'

'Little girl?' Dot took a step back. 'I grew up, Billy.' How could he expect her *not* to change? Everyone had changed. 'There's a war on, Billy. We've all had to grow up, and grow up bloody fast. At school I wasn't accustomed to pulling broken and bloody bodies out of collapsed, burned-out buildings, were you? Day after day during the May Blitz I helped my pa do that. But you were out of Liverpool then, weren't you, Billy? The nearest I got to danger as a kid was reading about William and his outlaws. But now death is everywhere, stalking us. Things have changed, Billy, and so have I. And I'm not going to be made to feel ashamed of that. And anyway, if it comes to that, what happened to the little boy *I* was at school with?'

Billy stood silently, staring at his boots.

'You even talk differently,' Billy said without looking up. 'Oh so posh now, aren't we, Dot? A couple of air-raid warnings, the odd bomb going off, and suddenly you turn into Princess Elizabeth.'

What a week! George said she was too common, and now Billy, who she'd known since she was five years old, telling her she was too posh.

'I think you should go and have a lie-down, Billy. I can't take it when you're like this.'

'In the way, am I?'

'Don't be ridiculous. But you're obviously tired. You might say I've changed but I can hardly recognise you now either.'

'Before you send me away, Dot, at least explain what your smug gum-chum meant when he called you "everybody's favourite nurse"? Are you spreading it about? Is that it, Dot? Is that the London way of doing things with those grinning, spoiled-brat Yanks?'

Dot swung round and slapped Billy's face.

Tears brimming in her eyes, she strode away. Unable to think where to go, she walked briskly in the direction of Vincent Square.

Billy did not follow.

*

Lilly had been wondering what was up with Dot. Was she actively avoiding her? It was a little catty to think, but she did question whether Dot was jealous of her engagement, as it was since then that Dot had changed.

That night! She laughed to herself. Watching George being a fan boy, hanging on Edward's every word: tales of childhood in New England, meeting Charles Lindbergh, his time at Harvard University and the day he impetuously bought his own plane. Anyone would have thought George was about to propose to Edward, not her! Lilly had been left to make small talk with Nancy. She felt intimidated by her languorous style and bitchy quips, even if some of them were rather witty, like referring to Edward as 'Superman crossed with Biggles'. Being in Nancy's presence made you feel part of something special. That way she tilted her head back when she laughed seemed as though she got the joke better than anyone else. People sitting at other tables surreptitiously looked over, seeming to admire you simply for sitting near her.

It had been bad luck that Jean-Claude had turned up just as George brought out the ring. It meant she hardly exchanged two words with him. She must have appeared very rude. They went off to the Savoy, leaving him behind. Lilly knew she had drunk too much. She could remember the pink-clothed table at the Savoy but had no memory of getting home.

Lilly glanced around the hostel bedroom, with its peeling, smoke-stained wallpaper and tired candlewick coverlets. How unsophisticated this scene was – sitting on the bed in a dressing gown and faux-fur slippers, nursing a cup of weak tea. 'No more than water bewitched,' she remembered her old Irish nanny saying when presented with a cup of tea stronger than this one. Her parents' char had used a more vulgar term for it: gnat's piss.

The front door slammed. Footsteps trudging up the stairs. Lilly hoped this was Dot, and she could discover the cause of the big freeze.

Dot came in.

Without looking at Lilly, she crossed the room, flung herself face down on her bed and started sobbing.

'Oh God, Dot!' Lilly put down her cup and clambered to her feet. 'Shall I get you some tea? Or would you prefer something stronger? I do have a flask of whisky in my kitbag.'

'A whisky would be lovely. Thank you, Lilly,' Dot mumbled into her pillow. 'I've had a trying day.'

Lilly poured a nip of whisky into a teacup and passed it to Dot.

'Another patient on the ward died. Second American boy this week. I wasn't supposed to be at work this afternoon. I volunteered. Poor man died in my arms. Worst thing was he was crying for his mammy.'

Dot took a swig while Lilly perched on the edge of her bed and put her arm around her.

'On top of that,' Dot continued, her voice shaking with emotion, 'I'd had a horrible row with Billy and now he's gone back to Liverpool. But you can't go round quarrelling with people any more … because, you know … these days, you might never see them again.'

Dot sobbed silently, tears rolling down her cheeks into her drink.

'Oh, Dot. The thing about this ghastly war is that we have to try and live as though everything is normal. If we don't do that, we'll all go mad. Then *they'll* have won.'

Dot let out another painful sob. Lilly pulled her closer.

'How long have you and Billy known each other?'

'Since infant school.'

'He can't simply chuck you away if you've been friends that long. There will be a bond.' Lilly doubted her own words. 'It's not my business, but why did you quarrel? Surely, it's nothing so bad you couldn't repair it with a heartfelt letter.'

'Cruel words were said.' Dot mopped her eyes with the corner of her sheet. 'He has the idea that London has changed me. But it's the war. It's changed all of us. We've all adapted to living on the edge. If we didn't we'd go under.'

'I know what you mean.'

Dot felt guilty for talking about Billy behind his back. 'He's defensive, gets the idea that everyone looks down on him. It's quite tiring.'

'Well, I'd say if Billy can be so cavalier, maybe *he's* not good enough for *you*.'

Lilly felt Dot freeze and knew she had gone too far.

'Poor Dot. You're really kind and thoughtful. It can't be easy working all day with the sick and dying.'

'I wish this war would finish.' Dot dried her eyes. 'That's all.'

Lilly seized her chance.

'Look, I have to say, you've not been the same since my engagement and I wonder whether that was because of your own situation with Billy?'

Dot pulled herself away, stood up and walked over to the dresser. She put the cup down. 'Not in the way you think, Lilly. If we're out in the open criticising each other's beaux, I'd say you're too good for George too. He's not a very nice person.'

Lilly regretted having started this conversation. Obviously, it was now going to plummet into a free-for-all.

'You can't judge George simply from watching him as you waltz by on a dance floor, Dot. That's ridiculous.'

But Dot's reply stunned her.

'George is a snob. He said that I'm not good enough to be your friend.'

'When did he do that?'

'On the doorstep, after he walked you back from the Savoy.'

'But why?' Lilly recalled being drunk but remembered nothing that was said. She also knew that George, like her, came from an upper-middle-class background where you never said cruel things to a person's face. 'You must be mistaken, Dot. After all, George doesn't know you.'

'Do you think I'm too common for you to share with cos I speak in a Liverpool accent?' she asked.

'Don't be absurd. If we all went around judging people by things like that, where would we be?'

'Your boyfriend's precise words were: "She's rather common. I hope it doesn't rub off."'

Lilly was appalled. Surely this couldn't have been what George said. She watched Dot, standing by the dresser looking down into her cup. Could she make up something as dreadful as this? Perhaps when she talked about Billy having a chip on his shoulder she really meant herself.

Dot wiped away a tear and looked Lilly in the eye.

'To be honest, Lilly, that remark floored me. I've been worried it was what you thought of me.'

'I would never think like that. I take a person on who they are, not how they talk. I really like you, and I thought we were lucky to be sharing with each other.'

'Till that night, I did too.'

'But George wouldn't...'

'George did.'

EIGHT

NEXT DAY DURING HER lunch hour, Dot started drafting a letter to Billy telling him how disappointed she was that the weekend had ended so badly. She cared for him, but the war was starting to wear her down. She knew that she was almost grovelling, but she needed Billy to see the truth. She wrote about the kiss on the beach at Crosby and explained that it meant nothing, the result of loneliness, of missing him.

The act of putting the truth down on paper made her feel better. When she was done, she folded the letter, put it into an envelope and tucked it into the inside pocket of her uniform jacket. She would hold onto it and only when she was certain it was the right thing to do would she post it.

Billy had been rude to Howard and Otis and she had been too flustered to intervene. That was wrong of her. She would apologise and ask Howard if he could investigate the worries about Rainbow Corner.

She didn't regret telling Lilly about George either. Lilly's opinions on Billy had inspired her to write that letter and clear her head.

As Dot applied dressings and gave blanket baths, she pondered it all. If she had been about to get embroiled with a man like George, she would like to be warned. Maybe one day Lilly would see she had done her a favour.

When clocking-off time came around, Dot felt much better. As if her vision had changed from black and white to colour.

Stung by Billy implying that she couldn't cope with a life under enemy fire, and embarrassed by the presence of her roommate, Dot knew what she needed to do. So, before clocking off, she went through to the staffroom and put her name down on a list of nurses available to go on active service.

*

While Lilly spent the morning drawing up a chart allocating rooms for bridge tournaments and classes, her mind kept going over Dot's outburst last night.

As she filed through a list of soldiers interested in the advertised classes in languages, wood-whittling and shorthand dictation, disturbing memories crept into her head: unkind comments George had made about ratings – the soldiers who had to work their way up from the bottom because, unlike him, they hadn't gone to Sandhurst. She recalled that he had laughed at his parents' cleaner when she bought him a birthday present and told Lilly that, whatever it was, he would donate it to some charity bazaar.

'How are you getting on, little Lilly?'

The general had his hands on Lilly's shoulders and was bending over her desk. She could feel his breath on her neck. She wondered how she could wiggle out of this one when he had her cornered. She turned to look to Controller Fergusson but she had left the room.

Lilly was about to open her mouth when the door opened, and Nancy entered.

The general leapt away, stumbled backwards and landed in his chair with a thud.

'There's some strange Frenchman at the desk wanting in. But the regs don't permit it, and the girl on desk duty, being rather rigorous, told him he can't enter unless accompanied by someone sporting a US uniform. Then he claimed he knows you.'

'That'll be Jean-Claude.'

'Oh, the bloke who ruined your romantic engagement scenario.' Nancy leaned back against the open door. 'Well, Lilly, you'd better go down and tackle Miss Cerberus and save your French friend from further *ennui*.'

'Right.' Lilly screwed the top on her pen and stood up.

'Trot on, Hopalong, the Frog prince awaits you!'

Nancy stepped back to let Lilly pass, just as Fergusson arrived on the landing.

'Off somewhere?'

'Front desk problems,' said Nancy.

Nancy followed Fergusson inside and slammed the door behind her.

Limping down the stairs, Lilly felt relieved to be out of whatever drama was about to unfold up on the fourth floor.

Jean-Claude was waiting in the hall, pointing at the large map of the USA.

'Nouvelle Orleans!' he cried. 'The hometown of Earl.'

The girl behind the desk was frantically indicating to Jean-Claude that he should not pass so far into the club.

'Don't worry.' Lilly took Jean-Claude's arm. 'He's with me.'

Jean-Claude loomed in to kiss her cheek. She swerved it, forgetting that in France a kiss on each cheek was the usual formality for a casual meeting between friends. She led him down the corridor.

'I needed to come back to say *félicitations*.' Jean-Claude spoke earnestly. 'Pearl explained you have made betrothal to marry an English lord.'

'George is hardly a lord.'

'I also want to say hello, goodbye, because next week I leave London and perhaps I won't be back.'

'Where are you off to?'

Jean-Claude shrugged. 'Who knows?'

'Well dodged, getting him past the doorkeeper!' Peggy passed by, bearing a tray of dirty dishes. 'She's a stickler, that girl!'

Lilly waved as Peggy turned a corner, heading back towards the cafeteria.

'I am worried for Earl too,' said Jean-Claude. 'He has been forbidden to marry Pearl.'

'Forbidden? By whom?'

'His commanding officer.'

'You can't go round forbidding people to marry! Is she underage or something?'

'No. She and Earl are much older than me. Both of them mid-thirties now. I was the baby in the group. Pearl is very upset. I tell you so you can talk wiz her.'

'What will happen? Will Earl go home to America without her?'

'She had wanted, when this catastrophe is over, we *all* three go live in America and play in Chicago and New York.'

Lilly glanced up at the clock. She shouldn't stay out of the office too long.

'Look, Jean-Claude, why don't you come and eat with us tomorrow night. Edward has invited George. They're going to watch some boxing match and afterwards we're meeting for dinner. I'm sure between them, those two powerful men can come up with something to help. Come latish, around desserts and coffee.'

When Lilly got back upstairs, she found Nancy lounging in her chair.

Fergusson was beaming at Sydney, who stood gripping a handful of papers from men who had signed up for a day trip to Windsor Castle.

'I don't know anything about castles or kings,' Sydney was saying, 'but as George Washington once said, "I would rather be on my farm than be emperor of the world."'

'That's jolly lucky, Sydney,' said Nancy, deadpan, 'as the latter option seems highly unlikely.'

From the look on his face, Sydney wasn't sure whether to laugh or be affronted. He said: 'You're funny!'

Nancy came back at him with 'I know', before regally allowing Lilly to sit in her own place.

'I tidied up some of your papers, Lilly. A neat desk, they say, is the sign of a well-ordered mind. By the way, you do realise, darling, don't you, that kissing a Frog won't really turn him into a prince.'

'I'll be going then, General, Controller.' Sydney saluted and left the office.

'My word, Sergeant Newton, you are quite the uppity madam.' The general stretched out his legs, exposing furry ankles. 'That pilot of yours must be a brave man. Anyone wanting to take you home would as soon take a wild colt into his house. You need breaking in, woman.'

Nancy turned and gave the general a filthy look. 'General Smith, I might not be tame enough for you to mount me, but, unlike you, I'm years away from the knacker's yard.'

The general was shocked into stunned silence. Lilly glanced at Fergusson and held her breath. But she didn't make a comment.

Nancy turned at the door. 'I'll see you later, Gloria, darling.'

And she was gone.

General Smith coughed, picked up a magazine and started flicking through the pages.

As though on cue, Fergusson said rather loudly, 'There was some sabotage last week in Kent.'

'Really?' Lilly replied.

'At the US airbases at Headcorn and Penshurst. Also, I'm told that the day before you arrived, there was an episode in Brighton. Didn't you come up to London on the Brighton line? A person of suspicion was picked up there yesterday, prominent Mosleyite member of the January Club. Police found papers emanating from here – Rainbow Corner.' She patted the filing cabinet.

What was Fergusson implying? That Lilly herself had popped down to Brighton to give information to a man she didn't know with papers from somewhere she'd not been yet? Lilly glanced at the general, who put his feet up on the coffee table and started paring his nails with a hunting knife.

'Didn't you notice anything or anyone suspicious on your journey?'

'I didn't see anyone with a camouflaged face gripping a large pair of wire cutters, if that's what you mean. Nor have I visited Kent since a school trip to Scotney Castle.'

'There's no need to be flip, young lady,' Fergusson snapped. 'Sabotage is a serious business, especially as we are leading up to … Well, let's say, though it might not look like it, the Americans haven't come over here to lounge around eating donuts.'

'I'm sorry, Controller, but I have been working here two weeks. If there is anyone unpatriotic working in this place, you'd do better to look elsewhere.'

Without a word, Fergusson rose, grabbed a pile of papers, strode over to Lilly's desk and slammed them down. 'These are the posters for tomorrow's quiz night, the chess tournament, and some lists for people to sign up for the talent show. Can you make sure that one of each is put up on every noticeboard?'

Lilly took the pile of papers and started sorting through them.

'Not in here, girl,' said Fergusson, opening the door. 'All over the building. Stop shilly-shallying. I mean now!'

*

As Dot came into Rainbow Corner that night, Howard was chatting with the boy on the desk. When he saw her, he jumped away and rushed over.

'I have to apologise for the other day, but I wondered…'

Dot put out her hand to stop him. 'No, Howard. It's me who should apologise. I realise that my boyfriend put you on the spot. I wondered whether I could depend on you to follow up on the…' Careless Talk Costs Lives, thought Dot. She looked around to make sure they could not be overheard before continuing in a low voice: '… follow up on the information my deceased patient Joe passed to me.'

'Here's the thing, Dot,' whispered Howard. 'I was looking for you so that I could ask you the same thing.'

'I won't be able to do anything, Howard. I'm sorry. I've signed up on a ship.'

'Ah!' Howard sighed. 'I'm heading out of London tomorrow, myself, so…'

They stood in silence for a few moments.

'You could ask…' Dot didn't want to use Otis's name, but Howard latched on straight away.

'No, I could not ask Otis. He's…' Howard shrugged. '… incompatible with stuff like this. Doesn't your roommate work up in the office?'

'I'll speak to her tonight,' she said. 'After work.'

'Work?'

'The dance.'

'Aw, come on, Dot.' Howard winked. 'For a perfect Ginger Rogers like yourself, don't call it work!'

'I'd better hurry up.' Dot blushed. 'Got to get smartened up. Take care, Howard. Come back safe.'

'You too, Dot.'

That night the dressing room at Rainbow Corner was less busy than usual as the band, Stars in Battledress, was all-male and had their own changing room.

As Dot laid out her make-up, she felt an urgent obligation to follow through on the Joe business. She had no idea why she hadn't marched straight up to the office and told the people at the top. But she had felt intimidated. She, who in Liverpool had always felt at ease with everyone, was frightened of southern posh people. That gave her a start. Wasn't fear of them exactly the same thing in reverse of George with his remarks about her being common?

'Farming isn't a job. It's a life. That's what he says.' Violet leaned against the architrave of the stage door, holding forth. 'But Sydney also says "a farmer has to be an optimist or he wouldn't be a farmer"…'

'I think you'll find that's a quote by Will Rogers.' Nancy didn't look round from drawing on her eyebrow liner. 'Actor, vaudevillian, cowboy.'

'I love hearing about Sydney's farm,' added Violet, deliberately ignoring Nancy. 'The idea that a vast emptiness like that exists. Green and blue, land and sky, and nothing else. It'll be surreal for a Bermondsey girl like me.'

As Dot applied her mascara she noticed that June was staring at her.

'Are you married, Dot?' she asked quietly.

'I have a beau. Merchant navy. And you, June?'

'No, no.' Dot noticed that June slightly shifted before replying: 'I am that creature nature abhors – a spinster.'

Dot leaned towards her and whispered, 'But you're very pretty, June. I'm sure you'll find someone soon.' She really wanted to suggest that perhaps June should wear a little less make-up, as being so painted gave the wrong image, but couldn't find words which wouldn't be hurtful.

'Whereabouts do you live, June?'

'Why do you ask?'

'I'm in a hostel, living away from home. I wondered whether you had the luxury of going to your own place at night. It's the little comforts that make all the difference.'

'Yes, petal,' replied June, non-committal. 'They do.'

Dot wasn't sure what June was agreeing with. One thing was for certain, June wasn't fond of being asked questions.

Later, when Dot flopped down at the hostesses' table during the band break, she mentioned casually to Nancy that it was very sad about June being a spinster.

'Spinster equals euphemism for "on the shelf".'

'I wish June wouldn't wear so much make-up…'

'Ah, Dot. Has it never occurred to you that perhaps it's necessary? Maybe under all that war paint she's a gorgon. Who knows? Who cares? Perhaps she had childhood smallpox. A person would only discover what lies beneath after they married her.'

In what she realised was a pathetic attempt to change the subject, Dot said, 'Sydney and Vi are a sweet couple, aren't they?'

'Oh God, don't start me – the "as far as the eye can see" pair. They won't lose each other in a crowd, that's for sure…'

'Enjoying your break, girls?' Art loomed over them, bearing a tray piled high with donuts. 'You'll need to stoke up with some good ole Yankee fayre. Tuck in, ladies.'

'I really shouldn't.' Nonetheless Nancy picked one and took a huge bite. 'They are so delicious.'

'In America we believe in a plentiful table. It's what the good Lord intended. As you'll see for yourself when you come to live in the greatest country in the world.' Art wiped the sugar from his fingers down the side of his trousers. 'Is your fiancé not with you tonight?'

'Edward is off on some mission. Bombing Berlin or Heidelberg or somewhere.'

'I knew his family way back, you know, when I was just a little squirt.' Art grinned and pushed his specs up. 'My father was a cutter in the tailor shop which his father frequented. I helped do the measurements.'

'Not too far up the inside leg, I hope?'

Seemingly unaware of Nancy's innuendo, Art pressed on: 'The whole family came to my church a few times…'

'I didn't know you were a priest?'

Nancy had put on the seemingly simple face which meant she was mocking him.

'Oh, no. I'm no pastor.'

'Could have fooled me…' Nancy said under her breath.

'I meant the church I attended as a youngster.'

'Easy mistake to make – you regale us with so many Biblical quotations.'

'As I always say, the good Lord will guard over the righteous. Keep smiling, girls…'

Art moved off briskly.

'*Quel ennui*.' Nancy sighed. 'Here's my own personal daily prayer: "God, please deliver us from ghastly, self-righteous bores like Art!"'

Dot was thankful that at that moment the band struck up 'C Jam Blues' and a tall grinning boy with tousled red hair was standing before her, holding out his hand for a dance.

*

Lilly sat on her bed dreading the sound of Dot's tread on the stairs. She also looked forward to it – so that they could clear the air. Living through a war was bad enough without falling out with your roommate.

Wearing her pyjamas and dressing gown, at eleven o'clock she went down to the common room to make a cup of tea.

When she came back up, Dot was undressing.

'I'm so sorry!'

They said it in unison, then laughed.

Lilly offered her cup. 'You have this one while you put on your nightie. I'll pop down and get another.'

Returning with the second cup, Lilly said: 'Guess what happened? The general and Fergusson all but accused ME of being a traitor! Something about dropping off papers at Brighton, and stealing papers from Rainbow Corner to dispatch to the enemy!'

Lilly was surprised that Dot looked perturbed by this.

'I thought you'd laugh, Dot. Don't tell me on top of everything you think I'm a spy!'

'Of course I don't.' Dot spoke deliberately. 'It's just that … the people must *know* something is going on.'

'What do you mean?' From her tone Lilly knew that Dot was totally serious.

'I shall go in tomorrow and tell them.' Dot ran her hand across her forehead. 'I should have done it days ago. But it seemed…' Dot shook her head and didn't finish the sentence.

'What do you know, Dot?'

'At first I put it down to a man being very ill and incoherent. It must go no further, except to people who can do something about it, but I'll share this with you.'

For the next five minutes, Dot poured out the whole tale of Joe, and his dying words about a pair of traitors working from Rainbow Corner.

'Who would do such a thing?'

Dot shrugged.

'I can't imagine who it could be?' At first Lilly imagined someone speaking in a German accent but appreciated that you'd only find that kind of spy in a comic like *The Wizard* or *The Dandy*. This would be just an ordinary person. Nobody who stood out. The whole technique of espionage was to be invisible, cover your tracks. Lilly suspected that this would be a case of someone with big ears, listening in for careless talk, which, in a place like Rainbow Corner, was easy enough to overhear, and disseminating information about troop movements of the soldiers there could certainly cost lives.

'I feel so bad for not telling you days ago.'

'This is not going to be some top-level spy ring with a direct line to Hitler, is it? Low-level spying is rife. That's why the posters are everywhere…'

'Keep Mum, She's Not So Dumb?'

'Careless Talk Costs Lives. Loose Lips Sink Ships. I'll bet those Mosley types are still at it.' Lilly plumped up her pillow and sat with her back to the wall, her feet hanging over the side of the bed. 'George's brother, who's a barrister, is constantly in court prosecuting housewives and toffs for these things.'

'Really? It's not in the papers.'

'Bad for morale. A few years back some woman on the Isle of Wight was picked up. She walked her dog every day. Seemed harmless enough. Turned out she was drawing an accurate map of possible landing places for an invading German army. God knows who she was going to pass it to. Anyway, they locked her up, and the case never made the papers, cos the trial was held in secret, but George's brother told us all about it.'

'There we are,' said Dot. 'That's how this spying thing works. If it's secret, he shouldn't have told you. The brother, I mean. That's careless talk too.'

'I agree, Dot. This is going to be that type of thing. Someone who listens in then passes on info. Like you know such-and-such a soldier is moving out of London, therefore his whole group must be on the go. To whoever operates panzer divisions, that information would be invaluable.'

'From what you just said, they already know that someone inside the club is a rotter.'

Lilly thought back to Fergusson's demeanour that afternoon.

'Yes, they do.'

'I have a number-one suspect,' said Dot.

'So do I.'

'Let's say it together – one, two, three…'

Simultaneously Dot said, 'Liz Webb', while Lilly said, 'Nancy Newton'.

'Really!' Lilly turned around on the bed and lay back against her pillow.

'Can I add my fellow dancer, June?' said Dot. 'Very evasive. Always questioning everyone else but won't reply to any enquiries about herself.'

Lilly raised herself, leaning on one elbow. 'I can't tell you anything suspicious about Nancy except I can't stand her. She's such a cat. But I can't see Nancy cutting telephone lines, can you?'

The idea of Nancy risking a broken nail made Dot laugh out loud.

'Tell me about Liz Webb?'

'She was terribly nervous when asked about having been in Kent.'

'Fergusson said something about Kent today…'

'And though Liz said she'd just been walking in the countryside, there was paint on her clothes and she looked exhausted.'

'Doesn't she teach art?'

'Yes. But she said she'd been having a day off. Surely it's against the law to take a train out of town just for a walk?'

'I tell you something, Dot. Together we could crack this. We both work at different times and move among different people, and between us we have all-round access.'

'I'm sorry, but I may not be here, Lilly. I've signed up for overseas. A hospital or troop ship.'

'How long will you be away?'

'Six weeks to two months.'

'This isn't because of me, is it? And George?'

Dot couldn't answer. It was, in part. And Joe and Billy and Otis. She just felt the need to run.

NINE

FEBRUARY 1944

Next morning Sister Sullivan handed Dot two letters – one from Billy, the other an official letter with details of her upcoming travel. Tomorrow morning Dot would report to HMS *Vernon*, prior to being assigned to a ship.

She hadn't expected things to move so fast.

Sister took Dot to the staffroom and administered the necessary inoculations.

'Do these give you any clue as to where I'll be sent?'

'I imagine it will be the Mediterranean or North Africa, rather than the Atlantic.'

Sister put the needle into the refuse box and applied a plaster to Dot's arm. 'Would you like the rest of the day off?'

Dorothy pulled down her sleeve. 'I'd get very nervous sitting on my own doing nothing.'

'Your arm will ache, and you may suffer headaches, fatigue and possibly a slight fever. If it gets bad, go home and lie down. I imagine tomorrow will be an early start.'

Fearing the worst, Dot saved Billy's letter until the lunch break. But it wasn't so bad. He apologised for being abrupt, explaining that Yanks always rubbed him up the wrong way. It was bad enough being made to feel inferior to British Royal Navy men. Those brown-jobs on the street had really got his goat, along with those spoiled brats from America who thought they could lord it over him. He was due to go back on board any day, and asked Dot to make sure she wrote him lots of letters. In a PS, he said he'd bumped into an old school friend of theirs, Clarice Titchmarsh. They'd gone out for a lovely dinner at Reece's. She sent her regards.

Dot remembered Clarice as a tubby little girl with rosy cheeks who cried a lot, while being rather mean. Clarice's line in snide remarks reminded her of Nancy!

Dot spent the evening packing. She looked at the letter she had written to Billy and decided not to send it. Instead she put it into one of the drawers, with everything she wouldn't take on board, like her dancing shoes. She slipped the snaps of her parents and Billy into the side pocket of her case. These were the only essentials. Everything else could be replaced.

Tonight was boxing night at Rainbow Corner. Dot couldn't imagine anything worse. But that meant she wouldn't be able to say goodbye to the other hostesses.

She flopped down on the bed. It wasn't so bad, this room. And Lilly had been a very amenable roommate.

Why had she offered to go away like this? What was she running from? It was as though by rushing headlong into the firing line, she alone hoped to end the war and the chaos it had brought into her life.

But it wasn't right to blame all her troubles on the war. Perhaps it was part of growing up. She had known nothing but living at home with her parents and school. Then suddenly, after one month's holiday, war was declared and she had grown up overnight.

What did she really want?

The war to be over, certainly.

Then?

She couldn't live with her parents till she was an old maid. Lilly had said she wanted a bit of an adventure before settling down. So did Dot. Maybe active service would satisfy that and then, when peace came, she would marry Billy and live happily ever after.

Something like that. That was what she wanted. To live with a nice man in a comfortable house. Someone to laugh with. Someone who cared. Go to the pictures together, dance now and then. A record player and all the latest hits in the corner. Then children.

When Dot finished packing and tidying up, she went downstairs and made herself a cup of Ovaltine. She started humming the Ovaltineys' song.

"'Because we all drink Ovaltine, we're happy girls and boys.'"

O is for Ovaltine. O is for Otis.

She shook her head. If Howard was going away, Otis would too. And what did Otis matter anyway?

It wasn't till she was lying in bed, rereading Billy's letter, that Dot's arm really started hurting and she was overcome by a wave of tiredness. She pulled the cover up over her shoulders and fell into a deep sleep.

*

Lilly sat patiently in the restaurant. George was still at the boxing. She could have gone into the auditorium with them but couldn't stand the crush or the sheer masculinity of the room.

All day long she had wanted to tell General Smith Dot's story. But as soon as she came in, he left the office. In the afternoon when he returned, Lilly started with 'I have heard some disturbing rumours about Rainbow Corner which I feel I should share with you, General Smith…' but Fergusson leapt to her feet and snapped brusquely, 'Get on with your work, Corporal Deane. We have no time for idle chat and rumour.'

Lilly decided she would wait until she got the general alone.

The restaurant tables were laid with white tablecloths. One desultory waiter strolled between them, slightly adjusting knives and forks. Only two were occupied. At one, a pair of GIs sat anxiously with two girls who were inspecting their faces in their compacts. In the corner, two beefy women Lilly recognised from Dabbler's Den hobbies room tucked into a hearty supper.

Lilly wished she hadn't been so early. Either that or she should have brought a book.

'Like a little aperitif while you wait?' The lingering waiter had a thick Liverpool accent. 'I always say you need *a pair o' teef* to eat your meal.' He pressed his thumb up against his front teeth. 'I like a cocktail, me. Can't I tempt you? Whisky sour? Pink gin? Martini? Americano?'

What would be the harm? Lilly was fed up waiting. Why not have something lovely to drink? She glanced up at his name badge.

'You've tempted me, Paul. I'll have an Americano.'

'I think we'd all like one of them. And this is certainly the place to find one.' As he scribbled down the order, he leaned in to whisper in her ear, 'The ladies from the arts and crafts were on the verge of heading over to ask you to join them. I knew if I loomed in they'd leave you alone. You don't want to spend an evening talking basket-weaving and upholstery.' He gave a wink and sidled off, wending through the tables and out through the swing door.

Lilly studied the menu.

'I've not seen you about.' Paul brought her drink, then, pretending to polish a spoon on the next table, asked: 'Are you new?'

'I've been here two weeks.'

'Managed to hook yourself a Yank yet?'

'I'm engaged to a British soldier.' She presented her ring. 'He's down at the match with an American pilot.'

Paul raised his eyebrows.

A sudden burst of shouting and applause from downstairs. She hoped this meant it was all over, but no.

'Come on, girl, chin up!' Seeing that she had almost finished her drink, Paul snatched away the glass. 'I'll get you another.'

After a quarter of an hour, another gust of cheering reverberated through the floor, followed by men running into the restaurant and settling themselves down at tables all around her. Minutes later the place was full.

George swaggered in with Nancy on his arm. Edward lagged a few steps behind, signing autographs for eager GIs.

As the party assembled, Lilly relaxed.

'A glass of Minnehaha, please, Edward.' Nancy didn't bother to check the list.

'Minnehaha?' said George. 'Is that a cocktail? I've never heard of it.'

'Champagne, darling. Laughing water.'

George looked perplexed.

Lilly got the joke and laughed slightly too loudly. 'From now on, champagne will always be Minnehaha.'

'"Minnehaha, Laughing Water",' Nancy recited, '"Handsomest of all the women/In the land of the Dacotahs/In the land of handsome women." It's by Longfellow. An American poet.'

Lilly gazed at George, so handsome in his uniform, and felt content. This would all work out. When the war was over, they would marry and it would be wonderful.

Paul swished by, serving rolls to accompany the soup.

Along with Nancy's glass of champagne, Edward ordered wine. 'Pity we can't import some American wine,' he announced. 'Even though this is the American Red Cross Club, we're limited to what's available from the cellars of London. Back home we have some great wineries. My mom and dad have invested in a huge winery in California. Wine isn't simply the prerogative of the French, you know.'

'I won't challenge you on zat claim, though I could!'

Jean-Claude stood by the table. Lilly had quite forgotten she had asked him to join them.

She heard George quietly groan.

After shaking hands with the men, Jean-Claude kissed Nancy's hand.

Clicking his fingers, George tried to attract the waiter's attention. 'Another chair here!'

Lilly wished he hadn't done that. Paul shot her a look, pursed his lips, took an empty seat, placed it at their table and snapped his heels together.

'Voici la chaise de ma tante.' Paul spoke with an exaggerated French accent. *'Allez-vous en.'*

Dismissing Paul with a wave of his hand, George started chatting to Jean-Claude. 'So what are you boys up to with old de Gaulle?'

'I go back and forth to my country.'

'Had any truck with those wretched collaborators?'

'I can't talk about zat.'

'And how do you feel about your Marshal Pétain handing your country over to Herr Hitler?'

'People were blinded by the heroism of his past, mistaking it for patriotism. Pétain was once a hero. Now he is a traitor.'

'And the French people just threw in the towel and surrendered. Right?'

Lilly felt Jean-Claude flinch. She was very uncomfortable at how this was going. She gestured to George to change the subject. He did.

'You're a musician, Lilly said?'

'Guitarist. Yes.' Jean-Claude shuffled his chair. 'Strangely useful in time of war. I've been doing some work with Bertram Mills Circus.'

Lilly noticed George exchange a sneaky look with Edward. They both smirked like schoolboys.

'Perhaps I could clear some of this away?' Paul was hovering. 'Will you be continuing with the second course?'

'Naturally!' George smiled. 'Perhaps wherever you come from, only one course is served at dinner – or up there it would be yer tea, wouldn't it?'

Paul flared his nostrils and sidled away. Lilly cringed. She couldn't believe that George had been so rude.

She whispered to him. He whispered back, 'Something about those Liverpool people I don't trust.'

Lilly leaned across to Edward. 'Was it an enjoyable fight?' She blundered on, making even more stilted small talk. 'We've been lucky for the last few days, haven't we? No more air raids.'

'I believe you can thank our brave pilots for that.' Beneath the tablecloth George took Lilly's hand and squeezed it. 'It's Edward and his boys who, day after day, are destroying the Nazi airbases in Europe, ready for us to go in.'

For the rest of the meal, conversation was bland – the weather, the setbacks in the Italian campaign, whether anyone had seen the new play on up the road, *Blithe Spirit*.

Nancy was the quietest Lilly had ever seen her. Occasionally she turned to give Edward a fawning smile. He smiled back. Was she listening out for information to pass on?

While waiting for desserts, George opened a packet of cigarettes and offered them round the table. Nancy took one. Lilly did too, even though she hadn't really started smoking. When it came to Edward, he pulled out a packet of Lucky Strikes.

'I prefer American smokes.' He nodded in Jean-Claude's direction. 'And I'll bet you have a taste for those fancy Gauloises. I'd say, apart from beer, nothing divides the nations so strongly as tobacco. You limeys with your warm beer!' He pulled a face of disgust and offered around the Lucky Strikes. Jean-Claude took one.

Lilly was relieved at the sense of calm which fell as everyone lit up and took their first puff.

'Before the war, Jean-Claude played in a café in Montmartre with Pearl Heaton,' said Lilly, tipping some ash from the end of her cigarette. 'Pearl is the drummer with the band who played here the other night.' Music had to be a safe subject. Then she remembered Nancy's snide remark about the all-girl orchestra. But Nancy was oddly silent on the subject, occasionally dragging on the cigarette elegantly poised between her forefingers.

'Pearl flies with the Air Transport Auxiliary.'

'She's a pilot?' Edward looked up, blowing out a cloud of tobacco smoke. 'I'd love to meet her.'

'She's a very glamorous blue-eyed, blonde pilot,' said Lilly. 'She's formidable.'

'Pearl is the reason why Lilly suggested I come here to talk to you.' Jean-Claude turned to Edward. 'Perhaps you might be able to help.'

'Why, sure.' Edward's face lit up. 'Those girls do a great job for us. What's the problem?'

'It's my American friend, Earl, who needs help. He played the bass in our group in Paris. He's currently serving in Italy.'

'They're brave guys. They're having quite a tough time trying to reach Rome, I read.'

'Earl is a very gentle man.'

'You must be proud.' Edward leaned back in his chair. 'What can I do for your friend?'

'His commanding officer has forbidden him to marry Pearl.'

'That's pretty tough. When a guy is serving on foreign fields, you'd think his officer would want to keep him happy.'

Edward stubbed out his cigarette and lit another.

'Zey were due to marry here in London when he gets leave.'

'Was the plan that Pearl should go back to live with him in the States when this farrago is over?'

'Zat's right.' Jean-Claude nodded. 'We all three wanted to play together again in New York, Chicago, New Orleans.'

'New Orleans is a dump.'

'It's the home of the jazz,' said Jean-Claude. 'Also the birthplace of Earl.'

'I wouldn't envy him that,' said Edward. 'So did this overreaching commander give a reason why they couldn't marry?'

'Yes.' Jean-Claude held his hands up. 'Because he is black and she is white.'

Edward took the cigarette from his lips and crushed it out in the glass ashtray.

'Earl is a Negro?'

Jean-Claude nodded.

'And Pearl is a blue-eyed blonde?'

'*Exacte!*' said Jean-Claude. 'And quite old enough to make her own decisions.'

'Then my sympathy is with the commanding officer. Let's put it this way…' Edward wore a fixed grin, cold and forbidding. 'Back in the States, it's not encouraged, mixing the races … It doesn't work.'

'I'm sorry,' Lilly interjected, 'but that sounds remarkably like something Hitler might say. Isn't that one of the reasons we're fighting this war?'

Lilly turned to George for support. But he was looking down, white-lipped, muttering under his breath: 'Leave it, Lilly. Not your problem.'

Lilly glanced across at Nancy. They caught eyes and Nancy slightly shook her head.

'Look, my French friend.' Edward leaned back in his chair, confident and unabashed. 'Sorry, I forget your name…'

'Jean-Claude.'

'Yeah. Jean-Claude. It can't happen. In certain areas of the USA, the Negro areas, we keep things separate. Separate hotels, restrooms, schools, transportation, theatres, bars, clubs. You and Pearl could not play together with this man. On top of that, in some neighbourhoods, it's against the law to mix races within apartments – there, they couldn't even live together. Even in the unlikely event that they were man and wife.'

Lilly glanced at George. Surely as a man of honour, a British officer from a good family, he could not stay silent on a subject as important as this. She elbowed him. 'George! Say something.'

'Mixing with blacks is one thing. But marriage,' George spoke in a magisterial tone, 'I'm with Edward and this Negro bloke's CO.'

'George, you can't say that.' Lilly grabbed his hand. He couldn't be so subservient to this American pilot that he'd lost all his values. 'We're talking about two wonderful people who love each other.'

George put his cigarette to his lips and inhaled. 'To be frank, Lilly, I wouldn't like the idea of you kissing a Negro either.'

'I'm shocked.' Jean-Claude stood up and turned to Lilly. 'How can zese people be your friends?'

'Oh, do shut up, circus boy.' George calmly flicked ash from the end of his cigarette.

'Tell me something, George.' Dot's comment came back into Lilly's mind. 'What do you think of my roommate, Dot?' she asked.

'Beneath you. Common. You should ask to be reassigned rooms.'

'I am going to be.'

'Good.'

'Only because she is going to sea on a troop ship. And she's doing that because of you.'

'Don't be absurd. She's Royal Navy. She goes where they send her.'

'I can't marry you, George.' Pulling the engagement ring from her finger, Lilly rose. 'It's a terrible mistake. Here. Take your ring.'

She flung it onto the table, where it bounced off the white cloth and landed in the butter dish.

With a roar, George jumped to his feet and grabbed Jean-Claude by the lapel. 'You bloody interfering little Frog,' he growled. 'You caused this!'

Then, to Lilly's horror, George punched him in the face.

Lilly pulled at George's jacket but he continued laying into Jean-Claude.

On the other side of the room, Paul put two fingers in his mouth and let out a piercing whistle. The burly men he had been chatting with put on their white helmets and ran towards them.

Smashing two chairs as he fell, Jean-Claude lay on the floor, dabbing at his bleeding lip, trying to fend George off.

'Coward.' George loomed over Jean-Claude's prostrate body. 'Typical Frog. Hands in the air, white flags, don't even try and fight back. The British are only in this mess cos you lot ran away.'

Lilly kicked George off, then threw herself to her knees beside Jean-Claude, cradling his head.

'Lilly! Let go of that man.' George spoke in his best military manner. 'I forbid you to touch him.'

'You can't tell me what to do, George.' Lilly turned and glared.

As the military policemen closed in on them, Lilly pulled Jean-Claude to his feet and addressed George.

'Goodbye, George. And don't be in touch.'

TEN

AFTER THE GHASTLY FRACAS, Lilly took Jean-Claude to a late-night café. Applying ice to his cut lip, they sat and talked, consoling one another.

Jean-Claude stretched his arm across the table and held Lilly's hand.

When the waitress finally showed them the door, they strolled along the banks of the Thames, arm in arm, reminiscing about Lilly's wonderful week in Montmartre. They both hoped that one day they would know carefree days like that again.

'When she is liberated I must go back to France,' said Lilly. 'I felt so at home there.'

'It was a magical time. We didn't realise how soon it would all disappear.'

Lilly looked into Jean-Claude's eyes and she let him kiss her. It was a delicious kiss which confirmed George was not the man for her.

They held each other close, warm against the cold of dawn.

'He called me a coward,' said Jean-Claude. 'I love my country and will fight until we get her back.'

'He's one of those traditional Englishmen who enjoy generalisations.' Lilly apologised not only for George but for many others. 'I often wonder how we Brits would have reacted faced with a panzer division rolling up our street. Would my family have held up their arms in surrender or put up a fight and been shot? Perhaps they'd have invited them in for tea and scones. Who knows? Everyone thinks they would do the right thing. Until it happens to them.' Lilly rested her head on Jean-Claude's shoulder. 'The English Channel is a blessing. Imagine if at Dunkirk the tanks had been able to push on … into Dover, Canterbury, Ashford, London. It doesn't bear thinking about.'

The dawn light spilled across the dirty river.

Lilly and Jean-Claude watched the sun rise beyond Tower Bridge.

'Are you really working with the circus?' Lilly knew that that was one of the subjects which had irked George. 'Can you justify that in times like these?'

'Nothing is what it seems.' Jean-Claude scrutinised her face. 'I can trust you?'

Lilly nodded.

'You won't share this with your English boyfriend?'

'He's not my boyfriend.' By saying this, Lilly realised what a huge step she had taken tonight. The real mistake had been in saying yes in the first place. Why had she been so impulsive? Was this the effect war was having on everyone? Would they all leap into situations which they would have approached warily if they were not living on the brim of a powder keg?

'From now on, I'm sticking to friendship,' she said. 'Friends like you.'

She squeezed him tightly.

'I am working with the Free French. Bertram Mills Circus headquarters are my base. Would anyone imagine that a circus troupe was slowly infiltrating France? In a week or two, I'm going to leave for somewhere in France where…' He let the sentence fade out without finishing it. 'Let's simply say I am going to liberate my country.'

Lilly tried to imagine dropping from the sky in the black of night, knowing that you could be shot or, if you survived, denounced by the people giving you shelter.

Realising that she might never see him again, she shivered. Jean-Claude pulled her to him and they kissed once more.

When Lilly came back to her room in the early morning, she was hoping to find Dot there, getting dressed.

She wanted to tell her about last night and how Dot had been proved right.

But Dot was gone, leaving a farewell note on Lilly's pillow. Off on some voyage to who knows where. The thought made Lilly's heart skip a beat. Dot was putting herself in the front line. And part of the reason was George, and therefore herself. She wished she could apologise. But it was too late.

In a couple of hours Lilly should be on her way to work, but after last night, she dreaded facing anyone at Rainbow Corner.

With these thoughts spinning round in her head, Lilly drifted off into a deep sleep.

Around lunchtime she dragged herself out of bed.

She decided not to make an excuse, simply arrive in the office as though it was the normal thing. But she need not have worried, for Fergusson was not there.

The general stretched out in his usual seat with Peggy at his side, holding a tray. Peggy gathered a few dirty cups and left. The general, as usual, said nothing, just picked up his newspaper and hid behind it.

How aware was he of last night's fracas, Lilly wondered?

After an hour or so writing notices about a forthcoming bicycle tour of London and a quiz in Rainbow Hall, Lilly looked up. General Smith was again giving himself a manicure. When he saw her watching, he yawned loudly, slipped the hunting knife back into his jacket pocket and stretched.

'What's that you're up to, young lady?' he asked, padding over to stand behind her.

He seemed too near, but perhaps that was old age and short sight. He bent over her, resting his hands on her shoulders as before, breathing rather loudly.

'You have good, strong handwriting,' he said.

Feeling the dampness of his breath on her ears, Lilly stood up quickly and offered to get him a coffee.

He eyed her shrewdly.

'You're one of those, aren't you?'

She had no idea what he meant but said 'no' anyway, as, whatever he meant, it was clearly something of which he disapproved.

'Yes, you are. As an Amarillo man I can always tell…'

'Black, one sugar? Is that right?'

'Definitely one of those…'

Lilly moved briskly towards the door just as Controller Fergusson entered.

'Excuse me, General, but I have some information to impart which may be of a serious nature…' said Lilly, suddenly remembering what she wanted to discuss yesterday.

'Really?'

'It concerns security here, at Rainbow Corner.'

'Not now. Not here.' Fergusson clapped her hands. 'Take as long as you please on your break, Corporal Deane. I don't want to see you up here for at least half an hour.'

Lilly wondered what was up. Was Fergusson angry with her? Could it be because of last night?

The canteen was almost deserted. Thelma, looking as pale as ever, was giving the tops a desultory wipe-down. Violet sat alone at a table, stitching a pair of uniform trousers.

'Oh lawks,' she cried as Lilly walked past. 'You certainly made a splash, dear. I was hearing all about it from the MPs who broke up the fight. These trousers – or pants, as the Yank prefers to call them – got ripped when your boyfriend shoved him over.'

'George hit a security guard?'

'Were you too blotto to register that portion of the evening? Honestly, it's given me the biggest laugh in weeks.'

'I left straight after the first punch.'

'It's a pity I missed it but last night I went down to Richmond to see Sydney's quarters. Gawd, I couldn't be a soldier. I like me home comforts. My little rooms in the Aldwych, bar heater, cosy quilt, glass of sherry before bed. But then, men are tougher than us, eh?' She reached into her bag for a pair of scissors and snipped the end of the cotton, then tied it into a tight knot. 'He's dishy, that Frenchman. I was chatting to him down in the hall the other day. Anyhow, Paul told me all the juicy details this morning. And I got the rest from the Snowdrops this afternoon. You'd think them blokes covered in scrambled egg would know better, wouldn't you?'

'Scrambled egg?' Lilly had no idea what Violet meant.

Violet indicated her shoulders and forehead. 'All that gold braid over their uniforms. Commanding officers!'

She meant George! How embarrassing.

'What happened to Nancy, do you know?'

'She sat impassive throughout the fight.' Violet lowered her voice. 'Came in this morning with barely a smear of make-up and went straight up to the office, spoiling for a fight, I'd say. Her Majesty wasn't in there, though. So, after a few words with the general, she skedaddled.' Violet suddenly raised her voice. 'Oi, Virgil! Yer pants are patched.'

From behind the counter, the skinnier of the two MPs emerged. He had a tea towel dangling from the front of his underpants.

'You auditioning for the role of an Egyptian slave, Virgil, dear? 'Ere!' Violet threw the trousers but they landed well clear of him, so Lilly picked them up.

'Thank you for coming to our rescue last night, Officer. I'm embarrassed to have been part of it.'

'All in the day's work. Your boyfriend should have realised that boxing matches never take place in the restaurant. Now, thanks, ma'am, but I'll take my pants back.' He snatched the trousers and ran back behind the counter.

'Never mind the gum, Virgil, anyone ever tell you you got a lovely bum, chum.' Violet cackled to herself. 'Bum chum!'

While Lilly waited for Thelma to pour the coffee, she wondered whether she would get a written apology from George. Or if she would ever see Edward again. She couldn't imagine Nancy being that keen on showing him off in here now. But then, when she thought about it, Edward had just sat smirking, spurring everyone else on.

'Hey, Virgil,' Lilly called across the counter. 'Did Lieutenant Colonel Cornell leave with Sergeant Newton?'

'Oh, yeah. She was draped over him like poison ivy.'

'They were braying about going to the Savoy for "drinkipoos",' added Violet.

'It was only your limey colonel who ran amok.' Virgil was dressed now, pulling his belt tight. 'Tried to land one on my partner, Marty. But Marty used to be an all-in wrestler, so your boyfriend got grappled to the floor, while the other two sidled out, leaving the limey to face the music on his ownsome. You did good to get out quick with that poor French fellah.' Virgil strode past Lilly and called to Violet as he left the room, 'Owe ya one, babes.'

'No, you don't, Virgin, erm, I mean Virgil!' Violet laughed and said quietly to herself, 'Stupid names these Yanks have. And that Marty has set me a puzzle. Says you, me and him have something in common. And it's connected to our names.'

'Deane, Beckton? What's Marty's surname?'

'Joyce. No. It could be Lilly, Violet, Marty?'

'Well, two of them end in Y. Perhaps he thinks Vi is spelled VY. Like Vyella.' Violet pursed her lips and took on a pose of thought. 'There's an idea! I'll change my name to Vyella Winceyette.'

Back in the office, the controller was at her desk.

'Good afternoon, Corporal. A few changes underway. May I present Chief Warrant Officer Jack Kirk. For the next few weeks, he'll be sharing our office.'

A tall man in his mid-thirties held out his hand.

Lilly saluted. 'Good afternoon, Chief Warrant Officer.'

'No need for that.' An imposing figure with a bold profile, his black hair scraped back from his high forehead, long for a GI, Chief Warrant Officer Kirk nodded slightly and patted his chest. He did not smile.

Fergusson snatched the cup from Lilly's other hand, took it to the corner sink and emptied it away. 'The general won't be needing that.'

It was only then that Lilly noticed that both the general and his armchair were gone; in their place stood a new desk, piled up with complex-looking radio equipment.

'The general has moved to another, smaller Red Cross Club. Meanwhile I have suggested that you will assist Chief Warrant Officer Kirk. He will need someone to transcribe. He'll give you all the gen.'

PART TWO

At Sea

ELEVEN

MARCH 1944

Despite its name, Dot's training establishment was not a ship. It was a requisitioned school building, with classrooms and dormitories. She learned boat drills, how to operate grappling hooks and how to haul bosun's chairs and scrambling nets up the side of a ship. When she and her fellow nurses asked why they were expected to learn how to do such things, they received a stony glare from the sturdy woman who led her team.

Three weeks later Dot boarded her allocated ship, having no idea what lay ahead.

She had expected to be part of a large team on a hospital ship, but found herself part of a very small team on a huge American aircraft carrier loaded with thousands of troops. Where they were heading, no one knew.

There were only four nurses on each of the two on-board wards. For the first weeks they would share a berth with the nurse on the alternate watch. When one was in bed, the other would be up and working.

Once they arrived at their first destination, troops would unload and there would be more space.

At the end of the first day at sea, the chief medical officer took Dot up on deck. Although it was a hazy evening, she saw their ship was not alone. The horizon was filled with other, smaller ships, all moving steadily and stealthily south. Through the mist she counted fourteen but was sure there were more. She wondered if Billy's ship, *City of Boston*, might be out there.

'Do you think there are U-boats around?' she asked, hoping for a negative reply.

'Hundreds. If any of them get a sniff of us, they'll come a-hunting.'

Next day, crossing the Bay of Biscay, the ship pitched and rolled. With no windows in the medical quarters, Dot was glad she had sea legs. Many men were brought in suffering from acute seasickness.

Dot got used to moving along the low gangways, ducking under cross-pipes, nipping down to the supply room on the fourth deck, racing up to the canteen on the second, taking messages to the officers' wardroom. By noon on the third day, when it was announced they were about to go through the straits of Gibraltar and that things might get tricky, she was well acquainted with the vast area below deck.

It was strange that only when frissons of terror at the threat of action gripped her, had she thought of home, or Billy. She was too busy to be sentimental.

Having gone off duty at midday to be ready for service again in eight hours, Dot lay on her shared bunk, wide awake. She couldn't possibly sleep, so wandered into the mess room to grab some food.

'Nurse Gallagher! If I'd known you were on board I might have got myself seasick!'

Before her stood Captain Howard Hopkins.

He quickly added: 'Don't worry, our friend First Lieutenant Oakewood is not on board.' He patted his leg. 'Ankle playing up. Though whether it was entirely accidental, we are yet to judge. But he neatly got himself out of service again, for a few months at least. Might I join you for a coffee?'

'Sure!'

Howard's company was really welcome. A friendly face, someone comfortable to chat with.

'In a day or so you'll drop us off,' he said, carrying the tray of coffees and sandwiches to the table. 'My guess is Sicily. If it was Morocco it would be later today. On my map, Morocco is less than a quarter of an inch away from Gibraltar!'

'Are there any other people I might know?' asked Dot.

'Did you meet Tony Caruso?'

'Married to Barbara, with the baby?'

'Poor Barbara'll be at her wit's end.' Howard laid the plates and cups on the table. 'It was bad enough when Tony was let loose in London. They met and married while he was stationed up north. She moved down to London with him, but now imagines, because they got hitched so fast, that he beds every girl he winks at. But she's wrong. Tony's just a typical Bronx kid. All Italian swagger. And he really does love her. We're not all how your rhyme describes us: "overpaid and oversexed".'

'My boyfriend thinks you are.'

'He could be right about the pay, but not the other...' Howard slowly stirred his coffee. 'Maybe with one or two exceptions.' He dipped his eyes, averting his gaze.

She said aloud what he hadn't. 'I know you mean Otis. But he's there. I'm here. And I have a very nice fiancé.'

'Very glad to hear that. You deserve it, kid.' Howard edged away from her. 'We go back a long way, me and Oats. He's a fun guy. For other guys, that is. But for women, well ... that's another matter. I am only warning you for your own good.'

'I don't know why you are telling me all this, Howard. There is absolutely no danger of me going off with Otis.'

'In wartime, people do strange things, Dot. It's the intensity of the moment. Skating on thin ice, knowing that every minute could be your last. It explodes our feelings. Everything becomes more forceful.' Howard looked her in the eye. 'Have you ever read about the place in Italy called Pompeii?'

'With the volcano. Yes.'

'Well, there's a house there with a mosaic outside the front door which reads: "Cave Canem". Beware of the dog. When you next encounter our friend Otis, keep that in mind.'

'Otis, a wild dog?' Dot laughed. 'I don't think so.'

'He's not what he says he is. I can say no more. Please, keep your distance.'

'And when do you imagine I'm going to meet him?'

'He'll make sure of it.' Howard shrugged. 'But, beware. You're a very lovely girl, Dot. You deserve the world. Don't forget.' He stood up and tapped the end of his nose with his forefinger. 'Stay safe. And let's hope, like that English broad sings, "we'll meet again".' And with that, he started walking away.

The words of that song carried so much weight, so much yearning and hope. Dot knew that it was because, chances were, they would *not* meet again. Howard was going into battle. She was on a ship that might well get sunk by a U-boat or during an offshore manoeuvre. For all they knew, Howard would not get home. Nor would she.

Dot wanted to rush after Howard and hug him. She did take a few steps and touched his arm. 'Please promise me, Howard, that *you'll* take care of yourself.'

'God bless you, Dot. As my old dad always said: I've made no appointment in Samarra.'

'What does that mean?'

'It's an old Arab parable. Early one morning a man went shopping in the market at Baghdad. There he saw Death walking nearby. Death gave him an astonished glare. Scared out of his wits, the man hired a camel, or whatever they travelled on in those days, and galloped away. By dusk he arrived in a faraway town called Samarra, miles and miles from Baghdad. But there he met Death again. And Death took him, saying, "You know, I was so surprised when I saw you this morning in Baghdad. I couldn't imagine how you'd make it to Samarra, and I knew I had this appointment with you here, tonight."'

A shiver went down Dot's spine.

'Oh, Howard, let's neither of us try anything too clever like that.'

Suddenly, deafening alarms rang out throughout the ship. Men in the mess jumped up and ran out.

'Action stations! I gotta go.'

Dot reached out and squeezed his hand. 'Damn Samarra, Howard. We have an appointment in London, you and me. With the dance floor.'

Howard put his arms around Dot and gave her a hug.

'Dot, you really are a sweet and splendid woman.'

And he was gone.

*

The ship left the port of Gibraltar in the early evening. It was a short stop. Some British troops offloaded, more supplies were taken on. The chief medical officer advised everyone in the hospital department to observe the docks from the aircraft deck, because on the way back they would need to be familiar with loading in this difficult port.

When she returned to her berth, Dot found a letter on her pillow. The small neat writing was unknown to her. In black ink, almost like a typewritten note, the envelope was headed 'War Department, Official Business', followed by an RPO number. She read: 'Dearest, if I did not love you as I do, there would be no necessity for me to write. But I find

I can no longer reason with myself. I stare into the darkness all night long and see nothing but your eyes, and sense the well-remembered nearness of you, dear Skipper. How long has it been since I kissed you? So very long ago, yet somehow I still feel the warmth of your lips against mine. Oh, Skipper, I do love and miss you so!…'

The door opened and her fellow nurse came in. Dot quickly folded the letter and crammed it back into the envelope.

'I must be late.' She jumped from the bed. 'So sorry.'

As she hurried up the gangways to the hospital department, Dot wondered how Howard had known Otis would be in touch. She pulled on her scrubs and washed her hands, then pushed through the doors into theatre.

'Hurry along there, Nurse Gallagher!' The CMO was about to operate on an appendicitis patient.

Dot rolled up her sleeves.

She was in for a tough shift.

TWELVE

THE FIRST THING LILLY'S new roommate had done was to empty the contents of Dot's drawer all over Lilly's bed. Dot had asked Lilly to keep these things safe for her till she returned. The girl had been rather insensitive. It wasn't as though there was a load of stuff, only some mementoes and odd pieces of clothing unsuitable to take to sea.

Lilly went down to the caretaker for a box so she could stow it all away and store it under her own bed. As she sorted the sweaters, skirts, a pair of pyjamas and her dancing shoes, a letter fell to the floor. It was ready, stamped and addressed to a ship address: SS *City of Boston*.

She put it into her bag. On her way to work she posted it.

When Lilly came in, Jack Kirk was already working at his machinery.

'I notice you sometimes walk with a stick, Corporal. Have you a mobility problem?'

'No, sir. I sprained my ankle some weeks ago and, thank goodness, it's almost back to normal. Before this I was in pretty active jobs. I'm not great at office work.'

'You can read and write?'

'Of course.' Lilly laughed. 'I don't like being cooped up. I prefer a bit of adventure.'

He put a record onto a gramophone in the corner, blasting the music as loud as it would go, then grabbed a tin tray. As Lilly put down her bag, she wondered how Fergusson would react to this.

'I want you to take dictation, Corporal,' he said.

Lilly sat at her desk.

'No. You need to crouch down on the floor.' He thrust a pad and pencil into her hand. 'Here we go.'

The gramophone blared out 'Goody Goody'. Reeling off letters of the alphabet, Jack Kirk battered the tray with a handful of spoons. 'A, K, M, N, F, S, B, C, D, P, I, Y, Q, U.'

He stopped and grabbed the pad from her hands. 'Three mistakes. Let's go again.'

'Can't we turn off the record player, Chief Warrant Officer Kirk?'

'You have to learn to work through noise. And please address me as Jack or, if you must be formal, Chief. It's quicker.'

Lilly and Jack spent an hour doing this, then Jack put up the blackout curtains and turned off the light. 'Now we do it in the dark.'

Lilly was alarmed and hoped that this wasn't a cover for wandering hands. After about five minutes of continued dictation, the door opened, and light flooded in from the staircase.

Controller Fergusson stood on the threshold. She flicked on the light.

Instinctively Lilly leapt to her feet and saluted.

'Fail!' said Fergusson, closing the door behind her. 'Whatever goes on around you, you stick to transcribing.'

By following the rules, Lilly had flunked it.

'Am I not right, Chief?'

'Spot on, ma'am. Are you sure she's up to it?'

Fergusson glanced down to the wastepaper basket.

'Did you empty this, Lilly?'

'No, Controller.'

Fergusson turned to Jack Kirk. 'Did you?'

'When I came in this morning, some big brassy redhead was taking it.'

'What time would that have been?'

'Between 0730 and 0800 hours.'

'Interesting.' Fergusson sat at her desk. 'Please continue, Chief Kirk.'

'In the dark, ma'am?'

'Of course.' She turned the light off. 'May I continue my own work?'

'As loud as you like.'

As Fergusson sat at the desk and started typing, Jack Kirk put the record to the start.

Next morning Lilly arrived in the office to find the room to herself and a large note on her desk informing her of the death of Flying Officer Jim Webb while on service in southern Italy. 'His wife works here, in Dabbler's Den. Liz Webb. Please can you pass on the sad news before she gets it some other way. G. Fergusson.'

Lilly had seen Liz in the canteen, a cheery little cockney, always dressed very colourfully with scarves and a bright turban.

She had never had to do anything like this.

'Somebody died?'

Lilly had been so wrapped up in her thoughts she failed to see Nancy come in.

'Yes … um … Flying Officer Webb. I have to tell his wife.'

'Actually, I was making a joke about the flowers.'

A large bouquet lay on Fergusson's desk.

Nancy stooped to inspect the note. 'Goody! They're mine,' she said. 'Luckily I'm pals with the girl on the front desk. She told me Fergusson had brought them up here.'

Gripping the bouquet in one hand, Nancy nodded across the room at Chief Kirk, headphones still on, scribbling on a notepad.

'That's certainly an improvement on the former incumbent. Bet you're glad to see the back of old creeping hands?'

'It's not for me to comment.' Lilly stooped to fasten her shoelace.

Nancy laughed. 'Well, let's just say, you couldn't have taken a position like that with General Smith around. His hairy fingers would have been all over that pert little behind of yours.' She flicked her eyes in the direction of Jack's equipment. 'What's all that about?'

'The radios? No idea.'

'Edward didn't want to see me at all yesterday. We had a bit of a set-to. He went on one of his anti-Jew rants the night before and I walked out on him. Honestly, if he thinks he can get round me with a crass bouquet…'

So! Edward and Nancy had quarrelled, for much the same reasons as she and George. Not knowing how else to respond, Lilly said, 'Oh dear.'

'Don't worry, darling. I'll win him round, you'll see. Men are suckers.'

'If he's so anti-Semitic, why would you want him back? Or, for that matter, if he's a "sucker"?'

'Sweetheart, you are so naïve.' Nancy spoke intimately, as though not wanting Jack Kirk to overhear. 'I want a better life. Don't you? A fancy kitchen, a washing machine, servants, nice clothes, all that. Edward is from one of the richest families in America and, as we know, all Americans are richer than English blokes.' She glanced at her watch. 'Must rush, darling.' Resting the bouquet on her shoulder as though it was a rifle, Nancy marched out of the office and down the stairs.

Lilly glanced over at Jack Kirk to see his reaction. But it appeared that he hadn't even noticed Nancy and her little drama. His eyes were focussed on a small screen, while his long fingers twiddled various knobs.

If Nancy's views were like that, Lilly thought she should strike her from the list of suspects. Most of the Mosleyites and BUF members were proudly anti-Jew. That's one of the main reasons they so admired Hitler.

Now to business. Lilly put on her uniform cap and made her way down the stairs to Dabbler's Den. It was clear that Dot's suspicions were wrong. If Liz Webb's husband was a flying officer, of course she would spend her day off at an airbase in Kent. If people asked where she had been, naturally she was vague, thereby protecting him and his whereabouts. An exemplary woman. Now, sadly, to give her the worst possible news.

After it was done, Lilly climbed the stairs, realising how little she knew about their lives. Only Violet had mentioned her little rooms in the Aldwych – otherwise where did June, Thelma, Peggy or Fergusson go at the end of each working day? She presumed that they lived somewhere in London, not in a hostel like she did. Did they rent little flats, or own big houses in the suburbs? Did they have husbands, children, dogs or cats? Or did they perhaps return to a cold, lonely room?

*

Next morning when she got into work, Lilly paused at the top of the stairs to get her breath back. She didn't want any rude comments from Chief Kirk about being out of shape. As her breathing returned to normal, she could hear voices inside the office.

'God, yes. It is so much easier without G. Smith here.'

'Don't remind me.' Lilly recognised Nancy's voice. 'He was a real liability.'

'Not only in the obvious way.'

'Darling!' Nancy laughed. 'Tell me about it!'

The screech of Fergusson's chair scraping on the lino flooring meant she was standing up. Lilly heard her footsteps crossing the room. Was she about to open the door? Stealthily she took a step back and down a few steps so she could make out she was just arriving.

'How's the new bloke?' asked Nancy.

'I'm thinking of asking him to join us.'

'Really!'

What was going on? Heart pounding, Lilly strained forward, the better to hear. But her stick caught on the railing and tumbled down the stairs behind her.

Fergusson abruptly stopped talking. 'Shh!'

She yanked the door open. Lilly was caught trying to retreat. How to explain?

'Haven't you heard the saying, Corporal Deane, "Listeners hear no good of themselves"?'

'I just dropped my stick, that's all.' A banal response, but the truth. 'I don't know why I still carry it. I don't really need it.'

'Gets you a seat on the bus.' Nancy was putting on her service cap as she swished past Lilly. 'Good morning, Chief Kirk.'

She saluted as he passed her on his way up.

'I'm worried that she won't be ready, Controller,' he said, as soon as they were all in the office.

'Work harder.' Fergusson glowered in Lilly's direction, then followed Nancy down the stairs.

As she worked that morning, Lilly went over the conversation she had overheard. She found herself making mistake after mistake.

'Why are you so slow today, Deane?' Chief Kirk slammed his hands down on the desk. 'I need someone quick and bright. Controller Fergusson must be mistaken in you. Go back to riding your cosy little ponies along those leafy Surrey lanes.'

It was the hundredth time that morning that Chief Kirk had made a nasty dig at Lilly. She was starting to resent him. She was tired of the relentless insults and longed to go back to pinning up notices about table tennis tournaments in Dunker's Den or contact bridge in the quiet room.

Finally, Jack Kirk threw up his hands, pulled down the blackout cloth and told Lilly to go to lunch.

I hate him, I hate him, I hate him, she thought, as she went down the stairs. After waiting an age in the queue for a sandwich, she went to the steps of Piccadilly Circus, leaning against the Savings Bond posters. Since starting work with Chief Kirk, Lilly spent most lunch hours huddled up here, eating a sandwich, reading a newspaper. After a morning crazed with the darkness and noise, she was happy to get outside for some air and light, despite the cold.

She looked across to Swan & Edgar and noticed Chief Kirk standing on the pavement, laughing with Fergusson. Both of them holding their sides, in stitches about something or other. Probably her. Or maybe Fergusson had just asked him to join her mystery group. What were they up to? Perhaps they were the moles. Fergusson certainly had access to more information than anyone in the building, while Nancy could coax it out of the boys while she danced.

A discarded newspaper lay on the steps. Lilly picked it up and opened it, if only to make herself look busy should Fergusson and Jack glance her way. She didn't want to be accused of listening in a second time in one day.

Page one was all about the war, except for a small paragraph about a suspected fifth columnist who had been arrested in Onslow Square. Wasn't that where Joe told Dot he had followed some woman? The nameless man had been picked up a few days before the Baby Blitz started, back in January. She tore out the square and shoved it in her pocket to send to Dot. Page two had an article about sabotage in the GI camp at Richmond. Someone had maliciously cut the camp's telephone wires. Luckily, telephone engineers had been working on something else there, so it was repaired in no time and all danger averted.

Richmond?

Hadn't Violet said she'd been down there?

But that was absurd.

Violet was visiting her beau, Sydney. Why would she want to endanger him?

But then again, hadn't Fergusson seemed interested that Violet had come up to the office to empty the bin, assuming she was the big brassy redhead Jack had mentioned? Why would Violet do that? It wasn't her job, and the fourth floor office was hardly convenient when you normally worked in the basement.

Lilly realised that Violet seemed like the last person in Rainbow Corner to suspect.

But wasn't that the best cover?

She really hoped it wasn't true. She liked Violet.

She looked up from the newspaper and caught eyes with Jack, who was standing alone now, hands on hips, watching her.

A bus went by, obscuring him; when she saw him again, he was summoning her to cross the road.

She obeyed.

'Let's get back to work, Corporal. No time like the present.'

'I'm sorry I don't meet your standards, Chief Kirk...'

'... Jack.'

'But I wonder couldn't we try something else?'

'Dear Corporal.' Jack stopped, took Lilly's arm and looked into her eyes. 'We are going at your pace, not mine. I know not to snap the ears off the corn before they are ripe.'

'Well, here's another proverb for you, Chief. Bored, posh country girls don't know what you're talking about.'

'Not a very good proverb, if I may say so, except for spoiled brats.' He looked up at the front of the club. 'Look at that place. If you were expecting to discover a rainbow, it would be very disappointing. Have you ever stood alone in the rain, Lilly, no other creature in sight, watching the sun play at paints with the sky? Or do you prefer the more sophisticated colours of cocktails at the Dorchester?'

'To be honest, I don't think I've lived long enough to know what I really want. It's just been school, then this war.'

They climbed the stairs.

'So you *are* a spoiled brat? Tied to Mommy's apron strings, never straying far from home except on the odd pony trek?'

'I've not been off fighting, if that's what you mean. Few women have.' Lilly felt really insulted by his tone. It was hardly her fault that she was young and inexperienced. 'But I've tried to do my bit, driving and so on. And why do you keep on about my riding ponies?'

'If you thought it was important enough to put into your curriculum vitae, it seems relevant to talk about. Are you a good horsewoman?'

'Good enough.'

'What size horse?'

'Thirteen hands.'

'Are you scared of the idea of battle?'

'Not now. Not while I'm safely here in London. I've been through a couple of air raids, but I'd bet that's not nearly as frightening as having to confront the enemy. The idea seems rather exciting. I'm not sure whether those feelings don't flee once you're down a trench, knee-deep in mud and blood, with bombs going off all around you, your companions lying dead at your feet.'

Chief Kirk made an almost imperceptible groan.

To break the ice a little, Lilly asked: 'Were you in Europe before you came to us?'

'I was in the Pacific.'

'I presume you witnessed "the monstrous anger of the guns" and "the stuttering rifles' rapid rattle"?'

'Anti-war poetry. Wilfred Owen, I believe.'

Lilly was surprised that Jack knew.

'Do you believe we should lay down our arms and let Hitler do what he likes with other people's countries, lock up the Jews and the Gypsies?'

'Of course not, but I...' Lilly had cornered herself. Looking up at Jack, she wondered – with his dark complexion, black hair and eyes, and strongly marked features – if he himself had Romani roots.

'You might believe in peace, Lilly, but there are times when you have no choice but to fight back.' As Jack opened the door to the office, he stopped. 'Perhaps one day you should hear thunder rumble in a purple sky, while your eyes can see nothing made by man on all the wide horizon.'

'Oh God, this is not going to be one of those "Big Sky America" sermons, is it?'

Jack looked down at her and laughed.

'Controller Fergusson was right. You are bright. But very naïve. And no, I'm not donut man. I won't wax on eternally about my country, although I could. Now let's get back to work.'

THIRTEEN

A LOUD EXPLOSION SHOOK DOT out of bed.

The action station alarms rang out, red lights flashed.

She hastily dressed and made her way to the medical ward. The ship was pitching and rolling. Men were running everywhere.

Another blast and the ship rocked to one side.

The convoy was under attack.

The CMO stood at the door of the ward. 'We're east of Sardinia, Nurse Gallagher, moving in towards Italy. Looks like Jerry was expecting us.' He stood back to let her pass. 'Probably being smashed to bits because some damned idiot couldn't hold his tongue.' He grabbed a portable first-aid kit from the counter and passed it to her. 'Flight deck, please.'

As Dot made her way up the gangways to the top deck, she passed a hall where hundreds of men were assembled ready to march onto landing craft.

From above, deafening sounds. The ship pitched.

In the distance she caught sight of Howard. He smiled and waved.

Her own terror was accelerated at the thought of what those boys were about to be in for.

As Dot made it into the open, a nearby plane took off from the flight deck, and she pressed her hands to cover her ears. The sky was black with smoke. Allied and Axis planes battled it out above.

Another bomb dropped, missing the ship by about 50 yards, but sending a plume of water smashing down onto the decks.

Dot gripped the handrail as the ship lurched to one side.

'Nurse!' An officer was climbing down the steps from the bridge. 'The captain's hand has been badly cut. This way.'

With thunderous blasts, the anti-aircraft guns fired; the officer hauled Dot up the metal ladder.

She cleaned the captain's wound and applied bandages, while over the noise he shouted orders to the crew on the bridge.

Outside, all hell was breaking loose. Smoky billows spewed from a plane as it plummeted from the sky.

'Another of theirs hits the drink,' said the captain, holding his binoculars with the unharmed hand. 'We've brought down around five now. And got one of their ships.'

At the side of the bridge window, a parachute opened.

'Yet another Jerry bails out. Looks like we've seen 'em off this time. We'll be going in soon to offload.'

By the time Dot got back, changed and scrubbed up again for the surgical ward, a man, black with burns and engine oil, lay on the table.

'Prepare me a syrette, please, Nurse Gallagher. He has to be sedated.'

Dot moved to the instrument table and passed the morphine syringe to the CMO.

The man on the table yelped and writhed in pain. His skin was ruptured, shiny with oil and blood.

'Hold down his arm, Gallagher. Third-degree. Four in some areas. Had to fish him out of the flaming sea.'

The other nurse was busily cutting away the man's scorched trousers. Dot grabbed the patient's arm and pressed it firmly against the operating table.

The patient turned his head in Dot's direction and opened his eyes. *'Lass mich los!'* he snarled.

'We're trying to help you,' she said calmly. 'It's all right. It's all right.'

As the man saw the painkilling syringe going into his arm, his eyes widened. *'Du dreckige Hure!'* He gathered up his lips and spat in Dot's face. *'Billiges Flittchen!'*

Calmly the CMO completed administering the injection, then, as the phlegm dripped down Dot's cheek, he said calmly, 'Go and clean your face, please, nurse.'

*

The rest of the passage back to Palermo was rough. And with nearly all the men gone, the ship felt ghostly. They docked briefly to pick up more wounded.

Dot tried to stop herself thinking of the contradictions of war. They set out to harm and kill people and then, whichever side they were on, had to help them. It was very difficult to reconcile the two. But as a nurse, it was her sworn duty to help and heal whoever was brought into the ward.

After another two days at sea, the ship moored once again at Gibraltar. As the crew tightened the mooring ropes, Dot looked down from the flight deck and was shocked to see that the length of the dockside was filled with rows and rows of stretchers.

'So many amputees,' she said quietly, surveying the hundreds, if not thousands, of injured men.

'They've been brought down from makeshift wards up in St Michael's Cave.' The CMO pointed his finger towards an area halfway up the great Rock of Gibraltar. 'A forty-minute walk at the best of times. God knows how they carried them all down.'

'Where have they come from?'

'Southern Italy – where we were a few days ago. Many brought here by faster vessels than us and given elementary first aid, then we carry the poor bastards home. Looks like there won't be much rest between here and Pompey.' He rolled up his sleeves. 'The moment the gangways go down, we'll start triage.'

By the time they pulled out of Gibraltar, every open space on the ship was filled with makeshift beds and men lying on blankets. The seriously wounded were put nearest the operating theatre and medical centre; further away lay the sick – men suffering from dysentery and malaria. At the other end of the ship were the cases suffering non-life-threatening injuries.

The German sailors and airmen who had been rescued from the sea in the Bay of Naples were by now all treated, wounds stitched up, burns under control. They had been locked up, prisoners of war.

As the nursing team started working on the worst cases, Dot was surprised to see that some men were still wearing filthy, caked field dressings which must have been put on days before, in Italy. On some of the amputations gangrene had set in.

Dot spent hours ladling maggots from buckets into the festering wounds, leaving the grubs to eat away the bad flesh.

Just before midnight, the CMO ordered Dot to bed. Reluctantly she obeyed, understanding that after a few hours' kip she would be more use.

As she curled up on her berth, a maggot fell from her hair and landed on the pillow. She jumped up, hitting her head on the bunk above. Although she had washed her hands as frantically as Lady Macbeth, she could still smell blood on them.

As she and Billy jokingly used to say, 'Wot a life!' She rolled over, facing the steel wall, remembering how Billy had talked to her in London. How on earth could he expect anyone living like this to stay a child? At dawn she was up again, this time working at the other end of the ship, tending the boys with broken fingers or superficial flesh wounds. She felt like an automaton, all emotion gone. The hardship of this work felt like an atonement, a penance for mistakes: petty, jealous remarks, silly little white lies, cheeky moments of laziness, like avoiding going to the corner shop when her mother had asked her, or pretending she had homework to do, when all she was really doing was sitting in her room reading *Melody Maker*.

'Hey! Scouser nurse. I know you!' The GI lying on the floor tugged at Dot's skirt as she passed. 'I danced with you at Rainbow Corner.'

Dot looked down at the grimy oil-stained face.

The GI burst into a bright smile. Once the teeth were on display, she recognised him.

'Tony!'

'That's right. Caruso. Like the singer.'

'How are you doing?'

'Could be better. Got a nick in my leg, a chunk out of my waist, a bullet in my arm and lost a finger. But I'm lucky it wasn't my heart, cos I'll be needing that when I see my new baby. Did they tell you? Barbara's made me a father again.'

'Congratulations!'

'Bouncing boy. I'm going to teach him to be a baseball whizz. Before you know it, he'll be joining the Brooklyn Dodgers.'

'Weren't you on this ship coming out, Tony? Didn't we just drop you off in Italy?'

'Sure did.' With a wince Tony pulled himself up and sat with his back resting against the grey metal wall. 'I had barely got 100 yards off the beach when I was hit. I was lucky. Soldier beside me ... a goner. Head blasted right off.'

He pointed down at his stained uniform shirt. 'That's his blood, not mine.'

Dot's heart lurched. She hoped Tony wasn't referring to Howard. She was surprised by the force of her reaction.

'Anyway, they loaded me back onto one of the landing craft and I was whizzed over to Gib in another ship to wait for this big one to carry me home. Well, not home, exactly, but to London, to my family. Which is a better form of home.'

Dot wondered how Tony had managed to get transported with such minor injuries. But before she could ask, he said: 'Compassionate leave. New father and all that.' He looked around. 'Can you keep a secret?'

Dot nodded.

'You'll have to come nearer.'

He plunged his fist into his trouser pocket.

'When they were cutting my sleeves off, in Gibraltar, I heard a ping. I looked down at the floor. Looked like a coin.'

Dot smiled. 'That'll be one of Vi's famous farthings. She sews them into the GI's stripes.'

Tony's face clouded over.

'From the back it looked like a coin, but when I flipped it over…' Surreptitiously he unfolded his fist and presented his palm to Dot.

He held a small circular lapel pin.

Dot glanced around to make sure no one had seen, while simultaneously folding Tony's fingers back.

'Oh, it's all right, nursey. I don't want anyone mistaking me for one of *them*. But I can just tell them I ripped it off one of those bastards who shot me on the streets at Nettuno. Battle booty.'

He unfolded his fingers again. Dot looked down. About half an inch in diameter, the badge was red enamel, with a white circle, in the centre of which was set a black swastika.

FOURTEEN

APRIL 1944

Lilly met up with the gang for dinner at Victory, a small Soho restaurant.

'Let's hope that name's a prediction for us,' said Paul, as they took places around a corner table.

Violet was in her Sunday best, everyone else in uniform. 'You lot are lucky,' she said. 'The WVS uniform is so ugly. It makes me look like a fat old char.'

'What's a char?' asked Sydney. 'Someone who makes tea?'

'A cleaner, Sydney, keep up!'

'You mean a janitor?' Sydney picked up the menu. 'I never understand a word you English speak.'

Lilly watched Violet from behind her own menu. It couldn't be possible that she was working against them. She was so open. Nothing furtive about her at all.

'Janitor? Oo-er.' Paul flapped his serviette open and lay it on his lap. 'To us, that sounds like someone who works down the drains.'

The waiter stood poised, pad and pencil in hand. He glanced down at the box of donuts which Art had brought with him.

'I'm afraid you can't eat those in here, sir.' He pointed to a sign on the wall. 'Only food bought on the premises.'

Art put one donut on a plate and offered it to the waiter, who glanced round to make sure nobody saw, before cramming it into his pocket. 'Put them away, then, and be discreet.' He looked at the two empty seats.

'Someone joining you? Over there we do have a table for five.'

'They're coming off duty,' said Paul. 'Or should I have said they're being fashionably late. The way those two always roll up ten minutes after everyone else makes you wonder if they haven't been sneaking peeks at

Euphemia McSmither's Guide to Etiquette, mistaking each vaguely social invitation for a solicitation to an intimate at-home soirée.'

'Cor blimey, Paul. You swallowed a dictionary? I fancy the fish. How about you, Lilly?'

'It all looks nice.'

'When d'you think you'll all be off then, Sydney?' Paul asked. 'I can never get a peep out of those two white helmets.'

'That's cos no one tells us anything,' Sydney replied. 'I think I'll have a meat pie.'

'Cooee!' Violet waved towards the windows. 'Here they come. The big hunks. Shove up, Sydney. Give the boys some room. They're burlier than you. Is that a word? Burlier?'

Virgil and Marty's faces were grim.

Lilly felt a shock of fear. It must be bad news.

As they came in, instead of taking off their helmets, they patted the tops of them, as though to make sure they were correctly in position.

Lilly prayed they would say something funny and the spell would be broken.

But no.

They stared down at the table.

'Violet May Beckton?'

'You're off duty now, boys.' Violet laughed.

There was no humour showing in their faces. Then a London bobby appeared behind them.

Violet patted the seat next to her. 'Sit your arses down, boys.'

She should stop joking. They were about to say something awful. Lilly was certain of it.

'Violet May Beckton. We are arresting you for crimes committed under the Treachery Act.'

'Wait a tick, what's going on?' Violet looked from one man to the other. 'This is a joke, right?'

'It's not true…' Sydney rose to his feet. 'You don't mean…'

But Marty was already trying to attach handcuffs to Violet's wrists.

She shook him off. 'You don't need to do that to me, Marty. I'll go with you peacefully, but only so I can prove my innocence. Take my arm if you like. If I made a run for it, you know you could overpower me in seconds.'

They led Violet out of the restaurant.

At the door she turned and shouted: 'I'll prove I didn't do anything, don't worry.'

Virgil tugged at her arm. The door slammed behind them.

Paul said, 'I've lost my appetite.'

'Me too,' said Sydney. 'Men have died because of what the posters glibly call "loose lips".'

Art threw down his napkin. 'If she's done this devilish thing, God damn her to hell.' From Art, this kind of language was shocking.

'Ready to order?' The waiter was back.

'I think we'll leave it for now,' said Lilly. 'We've had a bit of a shock.'

'As for you, Sydney,' Art towered over him, 'I pray you are not involved with this. And you'll not start defending her.'

Lilly looked at Sydney. His face was white. He was all-in.

'See you tomorrow.' Paul led Art out of the restaurant.

Sydney stood. 'We should go after her. It's gotta be one huge mistake. We know Vi. She would never … She was going to come and live with me, on my farm. Be my forever gal.'

He blinked away a tear which Lilly pretended not to notice.

'Come along, Sydney,' she said. 'Best go back to your quarters. And don't talk about it.'

'I have to talk about it, Lilly.'

Lilly's thoughts had been going in a similar direction. But what could they do?

'It all seems like some preposterous joke. I'll make enquiries tomorrow, see what I can find out.' They had reached Charing Cross Road. 'But from my experience, the officials are very cagy on such matters.'

Still shaking his head in disbelief, Sydney disappeared down into the tube.

Lilly had hardly got 500 yards down the road when the air-raid sirens rang out.

Rather than go back, she ran to Trafalgar Square and went down into the station there. Once she found somewhere to lie down, she pulled a notebook from her bag and started writing a letter to Dot. Their search for Joe's Rainbow Corner traitor was over.

*

Dot was changing dressings this evening. Winding bandages round arms and legs. Her ship was now sailing up the Channel towards Portsmouth. Tomorrow she would be back in England.

'Wake up, nurse!' The ship's senior sister had been addressing her. 'I was just saying that some letters came for you. They're in the mess room. And you're over your time. Go on your break before you drop.'

Dot picked up her letters, then went to grab some dinner. She sat at a small table to read them while she ate.

She opened her parents' letter first. Sweet tales of her neighbours and Trixy, who had escaped under the back fences and run down the jigger, where he knocked over a bin and caused an argument with the fussy old biddy at the end of the street. They'd been to the cinema to see *Fanny by Gaslight* starring Phyllis Calvert and James Mason. The story, they agreed, was pretty silly, but it was a nice escape from the rationing queues. They longed to see Dot and hoped all was well, wherever she was.

Billy's letter was written on one thin page and consisted of one sentence. 'If you can write things like that when I am on a ship under fire, while you're lounging about eating donuts in London with your Yank paramours, we're over. Goodbye.'

He hadn't even signed it.

Hadn't he got her letter where she told him that she too was at sea, also under enemy fire, and that she loved him?

Dot didn't know where to turn. She had no friends on board, no one with whom she could discuss things like this.

'Hey, nursey? Why you looking so sad? We can't have our smiling Liverpudlian wearing a long face. It upsets nature.' Tony was holding a tray, ready to sit down to eat. 'So, what's buggin' ya?'

'I've been chucked.'

Tony glanced down at the envelope on the table.

'In a letter? That's harsh.' He put the tray down at the adjacent table. 'Tell that fool from me that anyone who dumps a nice girl like you needs their head reading.'

He started tucking into his food. 'I heard they picked up that woman who sews the stripes on. Who'da thought it?'

'She always seemed so friendly.'

'Perhaps that's the thing. The cheery ones are more dangerous.' Tony shovelled another forkful of food into his mouth. 'Mind you, if that was a universal truth, it would mean we couldn't trust either you or me. And we're mint.' He shrugged his shoulders and grimaced. 'I give up.'

After dawn Dot queued with the other medical staff, ready to file off the ship. She'd been away for weeks and now she wanted nothing more than to go back to sea, to escape what awaited her on land. Billy's letter had depressed and angered her.

She had another couple of weeks here on shore base, then two weeks in London before she'd get a long enough leave to get up to Liverpool. Meanwhile she had one day off to settle down, then back to the wards.

She shuffled down the gangway. Ambulances stood on the quay to take the seriously wounded and sick straight to hospital. Further along the dockside a coach was waiting to bring the medical and service teams straight to shore base, outside the town.

It was pouring with rain.

Dot ran for the bus. Inside it was steamed up from the damp uniforms. With the condensation on the inside and the rain streaming down outside, it was impossible to see anything.

After about twenty minutes' drive, the coach pulled in at a large house which might once have been a hotel or school. People ahead of her formed a scrum to retrieve their kitbags as the driver chucked them out into the rain.

Dot didn't care. If you hung them up, clothes dried. Most of her things needed a good wash anyway. So what if the ink on Billy's letter got smudged? She didn't want to read it again, ever.

As she climbed down the steps from the coach onto the gravel driveway, she felt terribly lonely.

Her kitbag was leaning up against the side of the front wheel, so she slung it over her shoulder.

'I think I can take that weight from your shoulders, Nurse Gallagher.'

Dot was about to argue with whoever had pulled the bag from her back.

'Hey, Skipper, how ya doing? You look all in.'

'Otis?'

Dot was shocked to see him. But perhaps it would be nice to have someone to talk to.

'Come along, Skip, let me get you dried out and a hot drink inside you. I hear that this place is so great they even serve English tea. How about that? Tea and toast. Just like your folks made for me.'

'What are you doing here, Otis?'

'Can't a guy spend his one day's leave visiting the gal he adores? I tell you it took a lot of sucking up to get a travel warrant to come down here.'

'I didn't ask you to.'

'But it's been an age since you went away. What I really mean to say is I missed you.'

They passed through the large front door into a hall where the others were crowded round a noticeboard searching the lists to find their room numbers.

'Eighty-eight! What d'ya know. My lucky number.' Otis steered Dot through the crowd towards a large wooden staircase. 'Got to get you settled in so your personal steward can bring you tea.'

Dot was too tired to fight him.

Otis laid her kitbag on the bed and went down to the canteen, leaving her to unpack.

When she had finished hanging her few things out to dry on chairs and hooks on the door, Dot perched on the bed. She felt empty and numb. As for Billy…

The door opened and Otis came in bearing a tray. He burst into the song 'Tea for Two'.

When Dot smiled, he stopped.

'Don't worry, Skipper, you don't have to listen to me singing. As you British folks say, "Wait a tick"!'

He went out of the room and returned bearing a gramophone, which he placed on the floor and wound up with a handle on the side.

'It occurred to me, Skipper, that the one thing you don't get on a ship is music, and we all know you love it … so here you are. My gift.'

He ran out of the door once more and returned with a pile of records.

'But I'm only here two weeks, Otis, I can't lug that thing back to London on the train…'

'That's good, Skip. You're putting up a fight. What d'you know, when I said *my gift*, I really should have said *my loan*. I borrowed it for two weeks, then my pal will come take it back. Meanwhile,' he had plopped a record onto the turntable and laid the arm ready to play, 'may I have the pleasure of the next dance?'

After half an hour jitterbugging in the confines of the small room, they collapsed on the bed, out of breath. How wonderful it was to dance again. Otis jumped straight up again. 'Have to spin another disc…'

'But I'm exhausted…' Dot raised herself on her elbows. The man was impossible. 'I couldn't dance another step.'

'Nor me.' Otis sat next to her on the bed. 'That's why I'm putting on this corny old thing.'

The disc crackled for a second, then, after a chord on the steel guitar, the mellifluous voice of Bing Crosby started singing 'Blue Hawaii'.

Otis put his arm around her shoulder and splayed the other out before him as though setting the scene. 'We're going to have them sing this on the beach in Waikiki, on our honeymoon.'

'Please don't get fresh with me, Otis.'

'Would I do such a thing?' Otis held up his hands. 'No, Skipper. I'm only here to make you smile. I gather Howard was on board with you. Can't wait till the pair of us are back on that big shiny train steaming down to California.' Adding, 'Of course you'll be with us, we couldn't leave our darling Skipper behind.'

Otis told her that in California the sun always shines, and that women have modern kitchen gadgets, no mangles or washboards, so they live the life of Riley, sunbathing and painting their nails, while all the men drive huge cars with open tops.

After Otis had left for London that evening, Dot felt sad. He had brightened the day with his chatter and impulsive ideas.

In the morning, a letter from Lilly arrived, dated just after Dot had left for the Med. It had certainly taken its time getting to her. The news (or should it be the 'olds'?) was that Lilly had broken off her engagement with George. Glued to the bottom of the page, a small cutting about the arrest of a man in Onslow Square. Joe had been right all along. A second letter was from Howard. He wrote with a strong hand in black ink, filling five sheets of onion skin. The men of the US army, he wrote, were followed everywhere by local kids who'd learned to say 'Hey, GI!', which came out all strange in their accent. It was tough, he said, but he was confident that they would win through. He'd not been tempted to take a ride on a camel, as there was none available in that part of the world, and please could Dot make sure she avoided them too. He signed off: "'I'll be looking at the moon, but I'll be seeing…" a swell gal from Liverpool, my love, Howard.' Adding beneath his signature, in capital letters: 'PLEASE REMEMBER – CAVE CANEM.'

Beware of Otis, indeed! Hadn't Otis been the one bright moment in the last month? Howard had to be jealous of him. Why else warn her off a friend?

Dot now prayed that when her two weeks were up and she could make it back to London that Otis would still be there and not have been sent off to take part in the Allied invasion of Europe, which everyone sensed was imminent.

FIFTEEN

NOW THAT PEOPLE HAD worked out that Lilly always went there, she didn't fancy being such a sitting target for random chats during her lunch break, so instead of the steps at Piccadilly, she went up the road for a snack in Fortes café on Leicester Square.

She was almost finished when, at a distant table, she noticed Art talking intently with June. June was resting her face in the palms of her hands. Was she crying?

Art placed his arm around her shoulder.

Well!

Art and June!

That was something Lilly wouldn't have expected. The Holy Joe and the painted Jezebel. Perhaps June's spinster days were over.

Not wanting them to know she'd seen them, Lilly quickly paid and left.

To fill the rest of the lunch hour, she strolled up and down Shaftesbury Avenue looking at the photos outside theatres, then browsed at a news stand, choosing a magazine to take home and read that night.

On the stairs up to the office, she met Nancy coming down. More furtive meetings with Fergusson, no doubt.

'How are you doing, Nancy?' she asked.

'Getting along.' Nancy sighed. 'If we're going to go into Europe, I wish we'd just get on with it.'

'Afternoon, girls!' They made way for Art, who was heading up the stairs, his long legs taking the steps three at a time. He was clutching a huge pile of paperwork. He passed, then hesitated, before turning back and saying in a sombre tone: 'I'm so sorry, Nancy.'

'Don't worry, you didn't tread on my toes.' She laughed. 'Not this time, anyway.'

Art gingerly came down a few steps to be on a level.

'I don't think you can have heard the news.'

'Don't tell me they're not going to put on any extra trains over Easter?'

Lilly wished that Nancy would stop making quips. Art was obviously about to say something very serious.

'I'm sorry, Sergeant Newton.' He put out his hand and gently touched Nancy's sleeve. 'But we've just heard. Colonel Cornell's plane was shot down.'

'But he bailed out? Didn't he? Yes?' Nancy grasped the handrail and leaned against it. 'He's safe? Taken prisoner?'

Art slowly shook his head. 'It's the very worst possible news, I'm afraid.'

'No, no, no!' Nancy shot out her hand to cover Art's mouth. 'That's not possible. No. No. Edward isn't dead. No. He isn't. He can't be.'

Art cast a look at Lilly, and she put her arm around Nancy. But Nancy pushed her away.

For a moment Nancy stood deathly still, staring straight ahead. Then she slid down the wall and crouched in a ball on the steps. She started to wail.

Fergusson came out of the office.

'I'll take care of this, Corporal. You get back to work. I'll take her down to the nurse in Dunker's Den.'

Fergusson put her arm around Nancy's waist and hauled her to her feet.

She then turned back to address Lilly. 'Chief Kirk is attending a meeting with the bigwigs at Grosvenor Square. Find something to occupy yourself.'

Lilly sat at her desk. What could she do on her own without Chief Kirk?

She decided to go back to the things she had done previously. Taking a pile of quiz forms from Fergusson's desk, she went through them, then checked through the diary of upcoming events: a tea dance, a golf tournament, dramatic classes with an actress from a play on up the road. Lilly spent half an hour preparing lists to go up. She was surprised that she now longed for the pressure of Kirk's curt orders; this old job was tedious beyond words.

Flicking through a list of current hostesses, she presumed that they needed filing, so moved over to the cabinet.

Then she paused.

She'd never actually looked inside. It was always a case of Fergusson opening the drawer for her to drop papers into the open folder.

Would she find a file on herself? Or on Dot?

She pulled open the hostess folder.

No file on Nancy. She only seemed to appear on lists. There was no character reference on her either, as there was for Dot (Ward Sister Sullivan, Vincent Square) and all the others.

She pulled out June's file. She was older than she looked. She'd been born during the Great War, which made her almost thirty. Married to a warrant officer in the RAF, based at Hornchurch.

Hadn't Dot said that June was a spinster? Who on earth pretended *not* to be married? And to an RAF man? That would be most girls' dream. What was June hiding?

Behind her the door opened. Lilly shoved the papers back into the folder, slammed the drawer shut and turned, trying to look nonchalant. Failing to hide her shaking hands, she turned to face Thelma on the threshold.

'Any stray cups?'

Relieved that it hadn't been Fergusson, Lilly glanced around at the desktops. On Jack's desk, there was one solitary mug.

She placed it on Thelma's tray.

'Terrible news for poor Nancy, isn't it?' Thelma walked to the door.

'Terrible,' added Lilly, as the door closed behind her.

She sat and thought back on everything Dot had said about June. She wasn't going home alone each night to the lonely hostel as she had implied to Dot. She must live in married quarters, on an airbase. Why lie? Nancy had wanted the world to know she had been going out with a high-ranking pilot. Why would June want to hide her position?

Then a thought occurred – perhaps Art had his arm around June because he was breaking bad news to her too.

Maybe they had all been wrong about Violet. Perhaps June *did* have something to hide and Violet had been framed for something she hadn't done.

Lilly wanted answers but knew she'd never get a pass to visit Violet in prison. However, she could write. She took a clean piece of paper and popped it into the typewriter. While making the letter seem chatty and inconsequential, she tried to be factual. Unimportant events at Rainbow

Corner. Wondering what to do with her own upcoming two-day leave, she asked if Violet could recommend Brighton. Wasn't that where Fergusson had said some member of the January Club had been picked up, and papers found in their house, papers which had come from here, Rainbow Corner? As Lilly sealed the letter, she understood that if Violet was guilty she wouldn't admit anything. But how would an innocent person reply?

As she left for the evening, Lilly popped the letter into the outgoing mailbox in the front hall.

Pearl had invited Lilly to join her at Feldman's Club in Oxford Street and left her a free pass. So Lilly joined the queue leading down the steep staircase to the clubroom. She took a little table for two near the front, good for seeing the band. A small drum kit, lit in shades of pink, stood ready on the stage. A guitar and double bass waited on stands.

Lilly perused the menu then glanced back to the entrance. The club was busy. All the tables were full. Some people were standing near the bar at the back.

The lights flickered, indicating that the show would soon start. But no Pearl. Lilly wondered whether she might have misread the message. Had Pearl meant for them to meet outside? Perhaps she had got the day wrong.

Lilly faced the door, anxious to catch Pearl's eye the moment she entered.

A drum roll.

Lilly took another glance towards the door.

Then she saw Chief Kirk, standing at the bar.

She hastily turned away to face the stage.

And there was Pearl, behind her drum kit. Jean-Claude on guitar. And beside him, resplendent in a sparkly blue-sequinned jacket, stood Earl, fiddling with the tuning pegs of his double bass. The band was back together.

At the break, Pearl came down to Lilly's table and apologised for having been so vague.

'You see, love, we're so excited cos Earl is back in one piece, and we're playing together again but…' she whispered in Lilly's ear, 'we disobeyed the CO and, this afternoon, at Caxton Hall, we got married.' She waved a wedding ring in front of Lilly, then perched on the edge of the empty chair. 'They'll never know. And what business is it of theirs, anyway? Earl's got a few weeks' leave now, so this gig will pass for our honeymoon.'

'What about the future, Pearl? When we go back to peacetime, where will you live?'

'We'll have to wait and see.'

A bell rang; people hurried from the bars back to their seats.

'You'll be here when we finish the set, won't you, Lil, love? Stay put, then we can all raise a toast together?'

Pearl climbed back onto the stage.

The house lights dimmed.

'Good evening, English Rose.' A tap on Lilly's shoulder. 'If that seat is still empty, I don't suppose you would consider letting me sit for part two?'

It would be churlish to refuse.

As Jack sat, he whispered, 'I had no idea you had such good taste in music. Or glamorous friends in such high places.'

Lilly put her finger to her lips. The band had started playing.

When the concert was over, Jack asked how she knew the musicians. She explained how, before the war, she'd seen them play in Montmartre and they'd got to know one another. She, Jean-Claude, Earl and Pearl had stayed in touch, as much as that was possible these days.

Jack asked if she might introduce him. Lilly felt reluctant to bring another man into the racial mix after the episode with Edward and George, but didn't know how to refuse.

To her surprise, when the trio arrived at the table, now back in uniform, Jack made straight for Earl, falling straight into deep conversation about their military world. Pearl went off to get drinks, leaving Lilly to chat with Jean-Claude.

'I missed you,' she said. 'I was so worried while you were away.'

Under the table, Jean-Claude took her hand and squeezed it.

'Me too. I thought about you.'

Lilly suggested that they meet up again, perhaps spend an evening at the theatre. The Rattigan play, maybe, or *Arsenic and Old Lace.*

Jean-Claude flinched.

'Tonight is my last night in London. Tomorrow I leave.'

'What's that?' said Jack, breaking away from his conversation with Earl. 'You're off?'

Jean-Claude nodded. Pearl arrived back at the table with a tray of drinks.

'I won't ask where, but I can guess. A dangerous engagement.' Jack waved to a passing waiter. 'Do you have champagne? A bottle, please. We need a toast. A toast that we all come back safe.'

Earl and Pearl looked into each other's eyes as they raised their glasses.

'To peace,' said Jack.

'To peace,' they echoed.

What had Jack meant by a 'dangerous engagement'? Jean-Claude had nodded, implying that it was. As Lilly clinked glasses with Jean-Claude, she imagined him falling in the darkness, landing in a black field, surrounded by Nazi soldiers.

'Take enormous care of yourself, please,' she whispered.

Jean-Claude tore a thin strip from the bottom of the menu card. He pulled a pencil from his pocket and hastily scribbled J-C ♥ L, then wrapped it around Lilly's engagement finger. 'You have tape in the office? Tomorrow you can make it whole. But from tonight we are linked together, OK? I need someone to come back for.'

Lilly kissed him on his cheek.

She raised her glass. 'To us!'

'To you two!' Pearl raised her glass high. 'And to us.'

As she glanced around at the grinning faces, Lilly could sense the charge of fear behind the smiles.

This was no drill.

Jean-Claude was leaving on some perilous campaign and soon she would be joining Chief Kirk, on their own special service.

She raised her glass once more: 'To life.'

'To life.' Jean-Claude clinked her glass.

SIXTEEN

JUNE 1944

Lilly received a reply from Violet. It had been opened by the censor and passed with no cuts or blackouts. She read it as she climbed the stairs to the office.

'Brighton? You're joking, aren't you? I thought people only went there for dirty weekends or to set up grounds for a divorce. A few days' hop-picking down in Kent was what we called a holiday. It always rained, was back-breaking, and we came home with bloody fingers. Never fancied Brighton. I know everyone in here claims they're innocent, but I didn't do it, you know. My bet is that Nancy framed me because I'm always mocking her. I hear Sydney's forgotten all about me now and is stepping out with her. But the truth is, Lilly, I never did nothing against anyone, and thank you for having faith in me. Pity Sydney couldn't do the same.'

She pushed into the room to find Jack packing up his equipment.

'Time to go.'

'Where are you going, Chief?'

'Where are *we* going.'

'But I...'

'Haven't got your things together. No? Well, that's what you'll be doing this morning.' He put one of the metal boxes by the door. 'Your leg is now fully recovered, I hope, and you will be fit to drive?'

Lilly nodded.

'Back here for early lunch. You'll take us out of London this afternoon. Bare minimum, English Rose. No frills or furbelows.'

'No problem, sir. I have no idea what a furbelow is.'

Back in her room she wasn't sure what to do with her things or with Dot's box, so she took a cab back to the club with everything, hoping that Fergusson would let her stow these things until she was back.

She wrote a quick note for Fergusson and started a brief letter to Dot to leave in her box.

As she changed into her khaki overalls, she thought of Chief Kirk. English Rose, indeed! She'd have to put an end to that.

At four o' clock, Lilly sat in the driver's seat. The van pulled away from Rainbow Corner, heading west. The stretch out of town was slow and difficult, so many army trucks were on the same road. Only when they passed Chertsey was it possible to stay in top gear for more than two minutes.

Beside her in the cab sat Jack, a book of maps on his lap, torch poised ready for nightfall. Four soldiers had loaded their equipment into the canvas-covered back section of the van. Lilly did not envy them the ride, sitting sideways on wooden benches, but they seemed happy enough. It was just possible to hear them over the engine noise, chatting and laughing.

At Woking, Jack demanded a short breather for the boys, but ordered Lilly to stay at the wheel. After a quarter of an hour, they set off again on the winding road.

Rain pouring down, the rhythm of the windscreen wipers was hypnotic. Not wanting to lose this job, Lilly decided not to comment on her tiredness or the discomfort of long periods without a break.

When they came into Salisbury it was already dark. Lilly finally broke the silence to ask if she could have a short break. Jack sighed and said yes.

Lilly darted across the market square to the public conveniences. Afterwards she ran around the square for a minute to stretch her legs.

Damp from the rain, she climbed back into the cab, and spent five minutes searching for a petrol station to fill up.

Her wet uniform fogged up the windscreen. At regular intervals, Jack wiped the inside with an old chamois, saying nothing.

It was getting on for midnight by the time they reached Crewkerne. Jack demanded another break for the boys. Lilly was exhausted. She imagined pulling into Land's End at dawn.

She wished the chief would say something, anything.

As she cleared the windscreen again, she saw that he was standing on the pavement, laughing. She wound down the window and tried to listen. She wasn't sure if it was just their accents, but she couldn't understand a word they were saying. It sounded like a foreign language. How could that be? Chief Kirk and his men wore US army uniforms.

Perhaps it was her tiredness. Driving at night was hard enough, but with dimmed blackout headlights and no street lighting, it had been gruelling.

She knew that Jack thought she was some rich, privileged English girl who hadn't a clue. She felt left out and punished. But for what? What had she done?

Slapping the four men on the back, Jack signalled them to get back inside. He tapped the dashboard with his leather gloves and Lilly turned the ignition.

Jack looked down at his map and pointed forward. 'That way.'

In the early hours they pulled up outside a bleak-looking building the other side of Exeter.

'All right, Corporal. You can stand down.'

As Lilly climbed out of the cab, the four men were already lugging the metal boxes of equipment into the building.

'Where do I go, sir?'

'Into the house. First door on the left.'

Lilly felt near to collapse.

Hauling her kitbag from the rear of the truck, she trundled it inside and turned into the room, expecting a dormitory.

Instead it was a dusty, dirty room, the floor scattered with old newspaper pages. In the centre stood a desk, upon which stood an ashtray full of butts, and a large lamp, which was off. Tucked behind, a creaky wooden chair. The only lighting flickered in from the torchlight of the men passing through the hall.

Lilly turned back to see what was going on.

Jack entered, locked the door behind him and pocketed the key. He walked calmly to the table and turned on the lamp, a very dim blue nightlight.

'Take a seat, Corporal.'

What was this?

Lilly felt panic rising.

Chief Kirk walked back to the door.

'I said sit!'

Lilly sat. The chair wobbled. She feared it would collapse beneath her.

'Tell me everything about the espionage at Rainbow Corner.'

Jack's voice was cold, impenetrable.

'I don't know anything about it.'

'Yes, you do. Tell me.'

'They arrested a woman called Violet Beckton under the Treachery Act. That's all I know.'

'Do you think Violet Beckton is guilty?'

'I have no idea.'

'So she might be innocent.'

'I told you. I have no idea.'

'Why did you write her a letter?'

'Because I like her.'

'Even when she is accused of spying?'

'I like her, and I hope it wasn't her. She doesn't seem the type.'

'Who is the type, in your opinion?'

'Well, I suppose Mosley, and all those black-shirt sorts.'

'People like your own family and acquaintances?'

'Much posher than them. Perhaps also their servants. And people who lived in Germany before the war, or who were married to somebody German. But Vi doesn't sit right. I mean, why would she do such a thing?'

'Why would anyone?'

'Three reasons: money, hate for their own country or love of Hitler.'

Jack glanced down.

'Any other suspects?'

'It could be anyone. June, Nancy, Peggy, Thelma…'

'Not your friend Dorothy?'

'No. Nor me. We arrived after it started.'

'What does Brighton mean to you?'

'It's where they picked someone up last month for being a fifth columnist.'

'And who was that person?'

'No idea.'

'Brunswick Terrace?'

Lilly shook her head.

'You had a mock engagement a few days ago to a Frenchman, serving under de Gaulle.'

'Something like it. I wanted the man to have someone to come back for.'

'You knew him from before the war, in Paris?'

'I told you, the Butte Montmartre.'

'The Butte?' The shadow of a smile played on his lips. 'What is this man's role in the Resistance?'

Whatever was going on here, Lilly had no desire to put Jean-Claude at risk. 'I only know him as a guitar player and think that lately he's been working with the circus.'

'As a clown?'

'He's a professional entertainer. In the circuses I went to as a child, clowns played instruments.'

'And what do you think you have been working on with me these last weeks?'

'Dictation, of a very basic kind, sir.'

Jack Kirk laughed.

'What interested you in the personal filing cabinet of Controller Fergusson?'

Lilly's mind raced. Who had seen her at the filing cabinet? Only Thelma. Had she informed against her? If so, what did *she* think Lilly had been doing? Thelma had no idea what Lilly's job involved, so for all she knew, it was part of her work to be rooting in the office filing cabinet. Or perhaps Fergusson had some secret thread or something which indicated whenever someone had opened the drawers in her absence.

'Nothing that would interest you.'

'How do you know what interests me?'

'I was simply looking up the hostesses' files. To see if one was married or not.'

'Good try.' Chief Kirk laughed. 'I don't think you're interested in the marital status of the hostesses.'

'Well, that's what I looked up. A lady called June. Doesn't want anyone to know where she lives or what she does outside Rainbow Corner. Says she's a spinster, but I discovered she's actually married to an RAF pilot.'

Chief Kirk remained silent. Staring at her.

'But you're right, Chief. You have no idea what interests me and I have no idea what interests you, apart from Le Jazz Hot, as they call it in France. In fact, to be totally honest, Chief, I don't know why this is happening, nor who you are.'

Jack stood up. Only then did she fully realise how big he was.

She looked him straight in the eye.

'Are you a Nazi, Jack? Are you the mystery spy in Rainbow Corner? Have Nancy and Fergusson embroiled you in some plot against us all?'

His lip curled in amusement.

'Who are those men with you, Chief? And why don't they communicate in English?'

'I'm asking the questions here, Corporal.'

Jack gazed at her for a moment, then unplugged the lamp, put it under his arm and strode towards the door. Was he going to leave her here with no light? Lilly panicked. She shouted after him: 'Tell me one thing, Chief Kirk, or whatever you are – does Controller Fergusson know what's happening here? Has she condoned this?'

'She has no jurisdiction over you now.' He opened the door. 'Make yourself comfortable, Corporal. This is your lodging for the night. There's a bucket in the corner.'

SEVENTEEN

WHEN DOT GOT OFF the train in London, she was alarmed how empty everywhere seemed. Piccadilly Circus was still a bustle, but there were far fewer uniformed men in the streets. The atmosphere inside Rainbow Corner was different too.

The first thing she noticed was that the outgoing mailbox in the entrance hall was crammed full. The men were obviously writing home before they left for action.

Anticipation was in the air.

She spent the morning dealing with sprains and cuts, and took the temperatures of a few young men who, now the reality of impending battle had set in, had worked themselves into a state.

At one she went to the canteen for lunch.

'Welcome back, Nurse Gallagher.' It was Art, standing at the door with his usual tray. 'Can I tempt you with a delicious all-American donut?'

Actually, he could, so Dot took one. The plan was not to eat it herself, but to squash it into a little box and post it to her parents in Liverpool. They wouldn't have eaten anything as lush for years.

She looked around for Lilly. But the only person she recognised was Nancy, sitting at a side table in intense conversation with Sydney.

From behind the counter Thelma said: 'Poor love. Since her fiancé was killed, she's a changed woman. Did you hear, shot down over France? Plane exploded mid-air. Poor bloke didn't have a chance.'

Dot felt another rush of terror for all the boys overseas in action and those about to join them.

Peggy murmured, sotto voce: 'And that Vi, his ex-fiancée, got banged up for spying. How about that, Dot? Violet Beckton a spy! Reckon Sydney and Nancy are consoling one another.'

Dot was about to pass on her own information about the badge that Violet had sewn into Tony's stripes but thought again. Even information like that must qualify as careless talk. But Dot knew she had to report it to someone in authority here at Rainbow Corner. She could have reported it to the CMO on the ship, but he wouldn't have understood the implications of the club and Violet's job here. The only person who would have the means to deal with it had to be Controller Fergusson. It would also give her a chance to catch up with Lilly.

Before her hour was up, she went upstairs. Getting no reply when she knocked, she pushed the door open and peered in.

Lilly's desk had been cleared and the general's chair was gone.

Dot scribbled a note addressed to the controller, explaining that she had important information to impart, and that she could be found during daylight hours in Dunker's Den. In the evenings, she added, she would be glad to offer her services again as a hostess.

Dot wasn't sure where to put the note, so moved to Fergusson's desk, which was strewn with piles of paperwork. It certainly would not be seen among the other notes and lists, so she looked around for some empty space where it would be more obvious. In the end she balanced it on the keyboard of the typewriter.

'What are you doing in here?'

Dot spun around to face Fergusson herself.

'I was … I was writing you a note, ma'am. I have something to tell you.'

'So tell…' Fergusson sat. Dot stood before her like a witness in court.

When she finished telling of Tony and the Nazi badge, Fergusson sat for some time, fingers steepled, eyes closed.

'Is there any particular reason you feel this is very important, especially now that Miss Beckton is imprisoned?'

Dot finally told Fergusson all about Joe, and the things which he had said fearing treacherous acts at the club.

'So ultimately you suspect Violet Beckton of being the said spy or saboteur or however you like to see it. But that lady has already been locked away. So, nothing to worry about now, Nurse Gallagher.' She spun her chair around to face the desk, dismissing Dot. 'I suggest you leave your private-eye act to the professionals.'

Dot noticed a box under Lilly's desk.

'Why has that box got my name on it?'

Fergusson bent down to look and quickly read the note Lilly had taped to the top.

'Because it's yours.'

She passed the box across.

Dot took the moment to ask after Lilly.

'She no longer works here, Nurse Gallagher. I cannot locate her for you as her posting is top secret, but you could write c/o the club and I will be sure to forward it.'

At the end of the afternoon a new secretary brought down an official letter informing Dot that, due to a suggestion of the nursing sister, from tomorrow she should no longer report to Rainbow Corner. Tonight's digs would be a room at the Regent Palace Hotel. From tomorrow accommodation would be provided by the hospital in Southend.

What was going on? Being removed from the club before twenty-four hours had passed was a terrible blow. And now, when companionship was more necessary than ever, she was heading somewhere she'd never heard of, to start all over again.

On her way out, as she passed the front desk, Dot was handed another letter.

She crammed it into her bag and, with her box under her arm, took the short walk around the corner to the hotel.

Once in the room, she rummaged through the box Lilly had left and crammed everything into her kitbag ready for tomorrow, then she flopped down on her bed to read the letter. It was from her parents' neighbour, Mrs Carey. For a moment Dot could barely breath. She read on quickly, dreading that this must be bad news about her parents. But it was only two pages of silly local gossip. Until the last sentence. Mrs Carey was sorry to hear that Trixy had got out and run down the jigger onto Queens Drive, where he had been fatally hit by a car.

The bloody woman.

Dot thought back to her parents' letter. They had obviously tried to protect her because they knew what she was going through and how upset she'd be.

Trixy!

Dot sobbed into her hands.

Her first thought was to write to Billy. But how could she? Then she remembered the letter she had written but decided not to send. She rifled through the box, but the letter wasn't there. Lilly must have come upon it, thinking Dot had meant her to post it.

That would explain Billy's coldness.

Momentarily Dot considered writing again, but instead started writing a letter to her parents – but after a few sentences, she left that too.

Now that she knew they had lied to her, everything felt different. From now on she'd be unable to believe any good news from them. She finished the letter, telling them she needed to hear the truth from them, however painful.

It was the first time she had been harsh towards her parents. It made her feel bad, but it was necessary, so she dropped the letter in the postbox in the hall.

As she walked back towards her room, she felt utterly empty and alone.

She could feel the rhythm of music, coming very faintly from downstairs.

That would be better than sitting alone. A drink among other people.

The bar was crowded, a jukebox in the corner blaring out American songs. GIs huddled, talking loudly. A sense of excitement filled the air.

Dot asked a passing waitress what was the cause of the celebration.

'It's not a celebration. More like a wake. They all got their papers this afternoon. They're leaving tomorrow.'

'For America?' asked Dot.

'No, silly. They're off on preparations for … you know what.' The girl tapped her nose. 'No names, no pack drill. You get me?'

The invasion. It had to be. Only something enormous would have caused a mass evacuation of military on such a scale.

Dot ordered a drink, a whisky and soda. She found a seat, closed her eyes and tried not to think.

'Drowning your sorrows, luv?'

A slender white-haired man sat beside her.

'I'm not … I don't…' Knowing that all the hotels around Piccadilly were famous for prostitution, Dot had no idea how to let this man know that she wasn't one. 'There are women outside … who … provide…'

The man laughed.

'No, girl, I wasn't – as they say – "looking for company". I recognise you from round the corner. Dance hostess, weren't you? I'm Paul, by the way. I'm a waiter there.'

'Scouser?'

'Snap, Sherlock.'

'I'm ever so homesick, Paul.'

'It's brutal.' Paul knocked back his drink. 'Can I get you another?'

Dot nodded.

'What's up?'

'I got a letter. My dog got run over on Queens Drive.'

'It's notorious, that road. You live near there?'

'Yeah. Walton. By the cemetery.'

'Sounds attractive!' Paul turned and grabbed Dot's leg. 'Uh-oh! Nine o'clock.'

'No, it's only about seven.'

'I mean, take a decko. Nine o'clock.' He inclined his head in the direction of the doorway. 'Attila the Hen. Dolores the Donut Dolly from Des Moines.'

In the doorway stood a tall, confident brunette, whose uniform skirt was just a fraction too short, whose heels were just a little too high, and whose bust was pushing out of the uniform shirt. As she wiggled across the barroom, Dolores pouted her blood-red lips and fluttered her dark eyelashes.

'Arrived a few weeks ago,' whispered Paul. 'Of course, all the men are too stupid to see she's just a shallow hussy on the prowl.'

'American?'

'What do you think? Since you were last here, there's been a few American girls arriving. Very popular they are, on the dance floor. I wonder who Dolores is gunning for tonight? Have a gander, will you.'

Though there was a lot of rowdy cheering from the GIs gathered around the counter, no one seemed to be looking in Dolores's direction. Paul jabbed Dot in the ribs.

'She's on the move. Look. Missile trajectory engaged. Note the discreet wave of the fingers without raising her hand. Who's her target?'

They both leaned to the side to get a better view.

'My God! Who'da thunk it? It's the posh pugilist himself. Colonel Blimp. "Gad, sir, if I see a pair of knockers I knobble 'em."'

Dot looked over. Lilly's ex, George, was sitting at a table, grinning at the oncoming female. He rose and, with a gentlemanly bow, took Dolores's hand, assisting her to sit.

'George Widmer. I hate him,' said Dot. 'He said I was too common to be Lilly's friend.'

'He said a lot worse the last time I was in his company. Had to set the police on him.'

'I think Lilly would be shocked that he's going out with that type of woman, don't you?'

'No, I don't. She had a gobful of his darker side and chucked him.'

The waitress finally arrived with the drinks. They clinked.

'Here's to Liverpool and everyone who sails in her.'

'Here's to you, Paul, for putting a smile back on my miserable face. Thank you.'

A loud cheer from the corner and all the GIs started jumping up and down to the music booming from the jukebox.

'They're excited cos they're leaving.' Dot put her glass down on the low table. 'Why can't I feel like that?'

'Are you leaving?'

'Only just got back to the Smoke today and they've posted me to Essex.'

'The arsehole of London.'

'Southend.'

'Blackpool on sedatives. Good luck with that, kid. I prefer a metropolis.'

'Me too.'

Paul looked at all the men jigging up and down, laughing, spraying each other with their drinks. 'Do they know there's a strong likelihood they won't be coming back from where they're heading?'

A shock went through Dot. 'You think they're all going to be killed?'

'Many will. But, once this charade of manly conflict is over, the survivors will be sent straight back to the USA – to parents, brothers, sisters, wives. Normal life. Not to this hothouse.'

'We may never see them again?'

'Probably not. Actually, I'll qualify that. Maybe when they're fifty, the ones who make it will come back, bringing their second, much younger, wives for a tour down memory lane. But, for most of them, that's it. Bye-bye, Blighty.'

Dot was suddenly full of grief that she wouldn't be seeing those cheerful, smiling faces anymore.

'So are you "seeing anyone", as they put it?' Paul took a sip of his drink. 'Or, as we put it, "Have you hooked yourself a Yank?"'

Dot thought of Billy. He'd made it quite clear he'd have nothing to do with her. Well, two could play at that game. Perhaps she really would have a Yank. If you were being blamed for something, why not have the fun of actually doing it? It might even make Billy feel jealous enough to want her again.

'Yes, Paul,' she said. 'There is someone I've been seeing. He's nice. He makes me laugh.'

'That's the most important thing. Never look for anything more than that. Might I know him?'

'He's a GI.'

'Like the six thousand others who came in the club yesterday! Name?'

'Otis.'

'Oh!' Paul made the one syllable last a very long time. 'Handsome one, that. Well caught, luv.'

Just then, a man flopped down on the seat beside Paul.

'Not interrupting, am I?' Dot recognised him as the squatter of the two Snowdrops.

'Hey there, Marty! I'd like you to meet my new friend, Dot. She hates Colonel Blimp as much as we do! He's over there, by the way, with Mata Doloroso, the Des Moines dynamo. And listen to this – our Dot's pulled the flashing-smiled Otis!'

Dot didn't contradict him.

EIGHTEEN

LILLY WOKE IN THE cold of dawn. She had slept on the concrete floor and was starving. She'd only eaten the snacks provided for the drive, no real meal since yesterday's lunch.

Had she been taken prisoner by some fifth column group, who were going to hold her here in the middle of nowhere? But why? She wasn't important. No one would pay a ransom, nor would they even miss her. Perhaps the Rainbow Corner gang knew she was onto something. In which case they didn't realise that she hadn't a clue about anything.

She shuffled over to the door and put her ear to the flaked paint. She could hear nothing. She moved to the window. It was dirty, caked with mud, dust and cobwebs. She wiped it as clear as she could. The truck was no longer on the driveway.

She should try to escape. She scouted the room for something to use to break the glass and decided on the chair. But that would make such a noise, and before she had a chance to get the glass out of the way and climb through, they'd be down.

Placing the chair by the window, Lilly took off her uniform jacket and rolled it into a ball. Then, putting her fist in the middle of the ball, she bashed at the glass. But nothing happened. Glass had to be etched. She went through her pockets and then saw the small metal badge on her cap. She unpinned it and, using the sharp edge, scraped at the glass till she had carved four distinct lines. Then she punched again with the jacket around her fist.

This time it worked. A square of glass fell out and landed in the shrubs beneath the window. She climbed onto the chair and jumped out.

The drive was gravel, which would be noisy to walk on, so she tightrope-walked along the narrow stone border, tiptoed briskly through the gates and turned into the lane.

She looked around for a road sign, anything to help her find the nearest town.

'Congratulations, Corporal.' Jack Kirk was leaning against a jeep parked under the shadow of a chestnut tree. 'Timing pretty *spot on*, as your compatriots would say. Now hop in. It's time for chow.'

Over porridge with honey, hot toast and tea, Lilly eyed Jack Kirk suspiciously. He had brought her to a small country hotel. The only other guest was an old lady with a large hearing aid, who shouted sporadically at the waitress.

Chief Kirk was all smiles but explaining nothing.

'Is this a test, Chief, or are you some kind of traitor?'

'Which do you think?'

'If you were a Nazi, I can't imagine you could have infiltrated Rainbow Corner or Grosvenor Square at such a high level. And if you wanted rid of me, it would have been easier to shoot me, though I wouldn't know why you'd want to. And anyway, if you wanted to cause trouble, why pick me? I'm nobody. So I can only presume this a test.'

'Controller Fergusson has confidence in you. I'm simply making sure she's right. You'd better not let me down, English Rose.'

'That's another thing, sir. I'd prefer it if you stopped referring to me as English Rose.'

'It's what you are, isn't it? The peachy complexion, what they tell me is a Home Counties accent, ponies and a comfortable background?'

'I've always been a tomboy. Not rose-like at all. Anyhow, my name is another flower, Lilly. Why not stick with that, sir?'

'All right, English Lilly. A significant flower, where I come from. Sego Lilly, the others call you. The life plant. And how many times have I told you? No "sir".'

'Yes, Chief.' Lilly wiped her mouth with a linen napkin and stirred her tea. 'Who are they, those four men?'

'Signallers. Like us.'

'Where from?'

'America.'

'So what language were they speaking? Spanish? Mexican?'

Jack just shook his head and laughed.

As Lilly sipped her tea, she asked Jack what he had been discussing so earnestly with Earl and Jean-Claude while she was chatting to Pearl in the jazz club.

He simply put his finger to his nose and tapped it.

After breakfast she followed Jack back to the jeep. This time he drove.

'I could always write to Earl or Jean-Claude and ask,' said Lilly, feeling that by saying that she had got one over him.

'Your letter would never reach Jean-Claude, and Earl certainly wouldn't share the information with you. The three of us are outsiders. That's all.'

Another thing had been puzzling Lilly. Why was a man with such a high rank travelling alone with such a small squad and herself?

'We are unique,' he said, 'with a special mission. And you are joining us only because one of my men was killed during that bombing spree in London, and it has proved impossible to find anyone else or bring another of us across in time.'

Lilly was perplexed by this. There were so many GIs in London. Surely one would have been suitable. The jeep turned into a narrow lane leading to a large empty space on the Devon moors, and Jack turned to her.

'Test two.'

He handed her a heavy backpack and told her to run to the top of the hill, then to find the nearest hiding place – a ditch, a bush, wherever she could make herself invisible. There she must count to sixty. She would hear him drive away. Then she must find her way back to the house they had just left, with a rucksack, using only the tools provided. She must not discard anything.

Lilly ran up the hill and crouched behind a gorse bush. She felt a shiver when she heard the engine of the jeep get further and further away, leaving nothing behind but the wail of the wind.

She peered into the rucksack. She was expecting a compass, a map and perhaps some money. But inside were six red builders' bricks.

Her first instinct was to jettison them, but that was against the rules. Presumably they had been put there to simulate the weight of something which another day she might carry.

Balancing the bag over her shoulder, she ran down the hill, crossed a field and ran on until she reached a tree-lined lane. She had no idea which direction to take.

After half an hour's walking, she started to panic. Chief Kirk had said to use whatever was there. But there was nothing. She perched on an old stone wall enclosing a churchyard. How could you find your way from somewhere when you had no idea where you were to start with?

Opening the rucksack again, she felt around inside the pockets and found a small leatherette ration-book holder. But there was nothing in it. No ration book, no ID card, nothing. What was the point of that? Furious with him and herself, Lilly tried to tear the holder, but the leatherette was too tough. She turned it inside out. The inside was lined in silk. That was weird. She put her fingers inside to see whether there might be something sewn inside, like a card. The lining was loose. She pulled at the fabric. It unfolded over and over, and on the reverse side was an OS map. A map drawn on silk.

She could see the EX of Exeter. Lilly searched for the symbols for churches and churchyards. There were only two, so she had to be at one or the other. The symbols were different, one round, one square. She seemed to remember from geography classes that one represented a tower, the other a spire. She prayed that this one, the one with a tower, was the square symbol.

She started to run.

*

When Lilly arrived back at HQ, she expected praise. But all she got from Chief Kirk was, 'Grab a quick lunch before we press on.'

There was no let-up.

A military wagon rolled up bearing mail, including a letter for her.

Lilly had been starting to feel sorry for George. But after reading his letter – which was 'to let her know before she heard it from any other source' that he was walking out with a lovely young American girl, who had admirably volunteered to come over and help out in London – she decided he needed no sympathy. It took him three pages to extol this girl's extraordinary social abilities and sympathetic, listening, feminine ways, qualities so perfect in an army wife. Lilly took this to mean that she herself would *not* have fitted the bill. Weirdly, George added a postscript saying that his father was seriously ill and not likely to last the week.

Poor George. And poor Sir William and Lady Widmer.

All weekend, Lilly and the four men worked in separate rooms, sending and receiving messages, handing Chief Kirk the transcripts for checking.

He warned them to be prepared to leave at any moment, for on Tuesday the moon would be full.

It seemed a strange reason to be moving on, but in military affairs night visibility must matter. Lilly noticed that at the mention of the moon, Jack and the four men tapped the centre of their chest twice. She wondered if that was an American good luck thing, like throwing salt over your shoulder or touching wood.

Later that evening, Jack put his head round the door. 'Everything's been postponed. Bad weather. Another day in hand. We move to the coast tomorrow, then, if all goes well, we set off a few days after that.' He came inside and lowered his voice. 'I've heard word that your friend Jean-Claude has landed in France. He is ahead of us all, preparing the way.'

'He's safe?'

Jack shrugged.

'Can't you tell me a little more.'

'Not possible. Sorry. We head for Dartmouth. It's possible that we'll meet some Free French there. Their HQ is next to ours. Prepare to move at a moment's notice. And keep working on those codes.'

*

As she sat on the train out of London, Dot felt sorry for all those soldiers waking this morning with throbbing heads, yanking their kitbags into jeeps, lorries and trains, heading off to training stations near the coast, to prepare for … what?

She shuddered with hope and dread. All those servicemen who had been wanting, in their own words, to 'get it over and done with' were about to start doing just that, whatever the outcome.

It had been bad enough taking the flak at sea, but she couldn't imagine what it must be like to run through the streets of some strange town, shells exploding all around you, snipers round every corner. Tony had done it. Howard was still out there doing it. And thousands of other young men were now about to join them.

She wished she could think about something else and felt stupid that she hadn't bought a newspaper at Fenchurch Street. But she hadn't, so made do with staring out of the window at the bleak, drab suburbs. Every now and then she'd see another street reduced to rubble, the desolate landscape of a bombsite, buildings missing walls, people's kitchens and bedrooms open for all the world to see, their blasted curtains flapping pointlessly in the breeze. Occasionally there would be a table and chairs, set for dinner, balanced on a mere ledge in the open air on the second floor of a house with only the painted reminder of a staircase beside it.

Eventually the train pulled in at Southend Station. To cross to the exit, Dot had to climb over a steep iron bridge crossing the lines. She paused at the top and stood, watching trains pass beneath, steam puffing around her as each engine ducked underneath. She thought about the people inside them. People with ordinary lives, who she would never meet, glancing out, as she had done. Humans were little different from ants. Carrying on, best they could. And here they all were, thrown into a frenzied, capricious life, which none of them had predicted.

Jacking the kitbag up over her shoulder and grabbing the handrail, Dot made her way down the steep rusty steps and out through the ticket hall.

She wondered why they had posted her here. She'd only been in London a day. Had she upset someone? She couldn't imagine anyone in Southend asking for her particularly, so it seemed more likely that somehow she had failed at Rainbow Corner.

*

The jeep issued for Lilly's drive to Dartmouth had the driver's seat on the wrong side. When Lilly pointed it out, Jack Kirk raised an eyebrow. 'Depends whether you think that Great Britain or the rest of the world is on the right side.'

Even social chit-chat with this man was a minefield.

At the Dartmouth HQ, another large country house, Chief Kirk announced that from now until further notice, nobody could leave the building, but that they were free to make the most of the facilities provided. Lilly quickly found the kitchen, a huge room with a gigantic iron range. Many uniformed men were gathered around a large table, talking and laughing. When she came in they turned to look, then went on talking. While she brewed some tea, she listened in. They were billeted here: marines, GIs, supply troops, medical teams, all feeling left out. It seemed that something big would be happening tonight, but without them.

She shared a room with three nurses from a hospital ship which was scheduled to sail within the next forty-eight hours, but was currently moored further up the coast.

Lilly had the top bunk. She spent most of the night staring at the dusty, flaking paint on the ceiling. What was this war doing to everyone? The constant imminent sense of danger which made them all need to get engaged, to marry, to make babies. Was everybody living out their volatile existence on a short fuse, silently fearing the worst, doing anything to make it feel better, or doing things now which they might never get the chance to do again … ever? There was no point pretending that this life – or, rather, this dance with death – was normal.

*

Dot felt a certain elation working in the large hospital. The day was gruelling, as it always was, but here in Essex she was faced with the additional burden of countless burn patients, mainly men who had worked at the nearby aerodromes. Every morning a stream of pilots and gunners, who had flown out the night before on bombing missions over northern Europe, were brought in, looking more like a side of meat than a human being. But despite their wounds, they all felt lucky because they had made it back.

When Dot was about to go on her lunch break, Sister called her over and asked whether she would go to the female ward in the public wing to pick up a list of items. Anxious to make the most of her hour, Dot ran along and handed the note to the nurse in charge. As she waited, she noticed a woman lying in a nearby bed whose piercing blue eyes seemed familiar. It was impossible to see the whole of her face as it was bandaged across the nose.

Dot looked at the patient list chalked on a blackboard near the door. She counted the bed numbers and scanned the list. Mrs J. Jagger. Before she had a chance to look further, a nurse thrust a pile of boxes into Dot's arms.

That evening, Dot went down to the drab brown common room. A handful of nurses sat in frayed armchairs, reading books and writing home. Dot looked out of the window at the dismal view. She missed Liverpool, with its rows of red terraces and joking people. The truth was she really missed Billy. She knew in her heart, Otis was like Christmas tinsel to take out of the box once a year, exciting but ephemeral. Billy was more like bread and potatoes, something you needed every day, familiar and reassuring. But then she understood – Billy represented going back. He was life before the war, before everything had been changed by Hitler and his cronies.

She wondered how things were going up at Rainbow Corner. Where were Sydney and Art? What had Tony done with that Nazi token? Had he shown it to Barbara or to someone in authority? Then she thought about Howard. Poor Howard, battling his way up southern Italy. Day after day she read about the terrible difficulties the Allies were having reaching Rome. Howard was such a kind man. It didn't seem fair. But then … this was war. Nothing was fair.

'Are you Nurse Gallagher?' an orderly asked.

'Yes.'

'There's a man asking after you at the main desk.'

Her heart leapt. It had to be Otis. Who else would surprise her like this? Smoothing down her hair, she quickly ran down the stone staircase to ground level.

'Hello, old gal! How ya doing?'

She turned to see not Otis, but Paul, and was worried he would see the disappointment on her face.

'I got sent up this way to pick up a whole lot of supplies from a warehouse at Basildon for the old Rainbow, and I couldn't just drive past leaving you stranded – so instead of a lunch break, I popped in to fill you in on all the goss.' He put out his elbow for her to link arms and spoke confidentially: 'It's a bit depressing round here, isn't it? Do you know a good café? I'll stand you a high tea!'

'What passes as high tea these days, Paul?'

'Toast and marge!'

They walked down the street and settled down in a greasy spoon near the beach, which was barricaded off with barbed wire.

'Dodgy Dolores was telling all the hostesses that Blimpy old George had asked her to marry him.'

'Wow. I wonder where they'll live when it's over? His posh house in the middle of the countryside? She doesn't seem the huntin', shootin' and fishin' type.'

'You're right there.' Paul scratched his head like Stan Laurel. 'Perhaps he'll enlist as a GI bride, and sail over to join her in the US of A. She's brassy enough to pass as a bloke!'

'The GI brides and fiancées must be nervous now.'

'We all are. But there are an increasing number of women sitting around the canteen looking wan, you're right there.'

'Is Fergusson still barking at everyone?'

'Gone.'

'What do you mean, gone?'

'Just don't see her about anymore.' Paul bit into his toast.

'Who's running the place? Not the general?'

'He won't be back.' Paul stirred his tea, then took a sip. 'But now some high-up Yanks are in charge. Most of the blokes are gone too, you know. The place is almost deserted. The dances are a joke. Like a wet November weekend in the Birkenhead Majestic. Three or four couples shuffling about on an empty dance floor. It's desolate.'

While Dot spread her toast with jam served in a small ramekin, Paul leaned in intimately. 'The big news at Rainbow Corner is that Nancy got engaged to Sydney.'

'Nancy! Sydney! But they're…' Dot had to pause to swallow her toast.

'Incompatible might be the word you were searching for, duck. But now she's practically swooning over his "as far as the eye can see" line. It's hilarious.'

'He must tower over her.'

'Yep.' Paul nodded. 'But she'd do anything to hook a Yank. And there aren't that many left.'

'Poor Vi. She adored Sydney.'

'Who cares if she's been selling us all up the Swanee?'

'Was it really her?'

'Don't you start too. Virgil has got it into his head that they made a mistake. I heard him and Marty squabbling about it the other day. I'm not so sure. No smoke without fire.'

They both chomped away in silence, then Dot felt she had no alternative but to ask, 'How's Otis?'

'I see him from time to time, moping at the front desk. He's managed to get out of it again, but all his friends are gone.'

'Howard not back?'

'No. Quite a few people I've not seen around the place lately. Barbara Caruso, but I suppose she's busy with the two babies, and with Tony making her new ones. June Jagger. She's not been in for a week or so…'

'June's surname is Jagger? I thought it was Worth.' Dot frowned. So that's why she recognised those eyes. J. Jagger was June.

'Fabulous, isn't it? Worth could be her maiden name or something.' Paul poured them both another cup. 'Jagger! Like something out of Charles Dickens. Only the Christian name should be Fanny or Agatha or something a bit more olde worlde. June. Fancy being called after a month. But I suppose it's a tad better than being called Hazel, after a ruddy nut.'

'Paul … do you think they wanted me out of Rainbow Corner? I have no idea why I'm here.'

'Oh darlin'.' Paul gave his usual shrug. 'Nothing makes sense anymore. Don't even try to work it out. The only thing we can do is to live for NOW. After all, there may be no tomorrow.'

NINETEEN

EARLY NEXT MORNING AN eruption of noise woke Lilly. It came from downstairs. People were yelling, clattering up and down the wooden staircase. She hastily dressed and ran down to see what was going on.

Men held up newspapers, shouting: 'The invasion has begun!'

Radios in some rooms blasted out the morning news. In the kitchen someone read aloud.

Four thousand large ships and countless small boats had crossed the Channel last night and landed on the shores of Normandy.

The liberation of France had begun.

Many US troops had sailed from here in Dartmouth. While Lilly was lying staring at the ceiling, all those men must have been embarking, then while she was still sleeping, landing in France.

Her heart lurched. The probability was that any day now she too would board a ship. Since the start of the war she'd longed for this, but now it was about to be reality she was terrified.

One of the orderlies announced that they were now free to leave the house. The curfew had been lifted.

As Lilly marched up the hill to get a better view of the long harbour, she noticed the sign of the cross of Lorraine on a gatepost. This must be the Free French Centre which Jack had talked about.

She went inside. The same manic atmosphere ruled. If anything, here it was even louder – after all, it was their country being liberated.

At the front desk she asked if anyone had news of Jean-Claude Toussaint. The lady took her name and said she would go and check.

After about ten minutes, a door opened and Jean-Claude came into the hall. He smiled widely when he saw her.

'Jean-Claude! I thought you were in France…'

'I was, day before yesterday. I've been working on the small fast ships, going back and forth, doing night raids, leaving supplies, doing small acts of sabotage. Preparing the way for last night.'

'I'm so happy that you're safe.'

They hugged in silence for a moment or two.

'Tonight I start a different mission. I'm leaving again.'

'We leave any time too. I think we'll be following the invasion troops.'

'I'm going to the south with the Resistance. It will be grim to see those SS officers goose-stepping down the promenade, taking coffee in the market cafés.'

Jean-Claude took Lilly's arm.

'Let's sit outside.'

Once seated on the lawns, Jean-Claude told her that the hope of seeing her again had helped him through the lonely nights performing dangerous operations in Normandy.

'So there was a point to keeping this with me at all times?' Lilly dug her hand deep into her pocket and pulled out the paper ring.

Jean-Claude leaned forward and kissed her.

*

By the time Dot found an opportunity to go back to the female ward next morning, June's bed was empty.

'She's gone back to him,' said the sister with a world-weary sigh.

'I'm sorry?' Dot didn't understand. She had assumed that June's injuries had been caused by being caught in an air raid.

'It's a different excuse every time, nurse: walked into a cupboard, fell down the stairs, elbowed in the rush down to the tube station during a raid. But her injuries were inflicted deliberately. One time I plainly saw the imprint of his knuckles in a bruise on her back.'

'Who's he?'

'Her husband. A pilot at the airbase up the road. Two or three nights a week Mrs Jagger goes up to London to do voluntary work. As good a way as any, I suppose, to be out of range of his flying fists.'

The ward sister sighed. 'I know pilots have to go through a lot, mentally speaking. They witness dreadful things, lose their companions daily … But there's no excuse for taking it out on her. She seems a sensible woman, but when you try and advise her, she won't hear a bad word about him, continues with the ridiculous stories about trips and falls.'

Dot remembered June's heavy make-up, and the way she flinched when Dot touched her. Everything now made perfect sense. Her lie about being single. If she had admitted being married, everyone would have expected her to bring the man into Rainbow Corner to show him off, especially if he was a pilot.

'Love is a strange bird,' said the sister. 'When people choose a marriage partner they make all the wrong choices. More often than not, they get themselves so trapped inside their idea of what love is that they don't see the wood for the trees. Don't you make the same mistake, will you? Life, my dear Nurse Gallagher, is not a Hollywood movie.'

As Dot walked back to her wing, she thought about June's situation and wondered what the husband looked like. She imagined some ugly, bald, fat thug, but knowing the pilots she'd met, it was more likely that he was a good-looking, slim, typical RAF man, with a mop of hair and a cheeky grin. She tried to imagine June's home life, dreading the sound of the key in the door.

She wondered what June had told her husband about her 'voluntary' work. Did he know that every night in London was spent dancing with strange men? Was that the reason for his violent rages? It all seemed so far from the idea of marriage Dot had from being in the company of her own parents, sitting contentedly chatting in front of the fire. She wished now that she had not been quite so harsh with them in her last letter. As soon as her shift ended, she planned to write another, apologising.

The last few days there had been even more burn victims than usual, mainly pilots who had covered the landings at Normandy. Though seriously hurt, they brought with them a sense of optimism, a promise that the end was in sight, that one day soon this hellish war would be over.

But the hope aroused by the Normandy landings was shattered a week later when Dot read accounts of new pilotless buzz-bomb rockets aimed at London.

Already feeling at quite a low ebb after holding hands with two patients while they died, Dot returned to her room to find a letter from her parents. She hoped this would be just the thing to brighten up the evening. And the opening pages were lovely, jolly tales of the city of Liverpool, comic goings-on of the neighbours and ribald comments overheard in ration queues and on city buses. But, as a PS, they had added, 'You said you wanted the whole truth, so we thought we ought to send this.' Glued beneath that was a tiny clipping from the *Liverpool*

Echo: a bald, official announcement of the engagement of Billy O'Brien to Clarice Titchmarsh. According to the cutting, the happy couple had known each other since they were kids, and hoped to tie the matrimonial knot within weeks.

Dot took a deep breath. Well! She had asked her parents to not hide anything from her, but this seemed brutal.

She lay back on her bed. If Billy had really felt about her the way he said he did, how could this other engagement have come about so quickly, with a wedding weeks away? While Dot had been fretting about one single kiss, had Billy been carrying on all this time with Clarice Titchmarsh?

She turned to the wall and sobbed. Why did everything keep going wrong? Every day she was dealing with awful things on the ward. A terrible new weapon was raining down terror on London. Her dog had died. And now her boyfriend of years had run off with a girl who hated her. Nothing seemed to offer any hope.

With a sickening sensation, Dot remembered the grovelling letter she had written to Billy and regretted it with all her heart. Had he laughed, tossing it aside to snuggle closer to Clarice? Had he read it aloud to her as they clutched their sides with laughter? Dot shed tears of self-pity, frustration, despair and anger. She felt like going to the nearest bar and drinking herself under the table. She had a miniature bottle of whisky in her bag, for emergencies. What was this if not just that? She downed it in one and lay back.

'Visitor for you!' one of the nurses called brightly through the door. 'Gentleman, waiting down in the hall.'

Paul, she hoped. Someone to make her laugh.

But it was not Paul.

'Hey, Skipper! Thought I'd escape those doodlebugs, get outta town and visit you.' He stood perfectly still, then moved softly towards her. 'Oh, Skipper darling, you've been crying. Come here, sweetheart. Let me kiss it better.'

TWENTY

SCORES OF AMBULANCES, JEEPS, mobile cafeterias, hundreds of men and a few women – mainly nurses, canteen workers and drivers, like Lilly – were crammed onto the boat. Sailing just after midnight, Jack Kirk advised his team to grab as much sleep as they could. Tomorrow would be a tough day.

That was an understatement. Lilly drove the jeep, which carried only herself and Jack. Gritting her teeth as they hurtled through bombed-out villages, she kept a firm grip on the wheel, shifting the gears up and down while rolling over roads pitted with holes and covered in debris. Thin grey mud, created by the incessant rain, was splashed up by the wheels of the Red Cross truck ahead, covering her windscreen with sludge.

Marching Allied troops trudged along the grass verges on either side. Other troops herded lines of prisoners of war back towards the beaches.

Occasional German snipers crouched in bell towers. Every now and then local people would run out of shattered buildings in front of the jeep to wave and cheer. The rattle of fire from Allied aircraft overhead, clearing the way for the convoy, deafened her.

At dusk, Jack signalled Lilly to pull in near the shell of an outbuilding where several US trucks were already parked. Troopers moved forward to check out the house, guns ready. Once cleared, Lilly and Jack's team carried the radio equipment inside and started work. Commanders from the other units ran in, handing her pieces of paper, top-secret messages to be transmitted by Jack.

They worked together long into the night, and just before dawn settled down to sleep. As Lilly curled up, fully clothed, in the corner, she saw why Jack had insisted on trying her mettle in that house in Exeter. He hadn't been sure she was up to this. To be fair, neither was she. But this was to be their life for weeks to come.

Though she tried to unwind, she found her thoughts drifting back to George. She wondered if he was among the British troops fighting elsewhere on this peninsula. It followed naturally that once again she imagined Jean-Claude, tumbling from the black sky, tramping for miles through forests, across rivers, scrambling across gorse-covered hillsides, ducking down into ditches. All along the way he'd be cutting communication wires, blowing up rail lines and bridges, doing anything to break the continuity of Nazi communications. His job was to disrupt.

What irony, Lilly thought.

The traitor at Rainbow Corner had been trying to do the same against them, maybe was still at it. With a shock, she realised that even Pearl must be suspect. As well as pinpointing Earl's unit, she had information concerning the whereabouts of fighter planes all over Britain. And the accomplice could well be a man. Perhaps an American.

Otis had been on the train coming up from Brighton on the day the papers were dropped, hadn't he? Dot had told her that Otis's friend, Howard, had warned her about him with the words 'cave canem'! Beware of the dog. Why would a fellow soldier do that unless he had his own suspicions? Miraculously, Otis had injured himself just in time to avoid going on active service in southern Italy.

Could it be?

Otis certainly could not be eliminated.

As soon as they joined a bigger company, one which had communication with London, she would fire off a telegram to Dot, warning her.

*

Dot was assisting at an operation. The patient, a sailor, had been caught in a rain of shrapnel during a raid just upriver on the banks of the Thames. She felt stupid. She had let Otis go much further than she had intended. Not that she had done the actual deed, but she'd gone much further than she ever had with Billy. Why had she knocked back that whisky before he arrived?

The smell of blood made her feel queasy.

'Nurse. I said forceps!'

Dot turned back to the instrument table. Her concentration was shot. She grabbed the forceps and passed them to Sister.

Otis had kept whispering that he was going to marry her and take her home to the States to be his bride.

'Let's get engaged,' he had sighed after a long kiss. 'Tomorrow I'll buy you a ring – real gold, a diamond, even.'

Though she had loved every second, Dot knew that she shouldn't. And that she had to stop him, because it was impossible to go further unless they were married.

What if she got pregnant? Dot had seen concerned mothers of young women shoving cushions up their fronts, pretending to be expecting, so that the child could be brought up without the stigma of being a bastard, while the pregnant daughter disappeared to the country for a few months. Dot couldn't expect her mammy to do that for her.

'I said needle and catgut, nurse!'

Dot hurriedly grabbed the needle and passed it to the sister.

When the procedure was complete and the patient taken back to the ward, the surgeon left the theatre. While Dot was wiping down the operating table, Sister spoke sharply.

'You are not happy down here, nurse?'

It wasn't that, but Dot said yes anyway. It was easier than the truth.

'You are far away from home. And these are particularly trying times.'

'I was promised leave weeks ago but they only seem to give me a day here and there, not long enough to get to Liverpool.'

'For the time being that's much the same for everyone, nurse. I was puzzled as to why they had sent you here. Might you be happier if I got you transferred back to London, to the thick of it?'

'I would, Sister.'

A week later, Dot was sitting at the station, her bag at her side, waiting for the evening London train.

'Hello, petal.'

'June!' Dot hoped that her face didn't betray the fact that she knew June's secret. 'Heading up to go hostessing?'

June furtively looked around before whispering: 'In London I do voluntary work.'

Dot nodded. 'Of course.'

How scared the poor woman must be of her husband if she even told that fib to her. Dot glanced down to June's finger and saw that her wedding ring was in place.

Instinctively June slid her hand inside her jacket.

'What are you doing down here, Dot?'

'I've been on a temporary job.' Dot stopped herself just in time from naming the hospital. 'Happy to be heading back up to the Smoke, actually. How about you?'

'Visiting friends.' June looked at her lap then said: 'The American boys are going off in droves, now. If we win, that'll be the last we'll see of them.' She lifted her eyes and stared up into the cloudy sky. Dot noticed that her eyes were brimming with tears. 'I keep wondering what life will be like when this bloody war is over.'

Dot felt an awful pang. What *would* become of them all when the war stopped? For Dot it would mean going home to Liverpool for good, she supposed, sitting by the fire every evening in her parents' home. Being reminded of Billy's marriage each time she left the house. Not even Trixy to tell her troubles to. No job either. And missing Otis. Dot had passed enough exams to become a voluntary nurse, but would she really be cut out for this job in peacetime? Her heart wasn't in it. She was only doing it because there was a war on.

Then she thought of June's life. In peacetime, what excuse could she possibly make for these twice-weekly forays into town? June would be stuck at home with a violent bully. She must dread the end of the war.

'I've missed the dances,' Dot said. 'The music.'

'Is that all?' June smiled. 'I don't know about you, petal, but if there's anything *I've* been missing, it's those ruddy donuts.'

*

The day was quiet. In Lilly's opinion, too quiet. She followed the convoy along deserted country lanes, on either side verdant fields, some with cows and horses. The occasional farmhouse stood in radiant sunlight. It was only when you drew close that you could see evidence of war: a missing wall, a burnt-out roof. After the hectic day yesterday, Lilly didn't want to be fooled into thinking this was simply a quiet drive through the countryside. They all knew that German troops were around. The Allies hadn't even managed to seize the port of Cherbourg yet and were fighting slowly forward, eastwards towards Paris.

'Pretty place,' said Jack, leaning nonchalantly out of the open jeep. 'Dairy farmland. I'll bet round here they do a good cheese.'

'Famous for it,' replied Lilly. 'Pont l'Évêque, Camembert, Livarot. Their butter is also renowned.'
'Naturally. And wine?'
'Further south for that. Up here it's cider.'
Lilly changed gears.
'We've passed many orchards.' Jack turned to Lilly. 'When all this is over, I shall come back.'
'Me too.'
'No rationing, no cost, what would be your favourite meal?'
Lilly thought. 'Sea bream, potatoes and peas, followed by a tarte Tatin. You'd get lots of that around here, it's a kind of upside-down apple pie.'
'Dang, and there's me thinking that apple pie was an all-American thing.' Jack yawned and stretched. 'I'd go for something a little spicier. Beans and chilli. Corncob with wild onions and the juice of a lime. Cornbread. Did you ever try cornbread?'
Lilly shook her head.
'One day.'
'Whereabouts in America do you live, Chief?'
'Middle, towards the south-west.'
'Isn't that all desert?'
'Mmmm. Pretty spectacular country.'
'Like in cowboy films?'
'Exactly.' Jack turned his head and gazed out at the land. Conversation over. Lilly knew that there had been a moment. But she wasn't sure what it was about. Homesickness, perhaps, or simply being overwhelmed with beauty after all the desolation.
She stayed silent.
A hissing in the air. Lilly looked up. A loud explosion rocked the Red Cross van they were following. Direct hit. The truck became an immense fireball.
Lilly jammed on the brakes and leapt out of the jeep.
Shielding their faces with their forearms, she and Jack ran forward, trying to haul people out of the burning vehicle and drag them to the hedgerow.
Sudden machine-gun fire ahead. The convoy was being targeted by an invisible enemy tucked away in a nearby barn.
A crackling noise and blinding blaze. Lilly's hair had caught the flame. In an instant Jack had ripped off his jacket and wrapped it around her head.

'You OK?'

Singed but unharmed, Lilly nodded.

'Get these two onto the back of the jeep,' Jack yelled, hauling the limp form of a nurse over his shoulder and lurching forward. 'Then get out of here.'

Lilly pulled the arm of the medical officer, who was half crouched in the ditch, his shirt bloody, a gaping wound in his side. She dragged him, stumbling on bent legs, to the jeep.

'How many others?' Jack yelled to the injured MO.

'That's it,' he croaked. 'Just us two. We're carrying supplies, not people.'

'Grab what we can,' Jack shouted back to Lilly who was standing at the back of the Red Cross van. 'Then turn round.'

'But we...'

'That's an order.'

After throwing crates into the jeep, Lilly jumped into the driver's seat, and turned, darting around the vans queued up behind them.

Lilly drove towards base camp at Bayeux. Her cheeks were starting to sting from the burns. Moving her hand to get a stray strand of hair out of her eyes, she found that a lot of her scalp was stubble.

When they arrived, Jack jumped out, grabbed his radio equipment and immediately started talking in code.

Lilly went to the back of the jeep, yelling to the guards in the car park for help.

'Get up!' she called to the injured medical officer. 'We're here.'

'Too late, I think,' said a voice behind her. It was a medic, reaching out to close the man's eyes.

Paralysed with shock, Lilly looked down at the dead man, pale as paper, lying in a pool of his own blood. He seemed to be smiling at her.

'The nurse, then.' Lilly turned to the medic. 'We must help the nurse.'

The nurse lay still, her eyes shut.

'You need to sit down,' the medic said calmly.

Lilly didn't move.

'Now!' He looked at the boxes packed up next to the bodies in the jeep. 'You saved the morphine. Well done, Corporal.'

Lilly climbed back into the driver's seat and the medic started work on her face, cleaning her burns.

Coming off the headset, Jack leaned against the jeep's engine. He pulled out a pack of cigarettes. 'Fancy a Lucky Strike?'

'I wouldn't normally, but yes, please, Chief.'

The medic relayed the cigarette to Lilly then started dabbing oily ointment onto her scalp.

'Elan sends his regards,' said Jack. Elan was the cheeriest of the four boys with whom they had travelled to Devon. 'I told him you had been a fleeting human torch. "Wo-chi," he replied.'

'Code for fire.' Lilly took a long drag and tried to control her shaking hand. 'Wo-chi.'

'Looks like we lost our division.' Jack blew smoke in a sequence of small rings.

'We can catch them up tomorrow, Chief.'

'Nah. Now that we've lost them, the plan is changed.' Jack slowly inhaled. 'We're heading back north to follow that section.'

'Cherbourg?'

'Eventually.'

As the horizon darkened with the setting sun, the officer in charge of the base camp strolled across and told Jack that there were no places left. If they slept here it would have to be in the jeep. Quite a few convoys before them had been hit or turned back. No one knew how many casualties would come in later.

Without waiting, Lilly walked over to the jeep. Someone had thoughtfully mopped away the blood from the metal floor. She climbed in and curled up on one side, her back resting against the cool steel wall.

A few moments later Jack climbed into the passenger's seat and stretched out, his head resting on the ledge of the door, his feet sticking out of the driver's side.

Lilly felt vaguely disappointed.

After everything that had happened today, she would have liked to have lain beside him.

TWENTY-ONE

JULY 1944

The first person Dot encountered at Rainbow Corner next morning was Tony. He thrust his hand into his inside pocket and whipped out some photos.

'The new baby. Another boy. We're going to call him Joseph after my pop, Giuseppe.'

She gazed down at the tiny mite nestling in Barbara's arms. She smiled at the baby's sleeping face.

'Congratulations!' She felt so happy for him. 'How's Barbara?'

'Fine, I guess. She's taken the two kids down to see her parents. I'm hoping she comes back before we set off.'

'Have you seen any of the others?'

'Everyone's rushing around cos we're all due to go off any day now.'

'Otis too?'

'You betcha!' Tony laughed, a full-throated holler. 'But this time it'll be pretty near impossible for him to wriggle out of it.'

Dot wasn't sure what he meant by that, but thought it was best not to ask him to explain as she was beginning to feel a little uneasy, remembering too what Paul had said in Southend. Instead, she suggested that Tony go down to Barbara's parents while he could and spend some time with her.

'No can do,' he replied. 'I've been roped in to be best man at a wedding this afternoon. Some place called Caxton Hall. Sydney's tying the knot with that mouthy firecracker.'

Nancy! Dot couldn't quite believe that this was actually happening. Nancy and Sydney? She then remembered she had an urgent question for him.

'I have to ask, Tony. What did you do about that token from your sleeve? Did you tell anyone else?'

'No point. I knew they picked up the broad that done it and put her in the slammer, so I threw it overboard. Didn't want the bad luck.' Tony glanced at his watch. 'Gotta rush. See ya round, nursey!'

'Nurse Gallagher?'

Dot turned.

Leaning casually against a column stood Howard, a wry smile on his face.

'Good to see you're looking so well, Dot. I heard your ship had quite a time of it coming home.' He moved over. 'Thanks for writing, babe,' he said quietly. 'It made all the difference.'

Dot saw that he had a scar running down across his cheek, making his smile slightly lopsided.

'You were injured?'

Involuntarily, Howard's fingers touched the side of his chin. 'I was lucky. We lost quite a few men.' He looked at her.

She felt a warm glow as they locked eyes.

'I'm really glad you're safe, Howard. I was worried about you.'

'Join me for elevenses, kid?'

'Why not?'

They walked silently to the cafeteria. Howard pulled the door open and ushered her through. 'When I was lying in that field hospital, wishing you were my nurse, I kept myself going by crooning that song. I must have driven the other patients mad.' He hummed the tune.

Dot knew the lyrics by heart:

I'll find you in the morning sun,
And when the night is new,
I'll be looking at the moon
But I'll be seeing you.

The cafeteria was all but deserted.

Up near the counter, Art was talking earnestly with Virgil. No doubt giving him one of his 'America is great, God is good – have a donut' talks.

'Have you been looking after yourself?' Howard put out a tray for her and then another for himself. 'I missed your sensational dancing.'

Dot looked back at him but when they caught eyes, he looked down.

Silently, they slid their trays along the counter.

Thelma loudly pointed out the special of the day: 'Spam fritters'.

Howard laughed. 'I don't know about you, Dot, but I'll pass. I've more of a sweet tooth.' He grabbed a coffee and a donut. She did the same.

Before she could mention it, Howard asked if Dot had seen Otis.

She felt ashamed. She didn't want him to know how close they had become.

'Seen him around.'

'Hope you've not got engaged or anything mad like that. Trust me, Dot. Don't get yourself embroiled.'

Dot felt the blood rise in her cheeks. Luckily Howard was stirring his coffee and didn't see.

'I'll warn you one more time. He is my oldest buddy, but ... take care.'

Dot wondered if Howard was jealous. Why else the endless warnings to keep away?

'There's a game I used to play with my mom.' Howard picked up his donut. 'You eat, but you're not allowed to wipe the sugar off your face, or to lick your lips. Like to play?'

'You're on!'

'OK? Ready, set, go!'

As they ate, Dot stared intently at Howard and he at her.

'It's hard!'

'Very!'

After a few chews, Howard's tongue darted out.

Dot pointed at him.

'I win!'

'Shucks. You do!'

Dot and Howard licked their lips clean, then Howard reached out to remove a grain of sugar from Dot's chin.

'I've missed your smile, Nurse Gallagher. Incidentally, I hope you enjoyed the loan of the gramophone and records I organised when you got off the ship...'

'Skipper! You've come back to me!' Otis stood at the side of the table. 'Put that woman down, Howard, you big ape.'

He grabbed a chair and sat between them.

'I hope you're not letting my revered captain lead you astray, Nurse Gallagher.'

Howard raised an eyebrow.

'Have you heard? As we speak, poor old Sydney's tying the knot. Imagine that!' Otis leaned back in his chair and guffawed. 'Poor deluded fool – "For what is wedlock forced but a hell, An age of discord and continual strife?"'

Howard coughed.

'Oops!' Otis glanced at him, an insolent grin across his face. 'What's needling you, old man?' He shuddered. 'Sydney's chosen his bed. I wouldn't fancy getting hitched to a dragon like Nancy, would you? Imagine being glued to that for life!'

'Each to his own, Otis. For most men marriage is a kind of security, a comfort. Women too. So, many of the guys are getting wed before they go off to face unknown dangers. I'm sure that's the case for Sydney and for Nancy. It's human instinct. And deserves a little respect.'

Howard pushed his plate away. Dot saw that, apart from that first competition bite, he had not touched the donut. 'This sense we have of being stalked by death makes everything more intense. We have to stay on guard, not be selfish, tell the truth and make sure we act with care of others. If anything good has come out of this war, it's that it may have made us realise we must be better people.'

Otis stood up and yawned. 'I don't know about you two, but I fancy some chow. Something dark, sweet and tasty!' He moved towards the counter. 'Right now, my motto is "eat, drink and be merry, for tomorrow…"'

'Don't finish that, Otis!' Howard jumped to his feet. 'Just don't!'

Otis turned and pushed Howard away, shouting, 'Dry up, old man, will ya? Stop needling me.'

'A little respect in front of a lady, my friend.'

Otis turned on him. 'Respectfully, Captain, I'll just say this: scram!'

Howard pushed Otis back with his fingertips, yelling: 'I know I am bound by the honour of my vow, Otis, but seriously, pal, you are *this close* to driving me to spill the beans. Tell her yourself, or I will…'

'Shut up! Shut up!' Otis lurched forward and thrust the flat of his hand over Howard's mouth, preventing him from speaking. 'I pegged you wrong, Howard. I thought you were an honourable guy.'

Otis started shoving Howard, pushing him in the chest.

'Are you jealous, Howard? That it? Cos I'm the pretty one, and you're getting nowhere fast?'

Dot tried to get between the two men, crying at them to stop.

As Otis rushed him, Howard kicked Otis's feet apart, causing him to lose balance, stagger and fall back.

Dot fell to her knees, trying to pull Otis away.

'Stop!' Pressing his white helmet onto his head, Virgil rushed over. 'Cool it, guys!' He stood over Otis, one hand spread out in Howard's direction, the other pointing to the letters on his lapel: MP. Military police. 'Simmer down, Captain, or I'll throw you in the pokey.' He pointed towards Dot. 'And you, little lady, can make yourself scarce. I need to sort out this brawl.'

'Otis didn't start it…' Dot took a step forward.

Howard grunted.

Virgil shot him a look and barked: 'Back off, lady! That's an order.'

As Dot reluctantly turned to leave the canteen, a mob of GIs ran in singing 'Here Comes the Bride'. In the middle of them towered Sydney. Resting on the other men's shoulders sat Nancy, arms in the air, laughing jubilantly: 'Minnehaha all round! Let's seal this wonderful day with some of that laughing water!'

*

Lilly prepared for another evening's drive. Now that Cherbourg had been taken, it was a case of moving south-east again towards St Lô, following the troops along with the ambulances and Red Cross vehicles. Even areas taken by the Allies had marauding stragglers, so it was difficult to relax. When tranquillity did come, Lilly frequently found herself feeling more nervous than when they were actually under fire.

This evening was no exception. As the hazy sun reddened and died to the west, the bucolic meadows with horses and cows made her hair stand on end with fear, her eyes darting, watching for tank tracks or low bushes hiding snipers.

In a nearby field a woman with a bucket strode across the grass and disappeared into a farmhouse. Normal life. Further on, a bunch of kids came running alongside the jeep shouting 'gum, chum' to Jack. As she and Jack had nothing to offer, the boys pelted them with stones.

At a fork in the road, Jack indicated to Lilly to take the lane rather than the main road. Either side the embankment rose high, and trees intertwined above, making it feel like driving through a verdant tunnel.

'I imagine this is like the countryside where you live, am I right?' Jack was stretched out in the passenger seat. 'Hedgerows, meadows, wild flowers. Where I live there's nothing like this.'

'Where is that exactly?' No harm in asking, thought Lilly, but Jack did not answer. 'I'm guessing it's a wild, dusty town with wooden houses and stoops.'

'Not a town at all. I live in the land of red rocks carved by the wind and water, a world of pronghorns, coyotes, bobcats and roadrunners.'

'Roadrunners? Isn't that us?'

Jack threw back his head and laughed. 'If you saw one ... it's quite funny to compare.'

Lilly slowed the jeep as they entered the near-ruins of a village. The church was still standing, but little else. People huddled in makeshift spaces created from hunks of wall, bricks, advertising hoardings, littered with random pieces of furniture and overhung by a sheet. At the side of the road, two children played in the turret hatch of a burned-out panzer tank. An overturned Nazi officers' car had had its tyres removed. An elderly couple sat on them smoking pipes as though it was the latest craze in furniture.

'Soon time to fill up, sir.'

'Pull in.'

'There's nothing here, sir.' Lilly went on driving.

'I said pull in, Deane. Order!'

Lilly slammed on the brakes.

Jack leapt out of the cab, and knelt on the scorched, sandy earth; he put his ear to the ground, then turned towards the people sheltering by the roadside.

'Allez!' he shouted. *'Va! Tanks! Cachez vous!'* He mimed shooters, while pointing at the burned-out tank, and leapt back inside the jeep. 'Let's go, Corporal.'

Lilly pushed the gears until the jeep was bowling along at full speed.

'Where to?' she yelled, the wind stifling her voice.

'We have to link up with the US division at St Lô,' Jack yelled. 'Twenty-five miles on. But there are planes I can hear, heading this way from the south-west, and lorries coming from that direction. They'll not be ours.'

Lilly glanced down at the dashboard. 'Not sure we'll make it on this tankful.'

'Foot down. If the time comes, we'll hike.'

*

There was no queue in Dunker's Den. Just a pair of empty chairs under the sign 'Nurse'. The long room was quieter than she had ever seen it. Not even anyone at the pinball machines. A few men lounged on sofas reading newspapers. The headlines were mainly about the campaign in northern France: 'Yanks Capture La Haye', 'British Close to Taking Caen'. The most worrying one was '10,000 Killed or Hurt in London by Robot Bombs'.

Dot pointed at the newspaper. 'Have you seen any of those?'

'Doodlebugs, we call 'em,' said the GI reading the paper. 'They come out of the sky at you, sounding like a badly tuned motorbike.' He made the noise. 'Then sudden silence, and a few seconds later – boom! It's quite disconcerting. While you can hear them, you're safe. It's a true case of silent but deadly.'

'Bit like your girl back in Seattle!' laughed the GI in the next chair.

'Whereas those raids always happened in the dark. These darned doodlebugs come any time, day or night. And no warning sirens.'

Dot felt something near despair. As soon as hope rose, it was always immediately quashed. She found herself reading the poster on the wall:

Mr Hitler wants to know!
He wants to know the unit's name
Where it's going – whence it came
Ships, guns and shells all make him curious
But silence makes him simply Fuehrious.
Don't discuss troop movements, ship sailings, war equipment.

That was the problem here in Rainbow Corner. Anyone with big ears could pass on so many details.

Liz Webb came in asking whether anyone would like to join her sketching class up in Dabbler's Den, but had no takers. Dot wondered how she could ever have thought Liz a suspect. She had glanced into the art room and watched Liz bending over the men's drawings, pointing out a tip here, suggesting a mistake there, always with a smile and a great deal of encouragement. And the poor woman had only recently lost her husband.

At the end of her shift, Dot made her way back to the dressing room to prepare for an evening hostessing.

She was surprised to see Nancy there.

'I want to party with my husband, darling.' While applying mascara, Nancy pursed her lips and gazed into her own eyes in the mirror. 'And to keep the other girls' hands off him.'

June sat in the corner. She patted the chair next to her, inviting Dot over, whispering, 'If Nancy was insufferable before, now it's off the scale.'

'I thought she despised Sydney?'

'She went for the best available, petal. Now she has her ticket to the States.' June gave Dot a friendly wink. 'Come on. It's going to be some night!'

TWENTY-TWO

DOT WAS DANCING A foxtrot with a young boy, very wet behind the ears, who talked of his mama and his little sisters, and how scared he was. She wanted to hug him and tell him everything would be OK. But that would be a lie.

Then, over the boy's shoulder, she caught sight of June. June's eyes filled with terror; she broke with her dancing partner and fled from the dance floor.

As Dot continued her dance with the quivering boy, she looked around to see what could have caused June's exit.

Then she saw him. A man in RAF uniform, sitting at a table of GIs, whom he was ignoring. He was staring at the women dancers, scanning their faces, his mouth set, his eyes hard.

Dot made her excuses and slipped away from her dancing partner. She rushed through to the dressing room. No one was there.

'June?'

Dot opened the far door, calling again.

'Shh!' A rustling behind her.

June peered out from the rack of hanging uniforms left behind by the band onstage tonight.

'I have to get out of here … You don't understand, Dot. It's not safe.'

'Actually, Mrs Jagger, I do,' said Dot. 'Stay there. Let me deal with this. Don't come out till someone comes for you.'

Trying to make it look quite usual, Dot hurried back to the ballroom and attracted the attention of Marty and Virgil. She explained June's story and surreptitiously pointed out the RAF man.

Virgil called across to Art.

'Ask the man to dance, Dot. See if he's looking for June, then tell him she was here earlier but that she left for the train station a short while ago, heading home.'

Dot went over to ask for a dance, but Wing Commander Jagger stood up, grabbed the front of her uniform lapel and shouted at her to back off. His breath reeked of alcohol.

Virgil and Art came across to calm him.

'Hey there, fellah. Leave the lady alone.'

'Where is June? I followed her in here.'

'An hour ago she was helping out in Dunker's Den,' said Dot.

'What in Christ's name is that?' Jagger leaned threateningly in Dot's direction.

'The nursing station. She brought me much-needed supplies from a hospital in Essex. She's heading right back there as we speak. She left, oh, about fifteen minutes ago.'

Virgil took a firm grip of Jagger's elbow. 'So, sir, if we saunter along to the railway station, you might be in time to catch the same train home.' He turned to Art. 'This is Sergeant Art Pemberton. He's going that way anyhow. So off we go, pal.'

'Let me go.' Jagger shook his arm free. 'And I'm not your pal, Yankee boy.'

'Fenchurch Station, isn't it?' said Art. 'Places over here have such quaint names.'

The two men guided the drunken pilot out of Rainbow Corner. At the front door, Dot slipped her own room key into Marty's hand, saying, 'Regent Palace, 251. Once we're out of sight, fetch June and take her up there. She's hiding in the dressing room wardrobe.'

Then, throwing her cape over her shoulders, Dot ran to catch up with the others.

Virgil pushed Jagger onto a bus heading east. Dot only just managed to grab the pole and leap onto the platform before the bus pulled out.

Swaying in the aisle, Jagger shouted at the other passengers, who shifted about, some moving upstairs to be out of his presence.

'I don't like inebriated men on my bus,' said the conductress, rolling out four tickets, which Dot paid for.

'He's had a belly-load, ma'am,' said Virgil. 'It won't be long before he collapses. I'll make sure he stays calm.'

'Any trouble and you're off.' The clippy moved on to take fares towards the front of the bus.

'I'm not so sure he's going to get any quieter.' Dot looked at Jagger, who was now growling abusive comments about women. Everyone knew pilots were doing a wonderful job, flying out each night to destroy the airbases in Belgium, France and Germany, but why did this man think it gave him the right to take his stress out on everyone else?

'Aldwych,' cried the clippy.

'Hey, fellahs!' Art shouted across the aisle to Virgil and Dot. 'Why don't we get him off here and walk a little. It might sober the guy up.'

Virgil shifted from one foot to the other: 'A couple of stops more, Art.'

'Didn't Vi live here…?' Dot had a memory of her saying she had rooms in the Aldwych, which, not knowing London, Dot had imagined was the name of a rooming house or cheap hotel. Only now she saw it was a crescent, recently bombed, most of the windows blown out, the buildings which had not collapsed black with soot.

'My wife is a whore!' Jagger shouted at the top of his voice as he slumped down next to a frail Chelsea pensioner. 'A whore!'

'Off!' The conductress pointed to them. 'Now! Off my bus!'

The two men pulled Jagger to his feet.

'I won't be manhandled.' Jagger writhed in Art's grasp. 'Hands off me, four-eyes!'

'Look, pal, we gotta sober you up before you reach the station or they won't let you on the train.'

Jagger shoved Virgil away. Art gripped him so that they wouldn't all three fall from the platform into the street. When the bus pulled in, they jumped off. Jagger pulled away, staggering up a side street.

'Come on,' yelled Art, running after him. 'We can't let him go.'

'Don't bother.' Virgil stood still, dusting himself down. 'We got him away from *her*. That's the important thing.'

'Look, Virgil, I *have* to make sure he's OK.' Art ran on, yelling back over his shoulder, 'For his wife's sake.'

'Careful!' Dot looked around. Although the street was empty, she thought she heard a motorbike coming up behind them. But there was nothing there but a parked van.

'Down!' yelled Virgil. 'Down! Down! Buzz bomb.'

Dot looked up to see something like a small aircraft directly above them.

It spluttered for a few seconds then cut out.

'To the ground! Art! To the ground! Buzz bomb!' Virgil grabbed Dot and threw her face down into a doorway, spreading himself on top of her. She felt crushed by his weight, unable to breathe.

Silence.

Then the explosion.

The impact threw Virgil several yards down the street.

Dot was showered with small pieces of brick but raised herself onto her elbows. There followed a loud hum, like a radio gone wrong. She could see, but not hear. She hauled herself to her feet.

Art had been smacked back against the building on the other side of the road, and sat upright, blood pouring down his face, his glasses shattered. About ten feet away, in the centre of the road, Virgil lay face down, immobile.

Dizzy from the humming in her ears, Dot ran to him and rolled him over. A thick layer of white dust covered his face. His eyes were open.

'Virgil!' Dot placed a hand on his chest.

He blinked.

Thank God. He seeming to be shouting, though Dot could hear nothing. He raised his arm, still mouthing words she could not hear. He pointed to Art.

Reaching in her pocket for a handkerchief, Dot went to Art and wiped the blood from his eyes.

She watched his lips move. He said: 'God bless you!'

She inspected the wound on the back of Art's head. Superficial.

Art was indicating further up the street where an office building had collapsed. Beneath the rubble she could see RAF blue trousers and black shoes.

Dot started heaving bricks away, desperate to uncover Jagger and pull him to safety. All around her, dazed people staggered from adjacent buildings, shocked but unharmed; others ran up the street to help. An ARP warden arrived and started organising groups to help clear away the rubble. They all shouted out for survivors.

Virgil yelled at Dot to stop digging.

'It's my duty as a nurse to save life, Virgil.'

'Too late for that, Nurse Gallagher.' Virgil pulled her to her feet. 'No one could survive an injury like that. He's a goner.'

'God save us!' Art loomed above them, his face chalk white, flame-red stripes of blood seeping from the cuts on his head. 'Someone has to tell June.'

*

Lilly had almost reached the main road when a barrage of machine-gun fire started up. She glanced at the petrol indicator. It was way past red.

Jack's eyes followed hers. He thrust out a hand. 'That way.'

Lilly drove off the lane into a track which ran through the fields towards a copse.

'Into the woods!'

Lilly yanked the steering wheel hard left and after a few bumps over lumpy tree roots, the jeep came to a sputtering stop.

They both leapt from the vehicle and crouched behind trees.

The plane flew overhead and continued northwards, while the sound of lorries and the occasional round of machine-gun fire grew nearer.

'How can we be sure they're not our boys?' asked Lilly.

'Listen. They sound different. Our guns sound like a drummer. Nazi guns sound like tearing fabric. Stay there!' Knees bent to stay low, Jack ran back to the jeep and pulled out the radio equipment, then squatted near Lilly. 'Whatever we do, we don't lose this.'

Lilly looked up. The treetops covered them.

'Let's go!' she said.

After about ten minutes, the undergrowth, a mix of ferns and brambles, became thick, making it necessary to wade through the bracken, rather than run.

Lilly could still hear the plane making circles above.

The light between the tree trunks grew brighter.

At the edge of the copse, Jack looked out.

'We stay here and wait for things to cool down, or move. What do you say?'

Lilly certainly didn't want to hang around. They had to rejoin a unit. They'd never survive alone.

Peering into the distance where the land swept down before them, Lilly could see the outline of a sizable roof.

'We could try our fortune at that farm?'

'Remember, not all the locals are grateful. Most grand houses like that were commandeered as billets for Nazi troops. They might still be there. We should go the other way.'

Lilly surveyed the meadows around them. In the nearest field, four hooves pointing to the sky, lay a cow, fresh blood running down its belly.

'Damned fool Nazis.' Jack started pulling up ferns and sticking them into his helmet band and across his shoulders. 'Why shoot a cow?'

Boredom, thought Lilly, as she too grabbed greenery to camouflage herself.

'Come on.' Hauling the radio equipment onto his back, Jack ran for the nearest hedge. Crouching down, Lilly followed.

The plane was far away now, still circling, but heading the other direction. It turned and came nearer.

Jack and Lilly lay flat until it went away, then got up and edged forward.

After about fifteen minutes, the plane did a sudden turn, dipped, waggled its wings and sped away. When it was less than a pinprick in the sky, both Lilly and Jack felt free to run upright along the centre of the lane.

There was a field of horses to one side. A smartly dressed woman led two bays towards outbuildings, presumably stables. They had to be racehorses, Lilly thought. It was an incongruous sight.

She looked up to the clear sky, wondering why the pilot had given up on them. Then it struck her. He must have known he didn't need to worry about them.

She looked along the lane ahead, at the level, neat sand.

'Stop!' she cried to Jack. 'Don't move!'

'No.' He turned to face her. 'We need to go forward.'

'It's mined.'

'What?'

As Lilly opened her mouth to reply, Jack, unbalanced by the radio kit, placed one foot back to steady himself, and turned to look at the surface of the lane.

As though in slow motion, a bunch of camouflage ferns tumbled from his helmet. Jack grabbed the air, trying to catch them before they landed.

He jumped back.

Boooooom!

The explosion flung Lilly back into the hedge.

She could see Jack lying further up the lane. He lay still. Lilly edged along the grass verge until she reached Jack's prostrate body, surrounded by bloody sand.

His shoulder and face were a mess of blood.

He wasn't breathing.

Lilly was momentarily immobilised.

Then suddenly Jack gasped.

Lilly was suddenly filled with super-strength. She rolled Jack to the verge, then, using leaves and grass, wiped the blood from his nose and mouth.

'Breathe!' she cried. 'Goddammit, Jack. Breathe, breathe, breathe!'

The sound of a distant motor, a small van or car, approaching.

They had to get away.

Lilly smashed a hole in the thicket, just big enough for Jack's inert body, then gingerly jumped over and pulled him through. She hauled him down the grassy slope towards a small pond surrounded by long reeds.

The motor grew louder. From where she sat, Lilly could see a small French farmer's van, driving right into the minefield.

She couldn't let them go to their certain death. She was about to get up and alert the driver to the danger, when the van pulled up, just short of the mines.

The driver knew.

Ducking behind the long grass, she thanked heavens that the khaki green of their uniforms blended in so well with the foliage at the water's edge.

She heard the van door open and someone walking around. The steps stopped. After a long minute, they went back to the car. The door slammed. The car reversed fast the way it had come.

Hardly daring to breathe, Lilly lay still, until the only sounds were the lapping of water and the buzz of insects.

She was certain that the van was going to come back with reinforcements.

Before that, she and Jack had to be gone.

Alone, she could easily run for it, but she wouldn't leave him.

A nearby thudding sound interrupted her thoughts.

She raised her head to see a horse ambling in their direction.

Jack lay motionless at her side. She felt his chest. His heart was still beating.

'Stay there, Chief. I won't leave you.'

Bent low, Lilly moved forward till she could touch the horse, then held her hand flat, as though she was offering a sugar lump. 'Good boy!'

The horse lowered his mouth to her hand, the velvet of his nose nuzzling her palm. She patted his muzzle, softly stroked his mane. The horse flared his nostrils and pawed the grass.

'Gently, boy.' Leading the horse across to Jack, she whispered, *'Allons! Doucement!'*

Jack stretched out a hand, feeling for her.

'Is that you, Lilly?' His voice was feeble. Blood caked his face and hands.

'I'm here.'

'I can't see you.'

'There's blood in your eyes, sir.' She knelt and was about to wipe his face when she saw a piece of shrapnel jutting out of his cheek. She could not move him with that left in. 'One moment, Chief. This will hurt.'

Swiftly she drew the crumpled metal from the wound, causing more blood to dribble down onto Jack's neck.

'You have to help me now, Chief.' She put her arms around his waist. 'You need to get to your feet.'

Once Jack was standing, leaning against the horse's side, Lilly placed his hands on the horse's croup.

'A horse!' he said quietly, running his hand along the horse's spine and murmuring indecipherable words.

Kneeling on one knee, Lilly made a step for Jack to climb. But he was too weak to mount.

'Keep hold, Chief. You'll need to throw yourself across. I'll push.'

She stood behind Jack, grabbed his thighs and thrust him up till he was lying across the horse like a saddlebag.

Then she climbed on behind him, sitting astride.

Once she was sure they were both balanced, she called to Jack, 'Hold on, Chief!'

Then, clutching the horse's mane, Lilly put her head down and rode.

TWENTY-THREE

DOT'S ROOM AT THE Regent Palace Hotel was dark, illuminated only by the flickering glare of the hall nightlights. Nervously knotting her fingers, June sat timidly on the edge of Dot's bed. She looked up, enquiring.

'Something's wrong!' June jumped to her feet. 'Is *he* with you? He knows I'm here, doesn't he? He's with you…' She rushed forward, trying to get out. 'You don't understand, he'll kill me…'

'June. Please…' Dot had no idea how to tell her.

'I'll do this.' As though to calm a wild animal, Art held up his hands and took a step forward. 'Please, June, sit down.'

There was laughter down the hall. Dot shut the door behind them, turned on a small table lamp, then backed away to stand guard.

'What happened to your glasses, Art?' June reached out to touch them.

'I'm so sorry, June.' Art knelt before June and took her hands in his. 'I have some very bad news. Your husband is dead. The victim of a buzz bomb. He didn't stand a chance.'

June said nothing, just stared at Art in incomprehension. Then she started crying, in loud, racking sobs.

Dot went to her kitbag, looking for her flask.

A brisk knock and the door flew open.

'Hey, Skipper! Why ain't you dancing tonight? I've been jigging about downstairs for hours, waiting for you.'

Otis flicked the main light switch, throwing the whole scene into bright, startling glare.

'Sorry, Art.' Virgil edged round the doorway from the corridor. 'Couldn't hold him back.' He tapped Otis on the forearm. 'Come on, pal, let's leave these folk alone now.'

'But, Dot, I'm leaving tomorrow for some camp in the country.' Otis whined like a child, as though he had not registered the atmosphere of the room. 'I gotta dance with you tonight, Skips.'

Without taking his eyes from June, Art yelled: 'Get that goddamned fool outta here!'

Dot looked across at Otis, all dishevelled and sweaty.

'You really have to go now, Otis.' She pushed him back. 'This is not the time.'

'Come on now, fellah!' Virgil gripped Otis's shoulders, but Otis struggled free and lurched towards Dot.

'You heard the lady.'

'Please, baby...' Otis grabbed Dot. She could smell alcohol on his breath.

'Another time, Otis!' How could he not see that she couldn't contemplate dancing when poor June's whole life had collapsed? 'Please go!'

'You're mean, Dot! That's what you are. Mean!'

'It's my fault,' June sobbed into her hands. 'It's all my fault.'

Running feet in the hallway.

'I got him!' Howard stepped into the room and took hold of Otis. 'Come on, Oats. Leave these poor folks alone.' He gently removed Otis's hold on Dot. 'I'm sorry, Dot. Until we meet again, take care of yourself. I'll write.'

Dragging Otis out of the room, Howard led him away.

Dot turned back to June.

*

Lilly perched on a fold-up stool outside a field hospital on the outskirts of St Lô. The medical team were treating Jack, his shirt and jacket black with caked blood, his pale disfigured face unrecognisable. Someone from the animal unit came to lead the horse away.

Face in hands, Lilly gazed at the earth, watching a line of ants scurrying back and forth bringing crumbs back to their nest. Helping each other, working as a fellowship, like the troops in this war.

Every time the green tent flap moved, Lilly sat up, hoping for news. Over and over they told her to go and rest. But she couldn't leave Jack.

Eventually a surgeon emerged.

'I'm afraid it's unlikely Chief Kirk will make it,' he said wearily. 'He's lost most of his blood.'

'He'll die?'

'We're out of blood. There's none here to give him. Sorry, Corporal. It's time to say goodbye.'

Lilly mouth went dry, her heart thumped.

She couldn't let Jack die.

Not when they'd come so far.

'Take mine.' Lilly rolled up her sleeve. 'I'm serious. Take my blood.'

'It might not be a match.'

'I'm O negative.'

'O negative?' The surgeon looked into her eyes. 'Sure?'

'Certain.' Lilly pulled out her ID card. 'Come on! There's no time to waste.' She finished rolling up her sleeve. 'Let's get on with it.'

'You understand there's no guarantee, Corporal?'

'Please.'

*

'I think we should leave them alone,' Virgil whispered.

Dot looked across to Art, still on his knees, holding June's hands in his. She was still weeping, tears dropping onto her lap.

Dot followed Virgil out. At the end of the corridor, they perched together on the top step.

'These religious fellows aren't always the joke that we think them,' he said. 'I gather that June had some secret which she had confided to him. I'd guess it was about her old man whacking her. But she couldn't leave him because he was a so-called hero.' Virgil sucked in his breath and shook his head. 'We see a lot of incomprehensible things, we MPs. What times we live in. No one can work out who's the hero and who's the villain.'

'For a while I thought June was the Rainbow Corner spy,' Dot said quietly. 'With her white lies and reticence to talk about her home life. Now we know why. Liz Webb too. I suspected her because she'd been down in Kent the day of a sabotage and tried to deny being there.'

'Liz Webb? She's a bit of hero, you know.' Virgil smoothed down his trousers with both hands. 'Her husband was a pilot, decent guy. Very droll. He was shot down. But even through her grief, Liz continued to spend her nights in Kent painting cardboard planes and inflatable tanks, decoys to fool the Nazis that the invasion would come from Kent.'

'Oh God!' Dot recalled the paint flecks on Liz's hands and clothing. 'That was why.'

With a loud click, the timed lights in the hall went out. They sat in the dark.

'Then they took Vi,' said Dot. 'Tony's Nazi button, the final proof.'

'What's that?'

Dot told Virgil about the Nazi badge.

'Vi didn't have anything to do with that. She's innocent.'

'So, why's she in prison, then?'

'She isn't.'

As soon as the words were out of Virgil's mouth, he shut up.

Dot looked at Virgil, lit only by the green light of the emergency exit sign.

'I knew that they knew Vi didn't do it, so I challenged them. They took her, see, because of the wastepaper basket. But they knew it wasn't her. They wanted to make the real enemy feel easy. A well-managed trap. A few days after Vi was put in the slammer, she was secretly released into my care. I've been staying with her some nights in her little apartment, bringing supplies, helping keep her out of the public eye.'

'I don't understand?'

'Whoever has been leaking information is still working at Rainbow Corner. The powers-that-be want them to believe they're off the hook. All the easier to feed them false information, or to discover them...'

*

When Dot finally made it back to Rainbow Corner, the dance floor was almost empty, the band packed up and gone. The only music came from a jukebox.

Nancy was there, jitterbugging with some American sailor.

Otis was gone.

However brash and insensitive he'd been, Dot couldn't let him go off without a goodbye.

She went to the front desk, where Paul perched on a stool behind the counter, idly doodling on today's newspaper.

'Hello, Scouser!' he called. 'I'm sitting in for the girl while she takes five. What can I do you for?'

'I wondered if you might have seen...'

'Otis? Yes. Gone back to the hotel with Howard and a few others. I gather they're off tomorrow, the lot of them.'

Dot moved away but Paul shouted after her.

'Letter for you. It's been in the post room forever but someone saw you round so brought it down here.'

Lilly's writing. Dot shoved the envelope into her pocket and went back to the hotel.

In the hotel bar she found Howard sitting in a corner, Otis slumped beside him, asleep.

'I wanted to say goodbye.'

'I'll pass on the message.'

Dot took a seat next to Howard.

All around the room people talked intently, the atmosphere charged.

'Do you know where you're going?'

'A training camp, then a ship. I guess France, though, who knows, it could be North Africa, or Italy again.'

'I wish I was sailing with you.'

'Me too.'

A marine put a coin in the jukebox and the machinery rattled into action. The Andrews Sisters – 'Don't Sit Under the Apple Tree'.

Otis let out a loud snort.

'Otis will finally have to admit the reality of his situation. He seems incapable of facing the truth and has forgotten that we are only here in Europe to help liberate you all from the Nazis.'

Dot felt she was being lectured, as though it was her fault that Otis hadn't yet seen action.

'Why are you so against me going out with Otis?'

A pause.

'I'm looking out for you.'

'You mean you're envious?'

Howard said nothing.

'So you are.'

'Let's put it another way, Dot. I'm looking out for BOTH of you.'

That was a new one!

'We're both adults, you know, Howard. I really think you should mind your own business.'

For some moments Howard sat silently, then said:

'That gramophone, the one which I gave Otis to bring down to you in Portsmouth to cheer you up after your stint away … I can't bring it with me into battle so, if you'd like it, I'll get it sent to your room. You can hold onto it till we get back.'

Hardly listening to what Howard was saying, Dot was looking down at Otis, hair stuck to his forehead like a feverish infant. She reached out and stroked his damp cheek.

'That would be lovely. Thank you, Howard. I'll have to buy some records to play on it.'

'There are a few in the box.'

Howard waved. Dot looked up to see Earl leaving the bar, Pearl on his arm.

'See ya tomorrow, Captain.' He waved.

Howard whispered to Dot, 'He doesn't know it yet, but tomorrow morning Earl's being promoted to first lieutenant. While I'm to be a major.'

Otis snored, waking himself up. He raised himself onto his elbows and looked around.

'Hey, Skipper! What you doin' here? You should be tucked up in bed.'

'I came to say goodbye.'

'Yeah! Parting is such sweet sorrow, like your Bard has it. You just gotta promise me you won't get married to anyone. You need to wait for me.'

He flopped down onto the banquette.

'He doesn't know what he's saying.' Howard stood, pulling at Otis to stand up. 'Come on, pal. You must get some proper sleep. Tomorrow will be hard.'

'Tomorrow and tomorrow and tomorrow,' slurred Otis. 'Once more into the breach, dear friends!'

'Excuse me, Dot. I really wanted to sit and talk.' Howard looked down, biting his lip. 'I want your face to be the memory I'll carry in my head, to battle.'

'You still can, Howard. I'll pray for you. Take care, won't you?'

Otis slumped. Howard steadied him.

'I'm so sorry. I have to get this fellow into bed or he will regret it.'

Dot felt a pang of regret that she couldn't kiss Otis goodbye.

As Howard walked Otis to the exit, the jukebox started on 'I'll Be Seeing You'.

Howard glanced back over his shoulder.

'Look after yourself too, Dot, won't you?'

She followed them into the hall, watching Howard lead drunken Otis into the lift.

PART THREE

A New Year

TWENTY-FOUR

FEBRUARY 1945

New Year had felt like a day no one wanted to celebrate. The horrors of the previous year might be gone, but who knew what the next would bring?

By the end of January, Paris and the South of France had been liberated, but the Allied armies were still slugging it out with the German forces in the Ardennes.

Every day, news reached Rainbow Corner of the death in action of scores of more GIs. The poor American girl who had taken over Lilly's job had to mark so much of the incoming mail with the fateful sticker: 'Deceased – return to sender', then had to spend a good half an hour pulling out red flag-pins from the map in the front hall.

As February marched on, sporadic snowflakes floated down through the crisp air. Dot trudged the hundred yards round Piccadilly Circus and up Shaftesbury Avenue, tugging her scarf tightly around her neck. Her breath puffed out in grey clouds.

She would be glad to get inside and have a cup of coffee.

But at last she felt happy. Tomorrow, finally, she started her long-promised leave. Two whole weeks in Liverpool, a break from this relentless roundabout of work and worry.

She had written to Otis to let him know. Who knew, by now maybe he might also have leave? It would be awful if, while she was up north, he arrived at Rainbow Corner and they missed each other.

Before her shift began she went to the canteen and had that coffee with Paul. He nodded in the direction of Nancy, who was talking seriously with Sydney, drawing something on a large notepad.

'Poor man.' Paul wore a tragic expression. 'Only back on one week's leave and she's got him writing his will.'

'Is that true?'

'Course not.' Paul blew on his cup to cool it. 'Perhaps she's swotting up on what Sydney knows of the battle plans. Then she can sell it for a bob or two to Lord Toffington of Hitlerdom.'

Dot laughed.

'I heard that Liz Webb met some lovely chap and got hitched again. That's nice, isn't it? US Marine. Sailed off on some huge ship across the Atlantic. Him, that is, obviously. Not her. She's moved out to Whitechapel now to be near her parents. Anyway, he's a sweet boy.'

Would people say that of Otis, Dot wondered? Sweet boy, that Otis?

'How is he anyway?' asked Paul, reading her thoughts.

'No idea.' Dot shrugged. 'He hasn't written. At one point, you know, Lilly thought he might be the spy.'

'Don't mean to be rude, love, but he hasn't got the brains. Got the looks, all right, but…' Paul swigged his coffee. 'I reckon it's that Gloria Fergusson. She's all but vanished off the planet. Why else did they get her out of the office?'

Next morning, as the first grey lights of dawn shimmered on the bleak horizon, Dot hurried onto a bus bound for Euston. A few hours later she was standing on her parents' doorstep.

She rang the bell. Her mother opened. She let out a cry and gave Dot a huge hug. Dot was so happy to see her.

'Why didn't you let yourself in?'

'I wanted to surprise you!'

'Who is it, Kate?'

'Our prodigal daughter.'

Pop emerged from the kitchen. He was wearing his ARP helmet, about to go on duty. 'I'll get the kettle on.'

'What a day,' said Mammy, as she helped Dot take off her coat. 'We have a surprise visitor. Just arrived by ship this morning.'

Oh God, thought Dot. Please, not Billy.

Dot stepped down into the kitchen. The warmth of the coal fire hit her.

'Come on in, love,' called her father. 'Get some heat in your bones.'

Her mother followed Dot in.

'Surprise for you, Otis. Our Dot's home.'

*

After lunch, Dot and Otis went for a walk. They sat together on a bench down at the pier head.

'You're telling me that Howard, Tony, Art and the others are still out there?'

'Well ... yes.'

'So how did you get leave, Otis?'

'It isn't exactly leave...'

'You've not gone AWOL?'

'Don't be silly.' Otis laughed and patted his leg. 'The old trouble flared up. They didn't think I was much use while I couldn't run, so I languished in a hospital in the South of France for a day or two, then they put me on a ship from Marseille to Liverpool. I'm going to see a specialist in London. If I get the all-clear, I'll be sent back.' Otis gave a sheepish grin. 'That's if the miracle Allied breakthrough doesn't happen by then and it's all over. I'm keeping my fingers crossed.'

Behind them a train rattled by on the overhead railway.

'I should be on my way down south, but ... how could I miss paying a call on my favourite Liverpudlian landlords,' he said. 'They've still got my suitcase, you know, under the bed in your room. I brought a whole lot more over from the States than I needed. They've promised they'll hold onto it till I get back.'

Now that she was sitting beside Otis, Dot was surprised she felt quite distant from him. It was all a bit too much. She had thought about him so often, but the dream was so different from the reality. The suitcase seemed like a ball and chain. Something which made Otis inescapable. Confused, she changed the subject.

'How's Howard?' she asked.

'Teacher's pet got promoted *again*. He's so high above us all now he sits on a cloud when he talks to me. Lieutenant Colonel Howard Hopkins, if you please. *And* he won two medals. *And* he earns twice as much dough as me. It's so unfair.'

Dot couldn't help feeling that being physically present on the battlefield might explain the disparity.

'Did you take part in *anything*, Otis?'

'Pity you don't have a piano, Dot. I'd play you some ragtime. I learned a tune or two when I was in hospital. Cheer you up. I know you love music.'

She wasn't going to let him get away with not replying.

'I asked if you took part in any action at all?'

'I was at the South of France landings and made my way up the Rhône or Rhine, or whatever that damned river's called. That was pretty scary, I can tell you. Those Germans don't give up without a hell of a fight. But then I got the old foot trouble…'

Dot thought of the devastated streets of Liverpool, the ruins and bombsites she had seen in Essex and London. If that was how everything looked in civilian cities, even a child could understand that German soldiers weren't going to let the Allied troops move forward without a struggle.

A seagull screeched overhead.

'I know what you're thinking, Dot.' Otis hung his head, twiddling his fingers. 'That I'm a heel. But as our friend Shakespeare has it, "We know what we are, but know not what we may be." I just didn't turn out to be much of a soldier.'

With a high-pitched hoot, the Wallasey ferry pulled out from the jetty. Dot watched it move into the swirling eddies of the Mersey like a soot-black swan.

'Before the war, Mammy, Pop and I used to go up to New Brighton on that boat.'

Brighton! Lilly's letter flashed through Dot's head.

'You may not be much of a soldier, Otis, but might you be a spy?'

He looked up, staring at her open-eyed. 'A spy?'

'I have a question about that night you came up on the train with Lilly.'

'Uh-huh?'

'Why were you in Brighton?'

'Well, yes. I fancied some air, so I went to the sea.'

'You need a special pass for that.'

'I had one.'

'How?'

'I asked for it.'

'Why Brighton?'

'A, it was easy to get to, and B, I was doing a favour for Thelma – you know, the girl in the commissary.'

'The what?'

'The canteen, as you lot call it. She needed someone to deliver a birthday present to her sister, Emily, at Brunswick Terrace, which is right on the ocean front…'

'I don't think there's an ocean near Brighton, Otis.' Dot was always amused by the dramatic turns of phrase Americans used. 'In Brighton, that would be the seafront, or just the front.'

'Anyhow, Thelma asked, I offered, and she got me the pass. I was only hanging around, doing nothing at the time. We all were. Like a weird vacation, minus the fun. To be honest, we imagined we'd been brought over on a lie. We hadn't seen one single air raid. It was as though you Brits had made it all up, just to get us there.' Otis took Dot's hand and squeezed it to his heart. 'Don't think badly of me, Dot. I had no idea when I joined up. Not until I was sent to the horror story they gaily call the French Riviera. Man, that was something else. Bombs going off all over the place, planes dropping things on us. We slept in shelters for animals, alongside cows and horses. Can you imagine? We had to bury scores of civilians that they'd massacred before they ran. Streets running with blood.' Otis moved Dot's hand from his heart to his lips and kissed it. 'The truth is, Skipper, the whole time I was out there, all I could think about was you. I couldn't concentrate. I'd have smashed my own ankle with a hammer to get back to you. Luckily all I needed to do was stumble in the grave I was digging.'

A tear spilled from Otis's eye and ran down his cheek.

'It's cold,' Dot said, meaning it in every possible way. 'Let's go somewhere and have a cuppa. There's a Reece's up the way.'

'Hello, Dorothy!' A bright female voice. 'Didn't know you were back in the Pool.'

It was hard to see through the clouds of breath, the loosely wound knitted scarves and the woolly hat pulled low over the woman's brow.

'It's Clarice O'Brien.'

Clarice O'Brien? Dot had no idea.

'You'll best remember me as Clarice Titchmarsh. I used to sit behind you in class, remember?'

Dot couldn't believe she'd come face to face with her ex-boyfriend's new wife. Memories of her came flooding back – the lumps of inky blotting paper Clarice threw into her hair, the time she'd unscrewed Dot's chair so that when she sat on it the whole thing collapsed, Clarice throwing a dart at the teacher then pointing at Dot, whining, 'It was her, Miss.'

'Billy probably told you that we're married now?' Clarice ran her mittened hand down the front of her tweed coat. 'In fact, we're expecting. We'll be hearing the patter of tiny O'Brien feet around April, May.'

'How lovely for you.' Surprised at how crushed she felt, Dot grabbed Otis's hand. 'This is my fiancé, Captain Otis Oakewood. He's with the US army. A very prestigious division. When we marry and this damned war finally comes to an end, we're moving to America, to live in Hollywood.' She turned to Otis. 'Isn't that right, darling?'

'Anything for you, Skip—'

Dot tugged his hand, and Otis corrected himself.

'Of course, my all-too-precious Dorothy. And in our home, my cherished betrothed will have a washing machine and a fridge, all the nylons she can wear and all the donuts she can eat.'

'Donuts! I hope they don't make her too fat.' Clarice wore a frigid smile. 'I have to say that most of us wouldn't dream of running away, spoiling ourselves, even when the war ends, especially if we have responsibilities to our parents and friends in this devastated country. We wouldn't let them fend for themselves in their old age, just so we could furnish a garish house with the latest gadgets.'

Rather than get dragged any further into the spat, Dot asked: 'How's Billy?'

'You know. The usual. Off at sea on board the *City of somewhere or other*, bound for India or Egypt or some ungodly metropolis crawling with foreigners.' Clarice gently rubbed her tummy. 'Darling Billy. Promised to bring me back some precious silks and exotic spices. So that'll be nice.' She looked at her watch. 'Anyhow, can't stand around all day gobbing. Got to get up to the butchers and queue for the Sunday joint, such as it will be these dreary days. We'll probably have to settle for some nasty inferior American muck, like Spam. See you around, Dorothy.'

As Clarice waddled away, Dot noted that she left in the same direction as she had come. Had she recognised Dot sitting here, then gone out of her way to 'bump' into her?

'If there's one thing I can't abide, it's not having respect,' said Otis, as he walked Dot away up Dale Street. 'It makes my blood boil when I think of your Billy playing around with that awful woman while he was betrothed to you ... playing you along, treating marriage as though he was buying a motorcar on a trial basis – a small down payment to hold onto you while he looked out other cheaper – and, may I say – drastically inferior models.' Otis slipped his arm around Dot's waist. 'If I was engaged to you, dearest Dot, I'd show a lot more appreciation and respect. Oh, by the way,' he added. 'Thanks for the promotion to captain. I don't deserve it.'

*

Next morning Mammy told Dot that she and Pop were out for the day visiting some friends in Talacre, North Wales.

'We'll be late back,' said Pop, putting on his hat.

Dot went through the pantry to brew up some tea. She had lain awake much of the night, stewing over Billy and Clarice. She felt stupid that she still cared. Otis followed her in.

'Hey, Skipper, where's Trixy? I thought we could take her for a walk on the beach.'

Grabbing the empty kettle from the gas ring, Dot moved across to the sink.

'Trixy's dead.' She turned on the cold tap. 'Hit by a car.'

Suppressing a sob, she was glad that the sound was covered by running water.

'Oh, honey, why didn't you tell me?' Otis slipped his arms round her. 'Poor baby. So many things to get upset about. Your fiancé and that awful woman and losing that lovely dog of yours.' He kissed her neck. 'Poor darling.'

Putting down the kettle, Dot turned, clinging to Otis.

'I'll bet you were really looking forward to coming back home too, Skip. But now you're finally here … the weight of the world on your pretty shoulders.'

Dot sobbed into Otis's chest.

He ran his hands up and down her back.

'Don't know about you, gal, but I'm near to freezing my feet off in here.'

They moved back into the kitchen, where the fire, set that morning by her father, was struggling to take.

A thin layer of frost lined the windows.

'It's really chilly in here too.' Otis sat Dot down on the couch. 'I'll try to get that fire going.'

He grabbed the poker and prodded the coal, with no effect.

'Here!' Snatching the *Liverpool Echo* from the table, Dot spread it out and held it up to the fire, covering the whole front of the fireplace.

'Watch out, gal! You'll burn down the house.'

'It works, Otis. Trust me.'

A roaring sound came from the grate. Dot pulled the newspaper away, revealing a cosy perfect glow.

'How does that work?' Otis held up the paper. 'Not even a scorch mark.'

Dot read the back-page headline. US troops make moderate progress – Nazis mass in Saar area.

'Is that your lot?'

Otis flipped the newspaper around and read the small print.

'That's my guys. And next week most likely I'll be back with them.'

'The trouble is that the papers only write about the successes, don't they?' Dot took the paper from him and put it back on the table. Did those words 'moderate progress' cover up human losses? She prayed they were all safe: Tony, Art and Howard. 'They don't dwell on the losses.'

'The truth is,' Otis flopped down on the couch, pulling Dot with him, 'I'm not cut out for soldiering.'

'Nor am I cut out to be a nurse, Otis.' Dot couldn't believe that he had dragged the subject back to himself. 'None of us are cut out for war. I hate the smell of blood, and whenever a patient on the ward dies I get very upset. But when I'm stuck doing minor first aid, like I do at Rainbow Corner, I wish I was doing something more serious. You see, Otis, it's our duty. If we don't do these things, the war will never end. As the papers keep saying, we need "one last push".'

'You're right.' Otis stroked Dot's face with the back of his fingers. 'I love you, Dot. You know that. That's why I'll get the first train tomorrow. I'll pass that physical and I'll be sent straight back to the front line.' Otis pulled her closer and gently kissed her lips. 'When I'm out there, I'll conjure up this moment,' he whispered. 'The feel of you, the scent of you, your warmth, your kindness. It will make me strong. You have inspired me to be a bigger person.' He got down on one knee. 'We've joked about it so many times. But go on, Dot. Marry me, darling. Go on! Before I go. Marry me, marry me, marry me.'

*

Next day, in the bleak early morning, Dot accompanied Otis to Lime Street Station.

People ran back and forth, heading into work, running for other trains, hats pulled down, scarves tight around their necks. Mist hung low over the platforms. The London train was waiting on platform one.

Otis leaned down from the carriage window, cap shoved back on his head, grinning.

'Until next time, Skipper. We're all but man and wife now, eh? When I get back, we'll have a huge wedding, and I'll take you to California, where the oranges come from.'

Dot stood on tiptoes, taking his hands. She felt a mix of elation and concern. Otis wanted to marry her, but yesterday she had certainly let him go too far.

A whistle blew.

Clouds of steam puffed up, hitting the blackened glass roof, and fell, blotting out the light.

Slamming doors. Two short blasts of the guard's whistle and the train pulled out.

'Bye, Skipper! See ya round.'

As the carriage moved, Dot ran along beside it, keeping a grip on Otis's hand. Suddenly the train was going too fast and she let go.

She remained there, watching Otis's grinning face grow smaller and smaller, till the carriage snaked round the bend and out of view.

Alone, she walked slowly back along the platform, moving through the pressing crowds heading out into Lime Street.

It was only after she crossed the road that she noticed how cold it was.

She tugged her cloak tightly around her and joined the queue at the row of bus stops outside Blacklers.

Otis did love her. Didn't he?

She hadn't given her virginity to some passing Lothario?

Cave canem.

But, no. This was Otis – mischievous, ever-smiling Otis. Otis who had told her a hundred times that he loved her.

Cave canem.

A newsboy yelled out the headlines: 'Red Army at the German border. Americans breaking though. Nazi defences cracking. Read all about it!'

Soon the war would be over.

Everything would work out just fine.

Otis would come back and she would become Mrs Dorothy Oakewood of California.

TWENTY-FIVE

SINCE JULY '44, WHEN JACK was hospitalised, Lilly had been paired up with Elan. He was difficult to talk to, his replies monosyllabic. He never uttered a word which wasn't practical, related to the job in hand.

They were sent off to follow the troops pushing east towards Germany, to continue sending coded messages behind the troops as they liberated Paris.

Sitting in a jeep on those late August days, riding along in the wake of good news, while cheering French crowds lined the boulevards and danced in the streets, thrusting tumblers of wine and pastis at them, had felt wonderful.

Lilly had taken Elan up to the little café on the Butte Montmartre. It was a sad sight. Swastikas scratched on the walls, all the paintings gone, the owners and staff cowed and grey. After years of subservience to Gestapo officers, there were no smiles left, and no music.

Lilly had known it would be disappointing. She wondered why she had gone at all. It was Jack she really wanted to take. But those heady summer days with him seemed part of another life, long ago.

Whenever anyone asked after Jean-Claude, Lilly felt like a fraud. She could barely picture his face.

Everyone had imagined the Allies would have taken Berlin by September.

But no. Christmas had been spent in a bombed-out village in the Ardennes. To celebrate, Lilly taped a bough of holly to the dashboard of the jeep. Now, in icy February, entrenched on the French side of the Rhine, they huddled around a stove in a little tavern in Alsace.

Lilly hadn't seen Jack since, unconscious, he was transported from the field hospital to a hospital ship bound for Portsmouth. She had prayed that Dot might be on board to care for him.

Every now and then a terse message arrived, via Elan: Jack had been released from hospital. Jack was convalescing in Wiltshire. Jack was back on duty, working from Grosvenor Square. She yearned for news of him. So happy that he survived. At the same time she feared he might already have trained up a new driver-secretary to replace her. Then she felt angry with herself for being jealous.

Finally, towards the end of August, she heard that Jack was back behind the lines in the South of France, part of Operation Dragoon.

Although she had sent many letters via the London office of the Free French, she had heard nothing from Jean-Claude. Not even a postcard to ask *'Ça va?'*

'Any takers for donuts?' A tall girl with crimson-painted lips entered the tavern. Wearing a neat bolero jacket, baggy trousers and heavy boots, she carried a tray, like a cinema usherette. 'Come on, boys, the Donut Dollies have arrived. Now you can make-believe you're home.'

'We won't feel at home till we *are* at home,' quipped a young GI near the door. 'Got a one-way ticket to New Jersey?'

Ignoring him, the Dolly continued her well-practised proclamation. 'In our Clubmobile we serve hot coffee, books, candy, gum, Camels, Lucky Strikes and good cheer. We play all the latest hit records – the Andrews Sisters, Harry James, Louis Jordan, Bing Crosby, the Mills Brothers, we got 'em all. So, boys … if any of you want to leave the wonderful heat of that stove to join us out in the miserable, cold bus, I would seriously imagine that you'd lost your senses.'

Lilly had to laugh.

A couple of men slouched towards the Donut Dolly.

'Some cigarettes would be great,' said one.

'I'd like a hot coffee.'

'Damn,' muttered the girl, immediately replacing her frown with a sparkling grin. 'Follow me, boys.'

As she opened the tavern door, a gust of wind swept in a flurry of sleet followed by a small gang of US soldiers. Wrapped up in mufflers and greatcoats, they pushed forward to the bar.

'The tank units are going in,' said one.

'Again!' came the cry from the room.

It was Elan who noticed. 'Your friend?' he said, pointing.

Lilly immediately recognised Earl. She called his name and indicated he should join her.

A cloud fell over his face.

'Lilly. How are you?'

The only reason for his sudden change of demeanour had to be that he was holding back bad news.

'Fine, thanks, Earl.' Lilly had trouble preventing her voice from betraying her fear. 'What are you up to?'

'Came up from the South of France.'

Please God, not Jack. Please, not Jack.

'Been back to London at all?' It was all she could think of to say.

'I was offered a furlough but stayed in the rear lines. It's too much of a thing. My time would have been taken up travelling.'

'How's Pearl?'

'Great. The girls' band came out and did some concerts for the troops. And she met Bette Davis.'

'Wow! I bet that was scary!'

'Yeah.' Earl took a sip of his beer.

A silence. Lilly had had enough small talk, but at the same time dreaded hearing what Earl was holding back.

'Look, Lilly, I do have something which I should share with you. Can we find a quieter place?'

Lilly's mouth went dry.

'If we want heat or light there's only this bar.' Her legs were shaking. It was difficult to walk. 'We could go to that corner.'

She followed Earl to a small empty table.

'I can see why no one wanted to sit here.' Lilly shivered. 'It's glacial.'

Earl put his hand up to the wall. 'The frame's been knocked off-kilter.'

Lilly saw the gaping hole between the masonry and the window frame.

Earl placed his beer down with precision, as though it was a chess piece.

Lilly gripped her knees with both hands.

'Well...' Earl stared into his glass, as though he might be able to read the future in it. 'It's about your dear friend...'

Lilly took a deep breath, then a slug of schnapps.

'Our little group bore east from St-Raphaël,' said Earl, 'fighting our way along the coast, heading for the Italian border, liberating town after town. The rest of the company moved northwards.'

A sudden cheer from a table of men in the centre of the room. Lilly glanced up. A group of GIs, playing cards, slamming their hands down.

Earl paused to let the frisson fade.

'There was a deal of fighting around the outskirts of Nice. But we learned, before crossing the Var River, that the folk of that city had put up an enormous fight. The bridges were blown, so we took a long time crossing in small boats, throwing down temporary bridges.'

He hung his head and took a deep breath.

Lilly was shaking so much she had to put her glass down.

'By the time we rolled in, the people of Nice cheered us, all right. The Nazis had already fled. But before they went, they'd gathered as many street fighters and soldiers as they could find and shot them in cold blood. As though that wasn't enough, they'd left their bodies strung up from lampposts, a warning to others. We cut them down.' Earl lay his hands flat on the table and inhaled.

'I'm sorry to be the one to tell you … one of those bodies was…'

Lilly's throat constricted.

'I'm so sorry, Lilly … It was Jean-Claude.'

Lilly breathed again, but she felt ashamed, appalled, because when Earl had said Jean-Claude, she had felt a rush of relief.

He hadn't said Jack.

*

Lilly lay in her hammock, strung up in an upstairs room of the tavern, surrounded by bunk and camp beds, each containing a sleeping woman – English ATS girls, Red Cross nurses and American Red Cross girls.

Dawn was a pink strip on the horizon.

It was difficult climbing out of a hammock without making any noise, but Lilly managed to slip out with barely a thud. Gathering her things, she tiptoed out to the wash-house – a stable with a cold tap.

By the washroom door, shivering, she pulled on her uniform, greatcoat and hat. She came back inside to dump her nightdress and washbag, passing the makeshift front desk, where a fresh-faced army boy, feet on a table, opened one eye.

'ATS Deane?'

Lilly nodded.

'Note for you.'

With thudding heart, Lilly tore open the envelope.

The front door opened behind her.

A wall of cold air hit her, setting her teeth chattering.

The letter was from HQ. As of this morning her assignment was changed. Details to follow.

She hoped she wouldn't be sent on some secretarial job, far behind the lines.

She ran upstairs and gathered her things. Glancing out of the window, she was glad to see that the American Red Cross food wagon was open.

She went there.

'Can I tempt you with a Spam roll?' The woman she had seen last night, already fully made-up as though for a dance, leaned out of the serving hatch.

The very thought of Spam made Lilly want to throw up.

'Oh, deary! You look all in.' The woman grimaced. 'How about you hop inside, sweety. I'll make you a pot of tea. That's what you limeys like, isn't it? I even have one of those teapot things in here … somewhere.'

Lilly went to the back door of the bus and climbed the metal steps.

The girl was working alone. The clock showed 5 a.m.

A bench lined one side, with a thin table and a few chairs. Lilly sat at the stove end, near the donut machine, where it was slightly warmer, while the girl busily worked at the counter.

'Have you been up all night?'

'Most of it. We're here to comfort.' The girl poured hot water into the pot. 'If one of our boys wants someone to talk to, well, here we are. Poor things. So young and so very far from home.' She brought the tea to Lilly. 'Would you like a donut with that?'

'Why not?'

The girl placed donuts on tin plates and flopped down opposite Lilly.

'They all say we're nearly there. I don't feel it. Do you?' The girl took a huge bite of donut, then lightly dabbed her mouth with her handkerchief, miraculously leaving her lipstick intact. 'I notice you were working with one of our guys. Where do you hail from, deary?'

'Just outside London.' Lilly knew that there was no point being specific with English geography. To most Yanks, Liverpool, Land's End and Edinburgh were only a few miles apart, and London was a country. 'They call it the "Home Counties", south of London.' She sipped her tea, grateful to wrap her fingers around the cup. 'I suppose you're looking forward to going home … to the States, I mean.'

'No siree bob. You ain't shunting me back to Des Moines in a hurry.' The girl raised her well-groomed eyebrows. 'It may surprise you to hear that I'll be making my home in good oldie England.' Although they were alone, she leaned forward confidentially. 'In fact, a few days ago I got myself hitched, wedding performed in a tent by the travelling pastor.' She held up a ringed finger. 'And I am now officially … a lady.' She threw her head back and laughed. 'Heaven knows what I was before. You know, sweety, since I was sixteen years old I always thought I was already a lady. But there you have it. I'm now Lady Dolores, if you please.' Looking over her shoulder as though for spies, she lowered her voice. 'Don't tell anyone but, listen to this: I'm really supposed to be Lady George. Look at me!' She threw open her arms, emphasising her ample bosom. 'Do I look to you like someone called George? I mean! And anyhoo, who's to know if I tell people I'm Lady Dolores?'

Dolores flashed her ring finger. 'George tells me it's actually a hair loom.'

'A what?' asked Lilly.

'Don't ask me. Hair loom? Air loom? Been in the family for years, he kept saying. But what's a loom got to do with it? To me it's just a plain ol' ring.'

Lilly bit her lip. She knew that her George had been dating an American girl, but … She took a closer look at the ring. Yes. *The* engagement ring. 'Your husband is Colonel Widmer? George Widmer?'

'How d'you know that, sweety? Controller SIR George Widmer, Bart, if you please,' said Dolores. 'He's pretty snippy about me using the correct etiquette. To be honest, it gets me in a bit of a tizz.' Dolores took another bite of donut. 'George tells me that after the war is over I'll get to open fates. Whatever that means. Sounds pretty doomy to me, like Pandora's box and all that old Greek mythology stuff from back in high school.'

Lilly polished off her donut and washed it down with the tea, weak but comforting. She was glad she'd met Dolores. George would never have let it happen without being around to supervise.

'When you next see George, please give him my regards. My parents live very near him and are quite friendly with his family. Sergeant Lilly Deane.'

'Well, darlin', I sure will.' Dolores gave a wide smile. 'You know, sweety, you don't seem nearly as snooty as he warned me the locals would be.'

*

'Sergeant Deane?'

While awaiting further orders Lilly had been hunched up in the mess room trying to read a book. It was hard to concentrate, her thoughts bouncing between poor Jean-Claude swinging dead from a lamppost, and newly promoted and titled George and his not-so-blushing bride, Lady Dolores.

'Report to Major Lockwood's aide-de-camp. You're being moved further back.'

Lilly's heart sank.

'Back?'

'Further behind the lines. To assist some disabled old general. They'll give you the exact details when you get there.'

Just what Lilly dreaded. Secretarial, perhaps, with a little driving thrown in, tucking a blanket round some old boy's knees.

She prayed it wouldn't be General Smith. She didn't fancy having her bottom fondled again by his gnarled, furry hands, even if it was in the line of duty.

'There's a van leaving with several wounded men. You'll be on that.' The sergeant indicated the vehicle beside the tavern.

Lilly grabbed her cap.

The journey was arduous. Mile after mile of towns reduced to rubble. The sides of the roads lined with crocodiles of German prisoners of war, being frogmarched away from the front line.

Dark and bitterly cold, the sight of a village of tents and buses was welcome. The Union Jack and the Stars and Stripes flew above. In the centre a bonfire glowed. Men stood around it, gazing into the flames.

Lilly jumped out first, getting out of the way so that the Red Cross workers could bring out the wounded.

'Sergeant Deane?'

'Present and correct.'

'Tent F.' The ATS girl pointed her pen towards a row of tents under the American flag. She leaned in and whispered: 'To be honest, I don't know why they let the old boy out here.'

Lilly's heart sank.

'Half blind. Walks with a stick.'

Lilly marched along the alley between tents. The flaps were all firmly closed against the cold.

She came to F and wasn't sure whether to bang the canvas, call out her name or just barge in.

She decided to call.

'Come!' A woman's voice.

Lilly entered the tent. At a desk, lit by the glow of a solitary lamp, sat Gloria Fergusson.

'Wonderful! Lilly! I got you.'

Lilly turned to fasten the tent flap behind her, hoping to cover the look of horror she couldn't hide. The old boy *had* to be General Smith.

'Get it tight, would you? It's brass monkeys in here.'

'I was told I was to be an aide.' Lilly let her kitbag flop to the ground.

'That's right.' Fergusson gave a wry smile. 'In you go.' She pointed to a further flap leading to an inner compartment. 'He's been way too demanding for me.'

Fergusson inclined her head towards the second chamber.

Lilly pulled open the curtain.

The inner room was dark, lit only by an oil lamp swinging from the ceiling. The general stood with his back to her, inspecting a map on the far wall. He leaned on a walking stick, his other hand drawing an imaginary line between two points on the map.

'Sergeant Deane, sir. Reporting for duty.'

The man turned.

For a few moments he stood utterly still, his silhouette haloed by the orange glow of the oil lamp.

'How many times, English Lilly, must I remind you I don't like being called sir? It's Jack, or, if you must be formal, Chief.'

Lilly could barely breathe. She wanted to run across and hug him.

'Sorry, sir. I mean Jack.'

'Forgive me for not welcoming you here sooner, Lilly. But, as you see, I lost an eye. We don't talk about that. Don't want to be repatriated quite yet. There's too much for me to do.'

Jack stepped into the light. A black patch covered one eye, rendering his hawkish face more handsome.

'Although I lost an eye and a great working companion, I gather you lost a few pints of blood, and gave them to some big idiot stupid enough to walk on a mine. I hope that in the coming weeks, I can make it up to you.'

'Anything you like, sir ... Jack.' Lilly wanted to punch the air.

Jack stepped forward to accompany her back to the other part of the tent.

'And when I say I'll make it up to you, I'm not offering to return the blood. Unless in these few months you've become a vampire.'

PART FOUR

GI Brides

TWENTY-SIX

MAY 1945

'"Hitler Dead!" Well, there's a headline we can all cheer.'

Dot sat alone at a table in the corner of the cafeteria, listening to the other girls reading out the good news. She wished she could feel as celebratory as they did, but she had missed three periods and her nightly prayer included 'please don't let there be a baby on the way'. Many women had similar symptoms brought on by stress and ration-book eating. Dot hoped it was simply that.

To allay her fears, two days ago, Dot had gone to St Thomas' hospital, where she knew no one, and taken a pregnancy test. The result would be ready later today.

'Not only Hitler dead, but can I say how lovely it is being back in Blighty, with china plates instead of tin trays.' Nancy took a long drag on her cigarette before stubbing it out in the gravy on her plate. 'Life behind the lines always made me feel as if I was in some awful play set in the fourteenth century. I only needed to black out my teeth and put on a dress sewn from a coal sack to complete the scene.'

'They'll be coming home now, won't they, our boys?' asked Thelma, cleaning down the counter.

'Depends who you mean by "our".' Nancy yawned and stretched. 'I guess the Brits will be back, but the Yanks will probably be sent straight home. Therefore, unless, like me, you have a ring on your finger, that'll be the last you see of them. And in the unlikely event you're engaged to a Kraut, he'll be banged up in a POW camp.'

Peggy let out a loud sob.

'Bloody hell,' muttered Nancy under her breath. 'I didn't realise we'd be getting amateur theatrics from the serving staff. What's she blubbing about now?'

'It's all right, love.' Thelma stretched out an arm to comfort Peggy. 'She got very close to those boys. She was like a second mother to many of them.'

'Course she was.' Nancy flicked her newspaper upright and mumbled into it, 'God spare us from the worthy!'

June piped up: 'I'd imagine the ships aren't going to sail directly to the USA from Germany, Nancy. Surely, they'd come back then sail from Southampton, Liverpool or Glasgow. That's where the Yanks all came in, isn't it?'

'I bet we won't be allowed to travel to the States on the same ships as our husbands.' Nancy folded the paper and laid it on the table. 'We'll be left behind, herded together, like milk cows.'

The canteen swing doors opened and a pram, pushed by Barbara, held them open.

'Talking of which…' Nancy sat back in her seat. 'Moooo!'

'Has anyone heard whether Tony is back?' Barbara was pregnant again. Ready to drop. Two babies, one sitting up sucking his thumb, the other lying asleep, were in the pram. A third infant staggered forward, tied to Barbara's waist by powder-blue reins. 'I heard a rumour that hundreds of GIs were seen streaming off trains at Waterloo.'

'I'd imagine Tony'd go straight home to you, Barbara,' said Peggy, wiping her eyes and glancing once more at the headlines.

'I'd imagine he'd go *anywhere else* first and get tanked up with booze,' muttered Nancy.

Barbara pulled the pram out of the room and left, letting the doors flap back and forth.

Dot stood. The sight of the babies had terrified her. And now news that troops were arriving at Waterloo. Should she go there and look for Otis?

'Churchill is about to announce plans for VE Day,' read June.

'Open bottle, pour alcohol into glass, apply glass to lips. Who needs a better plan than that?'

Dot sank down again on her chair and gazed into her cup of cold tea. She wished Lilly was here to talk to. But who knew where she might be now?

'It also says that Hitler, Mussolini and Goebbels are dead,' added June. 'And that Goering has gone mad and is roaming around Berlin dressed as a Roman emperor!'

'They should send him over here. We could do a re-enactment of *Julius Caesar* for the VE Day party. Et tu, Hermann.' Nancy slashed her knife in the air.

Peggy wailed.

'Dot?' June looked around. Dot saw how much prettier she looked without the thick coat of pancake and powder. 'We're all bona fide, but did you ever get engaged to that GI of yours?'

'When he gets back.' Dot hoped that once Otis heard, he would do the right thing. She crossed her fingers. A better solution was that the test would be negative.

'Art and I are engaged, but we're going to marry over there,' said June brightly. 'He sent me snaps of his house, soon to be ours! It even has a white fence, just like in the movies. You have a GI beau too, don't you, Thelma?'

'Oh yes,' Thelma replied. 'He doesn't come in here much, but he's very nice.'

'Got something to hide, darling?' Nancy peered over the top of the paper and looked at Thelma. 'Most of us parade our men about like horses in the ring at Ascot. How come you're hiding yours? Has he got jug ears or something?'

Dot watched a deep red spread from Thelma's non-existent bust, up her neck and across her cheeks.

'Personal reasons, he says. And who am I to question my fiancé?'

'Question him to hell and back, I say.'

The swing doors burst open again, and Paul appeared.

'Hold on to your ha'pennies, girls. General Gropius Smith is in the building.'

Peggy moved along the counter, taking off her apron, smoothing back her hair.

'Oh, Christ.' Nancy leapt to her feet. 'I thought we'd seen the last of Fingers McFiddler, the Werewolf of Westminster. What's he want?'

'God knows. Just thought I'd give you the heads up.'

Paul vanished in a flap of swing doors.

Dot noticed Thelma watching Peggy leaving the cafeteria, still crying.

'You know, Nancy,' Thelma stepped forward, 'you don't always have to be so rude about everyone.'

'In your humble opinion…'

'Some people might like General Smith.'

'If you have a penchant for fur-lined hands, you're welcome.' Nancy flopped back in her chair and sighed. 'Look at us all: the GI brides.' She pulled out another cigarette, lit it, breathed in and blew out a ribbon of smoke. 'What a motley crew we'll make, sailing across the ocean blue. Thank God America is big enough to keep us miles apart: me, Thelma, June, Vi, Barbara, Pearl, Liz, Peggy and Dot.'

'Didn't you hear, Nancy?' June said quietly. 'Liz was killed. About a month ago, in that huge V-2 explosion in Whitechapel.'

'Really?' said Nancy with a shrug. 'Doesn't change much, simply removes one of the saner names from the list.'

Dot was still watching Thelma. Pale, short, blonde, birdlike and gamine. The opposite of her. Otis had said he'd gone to Brighton on Thelma's behalf. Now she was talking about a mysterious fiancé.

'Thelma?' Dot asked. 'How's your sister?'

'What do you mean?' Thelma looked at her blankly.

'The one in Brighton?'

'What are you talking about?'

'Brunswick Terrace? Your sister? Emily? Emily Bowe?'

'I'm an only child.'

Dot felt her mouth go dry.

'One of the GIs told me he'd taken a packet to Brighton for your sister, Emily Bowe.'

'Which GI?'

'Otis Oake—'

'Oh, him?' Thelma wrung out the cloth and tossed it into the sink. 'Absolutely not. No thank you, ma'am. Wouldn't touch him with a ten-foot pole.'

This extreme reaction scared Dot even more. What was Otis to Thelma, or she to Otis? Why had Otis lied to Dot about Thelma? And what had he done to upset her? Dot realised that she knew nothing about him. Though she had written him many letters since their parting in Liverpool, he had not written one back.

Had he just used her? Now that he had had his way with her, was she nothing to him? She ran her hand over her belly and felt slightly faint at the thought of what might be inside. A wave of panic ran through her like a shock.

She had to get out of here.

Hastily she got up and slipped out through the swing doors. But she didn't miss the eruption of laughter which followed.

No doubt Nancy had made a hilarious quip.

*

By the time Lilly climbed up the gangplank onto the ferry at Calais, it was late evening. The steep wooden ramp was slippery from the tread of thousands of muddy boots.

She took a seat with Jack on the open deck and watched the dockers untying ropes, casting the ferry free.

She turned to look at Jack. His face was set.

'Will you be going straight to the USA?'

As she asked, Lilly fully realised the implication of his answer.

'I can't see why not.' Jack looked up, watching a seagull screech into the grey sky.

Lilly had longed for the war to end, but realised it wasn't going to be unmitigated joy. The Allies might have won, but she would lose.

'The US is still at war with Japan,' he said. 'They'll probably need my services in the Pacific.'

The words fell like lead into Lilly's soul. He would still be at risk.

'I suppose you wouldn't like my help?'

'Why would they take anyone British? There are so many American women available over there, I'd most likely be assigned one of them. Or one of my own men, like Elan.'

Lilly wanted to yell out: 'But I *need* to come with you.'

The day was clear. It wasn't long before Dover was visible. Despite the song's promise, there were no bluebirds. The dirty grey cliffs offered only dread.

'You'll be happy to be rid of me bossing you about,' Jack said.

Lilly wanted to reply, 'No, no, no. I want to stay with you forever.'

All that came out was, 'Certainly not, Chief.'

'I've been thinking of asking you ... Well, I did wonder whether you might like to come with me when this is all over ... But it could never work. You wouldn't care for my life.' Jack put his finger up to his eyepatch, adjusted it a little, then did the familiar double pat of his chest.

'I want to understand your life ... Tell me, Jack.'

'Hey, you folks!' Art Pemberton loomed over them. 'Great to bump into you. Me and the other guys, we're all London bound. Seems like you are too. Tony and Marty are looking to get us a crate of beer for the journey. Come and join us on the train.'

'Sounds lovely,' Lilly said. She didn't mean it.

'We're going to party till we drop. You?'

Lilly looked to Jack. Still wearing his inscrutable expression, he nodded. 'Sure am. I'm lucky that Lilly isn't so hot at the jitterbug cos I won't be much use: one eye, a stick and all.'

'What do you mean, Jack? I'm great at the jitterbug.'

'In my opinion,' Jack wavered his hand, 'only so-so!'

'I hate you, Jack Kirk.'

'Oh, Lilly!' Jack slipped his arm around Lilly's waist and pulled her close. 'You don't really mean that. I'll have lost the stick by autumn. Then if I'm around we'll dance.'

Military police started blowing whistles, forming the men into lines. Soldiers picked up their kitbags and shoved towards the gangways.

'Looks like we've arrived!' said Art, turning to join the others.

'Looks like we have!' Jack turned to face Lilly. 'I know you're going home now, and for you it's all over. But please … as long as you can bear to … stay with me.'

'I thought you'd never ask.' Lilly helped Jack to his feet. 'Come on, Chief. Let's go join the party.'

*

Dot had had to push her way through throngs of jubilant people in Piccadilly Circus. She came into work first thing, knowing that Rainbow Corner would be the obvious place for Otis to come looking for her. She had her results. She was carrying Otis's baby. Now they had to marry quickly, so that in four months' time when it became impossible to hide, only those with a calculator would figure out the truth.

Due to the wild party which had been going on all night in Dunker's Den, the nursing post had been moved up to the quiet of Dabbler's Den.

Dot sat on the windowsill looking out, hoping to catch sight of Otis before he came into the building. A conga line snaked up Shaftesbury Avenue. She could hear raucous singing. 'Roll Out the Barrel'.

During the afternoon a marine came in. He'd cut himself on a broken bottle in the street. When she told him she'd been up there all day, he brought her a sandwich.

It was like eating sand.

She left most of it.

'Hey, nursey!'

In hope, Dot swung round.

In the doorway stood Virgil.

'We can't leave you all on your own, babes. Not today.' He turned and yelled up the stairs. 'Come on down right now!'

Dot's heart leapt. She jumped to her feet.

A clatter of shoes on the steps.

She took a few nervous steps towards the door.

'Hi, darling! Long time, no see.' It was Violet, dressed top to toe in red, white and blue. 'I ran it up yesterday out of some old bunting, a sheet and the remains of a Nazi flag which his lordship brought back from his travels.'

Devastated with disappointment, Dot stood frozen to the spot.

Violet turned to Virgil. ''Ere, Virge, pop down to the canteen, would you, dear, and see if that grumpy madam behind the counter's got any donuts left.'

'I'm not hungry,' said Dot. 'Really I'm not.'

'Don't get ahead of yourself, dear, it's me what wants one.' She turned to Virgil and flicked him away. 'Go on, Virge. Don't hurry back.'

When he was gone, Violet pointed down to the sandwich missing only one bite.

'Trouble with days like these, love,' Violet put her arms around Dot and held her tight, 'they bring everything to the surface, don't they?'

Dot wept into Violet's chest.

'There now, dear. Let it all out.'

Between sobs, Dot said: 'It's not what you think, Vi.'

'I don't think anything, love. Not after what I gone through. Banged up for something I never did. Finger-pointing. Whispers. And you know what? Ruddy cow who really leaked all that stuff is still on the loose. Now the war's over they'll probably drop charges, won't they? How unfair is that?' Violet patted Dot's back. 'There, there, love. Things will get better. Really they will.'

'I don't think so.' Dot pulled away. 'You see, I'm going to have a baby.'

Violet took a deep breath. 'Some GI?'

Dot nodded.

'And you're waiting for him to come back?'

'Yes.'

'Now listen to me…' Violet held Dot by the shoulders and spoke to her as though addressing a child. 'There's no point piling misery on misery. If he cares for you, he'll find you. If he doesn't, he's not worth having.' She stroked Dot's cheek. 'You're a pretty little thing, Dot. Film-star looks, some would say. As the proverb has it and it's not wrong: "there are other fish in the sea".'

Dot felt as though the whole of her soul had drained from her body. 'I don't want "other fish". I want Otis.'

Violet stiffened. 'Otis Oakewood?'

'Don't you like him?'

'Don't know him, love. Only seen him around the place.' Violet led Dot to a chair. 'Listen to me. War blinds us to the truth. I thought Sydney was the man for me. Turns out I was wrong. He gave up on me. He believed I was the spy! Virgil, on the other hand … He fought my corner, right from the moment he was sent to arrest me. I wouldn't have lasted ten minutes on Sydney's ruddy "as far as the eye can see" farm. I know that now. But when you're up too close to things, you can't see the real picture.'

Dot noticed a shadow lurking near the door. Once more her heart thudded with hope.

'You can come in now, you big lug,' Violet shouted to Virgil, and he stepped forward, bearing a tray with coffee and donuts. 'And turn on the light. It's getting dark.'

'Blackout,' said Virgil.

'Keep up. Blackout's finished now, Virge, like the war. Now, Dot dear, you're going to wipe those tears off that lovely face, take one bite of a donut, then you're coming out on the town with us. This is a really important day in all our lives. You can't miss out because of silly Otis. You'll regret it forever if you're not part of it.'

'But I…'

'It'll be all right, Dot. You'll see. After all, as the song goes: "it's a lovely day tomorrow"…'

*

Instead of raking the dark skies for enemy aircraft, searchlights zigzagged beams over the crowds celebrating VE night.

Dot took a swig from Violet's whisky flask. The booze made her feel far less tense. She was glad too that she had come out to join the fun. Seeing unadulterated joy on everyone's faces filled her with happiness.

Pointing back towards the London Pavilion, Violet shouted out, 'Look at that, Virgil, I thought they'd put our names up.'

'"Wrigley's for Vim and Vigour,"' read Virgil. 'We could become Vim and Vigour.'

They both creased up with laughter.

A young marine grabbed Dot by the hand, pulling her out to dance a lively jive. Arms around each other, Violet and Virgil smooched. The marine kissed Dot on the cheek and disappeared back into the throng. A string of British sailors, a girl on each arm, surrounded them, singing 'Knees Up Mother Brown'. Violet broke away from Virgil to join in.

'Come on, Virgil. If you don't know the words, just make 'em up. No one'll mind.'

Someone was shouting Dot's name. She stood on tiptoes but couldn't see. Might it be…

Violet waved. 'Get over here, you pair of renegades.'

'"Knees up, knees up, don't get the breeze up…"'

Paul pushed through, Marty in tow. Right behind them came June, dragging Art by the hand.

'"Knees up, knees up, knees up, Mother Brown…"'

The line of sailors and their girlfriends snaked away.

Marty banged fists with Virgil. 'Evening, bro!'

'What a night!' shouted Paul. 'It's like an Everton/Liverpool derby coinciding with the Grand National and the Grand Prix, all set in a lunatic asylum. Hiya, Dot!'

'Hiya, Paul!'

'No Otis on your arm tonight…?'

Marty swung round to Paul and yelled: 'Roll up your flaps.'

When Paul shrugged a reply, and opened his mouth again, Marty bellowed: 'Shut up. SHUT UP!'

What was going on? Something concerning Otis. Dot fell back against Violet.

Art stepped forward, wearing his pious face.

Violet's arm tightened around Dot's waist.
The moment felt like eternity.
Nearby a woman screeched with high-pitched laughter.
The crowd roared.
'I'm so sorry, Dot,' Art shouted into her ear. 'Otis didn't make it.'

TWENTY-SEVEN

LILLY WOKE WITH A start. She was lying fully dressed on a bed in a hotel room, her head thumping.

Her memories of the night before were like a series of snapshots: coming straight from Charing Cross Hotel into drunken, celebratory crowds, walking through the dark London streets lit by streetlamps for the first time in years, standing with Jack outside the Athenaeum Club (surrounded brightly by a flickering, yellow glow of torches), pushing through crowds gathered round roaring bonfires of pallets and crates in the Haymarket, unable to penetrate the mob in Piccadilly, so squeezing through the heaving throng in Mayfair.

And … could it be? Standing in Berkeley Square, talking of nightingales, she had proposed to Jack.

When he had suggested taking her for a drink in a posh hotel in Park Lane, bold as brass, she had replied: 'Only if you marry me.'

She groaned. Had they gone for that drink? Had he stormed off and left her? How had she got to this room?

She had no idea where she was.

She hauled herself off the bed and looked around. Headed notepaper on the desk – Grosvenor House Hotel, Mayfair.

Grosvenor House Hotel!

She racked her brains. Crowds, lights, bonfires, bottles clinking in gutters, streamers in people's hair. Soldiers, sailors, pilots, ATS girls, ARP wardens, military police, bobbies, bonfires. Flags. Union Jacks, Stars and Stripes, Russian, Scottish, Belgian, Canadian, Australian, French, Polish, Czech, South African. Flags, flags, flags. Singing. So many songs. So many people.

But stepping inside this hotel? Not a clue.

From the corridor outside she could hear singing. The milky sunlight outside the window indicated it was around 6 a.m.

Lilly flopped back on the bed.

She had proposed to Jack.

Oh God!

What must he have made of that?

She dimly recalled the words of his response: 'Only if I can give you a "get-out".'

She staggered out of bed and opened her bedroom door. She popped her head out. The carpeted corridor was littered with bottles, streamers, bunting.

All she wanted was a cup of tea and an Alka-Seltzer.

Then she would find Jack. And apologise.

The grand staircase was difficult to navigate. American servicemen sprawled out, crooning sentimental ballads. Not all of them singing the same song.

Lilly threaded her way down the stairs.

It simply wasn't done, not in English society, anyway, for a woman to propose to a man. Had her proposal scared Jack away? Had she come here alone, to escape the fallout?

She found a waiter and asked him to please bring up a pot of tea and something for her head.

'Room number?'

She had no idea, so traipsed back up to the door with him on her tail.

'Ah! You're in 187,' said the waiter knowingly. 'Chief Kirk's room.'

'Chief Jack Kirk?'

'This has been his base for around two years.'

Lilly thanked him and went back inside.

Chief Kirk's room!

What had happened in here? The bed was made. She was fully clothed.

She looked out of the window. Revellers were still at it in Park Lane, staggering along in the cold light of dawn.

Lilly went to the bathroom, washed her face and looked at herself in the mirror. She was pale as a ghost. Using a hotel towel, she gave her cheeks a good rub till her cheeks had a slight blush of normality.

When she came back into the room, the tea was waiting.

So was Jack.

'Good morning, Sergeant.'

'Morning, Chief.'

'Shall I pour?'

'Please.'

'I'm not sure how much you remember of last night, Lilly. You may have said a few things, while inebriated, that you might not…'

'You mean proposing.' Lilly sat and cradled a cup between her hands. 'I remember it well. I'm just a little puzzled by your response. Was that a yes or a no?'

'It was a yes,' said Jack. 'A qualified one.'

'Qualified?'

'I need to explain a few things.'

'Don't tell me you're married and you have to get a divorce first, cos then the proposal is off.'

'No.'

'You're a Mormon. Can I put up with your thirty-nine other wives?'

'Absolutely not.' Jack laughed. 'It's just that … you need to see how I live and have the opportunity to change your mind. The GI in London is not the same as an ex-GI at home. So, I propose this – before I leave, we get engaged. A formal affair, with a contract, so that they'll let you cross the ocean to join me. Then, when you arrive at my home, have a look around. If you like it, stay and marry me. If you don't, we burn the contract and you're free to walk away.'

'Can't we just marry and be done with it?'

'No.'

'You're trying to wriggle out of committing?'

'I am not. I am allowing you an informed choice.'

'So "inform" me … Your life can't be that different.'

'America is not a huge version of Britain. Many have been spinning some fantastical tales. Take Tony Caruso…'

'"Caruso, like the singer"?'

'Tony boasts of owning a plush Italian restaurant in the heart of Manhattan. It's kinda true. His establishment is on the Great White Way…'

'Broadway? What could be plusher?'

'It's a hot dog stand.'

'Oh, poor Barbara!' Lilly couldn't help laughing. 'With all those kids to feed.'

'They'll be fine for bagels and knishes! I have no doubt that with Tony's stamina, his hot dog stalls will multiply the same way as his kids.'

'So, Chief, what's your big lie?'

'There is no lie. I'm proud of my home. I'm just not certain you will be. Though loving horses will be a bonus.'

'You run a ranch?'

'Let's leave it there. All I can tell you, Lilly, is that I love you, and I don't want to live without you. After all, I'm carrying around a pint or two of your blood.'

'Stop, thief!' Lilly grabbed and hugged him. 'I want my blood back!'

'Want to come over to the States and have a look?'

'I'm all yours, Chief. Let's do it!'

Lilly and Jack spent the morning in a solicitor's office and the afternoon at a jeweller's buying silver engagement rings. Jack insisted on wearing one too.

In the evening they went to the Foyer Bar at Claridge's and ordered a bottle of champagne.

'Still not opening up about your home life?' she asked. 'I tell you, I'm as good a rustler as your next cowboy.'

Jack rolled his eyes. 'You won't get it out of me, so stop trying. Just believe.'

*

Despite the unfamiliar glow of streetlights and sounds of joyful carousing coming through the window, Dot found the night too bleak and dreadful to escape into a world of dreams.

What would become of her?

She was carrying Otis's baby. But Otis was dead.

Violet wouldn't let Dot go to her hotel room – instead she and Virgil brought her back to her rooms in the Aldwych.

In the early hours Dot heard Violet talking on the hall phone.

'Whenever you can … I know you get things done … No, no … Water under the bridge … Thank you … Bye.'

The flat door clicked shut then Violet came in and sat on the edge of the bed.

'Pardon my humble abode.'

She took Dot's hand and patted it.

'I'll go now, Vi.' Dot struggled to get out of bed. 'Really. I should go back to my room.'

'Over my dead body.' Violet went silent. The words 'dead body' hung in the air. 'We're staying together. That's agreed. June and Art just arrived. Thanks to Art, we're drinking coffee.' Violet squeezed Dot's hand. 'Come on, love. We understand. Really, we do.' She whispered: 'And don't worry, I haven't told anyone about your ... condition.'

As Dot walked into the living room, conversation stopped.

June jumped up, opened a thermos flask and poured Dot a coffee.

'I put a lot of sugar in it. You'll need it, for the shock.'

Dot accepted the cup and cradled it between her hands. 'You're all being so kind.'

'No, we're not,' said Violet, matter-of-fact. 'We've all suffered loss during this war, but we have to move on.'

'It's so unfair.' Dot watched a tear drop into her coffee. 'He survived the whole war, then got killed in action hours before peace was declared.'

'He wasn't—'

Dot noticed Violet kick Virgil's foot, preventing him from finishing the sentence.

'He wasn't what, Virgil?'

Virgil licked his lips, then said very slowly, 'It wasn't hours before the end of the war. It was a couple of weeks.'

She saw Virgil's eyes dart to Art for approval.

'That's not the truth, is it?'

'It is the truth.' Art stood up, making the familiar gesture of pushing his spectacles up the bridge of his nose. 'Otis died before we took Leipzig, which was some weeks...'

Violet cut him off. 'The fact is, Dot, Otis died a hero's death. That's all you need to know.'

Art raised his eyebrows, but before he could speak, the doorbell rang with a loud, persistent clatter.

Virgil jumped up and loped down the stairs to open the front door. After a minute he led Nancy in.

'I'm so sorry, Dot.'

Dot felt tears coming again. Violet passed her a handkerchief.

'I've got you a travel warrant to Liverpool and a week's compassionate leave.' Nancy hastily unclicked her briefcase. 'The bastards were reluctant at first, telling me it wasn't priority because you weren't married or even engaged, but I put my foot down. How the hell did you manage working under those hospital harridans? They make Gloria Fergusson look like the fairy godmother.'

Nancy handed Dot the papers.

'Do you have any kitbag or things you'll want to be taken in to await your return?'

'Everything's in my room at the Regent Palace. I won't need it till I'm back.'

'The girl in the office has phoned Liverpool police and got a message to your parents letting them know you're on your way.'

Dot watched Nancy's lips moving. The words sounded like bubbles rising up through water.

'I have a jeep outside waiting to run you up to Euston.'

When the train arrived at Lime Street, Pop was waiting at the top of the platform. 'Come on then, kid. Let's get you home.'

'My life is over, Pop,' sobbed Dot. 'It's all fallen away.'

'It feels like that now.' His arm around her shoulder, he steered her out into the street. 'Time is a great healer. Time and love. And your mammy and I love the hide of you. We'll get through this. You'll see.'

But Dot knew that a shadow lay between them. By not telling Pop the whole truth, she was committing a sin – the sin of omission. But how could she admit to him, a fervent Catholic, she had allowed the man she was now mourning to get her pregnant?

*

Dot went up to her old bedroom, the scene of the crime.

The schoolgirl pictures she had cut out of *Film Pictorial* and *Photoplay* were still pinned to the walls: Clark Gable, Gary Cooper, Van Johnson, Cary Grant. They seemed to be leering at her. They knew. They had seen everything.

She ripped them down and chucked them into the wastepaper basket.

While her parents were downstairs preparing dinner, Dot hauled Otis's case from under the bed, laid it on the counterpane and opened it, hoping to find something of him among his discarded possessions.

On top was a large thick sweater. She pressed it to her face. It smelled not of Otis, but of her parents' house, where it had lain for the last four years. Shirts, formal clothing, a bow tie, a pair of shiny patent shoes.

At the bottom a brand-new tailored chalk-stripe suit. When Otis had packed for war, he obviously hadn't realised that there would be no opportunities for flashy civvies. Everyone always wore uniform.

What to do with it? Give it to the Red Cross, perhaps, for refugees and families who had been bombed out. She carefully repacked the case and clicked it shut.

What had she thought she would find? A letter, declaring his undying love? But why would he have left that? He believed he was coming back. He planned to marry her, take her off to California.

She had a sudden thought. Otis might have left something hidden inside the pockets of the suit.

She scrambled to open the case again, tossing everything onto the bed until she got down to the suit. She searched the trouser pockets first. Then the jacket. She fumbled in each side pocket. Nothing. Then her fingers hit something like card. She thrust her fingers deep into the inside pocket.

A business card. 'Walker, Anderson Inc., Tailors Outfitters, 377 Atlantic Avenue, Brooklyn, NY. Low prices for all your drapery needs.' Above the print was scrawled in pencil: 'Don't forget us! Kisses from all at—'

It must be where Otis worked before joining up.

Before he moved to California.

Perhaps it was his parents' business.

But then why wasn't it called Oakewood's?

She ran her fingers across the card, slipped it back inside the pocket and repacked the case, realising that she'd never know.

A few days later she helped her parents prepare lunch. Roast potatoes and carrots, with Yorkshire puddings whipped up using powdered eggs. And gravy to pour over it all. You barely missed the meat.

'Tonight we can use what's left over to make a blind scouse.' Her mother placed the remaining cooked vegetables in the pantry cupboard.

As they took their seats around the kitchen table, a wave of nausea ran through her.

'Are you all right, darlin' dote?' Her mother reached out a hand to feel Dot's forehead. 'You look awful pale.'

'It's hot. I'm not used to the heat.'

Pop pulled up the sash window, letting in a breeze from the side return.

But Dot knew it wasn't that.

'Nice weather for all those POWs arriving home today. Thousands of them coming in.' He sliced a roast potato, pouring gravy over it. 'Most of the ARP wardens have volunteered to help out. After all, we've nothing else to do now.'

A rap on the door.

Dot's parents exchanged a look.

'I'll get that.' Pop pulled his napkin from his collar. 'Probably someone from the church with another stranded foreign serviceman wanting the spare room.' He crossed into the hall.

'You must look after yourself, darlin'.' Mammy leaned in and stroked the back of Dot's hand. 'I don't want you fading away. Death *is* terrible, but life must go on.'

Dot thought of the baby growing inside her. Another life. A little Otis.

Dot could hear Pop in the hall, talking with some men. Their voices suddenly went into whispers.

'I'll go and see what's up with Pop.' Mammy stood up, anxious. 'Let's hope it's not more bad news.'

As she left the room, a shock ran through Dot.

What if it was Howard come to find her? Where was Howard? She'd not seen him on VE night. And no one had mentioned him. He'd not written back to her, not answered her letters for weeks now. Had he, like Otis, been killed in action? Was this someone come to pass on the bad news?

'Dot, darlin'?' Her father stood on the step down into the kitchen, his face set. 'Do you have that suitcase? You know. The one Otis left behind?'

'It's under my bed. Why?'

'You stay there, darlin'. I'll nip up and fetch it.'

'I'll go.' Dot stood up.

'No…' Her father put out a hand. 'Please, kid. Leave this to me.'

Pop seemed strange. What was happening? She followed him into the hall.

Two policemen stood on the doorstep. They'd taken off their helmets, like they did when they announce a death.

'We had no idea, Officer,' Mammy was whispering in a low voice. 'It'll come as a terrible shock to…'

'It's a story we're hearing all over the place, Mrs G.'

'What's going on?' Dot moved nearer to her mother.

'It's nothing, darlin'.' Her mother waved her away. 'You go back into the kitchen now.'

'No, Mammy. I won't go anywhere.'

'We're sorry about this.' One of the policemen made a placatory gesture. 'We don't like bringing news like this. But it's our job, Miss Gallagher.'

Dot's heart thundered.

From her parents' reaction, it was some news which affected her, not them.

It had to be another death.

'Who is it? Not Lieutenant Colonel Howard Hopkins?'

'No, no. We've been sent here by…' He read from an official paper in his hand. '… Mrs Jane Oakewood, of 377 Atlantic Avenue, Brooklyn, NY. We need to retrieve the belongings of a former lodger of your parents, First Lieutenant Otis Oakewood.'

'Otis's mother?' Dot tried to imagine what it would be like to lose a son in his twenties. 'She wants his things back?'

The policemen exchanged a look.

Pop clattered down the stairs and handed over the suitcase.

'You'll find it's all in the condition in which First Lieutenant Oakewood left it.' Adding sotto voce: 'You don't need to say anything more.'

'Why? Why don't they? What's going on? Pop? Pop?'

'We're sorry about this, Miss Gallagher, but…'

Pop interrupted them.

'Let me do this.' Pop put his arm around Dot's shoulder. 'It's not Otis's mother who wants the case, kid. It's Otis's wife.'

TWENTY-EIGHT

HOWARD HAD TRIED TO warn her. 'Cave canem'. Beware of the dog.

Beware of the bloody dog?

Why hadn't he simply told her the truth?

'Otis is married,' he could have said. 'Don't let him mess you about.'

Damn Howard. He knew.

They all did.

Oh, Otis! Otis, how could you?

How many other lies, she wondered? He'd always said he lived in Hollywood, California. It appeared that he really lived in Brooklyn, where many of her Irish neighbours had relatives. Near New York, nowhere near California.

Late in the afternoon, without knocking, Pop walked into her room, where, as soon as the police left, she had gone to be alone.

'Get your things,' he said. 'You're coming with me.'

'I can't, Pop. I can't face the world.'

'The least you can do is help out. These boys, they've been through a lot. It's our duty to give them a good welcome. Come along, Dot. It would lift their hearts to see your lovely face.'

'But Pop, I...'

'No buts, Dot. Your mother is going out this evening to visit the Winskills. They lost their son last year. Today's the anniversary. And I'm not leaving you on your own.'

How she wished they had not left her alone *that* day.

*

Under the shadow of battleships, hospital ships and troop carriers, the docks were heaving with people. Men filed down the gangways. The queue snaked into the customs hall. Dot stood beside her father at a long trestle table.

Lines of men waited to get their entry forms stamped. Some faces were worn and lined, others carefree and fancy-free, looking forward to being returned home. Officers, both British and American, were doing the paperwork. Pop and the other ARP people were there to direct the categorised troops to waiting coaches, trains, the medical room, or to army camps and private homes where they would await ships to take them home to America.

'We're doing the letters P and Q. Let's hope there aren't a lot of Pompadours, Quenelles or Quislings in the US services.'

Dot could only think of Otis. What game had he been playing? Had he planned to leave the Brooklyn wife and marry her? She couldn't have done that to another woman, faithfully waiting for her husband to come back from war. Or was the proposal only a ploy to get her to let him…?

Imagining that Pop could read her thoughts, she moved back and leaned against the wall.

'Hey!' A male voice ringing out above the din of the crowd.

'There's always one!' Her father glanced back at her.

A warden scuttled towards Pop, yelling: 'There's a bloke in my queue, letter O, wants to talk to your daughter.'

Letter O?

O for Oakewood?

Had they made a mistake? Was Otis alive after all?

'Yes.' Dot grabbed her father's elbow. 'I need to see him.'

Pop nodded at the warden, who scurried away.

Dot stood on tiptoes, trying to see.

Head and shoulders above the others, Sydney Olsen waved, pushing through rows of men to reach her.

'HEY! Dot! It's Sydney! Sydney Olsen! Remember me? From Rainbow Corner.' Sydney ducked his tall, wiry frame and crawled under the table to stand near Dot. 'How ya doin'?'

As Dot said, 'Fine,' she wondered how she could have deceived herself again.

'We just got in from Germany,' Sydney continued. 'I gather the other blokes in my division beat me to it. But I got taken prisoner…'

Dot was only part listening.

If this had been Otis, not Sydney, what could she have said? 'How's the wife?'

Sydney had stopped talking.

'I hope they didn't treat you too badly, Sydney.'

'Let's say I lost a pound or two.' Sydney grimaced. 'As though I wasn't skinny enough! Let's hope Nancy can fatten me up.'

Dot didn't imagine Nancy was the cooking type. The very thought of her behind a stove in a floral pinny made Dot smile.

'I feel quite bad that I suspected Vi, you know. I thought a lot about that while I was banged up.' He shuffled from foot to foot. 'Anyhow, Dot, it's so good to see a friendly face. We had an awful time of it. Mind you, I was one of the lucky ones. Lieutenant Colonel Hopkins gave it to those Nazi bastards, quoting the Geneva Convention, telling them to buck up. Didn't work, though. They dragged him off…' A pause. 'He never came back.'

It came like a kick in the guts.

'They killed him? They killed Howard?'

'Who knows? We never saw him again.'

'Olsen!' A male voice rang out. 'Sydney.'

'Better go,' yelled Sydney, ducking back under the counter. 'Don't want to lose my billet. Nice to see ya, Dot!'

Howard missing, perhaps dead. This was the final straw.

Dot told Pop she was going out to take some air.

'You look awful pale, kid. Back in five minutes or I'll send out a search party.'

Dot walked out onto Princes Parade. The rattle of the overhead railway drowned the seagulls. She leaned against the railing, gazing down at the murky water, watching the reflections of cranes swinging back and forth.

Howard was the only one who could fill the gaps, tell her the truth. And now he too was gone. Howard who had always been so kind, so sweet to her. Howard who got her dancing through her loneliness. Howard who had tried to warn her, tried to make her promise to keep away from Otis.

She felt such a fool.

'Well, well, well! Dot Gallagher!' A tap on the shoulder. 'Do you spend all your days watching the river?'

Dot turned to face Clarice wielding a pram, Billy at her side.

It was the first time Dot had seen Billy since that dreadful weekend in London over a year ago.

'No dashing Yankee captain escorting you today?'

Otis, Otis, Otis. Why couldn't people let her forget him?

'I'm with Pop. He's helping deal with the homecoming troops.'

'Always a hero, Mr Gallagher.'

Billy said nothing, just stared at Dot.

Remembering her manners, Dot directed her attention to the baby. 'How old?'

'Seven weeks.'

'She's called Joan,' said Billy. 'Joan Wilhelmina.'

'Joan for my mother,' added Clarice. 'Wilhelmina for William.'

For a few seconds Dot was lost, then remembered that Billy was William.

'Baptised last week in St Sylvester's.'

'How lovely.' Dot looked down at the pink, wriggling creature.

Billy, Clarice, a baby.

Another baby growing inside her.

It was hard to breathe.

Otis, the cheat, the liar, the husband, the father.

Nausea swept through her.

'Are you OK, Dot?'

Billy rushed to support Dot as she sank to the ground.

As though underwater, she heard Billy yell to Clarice to go and fetch Mr Gallagher.

*

Next morning Dot made her way to Vincent Square.

After she fainted Pop had tried to take her to hospital to be checked out, but she resisted, explaining that it was the heat of the crowded room, on top of not having eaten. It would be impossible to hide her condition from medical staff. More importantly, she knew that she didn't want this baby, a permanent reminder of someone who had taken her for a fool. Telling her parents that she felt her compassionate leave was no longer valid, Dot took the first train down next morning.

At Vincent Square she asked for Sister Sullivan.

'We've got a busy day,' said the duty nurse. 'So many men arriving back from the POW camps. Try surgical.'

The nurse in the surgical ward glanced down at her watch and said, 'Probably taking a late lunch.'

Down in the basement Dot peered through the diamond-shaped window of the staffroom door.

Sister Sullivan was inside, sitting chatting with a couple of doctors.

Dot pulled open the door. Sister Sullivan shouted across the room: 'Nurse Gallagher! I didn't think I'd see you again. How can I help?'

Dot was hardly going to yell her business out loud, so asked if she could have a few words in private.

'If you want your old job back, nurse, we'd be delighted,' Sister Sullivan called.

'Nothing like that…'

Sister Sullivan excused herself and led Dot to an adjacent storeroom.

Dot told her everything.

'I imagine you are looking to find an abortion?' Sister used the same hard voice with which she had once rebuked Dot for being overfamiliar with patients.

Dot nodded.

'Absolutely not going to happen. Even if I knew a doctor who would perform it, I wouldn't let you undergo an illegal procedure which, along with getting rid of the foetus, would most probably kill you.'

'What can I do? I can't bring up that man's baby, live as a single mother. I can't.'

'My only advice, Nurse Gallagher, is the age-old method, induced by gin, hot baths, ergot and shock. None of it assured. All of it downright dangerous.' She touched Dot's arm. 'Take care of yourself, nurse. Please don't try anything stupid.'

Dot pushed through scores of uniformed men tramping up and down the staircases, some in pyjamas and dressing gowns, some with arms in slings or bandaged heads.

Once outside Dot stood at the top of the steps looking out at the playing fields piled high with rubble. Since she was last here, whole buildings were missing.

London would never be the same.

Nor would she. Thanks to Otis, her future was inexorably changed.

Risk her life or bring up his baby.

Either way she was ruined.

She ran down the steps.

'Nurse!' A voice shouted from inside the hospital. 'Stop.'

Let whoever it was find another nurse. Dot didn't work here.

'Stop! Nurse!' The voice was insistent. 'Stop. Please! I can't run. Stop!'

Dot marched briskly away and turned the corner.

'Nurse! Stop.' The annoying man was still pursuing her. 'Stop!'

She turned into Rochester Row and realised the man was not yelling 'stop', but 'Dot'.

'Dot! Nurse Gallagher! Dot! Please! Dot!'

She couldn't make small talk with an ex-patient. Glancing back, she caught sight of a frail man in dressing gown and slippers, hobbling towards her with the aid of a crutch.

She ran across the road.

Then she recognised him.

It couldn't be.

'Howard?'

'Please, Dot.' He held up his hands, appeasing. 'Don't run from me.'

But the relief she felt at seeing him was overwhelmed by her anger. She swiftly crossed back towards him.

'You lied to me, Howard. You watched me fall into a fatal trap. You stood by and let Otis set it. You knew he was married. You knew he lived in Brooklyn. You knew every word which came out of his mouth was a lie.'

'I warned you.'

'Cave canem? Really? You thought that was enough? Cave bloody canem? If you cared for me at all, Howard, why didn't you tell me plainly: "Otis is married"?'

'I had promised him. We all had. I was trying to be true to you both.'

A police car roared past, bells ringing.

'You failed me, Howard.' Dot raised her voice above the din. 'You think a promise to a proven liar is more important than the truth to a friend?'

'We swore secrecy on the ship across. We'd been at sea for days. At the time it seemed like a game. No living human in England was more than an idea. But once I met you…'

'Thank you for that, Howard. Nice to know I was just a pawn. I hope you all had a bloody good laugh.'

'On the contrary, Dot. Otis had a bloody good laugh at the lot of us. When we tried to expose him, he called us dishonourable, unable to keep a sworn secret. He did it right under your nose, Dot, and fought me for it. You took his side against me, remember?'

Dot thought back. How had she not seen the truth?

'I paid too, you know, Dot.'

'How's that?'

'He stole *you*. From the first night we danced in the subway I adored you. I wrote you letters – Otis copied them out and sent them, making mine defunct. He told you he had arranged the gramophone in Portsmouth. He stole my life, my stories, where I live. He's never set foot in California. That's where *I* live. He's no actor. I am. He stole my stories, my quotations, my life. But when he stole you, he left me nothing.'

A bus rumbled past. A woman on the platform jeered at Howard, standing on the pavement in his dressing gown and slippers.

'If that's true, how come you said you went to school together?'

'We did. Elementary school in New York. Even then we called him the original Brooklyn Dodger. But my family moved west.'

Dot hung her head. Everything now made sense.

Horrible, glaring truth staring her in the face, laughing at her.

'Did I not try, Dot, time and again, to warn you?'

He had.

She had chosen not to listen.

But Howard didn't know that for Dot there was no 'over' or 'forget'. She had a lifetime ahead, a lifetime filled with Otis.

'Please.' Howard took a placatory step towards her. 'I love you, Dot. The very thought of you is what kept me going through all the hell…'

Dot turned and, momentarily unbalanced, her foot slipped off the edge of the kerb. She tumbled backwards.

Swerving to avoid her, a motorcyclist veered into the path of an oncoming bus.

In the crash which followed, everything seemed to move in slow motion.

The bike flipped and flew into the air, throwing the rider to the ground.

Howard ditched his crutch and launched himself forward, trying to pull Dot out of the path of the flying motorcycle. The bus ploughed into a wall.

With a loud crack, Dot hit the ground and lost consciousness.

TWENTY-NINE

'OUR HUSBANDS HAVE GONE home to America...' Barbara sat near the door of the cafeteria, one baby on her lap, the other two in the pram at her side. 'But no one will tell us when we get to join them? No one tells us anything.'

Lilly was running an informal Q&A session with women in Rainbow Corner who were married or engaged to US servicemen. Tomorrow the club was hosting a major event to which hundreds of GI wives and fiancées had been invited. Lilly's task was to find out the most obvious problems so that Controller Fergusson's speech could provide answers.

'It will only be for a short while, I'm sure.' Ever optimistic, Thelma leaned against the front of the counter, nibbling on a biscuit. 'We'll be with our men by the end of summer.'

'I'm not so sure,' drawled Nancy, one leg up on the chair opposite her. 'Logistics won't allow.'

'What are logistics, when they're at home?' Peggy, still behind the counter, presented a large jug. 'Anyone for a coffee top-up?'

'It's like one of those school maths problems.' Nancy yawned. 'If four ships can carry six thousand servicemen west across the Atlantic in five days but must take another five days to come back east, empty, and in between each voyage need a day to turn around, how many months before there's any room on one single westbound ship for the bloody wives?'

'I'm sure the powers-that-be have everything under control.' June smiled hopefully. 'Art assured me we'd be over in time for Christmas, which he says the Americans do better than anyone in the world.'

Lilly looked down to her notepad. What was perfectly clear was that the powers-that-be didn't give a damn about them, perceiving all of them as a lot of clinging, whiny women, or rats leaving a sinking ship.

Truth was, not one of them were likely to see their husbands and fiancés this side of 1945.

Tony had gone back to the States, along with Art, Earl and Virgil.

Nancy, Lilly knew, had had word from Sydney, who was in Liverpool, safe and well after his ordeal in a POW camp, waiting to hear when his ship would sail for the US.

'Whatever happened to Dot Gallagher?' asked Thelma. 'Here one moment, gone the next. Did she manage to wangle herself onto a ship?'

'Wouldn't put it past her,' said Peggy.

'She's at home with her parents.' It was Nancy who stood to defend Dot. 'She's not been well.'

'She'll be off to America soon enough though.'

'Dot is neither married nor engaged, Peggy.' Lilly sighed. 'So please explain to me how she would qualify as a war bride?'

'War brides! Ghastly term for us.' Nancy lit up another cigarette. 'War-bonded, war-painted, war-weary war brides – that's us.'

'Speak for yourself,' said Peggy. 'I heard Dot's as good as engaged.'

'Shut up about Dot.' Lilly couldn't take any more of this squabbling. 'The man she was seeing died.'

'She was a fool to have been chasing after that creepy married heel,' said Thelma. 'He was a thoroughbred rotter.'

Nancy shrugged. 'I don't think the cleverest of us can claim to have had a rotter-proof war.'

'There were worse rotters than Otis,' said Barbara. 'Tony told me that Dot knew about some spy in Rainbow Corner. And had proof of it.'

'If she had proof, they'd have picked someone up.'

'They picked up Vi...' said Peggy.

'Vi didn't do it. She was vindicated.'

'So why did they pick her up in the first place? No smoke without fire.'

Nancy turned to Lilly. 'Are you going to wind this up now, darling? Some of us have things to do.'

'Leave when you like,' said Lilly. 'I'm only here to find out what everyone wants.'

'You know what we want.' Lilly had never heard Thelma talk in such a loud voice. 'We want to go be with our men.'

'Got things to do. I'm off.' Nancy left the room.

'I don't care how busy Miss Fancypants is. We need to make arrangements,' said Peggy bluntly. 'ASAP. A passage to America.'

Lilly hadn't even realised that middle-aged Peggy had married. She only caught herself in time before saying it aloud.

'I'll bet that cow Vi gets over the Atlantic before we do,' said Thelma. 'Despite being a spy.'

'Vi wasn't a spy,' said Lilly. 'You heard Nancy. Vi was released without charge.'

'They do that to keep tabs on them,' said Peggy. 'Vi was guilty as sin.'

'If it wasn't her, then who?' June stood with her hands on her hips. 'We all heard the rumour.'

'Enough gossip!'

Lilly hadn't noticed Fergusson slip into the room and take a seat beside Barbara. 'Lilly! You're needed upstairs.' Fergusson addressed the rest of the room. 'I hope to respond to all of your concerns at tomorrow's meeting. Now, Lilly. Back to work.'

*

Dot woke lying on a bed in one of the women's wards. Her uniform jacket hung from the back of the bedside chair. Most of the other beds were empty.

Had she fallen asleep on duty?

She had no idea why she was here.

But when she tried to raise herself on her elbows, the pain was too much, and she had to lie down.

The nurse heard her groan.

'You were lucky. Only bruises. According to witnesses, the motorbike landed on you with some force.'

'Why do I feel so…' Dot lay back. Her head was swimming.

'Shock,' said the nurse who was now taking Dot's pulse. 'I need to check your blood pressure, then you're free to leave.'

'Do you work here?' The nurse pumped up the cuff. 'I've not seen you before.'

'I was visiting.' Dot watched the nurse apply the stethoscope to the crook of her arm.

'Of course.' Together they watched the mercury falling on the sphygmomanometer. 'On the low side, but that's not always a bad thing. All right, dear. You can go when you like.'

Dot swung her feet down over the side of the bed and stood up. She felt very strange. She took a few steps forward. The dizziness was so overwhelming she almost fell.

She hovered, then grabbed the foot of the bed before sinking to her knees.

'Good Lord … you're bleeding!' The nurse reached out to catch Dot and led her back to bed. When Dot was lying flat, she bent down and asked quietly: 'Are you, by any chance, pregnant?'

Dot nodded, closing her eyes in shame.

'I'd better fetch your husband.'

'But I'm not…'

'Lie still.' The nurse gently pushed Dot's hair off her face, calling loudly: 'Lieutenant Colonel Hopkins! Quickly.'

Howard limped in and hurried to Dot's side, taking her hand and kissing it. 'Come on, Dot. I've got you.'

'I'm so sorry, Lieutenant Colonel.' The nurse placed a chair for Howard. 'It looks like you're losing your baby.'

Howard's face remained inscrutable.

Dot felt humiliated, mortified. 'I was a fool, Howard…'

'I'll fetch a doctor.' The nurse swiftly left the ward.

Howard whispered into Dot's ear: 'I understand everything. Know, sweet girl, it makes no difference to me. I was to blame for not warning you. I'm so sorry. So sorry.'

'Oh, Howard.' A tear ran down the side of Dot's face. 'You don't want to be with a terrible girl like me.'

'Don't tell me what I want!' He wiped the tear away.

A cascade of emotions rose in Dot's chest. 'You must think me an awful slut.'

'My opinion of you, Dot, hasn't changed one iota. Why would it? I'm presuming the culpable was Otis, who wasn't in touch with you afterwards?'

Dot nodded.

'You were tricked by a master con man.'

Howard slid his hand over hers. She tightened her fingers around his.

'Please don't leave me alone, Howard.'

'I'll stay by your side till you tell me to go.' He kissed Dot gently on the cheek. 'You'll always be my dancing girl with the kind smile.

I'll find you in the morning sun
And when the night is new
I'll be looking at the moon
But I'll be seeing you.'

Howard sang low, almost a whisper, as Dot faded into sleep.

THIRTY

'WELL FIELDED, CONTROLLER,' SAID Nancy as Lilly arrived in the front hall.

She was standing by the front desk with Fergusson. But Fergusson did the strangest thing. Momentary, fleeting, but worrying. She raised a finger to her lips, eyes wide open, inclining her head towards Lilly.

What had Nancy thought well fielded? Her own comments on Violet? Why would that need fielding? Everyone knew Violet had been released.

Thinking back, Fergusson and Nancy had both put an abrupt end to conversations about the Rainbow Corner mole.

Were her old suspicions correct? Was it Fergusson and Nancy in league, leaking information from Rainbow Corner?

'I'm heading up to the office,' said Lilly, striding towards the staircase.

'Sergeant Newton and I are going out for a short while. I may not be back. There's plenty to be getting along with.'

Lilly walked up to the first landing, waited a moment, then tiptoed down, and perching on the bottom step, watched Fergusson exchange a few sentences with the girl at the front desk before walking out of the front door, Nancy at her side.

Once they were gone, Lilly dashed out to follow.

She watched them weave through the crowds as far as Piccadilly Circus, where they crossed Regent Street and stood at a bus stop, laughing.

Lilly dawdled in a shop doorway on the other side of the road, pretending to look at the goods inside, keeping her eyes focussed on the reflection.

A bus pulled in but neither Nancy nor Fergusson climbed aboard. Lilly glimpsed them using it to disappear down Air Street.

Pulling her cap low over her forehead, Lilly followed into Piccadilly, past the Albany, crossing to Fortnum & Mason, turning finally into St James's Street.

From the corner of Jermyn Street, she watched them cross.

A lorry passed. When the view was clear, both women had disappeared, seemingly into one of the four doors.

Lilly went over to inspect the brass door plaques. Nothing out of the ordinary. But a spy circle would hardly put their business on a sign. More likely they'd pass themselves off as art dealers, tobacco dealers or private couturiers.

Lilly waited on the other side of the road, trying to see into the upper windows. None of the buildings looked residential, all offices. One was empty, with dusty windows and a large 'TO LET' sign. Over the door the famous film company logo MGM.

Lilly waited. But what if they stayed here all night? Lilly had no desire to sleep in a doorway. She started walking back.

*

When Dot awoke it was dark, the ward illuminated only by a blue nightlamp. She looked to the empty chair where Howard had been sitting and hauled herself up. The night nurse came over.

'Are you all right, Nurse Gallagher? Sister Sullivan was worried about you.'

'Sister Sullivan was here?'

The night nurse nodded.

'Did I lose the baby?'

'I'm sorry.'

So that bit had been true.

'And the man who was here?'

'What man?'

Had she imagined it? Had Howard really been here, claiming to be her husband, holding her hand, telling her it would all be all right? Dot sank back against the pillows. Was it all a dream?

'Was I in an accident?'

'I have no idea. I only came on duty an hour ago.'

'Can I contact another patient in this hospital ... This is Vincent Square, isn't it?'

The nurse nodded.

'Lieutenant Colonel Howard Hopkins.'

'Of course.'

'Could you tell him that I'm here and I would love to see him.'

The nurse went.

Dot lay back and waited.

After a few minutes the nurse returned to Dot's bedside. 'I'm sorry, but there is no patient in this hospital under that name.'

'He's not here?'

'No.'

'Thank you, nurse.'

So it *was* all a dream. Though she was far from sleepy, Dot closed her eyes. A frisson of fear gripped her. Was she going mad? Had all that mess with Otis and the miscarriage left her unhinged? Hallucinations were brought on by feverish conditions. Like it was with Joe, all those months ago. No. She believed Joe. It was only she who was deluded.

No Howard. It was only a dream.

Dot felt an unfathomable emptiness.

Why on earth had she fallen for all that claptrap from Otis? She had never really wanted anyone like that. He was too flashy, too perfect, too false. All her life she had known what she wanted. Someone who would love her like her pop loved her mammy. Someone she could love as Mammy loved Pop. Not Otis. Not Billy either. Billy meant only one thing – going back, trying to remain a child. She didn't want life how it was before the war, because the world had changed and so had she. Anyway, even though the war was over, Billy would still be away on his merchant ship ten months every year. What kind of a life would that be? Not the life for her, a lonely wife, sitting alone in a house in Liverpool. Clarice was welcome to it. No, she didn't want Billy. No, she had never really wanted Otis. She had been blinded by his dazzling, boyish charm. But it had all been a lie anyhow. She wanted something real, something warm and yet exciting. She didn't want to go back. She needed to go forward. A new start.

With a dull realisation she saw that what she really wanted was a life with Howard. But that was not going to happen.

It had been just a dream.

She was wide awake now. All dizziness gone. A few bruises. That's what the nurse had said. Why was she taking up a bed when so many men were returning injured from battlefields and prison of war camps?

She knew how to nurse herself back from an early miscarriage.
She climbed out of bed and dressed.
As she left the ward, the night nurse asked Dot whether she shouldn't wait to be checked out by a doctor, but Dot said she simply needed to get home. Though where home was exactly, she had no idea. The poky room at the Regent Palace where she had left her bag, she supposed.
She felt so low.
She didn't want company.
She had been an utter fool.

*

Lilly knew that Fergusson wouldn't be checking on her, so decided to stop off at the ATS centre in Piccadilly for an evening drink. It was only after downing two gins while catching up with some girls from Sussex that the idea came to her.

Fergusson was a controller in the ATS. There must be someone here who knew her. Was she married? Did she live alone? What was her job before the war? Who was she?

Lilly knocked at the office door, not expecting to get a reply.

The secretary yelled a bored 'come in'.

'Sorry to disturb you…'

'Lucky for me you knocked.' The secretary jumped up off the sofa. 'I was dropping off. Only here to pick up some things before heading home. Made the mistake of lying down for a minute or two. What time is it?'

'Coming up for ten.'

'Oh Lord. I'll only just make the train.'

'I was wondering if you could help me.' Lilly stepped inside.

'As long as it takes less than five minutes. I really do have to get that train.'

'I'd like to get a leaving present for my boss,' said Lilly. 'She's zodiac mad, so I was wondering if you could get me her birthdate so that I can buy an appropriate present.'

'What fun,' said the secretary. 'Makes a change from issuing discharge papers. Rank?'

'Controller.'

'Phew!' The secretary crossed to the filing cabinets. 'Not so many of those.' She pulled open a drawer and pulled out a ledger. 'Name?'

'Fergusson. Gloria.'

'Fergusson, Fergusson.' The girl flipped the pages. 'Ewing, Fenwick, Ferdinand, Fergal, Gardner…' She turned the pages back. 'Fergusson, you said?'

'Gloria Fergusson.'

The secretary flicked back and forth through the register. 'I'm sorry to disappoint you, Sergeant. But there is no Fergusson, Gloria or otherwise, among the controllers of the ATS. Might she have a different rank?'

Lilly's thoughts were whizzing. Perhaps it *was* all a lie, a cover. Everything about her, invented…

'I'm so sorry to disturb you.' Lilly backed towards the door. 'I'm so stupid. She's in the WAAF, not the ATS … Pardon me.'

Lilly left the room, hearing the secretary muttering, 'If you're in the ATS and she's in the WAAF, how come she's your boss? And anyway the WAAF don't have controllers…'

*

Dot lay on her bed in the hotel. The yellow glow of streetlamps and flashing traffic lights illuminated the ceiling with colour, reminding her of Christmases at home before the war. Last time she had stayed here, when the war was still on, there had been no ambient light at night, only the void of blackout.

She thought back to that bleak night when Art had broken the news to June. Otis had given himself away that night, but Dot hadn't seen it. Once again Howard had come to the rescue.

She went to the window, watching people coming and going in the street below. All of them so cheery-looking. Drunk probably, arms linked, laughing, careering towards Piccadilly Circus. Happy.

War was over.

Life was almost normal.

Almost.

A rap on her door.

Whoever it was, Dot had no inclination to talk. The only people who *could* know she was here would be old friends from Rainbow Corner. She couldn't bear the thought of talking to any of them.

She stayed immobile by the window.

Another knock.

'Nurse Gallagher!' A female voice. 'If you don't open up, I will have to get the night manager.'

Dot didn't move.

'You shouldn't have discharged yourself.'

Dot recognised the voice. Sister Sullivan.

She opened up.

'What on earth were you thinking? So irresponsible.' Sister Sullivan flicked on the light and stepped into the room. The glare of the overhead bulb made Dot flinch. 'You, of all people, nurse, know how these things work.' Sister Sullivan closed the door behind her and moved to the bedside chair. 'Sit down. I'm going to take your blood pressure. I wouldn't want to lose a lovely girl like you, even if it was through your own negligence.' As she unpacked the equipment, Sister Sullivan continued. 'Feel free to criticise me for being overfamiliar with a patient. But you, Dot, were always more than that.'

Dot rolled up her sleeve, mortified to have caused this fuss.

'I should think you're feeling pretty relieved about the miscarriage.' Sister Sullivan wrapped the sleeve around Dot's arm and started pumping it up. 'I only hope you didn't deliberately run into the road and cause that accident.'

So she *had* been knocked down by the bike. At least that wasn't a dream.

'I was arguing. I lost my balance and stumbled back.'

'The offending father-to-be, I presume.'

'Not him.' Dot watched the mercury fall as Sister pressed the stethoscope against the inside of her elbow. 'He's dead.'

Sister Sullivan put away the sphygmomanometer.

Dot said quietly, 'I hope no one was hurt.'

'Only you.' Sister Sullivan took Dot's wrist and started counting her pulse. 'A bystander suffered a broken bone. Miraculously, the bike rider himself walked away unscathed and the bus was towed off with no one hurt.'

'My troubles really started when you had me sent away to Essex,' said Dot. 'That's when I started to feel so lonely and when that man got a grip of my mind.'

'I didn't send you to Southend.'

'They told me the order came from my superior.'

'That would have been Gloria Fergusson. Something to do with a security issue at Rainbow Corner.'

Dot remembered now. She had just arrived back in London and went to tell Fergusson about Joe – and hours later she was dispatched to Southend.

Sister Sullivan sighed as she took her fingers from Dot's wrist.

'You shouldn't have come all this way, Sister. I'm so sorry.'

'I was coming off duty when I heard you'd done a runner.' Sister started packing her things back into the bag. 'Decided to come into town, corner you and, while I was here, grab something to eat in one of the Soho late-night cafés. I hope you'll join me? I imagine you've not eaten.'

'I can't, really, Sister...' Dot couldn't bear to leave the room.

'Nonsense.' Sister Sullivan picked Dot's coat up from the end of the bed and handed it to her. 'You need to keep up your strength.' Sister Sullivan held the door open. 'I'm not taking no for an answer. And I warn you, Nurse Gallagher, I am very, very hungry. So hurry up.'

*

Though it was late, Lilly returned to Rainbow Corner to see if she could find any more clues in the filing cabinet or in Fergusson's desk drawers.

But to her shock Fergusson was there at her desk.

'Good evening, Lilly,' she said brightly, without looking up. 'I was wondering where you'd got to. What brings you back?'

'I forgot my ... pen.' Lilly grabbed a pen from the pot on her desk.

'Really? You've come back here for a silly, cheap government-issue pen, when I can see that you have another, superior one in your pocket.'

Lilly was grateful for the dim light so that Fergusson couldn't see her blush.

Fergusson stood and moved towards the door.

'The game's up, Lilly. You're going to have to come with us.' She raised her voice. 'Sergeant Olsen, open up, please.'

Sergeant Olsen? Sydney was in on this?

The door opened.

Nancy blocked the way. Of course, Nancy now had Sydney's surname.

Fergusson gripped Lilly's elbow. Nancy stepped forward and took the other. Together they frogmarched her out of the building. If anyone obstructed their path, Fergusson shouted 'gangway' and the path cleared.

Lilly tried calling out, but each time Fergusson murmured confidentially, 'She's had a few. We're taking her out for some air.'

Most people in the building were the few remaining servicemen celebrating the news of their imminent repatriation. Lilly looked like another case of too much booze.

'You can't kidnap me. People will miss me.'

'Who?'

'Jack.'

Fergusson ignored her.

A car waited on the kerb, sidelights blinking.

The two women bundled Lilly inside.

When Lilly leaned forward to call to the driver, she saw Elan behind the wheel, Jack at his side.

'What's going on? Jack? Tell me!'

'You were tailing us,' Fergusson replied. 'So we've been tailing you. Elan is remarkably good at it. You were getting dangerously close to discovering us, so, before you started blabbing your mouth off, we thought it safer to take control.'

The car roared along Piccadilly.

'Jack! Don't tell me that you're part of this dreadful mob.'

Jack craned his neck to look round. 'It really would be best, Lilly, if you stayed silent.'

'Let me tell you this then, Jack: we are officially unengaged.' She glared at him in the darkness and turned back to Fergusson. 'I suppose you're taking me to your seedy little HQ in St James's Street.'

'Well deduced.'

'I'm not frightened by you, Controller Fergusson, nor your henchmen and woman.' Lilly was not going to give up without putting up a fight. 'The war is over. I'm never going to join the Nazi party or the Union of Fascists or whatever you vermin call yourselves … Hitler's dead. Three cheers, hip, hip, hooray! I hope you all go to hell.'

The car pulled in under the MGM building's 'TO LET' sign.

While Nancy ran up the steps to open the front door, Jack said urgently, 'Don't make a scene, Lilly. Just come inside quietly.'

Lilly was tempted to yell at the top of her voice, but something in Jack's look made her resist.

Inside, Jack and Fergusson walked Lilly briskly along a dark, dusty corridor lined with fading movie posters. Elan locked the door behind them.

They pushed Lilly into a large, well-lit room at the back of the building.

Inside, a group of women sat at a row of desks, quietly typing. Others worked at a central table making diagrams on large writing pads. The far wall was lined with a row of telephones, above them clocks showing the time in Berlin, Paris, London and New York.

'Welcome to His Majesty's Special Security Services, London.' Fergusson led Lilly to a desk where one girl was busily typing up the notes which she herself had given her that morning. 'We work from Blenheim, Bletchley and all over Europe. Although the war may be over, we're still hard at it, uncovering the people who, for the last five years, have been undermining us. You almost ruined our current operation at Rainbow Corner. Now you will join us. Welcome to MI5.'

*

The café's walls were lined with faded, signed photographs of actors, actresses and boxing champs. Dot and Sister Sullivan sat at a Formica-topped table in the corner, cradling hot mugs of whisky toddy.

'I know you were badly affected by Joe's death. Your second day with us too. I also know why you were worried. He confided his fears about Rainbow Corner in me too. Naturally I telephoned Controller Fergusson and informed her of the poor man's concerns.' Sister Sullivan looked up. 'I hope you're still dancing, Dot. You can't let one rogue ne'er-do-well douse that bright spirit of yours. You were always a joy to have on the ward. The men adored you.'

'I don't have anything to dance about anymore.'

'Come, come. War may have battered our spirits, but if we give in to depression, they've won.'

'It's not that, Sister. It's been such a week. I think I'm losing my mind…'

'Why?'

'I don't know what's real anymore. Every day is like a dream – a nightmare more often. Sometimes I can't tell which is which. We've been living so near death for so long everything's got muddled in my head.'

'I understand.' Sister Sullivan took a long swig of her hot whisky. 'We lost another patient today. Lovely man. US officer. He'd been really abused in a prisoner of war camp. Managed to make it home in one piece … but…' She let out a long sigh.

Dot's heart thundered. Not Howard? He'd come back wounded from a POW camp. It would explain why the nurse told her there was no patient of that name in the hospital. He'd been moved to the morgue, his name rubbed off the ward list…

'It wasn't a lieutenant colonel, was it, the man who died? Lieutenant Colonel Howard Hopkins?'

Sister Sullivan looked up at Dot.

'Why on earth would you think that?'

'It's just that…' A tumble of words spilled out. 'He … I … I dreamed. He came to me. Helped me.'

Sister Sullivan smiled.

'Lieutenant Colonel Hopkins carried you into the ward. Despite his injuries. In fact, while hauling the motorbike off you, he broke a finger. And though he must have been in tremendous pain, he declined all treatment and refused to leave your side until he was certain you were all right…'

Howard *had* been there. He *had* cared. It wasn't a dream.

'And then he died?'

Sister Sullivan looked across at Dot and laughed.

'Not at all. As soon as we could pry him away, he was carted off to St Thomas'. They have more beds free for freshly broken bones as they handled the Blitz victims.'

'Howard is alive?'

Sister Sullivan nodded. 'And he appears utterly dedicated to you. He lied to the nurse on duty to be allowed in to see you. Told them he was your husband, apparently. And although we knew it wasn't true, we let him in anyway.'

'He's in St Thomas'!' Dot jumped up. 'I have to go there, now!'

Sister Sullivan put out a hand.

'For goodness' sake, let the poor man sleep. Go in the morning. First, we have a tasty fry-up to demolish. Come on, silly but adorable girl. Tuck in.'

PART FIVE

The New World

Happily coupled with men they adored, that could have been the end of Dot and Lilly's story.

But what happened next, changed everything…

THIRTY-ONE

FEBRUARY 1946

'If this is what America's like, you can stuff it.'

'It won't be like this, Vi.' Dot sat on her bunk watching Violet at an adjacent bunk bed unpacking her case. 'We've all seen snaps. It looks lovely.'

Dot shook off her shoes and lay back in her bunk. The dormitory, housed in one of the long, low buildings which made up the camp, was as it had been left after the army vacated: filthy.

What a roller coaster these last months had been. After Dot's accident, she and Howard had helped one another convalesce. Then, in early August, just when Howard was recovered, a letter arrived informing him that he would be leaving England one week later.

'Don't be sad,' said Howard, seeing Dot's face fall.

'How can I not be sad?' Sad wasn't anything near the despair she felt at losing him so soon after finding him.

Howard fell to his knees. Fearing that his war injury had flared up again, Dot rushed forward to help him.

'Hey, kid, give a man a chance. I was going to say – if you'd like to be Mrs Hopkins, we can do it tomorrow. Or better, the day after! We need time to get your mam and pop down to witness the proceedings.'

'But...'

'I'll pay their fare and put them up in a posh hotel for as many nights as they like. How does Grosvenor House sound? Used to be US HQ, so we have a bit of clout.'

'I meant the banns. We'd need weeks and you'll be gone.'

'Uh-uh!' Howard waved his letter in the air. 'With this I can get us a waiver.'

And so it was that on 15 August 1945, Dot married Howard at Caxton Hall. The civil ceremony was followed by a blessing by a Liverpudlian priest in the Lady Chapel of Westminster Cathedral, all flowers, as it coincided with the feast day of the Assumption. Mammy and Pop were dressed in their Sunday best, and Lilly, grinning from ear to ear, sat beside them in the front row. It was VJ day too, so everyone felt as though the whole world was celebrating.

A few weeks earlier, Rainbow Corner had closed its doors forever.

At the end of August, Howard went home but wrote long, funny letters, both on the journey and once he had arrived.

All summer and into the autumn, Dot, Lilly and the other wives and fiancées lobbied the US Embassy and held demonstrations in Grosvenor Square. They might be unwanted immigrants in the USA, they chanted, but they were wives and sweethearts of blue-blooded American men, war heroes, and needed to be treated with respect. The embassy replied, casually informing the war brides that most Americans resented them for stealing the best American boys at a time when their resistance was low.

If anything, this steeled the women to fight even harder.

Howard, Jack, Tony, Sydney, Art, Virgil and the other husbands, being spread over an enormous continent, were in no position to demonstrate. Instead, they wrote letters to the British and American embassies and badgered their local senators. The war was over. They wanted their wives and children with them. What had they fought this war for if not to preserve a decent life for their families?

Finally, soon after New Year 1946, the US government was roused from its apathy and, enlisting the help of the American Red Cross, and former workers from Rainbow Corner, things started to move.

As a wet and frosty January progressed, the women were presented with a pile of forms to fill in and went on a scavenger hunt of official documents, leading to a tangle of immigration red tape. Lilly and Dot went together to Somerset House to get multiple copies of their birth certificates. Afterwards they strolled down the Strand to look at their old digs, now being spruced up as a hotel, before going over the road for a cup of tea at Lyons'.

'Thelma not working here anymore?' Lilly asked the boss, who shook his head.

'Off filling forms,' he replied. 'She's hoping to be on the first ship over the ocean to Americky!'

'Fat chance of that,' said Dot under her breath. Lilly laughed.

A few days later, to their surprise, both Lilly and Dot received letters informing them that ships had been commissioned and that they were to be on the famous *Queen Mary*.

January came to a wet end, and Dot and Lilly, along with Barbara, Violet, June, Nancy, Pearl, Peggy and Thelma were sent further instructions. They must make ready for their imminent departure, with the promise that at last they would start their wedded life.

A date was given. They should assemble for trains which would carry them down to Wiltshire where they would finalise formalities.

Dot had agreed with her parents that the journey down to London just to wave her goodbye was an unwarranted expense and anyway would be too upsetting for all three of them. So she phoned, and they had a long talk with a few tears and the promise that one way or another they would meet again soon.

After the train journey, a bumpy bus ride and a lengthy welcome talk, Dot was exhausted. But at last, she and the other women were finally on their way. They were now at the embarkation camp at Tidworth, where all the official red tape was to be finalised before the GI brides finally boarded a ship to America and their loves.

'Tidworth Camp!' She looked at the sagging mattress above her and the graffiti scratched onto the wall. The familiar brick wall and long-nosed 'Kilroy was here'; a heart pierced with an arrow – 'Hank loves Betty'; a row of stars – 'LA Wildcats – best football team in the world!' She smiled. No more supporting the Liverpool team once she got to California.

How often during the last two years had she lain on a strange bed, she wondered, staring up, wondering what would come next?

'Do they ever let us eat, do you think?' asked Violet, testing out her own bunk. 'I'm starving.'

'I wouldn't get your hopes up.'

'Shall I go and ask?'

Dot shook her head. 'I wouldn't risk it!'

When the bus had pulled in at Tidworth barracks, Nancy had quipped: 'This place makes Wormwood Scrubs look like Versailles.' It certainly felt as convivial as a prison. The so-called 'welcome pack' included a luggage label for their name, 'to be worn at all times'.

'I feel like a parcel being sent freight,' Nancy had said, tying hers to her belt.

Their arrival had been followed by a 'welcome talk' given by an American staff sergeant who ended: 'You may not like the conditions here, but don't forget: no one asked you to come.'

One lone voice had piped up, a woman with a plump red-faced toddler struggling in her arms: 'We were promised there would be "ample and luxurious accommodation". Frankly, I wouldn't call this dump either ample or luxurious.' She was bluntly told she could take the next train to wherever she came from. After that no one dared comment.

At the far end of the dormitory a woman wailed.

'Oh Gawd, she's still at it,' muttered Violet. 'She's bawled her way through Waterloo Station, howled on the train journey down, same on the bus, and *still* she won't shut up.'

The poor girl had got it into her head that she would never see her parents again.

'I hope we won't be held in this place for long, Vi.' Dot sat up and perched on the side of the bed, looking down at the patched lino floor. 'Is Lilly here? I didn't see her at Waterloo or on the train, and she wasn't in our coach.'

'She'll be somewhere. Don't know how you'll find her, though. Did you see how many rows of buildings there were?'

'Thank God! Some friendly faces.' Nancy appeared in the doorway. 'I'm sharing with five thousand babies and a big-busted girl relentlessly playing "Greensleeves" on her zither. It'll end in bloodshed. Anyone wanna join me for chow?'

'Chow!' yelled Violet. 'The best word in the world!'

'Count me in,' said Dot, reaching down for her shoes.

A raised male voice came from the hallway behind her: *'Komm schon. Bringt diese billiges schlampen zum Essen.'*

'What did that man say?' The voice came from one of the upper bunks. Dot recognised Pearl, the blonde drummer from Rainbow Corner. 'It was incomprehensible.'

'Some kraut talk.' Nancy shouted over her shoulder, 'If you've got something to say, say it in bloody English!'

A gang of POWs walked past; one of them, a spindly man in a brown jacket marked with the large white letters PW, peeled off and thrust Nancy out of the way.

She pushed him back. 'Don't shove me, you Nazi pig.'

He spoke over her, in faltering English.

'Dinner. Now. Canteen. I am named Gerd. I can satisfy your wishes.'

'Oo-er, Gerd.' Violet rushed forward. 'My dream come true. The food, I mean.'

'Our current wishes are *only* for food!' said Nancy curtly to Gerd. 'Go on, then. Lead the way. Let's go, gals!'

In the canteen the same staff sergeant who had greeted them this afternoon banged on a tin tray. 'Ladies! I'd like to introduce to you our prisoners of war, who will be looking after you during your stay. Hans, Klaus, Gunter, Gerd, Wolfgang and Adolf. Give them a big hand.'

'I'll give them a big hand on their backside if I get the chance,' murmured Nancy. Dot looked along the line of POWs. Wolfgang? She recognised the face. Might he have been in Liverpool before the war? Sailors from Hamburg often banged around the city then.

Taking the foil tray of food, Dot followed the others to a long trestle table.

'Disgusting!' said Pearl after one mouthful. 'Excuse me,' she asked Gerd. 'What is this?'

'Sauerkraut,' replied Gerd, rubbing his stomach. 'Mmmm.'

'Sauerkraut?' Violet dropped her fork on the plate with a clatter. 'It's what I'd call cabbage what's gone off.'

'It's my new name for Gerd.' Nancy primly wiped her mouth with a paper napkin.

'What is?'

'The face on him. Sour kraut.'

'Mind if I join you?' Thelma hovered at the table. 'Did you hear that man in the corridor just now?' She put down her tray. 'He called us sluts.'

'Who did?' Nancy perked up.

'Wolfgang, I think he's called. The dark one. He called us *Billiges Schlampen*. That means sluts.'

Dot remembered now. *'Billiges Flittchen … dreckige Hure.'* She *had* met Wolfgang before, but it wasn't in Liverpool, it was in the operating theatre off the coast of Italy. He'd said those words as he spat in her face.

*

At 6 a.m. next morning bells went off. German POWs walked the dormitories calling the women to breakfast and switching on glaring overhead lights.

'You'd think *we* were the prisoners of war.' Lilly hauled herself down from the top bunk. 'I'm off for a shower before my medical.'

No one in her dorm replied. She heard only a series of groans as women turned over and pulled up the covers.

Lilly's last few months had been a mixed bag. Soon after her bizarre induction into MI5, Jack had been sent to the Pacific. While the US war with Japan raged, every day was full of fear. Even after VJ day Lilly couldn't relax until she received a telegram telling her Jack was safely at home in New Mexico.

As she pulled her washbag out of her suitcase, someone from the lower bunk squealed: 'Excuse me!'

'Yes?'

The woman's face was smothered in pale green cream.

'Not you,' said the green-faced woman. 'That guard. I wanted to ask him if I've time to do my curlers and everything before ... whatever comes next.'

'I'll fetch someone.'

'I'm Norah, by the way.' The green-faced woman thrust out a hand.

'Morning, Norah. Lilly.' Lilly shook hands, threw on her dressing gown and left the dorm.

The corridor was glacial.

A burly GI in a khaki jumpsuit was strolling towards her. Lilly told him that Norah wanted a word.

'What's she look like?'

'Viridian green face cream. You can't miss her.'

'Going for the Martian look?' He moved towards the door. 'I spy her.'

The washroom consisted of a row of dilapidated basins, facing a row of open showers with no curtains. Women were already in the first two cubicles, lathering themselves; another had her head in a basin, washing her hair.

Lilly stripped off, entered the third cubicle and turned on the tap, happy to feel the lukewarm water running down her body. After the hardships of Normandy, this seemed deluxe. And now that she was on the road, heading for Jack, she'd have willingly lived in a pigsty.

As she reached for the soap, she noticed Peggy scurry past, clutching a towel.

Lilly wondered if Dot was here. There were hundreds, if not thousands, of women here. She had tried to find her at Waterloo but had been shoved down to the front of the train by an over-efficient volunteer. But if Dot was here, Lilly hoped to find her in the communal areas.

'Niobe's left the camp, did you hear?' the woman in the adjacent cubicle said. 'In the middle of the night. Got herself a taxi, still wailing as she shoved her case into the boot. Sobbed all the way back to her parents, I presume. At least we finally got a few hours' kip.'

'I didn't know she was called Niobe. I thought she was called Susan.'

'Niobe was some ancient Greek woman who never stopped crying.'

'Susan was Greek?'

'Forget it.'

Lilly laughed to herself, wondering how Susan's husband would feel when he heard that his bride had left him to run back to Mum and Dad. She also felt rather put out after the hard graft and campaigning it had taken to get the war brides this far.

A sudden scream from the furthest cubicle.

'Shoo! Filthy letch! Get out!'

Lilly caught a glimpse of a POW running past. Grabbing her towel, she stepped out. 'Which one was it?' Lilly ran to make sure the woman was OK.

In the last cubicle, hiding her body with her hands, Peggy cringed in the corner.

'He came at me,' she said. 'He must have been in here, waiting.'

'You don't know his name?'

'No.'

'Would you recognise him?'

'Not sure. I tried to escape, but he grabbed me. It was such a shock.'

'Shall I get an officer?'

'It's all right.' Peggy straightened up. 'No damage done. Just a bit of a fright, that's all.'

After breakfast, Lilly went to the assembly hall for her medical. A small staircase on either side led up to the stage. The curtains were drawn. Lilly took a seat in the auditorium.

'Blimey, it's freezing in here,' she said, as she looked around at the rows of empty chairs. 'No wonder people are waiting elsewhere.'

'I dread to think what they're up to behind those drapes,' Thelma muttered. 'The women come out looking shell-shocked.'

Peggy sidled along the row and flopped down beside Lilly.

'You all right now, Peggy? After the peeping Tom?'

'Den spanner!' said Thelma. 'That's German for peeping Tom!'

'Thelma dear! How would you know such a thing.' Peggy leaned forward and shot Thelma a dirty look. 'Are you a secret German?'

'You know very well, Peggy. My husband's an interpreter. Seems to teach me only bad words, I'm afraid. I can swear like a trooper in German.'

'Please don't.' Peggy pulled her robe tighter and knotted the belt.

Lilly glanced up as another woman emerged from behind the stage curtains, clasping her dressing gown tightly around her, muttering: 'Perverts! Perverts!'

Lilly elbowed Peggy. 'You don't suppose they got Fingers Smith back to do the medicals?'

'The old boy was sent off to grass,' said Thelma. 'Best place for him.'

'He's in Texas,' added Peggy.

Lilly wondered whether Peggy had got the joke.

*

Dot drank coffee in the canteen. The anticipation of the journey had left her drained. Only today to get through, then tomorrow she would be on the ship, then the train ... Then Howard. Meanwhile, in these cold and depressing surroundings, she could think of nothing but Mammy and Pop. She shivered. How she'd love to be sitting on the hearth up in Liverpool with a book, or simply gazing into the flickering coals of a warm fire.

Violet let out a squawk. 'Hey! Look at this!' She held up her label. 'I never realised it till now, but there is one more delicious benefit of marrying my Virgil. Not only are we Vi and Virgil, which sounds like a radio comedy team, but look!'

'Violet King?'

'No one calls me Violet, Dot. No. Everyone knows me as Vi. So I'm now Vi King. Viking, get it?' She put her fingers up to the side of her head and sang a few bars of the 'Ride of the Valkyries'. 'Viking!'

The door opened and two infants on reins staggered through them, preceding a pram containing two babies. Barbara shoved them all forward.

'Can we wait in here before going for the medical?' Barbara tied the two reined children to a table leg and flopped down. 'That big hall is like an igloo and I'd kill for a cuppa.'

'Tea or coffee, Barbara love?' asked Violet, striding over to the huge electric urn in the corner.

'Tea, please.'

'Sorry. Couldn't get out of the habit of offering both, but there ain't no tea. When I asked for some earlier, that GI sergeant said we'd better get used to it cos Americans drink coffee not tea.'

'Charming!' Barbara yanked on a set of reins. The attached yowling child slumped down into sitting position and was silenced.

'If they're being so American about it all,' said June brightly, 'where are the donuts?'

'Oh, why did you say that, June?' Violet handed Barbara a coffee. 'I'd kill for one of them donuts right now.'

'They're punishing us for marrying their boys.'

'No. Don't you see what's happening?' asked June. 'That crying girl left last night. They're filtering out the genuine emigrants from those who might have regrets. To save everyone the bother later, I suppose.'

'They're not putting me off.' Barbara popped a piece of gum into her mouth and started chewing. 'That bloody Tony gave me all these brats. Now he can help me out with them. I've had enough of doing it all on my own.'

'Mrs Caruso?' a German-accented voice shouted from the corridor.

'Ah, well.' Barbara wrapped her robe tight around her and dragged the children towards the door. 'Now for the medical … then I'm done. Next stop, New York City. All steam ahead, kids!'

Dot looked up to see Wolfgang in the doorway, glaring at her.

'Dreckige Hure!' he muttered, his eyelids lowered. She knew he too had remembered their previous encounter. '*Billiges Flittchen.*'

'Don't you dare speak to me like that.' Dot walked over to Wolfgang so she wouldn't need to raise her voice. 'The surgical team on that ship saved your life. You had third-degree burns. Fourth-degree in some areas. If we'd left you there, you'd now be at the bottom of the Mediterranean Sea. Dead. So really, really … do not start on me.'

She tried to pass him but he blocked her path, pursing his lips. Dot knew what was going to happen. Hoping to avoid a face full of phlegm, she shoved Wolfgang away. He fell back through the open doorway.

'What's going on here?' The staff sergeant ran to help Wolfgang.

Pointing at Dorothy, Wolfgang muttered under his breath.

'Now, Mrs...?' The staff sergeant peered at the label dangling from her chest. 'Mrs Hopkins, I expect respect for my prisoners of war. If you want to be on the next train heading for London, you're welcome.'

A gang of women gathered round.

'He insulted her.' Violet spoke loudest.

'Really?' The staff sergeant squared up to Violet. 'What did he say?'

'Oh, *"Schlinken schlanken schlonken? Achtung, auf weidersehen, Heil Hitler?"* How the hell are we supposed to know? He was talking German.'

'So how do you know it was an insult?'

'Look at his face, for Gawd's sake.'

They all glanced at Wolfgang, who leaned against the door frame, his countenance now angelic, wounded, the martyr.

The staff sergeant grabbed Dot by the elbow and led her away.

'She only did what any of us would have done,' Peggy piped up. 'The bloody man followed me into the shower, for goodness' sake.'

The staff sergeant turned and said abruptly: 'Mrs Hopkins has committed assault. I'll have to see that you are checked very carefully before you can be allowed to enter the United States of America.'

Peggy and Violet had run up behind them.

'She did nothing wrong!'

'It's him what needs checking out!'

The staff sergeant turned and shouted: 'If you like, I can add you two to the list.'

'Shove it up your arse,' muttered Violet.

'I heard that, Mrs King. Take care.'

Dot pulled her elbow from the man's tightening grip. 'For goodness' sake. I'll come with you. Just let go of me.'

Ahead, Dot saw Lilly coming out of the assembly hall.

'Lilly!' Dot cried. 'Lilly!'

Lilly turned and, recognising Dot, ran forward.

'What's going on?'

'Remember, years ago, I wrote you a letter about the German who spat at me? He's called Wolfgang, he's here and he's out to get me...'

'Excuse me, Officer, this is unacceptable.' Lilly took the staff sergeant to one side and whispered a few sentences. He glanced at Dot and shrugged.

'Any more trouble from you, Mrs Hopkins, and you're barred from the States.' He turned to face the crowd that had gathered. 'And that goes for all of you.'

'We all contributed to this war against those dreadful people,' said Lilly. 'I'd like to point out, Officer, that there is a fine line between being reasonable with the enemy and colluding with them. These days I have my eyes peeled for that kind of thing.'

'Any more lip from you,' he glanced down at her label, '*Miss* Deane, and I shall recommend your transportation back to London tonight. That goes for all of you!'

The other women slunk away towards the cafeteria.

'How wonderful to find you. Come on.' Lilly seized Dot's arm. 'Let's go outside and catch up.'

'But it's freezing. Can't we go to the canteen?'

'We need to be alone.'

In a bus shelter some way from the huts, the two women huddled. 'I just needed you to know that the Rainbow Corner mole is still at large,' said Lilly. 'And she's here with us. Traps have been set, people watched, but they got nowhere in the hunt. Whoever it is is pretty smart. And I imagine by now they'd stop at nothing to avoid being shopped, especially as they're on the verge of a new life.'

'But the war is over. The spy must feel safe now.'

'They could still be banged up.' Lilly's breath came out in a round cloud. 'But only if we can discover them before they arrive in the US.'

'How did you get that sergeant off my back just now? I can't believe he'd defend that awful man.'

'Told him you were married to a man who'd been awarded the DSC for valour on the field and had himself been maltreated in a Nazi POW camp.'

It was true. Howard had won the Distinguished Service Cross. Dot was married to a true hero.

'Another thing we have in common, Dot,' added Lilly. 'Jack has one.'

'How far we've both come since that first night in the Charing Cross hostel,' said Dot.

'And now we're taking a giant step together, aren't we?'

Dot realised that this was true. There was a fear within the anticipation of their new lives on another continent.

'Do you have doubts, Lilly?'

'Jack's given me a get-out clause. If I don't fancy the life, I can come home. But, actually, that makes me feel quite uneasy.'

Dot thought of Howard. Could he be seeing things differently now that he was back living in familiar places?

'You're right. Now that the pressure of war is off, who knows what they think? It's an adventure for us – for them it must be more like an intrusion.'

'It's unreal, isn't it?' Lilly pulled Dot close. 'How can you measure feelings when all you have is a stream of letters and telegrams?'

Dot remembered how she had believed everything Otis wrote, even though it had all been a lie, stolen from Howard.

'Oh, well. We survived. And our prospects are good. And while there's life … I suppose the only thing we can ever depend on is hope.'

'It's all we ever have,' said Lilly.

'Which hut are you in?'

'D north.'

Dot laughed. 'I'm in D south. How come it took us all day to find one another?'

'Come on, gal.' Lilly linked arms and walked forward. 'We've got the whole boat and train journey to chat. Days and days of travelling. Let's get inside. But don't forget – someone we must know, who is here, is not our friend.'

The two women stamped their feet against the cold then walked briskly back into the hut.

THIRTY-TWO

THAT NIGHT LILLY WAS woken, along with everyone else, by an alarm bell ringing and searchlights flashing through the windows.

The corporal stood in the doorway with a torch. 'Anyone set eyes on the POW called Gerd? Looks like he made a break for it.'

Lilly jumped out of bed. 'I'll help search.'

Through the windows Lilly could see US soldiers with dogs and torches, walking the fences, looking for openings big enough for a man to crawl through.

All along the dormitory corridors, the screaming of babies rose to a crescendo.

'As if the bloody Germans haven't put us through enough,' sobbed Barbara, standing in a doorway, trying to placate her four wailing kids.

'Never got me clothes on so quick.' Violet stood, fully dressed, further down the hallway, pressing her hand to her chest. 'Thought it was another raid, love.'

'An escaped POW,' said Lilly.

'Found him, Corporal.' Gunter loped towards them, pointing towards the large hall. 'He's in there.'

Nancy peered out and swiftly joined them.

In the auditorium, the staff sergeant was tugging on the ropes opening the stage curtains when Lilly ran in, followed by Violet and Nancy. More women were huddled on the other side of the hall, holding their dressing gowns tight.

The curtains opened.

Onstage, a woman in a nightgown shielded her eyes from the sudden light. Naked but for his socks, Gerd cuddled her.

'Mrs Levinsky,' shouted the staff sergeant. 'Come down from that stage. You're heading back to your folks.'

'We're leaving now? For the ship?'

'No. You just failed the marriage test. You're going to London.'

'But Gerd promised me some nylons for the voyage. In exchange for a cuddle, that's all … *and* new high-heeled shoes. He showed me them. It didn't seem that much to do … I'm still fully dressed, aren't I?'

Gerd was furtively pulling up his trousers.

'Well, my dear,' sighed Nancy to Lilly, 'Mrs Levinsky has given us a whole new meaning to the phrase "Gerd up your loins".'

'There's more to this,' muttered Lilly. 'Where did Gerd find high-heeled shoes and nylons?'

'Point!' said Nancy. 'Our friend from RC?'

'Exactly.'

*

Before breakfast Dot sat on her bed. Her valise was packed and by the door ready for the weigh-in. She watched Thelma try to shut her own very full suitcase. Clothes bulged out of every corner.

'It's ridiculous that we were limited to these tiny cases,' she said. 'Are you any good at packing, Dot? Might you help? I was so panicked by all those talks about how the Americans won't understand that we were rationed, and that if we don't dress really well we'll be taken for peasants. So I packed far too much.'

Dot went over to Thelma's bunk. The case was crammed.

'Let's take everything out and put it all in again.'

For ten minutes Dot helped Thelma fold every item of clothing. Then the repack. Make-up bag rolled up in a skirt, shoes stuffed with bras, vests and pants, jumpers pressed flat.

All the while Dot was plucking up courage to ask Thelma to explain something which had worried her for some time.

They closed the case and clicked it shut.

'Thelma? Could I ask you something?'

'Of course, Dot.'

'On the day the news arrived that Hitler was dead…'

'I remember it well. We were all in the cafeteria.'

'I asked you about Otis Oakewood and…'

'He died, you know.'

'I heard. But you spoke with a certain tone, like "Oh, him!" Why?'

Thelma remained silent.

'I'd really like to know. You probably heard we were close. But it was a mistake. Please tell me what you knew then.'

'I didn't like him. He tried it on with everyone, but I knew he was married.'

Dot remembered Howard saying how all the men had sworn to secrecy on the ship. Had they warned Thelma, but not her?

'Did one of his company tell you that?'

'No, no. It was at the Lyons' Corner House I found out. Otis came in to ask me out on a date. He'd been flirty with me for some time. My old boss, Mr O'Kelly, whispered in my ear to refuse him. I was puzzled, but I told Otis that I was working late and off he went, tail between his legs. When he'd gone, my boss said he knew Otis's in-laws really well from when he'd worked in a restaurant in a town called Brooklyn in America. Lots of Irish go there. Anyhow, Mr and Mrs Anderson ran a big tailoring place and Otis was married to their daughter, Jane. He even lived in their house. "A cuckoo in the nest," Mr O'Kelly called him. A kept man, who used his social skills to milk people dry.'

Dot thought back to the loving note she'd found in his suit pocket, then at how comfortably Otis had settled in with her own parents.

'Next evening, Otis came back. I told him I knew he was married to Jane Anderson. It was the day before the Baby Blitz started. The Friday, remember, when the Houses of Parliament caught fire. January 1944. Anyway, from that day he kept away.'

And the following day he had resumed his campaign on Dot. She felt numb.

'He took me for a total fool, Thelma. I fell hook, line and sinker.'

'Don't feel stupid, Dot. You weren't the only one to be taken in. I was lucky.'

*

Lilly went through her folder once more, verifying the checklist: *inoculation certificates, birth certificate – full length (two certified copies), passport with US Embassy visa, military discharge papers, photographs with light background – two and a half inches square (three copies), UK ration book, ID card, letter of authority for bank exchange up to £15 sterling, £15 in notes,* plus all the affidavits and documents she and Jack had signed at the solicitor's office. What was missing? She skipped the page about babies and their supplies. *Certified and stamped confirmation of baggage weighed in at less than 200 lbs*. Yes, she had that. Then *50 lb of baggage allowance per child*. Not applicable.

Nancy had made Lilly laugh earlier at the luggage scales when she tapped a passing mother on the shoulder and said politely: 'My suitcase seems to be twenty pounds overweight. Might I borrow your kid? Just for the weigh-in? I'll give him back as soon as my luggage is passed.'

Declaration of personal jewellery – easy enough, Lilly possessed nothing but her engagement ring. *Three-page form letter*, completed. She hoped she hadn't missed anything.

Dot came out from her interview and, seeing Lilly, sat with her.

A subaltern popped his head out of one of the two office doors. 'Margaret Phyllis Velma Jaeger-Smith?'

Peggy got up and went inside.

'Oo-er. There's a moniker for you,' said Dot. 'Who knew?'

They both laughed.

'I got a telegram this morning. I'm to meet Jack on the platform at Albuquerque, New Mexico. Don't all American names sound so exotic!'

'Hollywood! Howard sent photos of his house. Not a bit like the terraces of Liverpool. Looks like a Spanish bungalow with palm trees out front. Have you seen Jack's place?'

'Not even a drawing.'

'Perhaps they're as nervous as we are.'

'I don't even know what Jack does. What does Howard do?'

'An actor. Not famous or anything. He says it's a pretty standard job in Hollywood.'

'I wonder what's a standard job in Albuquerque?'

'Teaching people how to spell Albuquerque?'

They both laughed.

'We must keep in touch, Dot. As far as American distances go, we're not *that* far apart. Only about 800 miles!'

'Don't you worry, Lilly. As you know, I'm a dedicated letter writer.'

'Lilly Anne Deane!' A head popped round the door.

'Here we go!' Lilly gathered up her things. 'See you tomorrow, honey, on the ship.'

'Pip, pip, Lilly! See you aboard.' As Lilly went into the office, Dot waved.

A disgruntled colonel sat idly flicking through an American magazine. He glanced at his watch and sighed.

'Good afternoon. RMS *Queen Mary* is waiting at Southampton. You'll be out of our hair early tomorrow morning, leaving us to prepare for the next batch of gold-diggers.'

Lilly wasn't sure whether he was joking. She decided she should laugh.

'Did I say something funny?'

'Quite funny,' she replied.

'What have we here?' Rifling through her folder, he was passing some papers to the subaltern, shoving others back to her, leaving the rest spread out on the desk.

'You served in Normandy. Me too. Unpleasant, wasn't it?' He ran his finger down the page. 'And the Ardennes, and the push over the Rhine. Very commendable. Good education too, I gather. Grades high. Rides horses and knows equine routines!' He laughed. 'Looking for a stint as a wrangler at a rodeo?'

'I'd give it a bash.'

'You bash horses?'

'English translation needed, Colonel. A bash is a try.'

'You have your money? Fifteen pounds. Not a penny more?'

Lilly rooted in her handbag and pulled out three five-pound notes.

'Passport?'

Lilly presented the booklet, open at the page previously stamped by the US Embassy in Grosvenor Square.

'No children?'

'No.'

'Ration book?'

Lilly slid her ration book across. The subaltern took it.

'Where you're heading, you won't need that. We don't have rationing.'

'Birth certificate?'

Lilly passed over the two copies.

'Two parents. How very satisfying. Marriage certificate?'

Lilly pulled out the solicitor's affidavit, certifying that she and Jack were legally engaged.

'I asked for a certificate of marriage.'

'We're not married.'

'Couldn't quite bring yourself to commit?'

'Nothing like that.' Once more Lilly wasn't sure whether the man was joking. 'I'd have married Jack in a shot. But he thought I should have the chance to see what I was signing up for before I chained myself.'

'Chained? Funny word for love.'

'Jack's word. He seemed to think there was something about him I might baulk at.'

'Is he a criminal?'

'The opposite.' She wanted to tell him how brave Jack was, how he had been awarded the DSC. 'I served under him for many months of war.'

'Oh, dear Miss Deane…' Lilly noted the stress on the word 'Miss'. 'I'll bet you served *under* him, and now he's gone his merry old way, leaving you here with no way of joining him.'

The colonel snatched the ration book from the subaltern and passed it back to Lilly.

'Sorry, Miss Deane. But neither tomorrow, nor any day soon, will you be travelling gratis across the Atlantic Ocean to New York on the *Queen Mary*. You'll be staying here in Britain for the foreseeable. Next!'

*

Just before Dot turned in for the night, one of the POWs arrived at her bunk bearing a telegram.

'Mrs Dorothy Mary Hopkins?'

Dot took the small square yellow envelope. So often during the war these brusque messages had arrived, some announcing death, others reassuring that a beloved person was safe. But a telegram always came with a frisson of fear.

As she tore open the envelope, Dot's hands trembled.

The strips of capital letters read: 'ALL A MISTAKE. DON'T BOARD SHIP. HOWARD.'

Dot sank back on her bunk and read the words again.

'All a mistake. Don't board ship. Howard.'

They were married. If she didn't board the ship, what would that entail? What had happened?

'Dot?' Violet sank down on the bed beside her. 'Bad news?'

Dot couldn't speak. The words wouldn't come out. She nodded.

'Not your parents, I hope.'

'No,' said Dorothy, showing her the telegram.

Violet read it then left the dormitory.

If Howard didn't want her, why had he waited till this late to let her know? She had gone through all the emigration procedures. She'd given in her ration book. How would she manage? Those brusque officials wouldn't be here again till the day after tomorrow, when the next batch of wives arrived to be processed. How would she get it back? Without a ration book she couldn't eat. Dot put her head in her hands. Why was she worrying about ration books! Surely Howard couldn't have become so hard he would dismiss her by telegram? She can't have been taken in twice.

Lilly arrived at the side of the bed, led by Violet.

'Let's see it.' She read, then pulled Dot up. She put her finger to her lips. 'Come with me.'

'If he doesn't want me...'

'Come with me, Dot!' she spoke firmly. 'Say nothing.'

Lilly took Dot out through the back door.

A dog started barking.

They walked briskly to the bus shelter, their breath billowing like cigarette smoke.

'Something's going on.' Lilly sat down on the bench. 'They've stopped me going too.'

'It's because of that trouble with Otis. I know it.' Dot wiped away a tear. 'Howard's had time to reconsider.'

'It's definitely not Howard. He's dependable and straightforward. He loves you. Real love, I mean, not romance or madness. He loves you.'

'So why did he send me that telegram?'

'As I said. Something's going on. Let me have another look at it. There'll be a clue somewhere.' Lilly took the telegram and read it back slowly. '"All a mistake. Don't board ship. Howard." It's the "Don't board ship" bit that worries me. No "I'll write a letter explaining"...'

'But that would be too late. I'd be in New York. How would I get back...?'

'Where is Howard now?' Lilly inspected the telegram more closely.

'At home in West Hollywood.'

'I've got it.' The dog suddenly stopped barking. Lilly looked around before continuing. 'Howard didn't send this telegram. Look.' Lilly pointed at a square at the bottom of the telegram. '"Office of Origin: USA OKL". If this had come from California, it would say USA CAL.'

Dot squinted at the tiny letters.

'Why would Howard travel thousands of miles to send a telegram?' asked Lilly. 'He didn't send it.'

'So who would have?'

'Someone trying to make you voluntarily fail to board.' Lilly folded the telegram and handed it back. 'Let's give them a shock ... You get on that ship.'

'I can't go all the way to America if Howard doesn't want me...'

'I swear to you, Dot, it wasn't Howard. It's going to be our old friend from Rainbow Corner. We must have seen or heard something and they don't like it. Either that or they think we're onto them.' Lilly gave a tired laugh. 'If only. If we had even a clue we would turn them in right away. But they obviously feel they need to get rid of us. They don't want us on that ship with them. Maybe something's going to happen on the ship?'

'But we know nothing.'

Lilly shrugged. 'They clearly don't think so. But, even if I'm not, you are leaving tomorrow. *Especially* if I'm not. This telegram proves that they are still scared of being exposed and they know we're onto them.'

'I'll be so wary of everyone.' Dot stood up and stamped her feet against the cold. 'Who can I talk to?'

Lilly said quietly, 'Nancy.'

'Nancy?'

'Trust her. No one else. They've stopped me leaving, Dot. But you must defy them and go.'

THIRTY-THREE

DOT LEANED OVER THE railings of the *Queen Mary*, watching the dockers release the last line, letting the majestic ship pull out. A desultory straggle of locals stood on the quayside waving off the most famous liner in the world and her cargo of women. No friends or family of the brides had been permitted.

Today the smell of seaweed and brine, which usually thrilled Dot, held no charm. What if Lilly had been wrong?

If Dot had obeyed her instincts, she would have been left behind. But here she was, sailing down the Solent, next stop New York. If Howard really had changed his mind and was divorcing her, it was too late now for Dot to jump ship.

For half an hour Dot stayed away from the others, under the shadow of the funnel, watching England slip away. As they passed the gaudy Italianate palazzo favoured by Queen Victoria, Nancy appeared at Dot's side.

'Can't skulk away the whole voyage, darling. Come on.' She put out an arm. 'Let's face the bitches!'

Reluctantly Dot took Nancy's arm and they strolled together to join the others nearer the bow of the ship.

'Where's Lilly?' asked June. 'I thought she was coming.'

'Problem with red tape,' said Nancy, steering Dot into the gaggle of women on the railings. 'She'll be on the next one.'

'Goodbye to Blighty!' Violet edged near Dot. 'Hey! Why are we slowing down? We're almost stock-still.'

'They'll be letting off the pilot,' said Dot.

'A pilot? You kidding?' Violet laughed. 'This is a ship not an aeroplane!'

'A pilot is a local seaman who knows the waters of difficult harbours,' said Dot, thinking about her previous voyages, where Howard had been so kind to her. 'He'll be getting into that tiny boat down there then going back to Southampton to see the next big ship out.'

'I forgot you were a navy girl.' Violet waved downwards as the little boat pulled away. 'It's fun being on a ship, isn't it? Especially near the front.'

'The bow.'

'Like "deck the hall with boughs of holly"? Is that where it comes from?'

'No.' Dot laughed. 'Different spelling. This one is spelled the same as bow and arrow but pronounced like "take a bow". The holly bough is pronounced the same way but spelled like the word "cough" but with a b.'

'Gawd, English is complicated, ain't it. Glad we don't have to learn it to go to America!'

'I may not be there long enough to find out.'

'Come on, dear.' Violet squeezed Dot's arm. 'We've said our goodbye. Let's find out where they dish up the grub.'

The voyage was rough. From the moment *Queen Mary* hit the English Channel, the ship pitched and rolled. As they moved into the Celtic Sea, conditions worsened. None of that bothered Dot. But the sound of retching and the rank smell of vomit mingled with the stench of dirty, damp nappies was hard to stomach.

Her cabin was no escape. She shared with three tearful girls from Norfolk, who, when they weren't being sick, spent their time sobbing about how they would miss the flat lines and the grey light of home. During the first night Dot had tried to make conversation, telling them about the ship, and how it had carried famous stars like Marlene Dietrich and Bob Hope. The girls looked at her blankly and went back to wailing about Gorleston-on-Sea.

Early next morning Dot went to the top deck to watch the sun rise over the slate grey water. She had been looking forward to this voyage for so long, but the telegram had put paid to that. Had Howard really thought better of their marriage? Was he a liar, too, with dark secrets? She couldn't bear to think that true.

But, if Lilly was right, someone was trying to sabotage them. And that person, most likely, was a fellow traveller and she hated them. How could anyone be so spiteful? And how could they benefit from ruining hers and Lilly's lives?

As she had done in those early days, Dot ran through the possible suspects: Pearl, Peggy, Thelma, June … Not Nancy now, according to

Lilly. But perhaps Violet? She might have been released from prison, but, if the powers-that-be were so fond of double-bluffing, couldn't it be true that they had released Violet to test her, to see whether she was still at it?

Ugh.

The whole thing made her feel mystified and furious.

When the cold began to bite, Dot came in, heading for the cafeteria to grab some breakfast. On the promenade deck she rounded a corner, bumping into Pearl, strolling arm in arm with Paul.

'My God! Dot! I thought ... So you're aboard?' Pearl pulled away from Paul, taking a step back. 'I was told you got a telegram from your beau...'

'False alarm.' Dot hoped she sounded convincing. 'I'm surprised to see you here, Paul.'

'Working the round trip but...' Paul leaned in and said sotto voce: 'New World beckons.'

'If the authorities know about that telegram, Dot,' said Pearl earnestly, 'you realise they won't let you disembark.'

'I'll take my chances.' Dot crossed her fingers behind her back. 'Like Paul.'

As Dot turned the corner, she heard Pearl hiss, 'Don't let her know! The fewer in on this the better.'

Dot stopped in her tracks and tiptoed back to listen. Barbara had joined them.

'Meeting at five,' said Pearl in a low voice. 'Third-class cinema. It's all roped off. In there no one will hear our homage to Berlin.'

Dot stifled a gasp and crept forward to hear better.

'Are there many of us?' Barbara asked.

'Quite a few. But as you know, you're either one of us or you're not. We don't want the captain finding out what we're planning. That would put the kibosh on everything.'

'I'm nervous,' said Barbara. 'I'm not sure where I'll find the space to prepare my ligatures.'

Berlin? Secret gatherings? Ligatures? What was going on? Dot ran swiftly down the stairs to C deck and the dull safety of her cabin. While the Norfolk girls wittered on about cockles and crabs and how they'd heard American mustard was nothing on the local stuff, Dot tried to digest what she had overheard.

If only Lilly was here to confide in. Had she accidentally stumbled on the most terrible plot? Should she go to the captain? Or would he laugh at her? She knew she had to investigate further before telling anyone else.

A rustle of paper under the door. The girls scrambled to pick up the small yellow envelope. They sighed and looked up at Dot.

'For you.'

Another telegram. What would this one reveal? Dot had no plans to read it in front of them, so jumped down and laced up her shoes.

A minute or two later a swift knock and, as she went to open, another envelope appeared on the carpet.

The three girls squealed in anticipation.

Dot looked down at the name, hoping it was for them. But it wasn't.

She let herself out, glimpsing the back of the bellboy disappearing round the corner. Perched on the top step of the nearest staircase, Dot opened the most recent telegram.

'Bon voyage, darling … Thinking of you.' Her eyes darted down to the sender's name. 'Mammy and Pop xxx.' She held it to her heart for a second before tearing into the next.

'I told you. Stay in UK. Angry. Howard.'

Another frisson of horror, before she remembered that Lilly told her to look out for the office of origin. OKL again. Oklahoma. She double-checked her parents' telegram. LIV 4. In other words, Walton, Liverpool.

So who was in Oklahoma? Could it be Howard? Surely not. And what was the point of sending a telegram to the ship telling her to stay in the UK when she was already on board? Was someone who had been at the camp and who was now on board been telegraphing someone in Oklahoma who then sent these?

'Penny for them?'

June and Violet were heading down from above.

Dot crammed the telegrams into her pocket and hastily stood.

'Escaping from my cabin mates.'

'Mothers or pukers?' asked Violet.

'Homesick whingers.'

'Oh dear,' June laughed. 'What were you reading? Not bad news, I hope.'

'Good wishes from my parents,' said Dot, gripping the papers in her pocket.

'Up in the lounge there's some woman giving a talk on American etiquette,' said Violet. 'We managed to escape.'

'I was heading up to take a stroll out on deck,' said Dot.

'Wouldn't bother, love,' replied Violet. 'It's Nappy Central. Strung up from every chair and railing. It's so white at first I thought it had snowed.'

'It's mean, isn't it,' said June, 'that they wouldn't let anyone wave us off yesterday. Now they want to bore us to tears with these incessant talks. Where's the fun?'

'Fun's forbidden,' said Violet. 'They don't like fun. They imagine fun is beetle drives and bingo.' Violet gave a mock yawn.

'Still,' said Dot. 'Three days, we'll be in New York.'

She noticed them exchange a look.

Just after five Dot made her way up the lino-clad forward stairs to B deck and the disused third-class cinema. The conspirators couldn't have picked a more obscure corner. Even the overhead lamps had been disconnected. She ducked under the red rope. Tiptoeing along the dark hall, she could hear Pearl's voice coming from a room at the end. So she had found the right place. Suddenly, Dot heard footsteps clattering down the stairs behind her, so darted through the nearest door, holding it open an inch to spy out. Barbara bustled past, bearing a long black case. What was inside? A gun? A sword?

When she had gone in, Dot followed, pressing her ear to the wooden door to listen.

'Sorry I'm late,' Barbara said. 'Kids! My turn to murder some good men. Is that the plural?'

The others in the room laughed. Dot estimated there were around twelve of them.

'It all goes off 9 p.m., Saturday. Agreed?'

'Night before we arrive, right?'

'There's no way they can stop us then. They'll be too busy prepping the debarkation and won't have the means to thwart our mutiny.'

The women cheered, but Pearl hushed them. 'Cave, girls.'

Cave! A simple 'beware'!

'Couldn't sleep a wink last night,' said Pearl. 'Too psyched up.'

'How deep is the ocean?' asked another woman whose voice Dot didn't recognise.

What the hell? Were they planning to sink the ship?

'Right, girls…' Pearl's voice. 'We'll start by massacring the canteen … One, two, three, four…'

Without considering the consequences, Dot pushed open the door and ran in.

Paul, who was standing just inside, tried to prevent her getting any further. She struggled with him, but over his shoulder, she saw the semicircle of women sitting staring at her. They each held a musical instrument. In the centre, Pearl perched at her drum kit.

'Oh, darling!' she said. 'This was going to be a surprise to cheer you up.'

The other women lowered their trumpets, trombones, saxophones, a guitar, a bass. Barbara held a clarinet to her lips and played a mocking riff.

'I thought…'

Pearl raised a finger to her lips. 'Don't tell *anyone*. When we asked permission, we were given a round "no". So I decided we'd do it anyway. A bit of a knees-up before parting company.'

'Paying homage to Berlin?' asked Dot, for clarification.

'Irving Berlin … and Ellington, Goodman, Strayhorn, Porter.'

It all made sense. 'How Deep is the Ocean', by Irving Berlin.

'You're massacring "Canteen Bounce"?'

'Opening number.'

*

In the cabin on the last night, under the fish-eyed stares of the Norfolk three, Dot did her hair and make-up.

'Why are you getting all tarted up?' asked the plump one.

'Just fancied it,' Dot replied.

'Liverpudlians are weird,' said the blonde girl on the opposite top bunk.

Dot wondered if she was weird. After all, she was on this ship despite having received a telegram telling her not to come, and if that really was a fake, she was on the trail of someone she had no way of exposing. She'd even suspected the band. Even if she had a hunch that June, Peggy, Thelma or Violet had it in for her and Lilly, as well as hiding Nazi sympathies, what was she to do? If she marched up to one of these women and asked them outright, they were hardly going to say yes, were they? How she wished Lilly was here to help her sleuth. But all she could do was keep her ears and eyes open and hope that Lilly was right.

She had no trouble finding the pretend ballroom. The band was warming up with a little 'Moonlight Serenade', the music swirling down the corridor.

Two cross-looking Red Cross matrons stood in the corridor, peering in and tutting, but doing nothing to stop it. In fact, Dot noticed their feet tapping in rhythm.

At one of the few tables, Nancy sat chatting with June, Thelma and a girl with red hair done up in a fancy chignon.

'Do you think they'll remember us?' asked Thelma.

'Who?'

'Our husbands. It all seems so long ago. Like a dream.'

'I bloody hope so. If my Sydney can't remember *me*, he should retire to a monastery. Talking of monasteries…' Nancy pulled a bottle from beneath her coat. 'Look what I managed to lay my hands on. A magnum of Minnehaha! Invented by monks, you know, so it has to be legal.' She whispered, 'I know we're not supposed to speak to the boys in the crew, but, apart from us, they seem to be the only people on board who haven't spent the last four days spewing their guts up. And those same boys hold the keys to the store cupboards! Paul is off getting us glasses, more booze, and even … drum roll … some snacks.' Seeing Dot, Nancy pulled up a chair beside her. 'Hooray! You escaped from the Norfolk broads!'

'At last.' Dot laughed.

'This is Maisie Froncek,' Nancy yelled above the music. 'She's wangled us another bottle of first grade pop.'

Another gaggle of women came tentatively to the door, peeked in, squealed and came in to join the fun.

Pearl's band struck up another of Dot's favourites: 'Sing, Sing, Sing'.

'Come on!' Dot jumped to her feet. 'How can anyone sit during this?' Taking a swig of champagne, she strode onto the dance floor. She knew everyone was wondering what she was playing at being here after that telegram. She had no idea what tomorrow would bring. Meanwhile, there was nothing to do but make the most of *now*. And, after all, this was the number which introduced her to Howard down at Charing Cross tube.

As the tune ended, Paul arrived bearing a large tray of sandwiches. 'Managed to finagle this lot. Shove up, gals…'

'Shouldn't you be working, Paul?'

'It's almost ten o'clock. I get off first thing tomorrow. What are they going to do? Keelhaul me? Make me walk the plank? Wrap your gobs round these.'

'It's lovely to have you back, Paul,' said June. 'In Tidworth we were served by German POWs.'

'*Achtung*, baby!' said Paul. 'Bet that was fun.'

'Peggy was attacked in the shower.'

'Is that right, Pegs?'

'He followed me in and, oh, his hands were everywhere. Luckily Lilly saved me.'

'I hear Lilly didn't have the right paperwork or something. Immigration bureaucracy is a devil.' Paul passed along plates of pineapple chunks, raisins and nuts. 'Now let's raise a glass and thank heaven all that nastiness is over.'

'All that Naziness, you mean?' Nancy swigged back her champagne.

Dot surveyed the faces around the table: June, Violet, Peggy, Thelma. Could one of them be a Nazi sympathiser? Or perhaps it was one of the women in the band, Pearl or Barbara.

As though to interrupt her thoughts, Nancy said loudly: 'What now?'

'Husbands game. Come on,' said Norah. 'Where did you meet your beau? I'll go first. Kardomah Café, Bristol. Over a Bath bun. John was a marine. In real life he runs an ice cream parlour in Holly, Colorado.'

'What about you?' Norah pointed at Dot.

'First night of the Baby Blitz. Platform of Charing Cross tube. He'd brought a gramophone. We danced to "I'll Be Seeing You".'

'Romantic! Nancy?'

'Dancing at Rainbow Corner. Sydney was army. In real life he owns a farm…'

'As far as the eye can see,' all six Rainbow Corner women choired.

'I went out with Sydney before her,' said Violet. 'But that was before I discovered my Virgil. He was a military policeman, but in real life he's a … police sergeant! And he lives in somewhere called Needles, which for me is appropriate, given that I'm a seamstress.'

Peggy hastily got up and left the table.

'We'll puke again…' sang Nancy. 'Don't know where, don't know when…'

'June?' asked Norah. 'Husband?'

'Same as them. Rainbow Corner. Art lured me with his donuts.'

'Is that a euphemism?' Maisie laughed. 'Very good reason to get hitched, I'd say. Paul?'

'Wouldn't you like to know? I'll give you one guess. Rainbow Corner.'

'Is she on board, Paul? Do we know her?' asked Norah.

'Let's just say my paramour is waiting for me in New York City.'

Nancy poured another round.

'Who hasn't had a turn?'

'Me,' said Maisie. 'And no. Not Rainbow Corner, which sounds delightful, but till I met you lot I'd never heard of the place. Mike and I met in a field hospital near a town called Erfurt.'

'Whose fart?' said Paul, pointing at Violet, then Dot. ''Ers? Or 'ers?'

'Anyhow, whoever's furt it was, it was a grim night. April '45, remember? Lots of casualties being sent back from the front. We were so near Berlin we felt we could touch it.' Maisie put her fingers up to her mouth. 'I shouldn't laugh. So, I'm looking after the wounded. At the end of my shift, I head down to the Clubmobile for a bite of supper. This louche type's hanging around, handsome, but dodgy ... He's got a limp. Injury on the phoney side, if you ask me. But he'd convinced the doc at the battle lines, so he was released back to safety. He tried chatting me up.'

'And reader, I married him,' said Nancy.

'No, no!' Maisie held up her hands. 'That ain't the hubby. Hear me through. I'm about to go to bed when this girl runs into the hospital tent, hysterical, screaming for a doctor to come to her tent. I wouldn't do, so I had to wake up the MO. Meanwhile I tried to shake some sense out of her.'

'This is a very long story, Maisie,' said Paul. 'I hope it's got a punchline.'

'Hold your horses. So, the bloke with the phoney limp had seduced the little nurse, and in the middle of it all, collapsed on top of her with a heart attack. She knew right away he was dead and had to haul herself out naked from under him. She was in quite a state.'

'Oh, my Gawd.' Violet fanned herself with an empty plate. 'Can you imagine! It's made me come over all queer!'

'Watch yourself, Vi,' said Paul.

'Anyhow, that MO was one Dr Mike Froncek, from Harrisburg, PA. He got the poor girl a new billet. Together we roped off the tent where the dead bloke lay, and kept guard till the MPs got there early next morning. Mike fetched us brandy from the medics cabinet, and handed it over, saying: "You'll be needing a stiff one after our brief encounter with the stiff" ... "With a stiffy," I added. We laughed. Staff stuffed after stiff stifles ... You get it. Neither of us could let the game go. And that's how I got to know the most gorgeous, beefy, brave, manly hubby. All that plus an IQ *and* a mean sense of humour.'

'What happened to the dead bloke?' Nancy knocked back the rest of her glass and started tearing at the metal collar of the next bottle with blood-red nails.

'Taken off and buried somewhere behind the lines, along with all the poor boys who fell in battle.' Maisie raised her glass. 'So here's a toast! To the stiff with a stiffy whose demise brought my hubby and me together. His name was—'

'Oh no!' Paul gripped the table and lurched forward. 'Stop! Stop! Maisie. No more. Stop there.'

'His name was funny too when you think about it. I know you're all dying to hear ... Oakewood.'

Silence. No one looked at Dot.

Somewhere in the middle of the tale she had feared it might be Otis.

'Thank you, Paul, for attempting to stop the name coming out,' she said. 'I know everyone wants to protect me. But I'm not a baby, I'm a fully grown woman who was seduced by flattery. Not the first, not the last. Thank you, Maisie. In many ways this has given me the ending I needed for him. You see, Maisie, I too was seduced by Lieutenant Oakewood. More fool me.'

'I'm sorry, Dot. I didn't realise...'

'I was told he'd died bravely on the battlefield. That was my one last worry. The fear that there might have been *some* decency behind the glittering façade. But this sordid little tale has taken a huge burden from my mind, so thank you, Maisie. My only regret is that I didn't work it out much earlier myself and save myself a lot of pain.'

Nancy grabbed Dot's hand.

'We can't have our last night ending like this, Dot. Come on, darling. Let's dance!' She dragged Dot to her feet.

The number was a slowish one. Nancy put her arm around Dot's waist and pulled her close enough to talk into her ear.

'Mea culpa. I thought that Maisie dame would be fun. Didn't realise she came loaded with that bunkum.'

'I'm over Otis. It's Howard I worry about. I'm praying he's not the same.'

'Dot, listen to me.' Nancy pulled her closer. 'If it doesn't happen, it's not meant to be. Like me and Edward Cornell. That could never have worked, even though, in my dreams, it did. One day I'll tell you why.'

'I hope I've not been twice duped.'

'I'll be honest. Tomorrow *could* be ghastly. But think of poor Liz Webb. It's not the end of the world. Keep positive. If they send you back, it'll be on a ship without nappies!'

Dot laughed. She hoped she would still be laughing tomorrow night.

THIRTY-FOUR

THE *QUEEN MARY* STEAMED up the Hudson at dawn. Dot had stood alone on deck for hours, watching the approaching skyline in the cold darkness, fearing what might come next.

A welcoming flotilla of tugs surrounded the ship as she passed the Statue of Liberty and pulled into her berth. By the time the ship docked, the decks were crammed with hordes of women jumping up and down, yelling, trying to get a glimpse of their husbands on the quay and marvelling at the famed New York skyline, the Empire State soaring high above the mist, the Chrysler Building glittering like a sixpence in the morning sun. Down on the pier a band played 'I'm a Yankee Doodle Dandy'.

Being surrounded by such unbounded jollity only added to the fear gripping Dot's heart.

'Look, there's Tony!' Everyone around Dot waved down at the little guy in the wide-lapelled suit and trilby hat, who stood wielding a large hand trolley painted with the logo 'Caruso's Famed Hot Dogs'.

'Aren't the husbands meant to wait for the wives inside at some holding centre?' asked June. 'That's what I read in the instruction pack. Why are so many here?'

'I barely recognised him from above.' Paul suddenly started waving frantically. 'HEY! I can't get his attention!'

'Whose attention?'

'Marty's!'

In full uniform, complete with white MP helmet, Marty stood on the quay, looking perplexed. Violet leaned over the rails, cupped her hands and roared: 'Oi! Marty!'

He still didn't hear.

An announcement came over the ship's loudspeakers, but, with the noise of shouting and the band, which was now blasting out 'Here Comes the Bride', no one had a clue what had been said.

Picking up her valise, Dot pulled out her papers and passport and joined the crowd surging down the stairs. Her mouth was dry.

'Come on, Dot,' yelled Nancy, linking arms. 'Time to face the music.'

At the open door to the gangway, officers stood checking off names.

Dot presented her label, still attached to her collar.

The officer waved her forward.

A shout: 'Wait!'

She turned.

But the officer was holding up a hand to stop Paul.

'Aren't you staff?'

'Yes.' Paul stepped forward and grabbed Dot's valise. 'This lady was feeling a little faint so I said I'd carry her case and assist her down to the quay.'

The officer reluctantly let him pass, a suitcase in either hand.

'They can't understand our accents,' Paul whispered into Dot's ear, thrusting her forward down the gangway. 'He had no idea what I just said.'

They followed the crowd pushing into the immigration hall.

Violet, Nancy and Pearl were ahead of them, shoving a path through.

'Hello, sailor!' Marty stepped forward and swiped the case out of Paul's hand.

'Give that back, you swine! It's Dot's. It's my prop. They're trying to get me back on board. Take this one. Pretend it's yours.' Paul handed him the other case as Marty flung his arm round Paul's neck and pulled him over.

'Enough with the quarter nelsons,' quipped Paul. 'I'm not joking. Listen.'

'Mr Paul Rigby. Please return to the ship.' A voice over the loudspeaker inside the hall, competing with 'Stars and Stripes Forever'.

'Paul Rigby? I have him!' Marty shouted, whipping his handcuffs from his belt and applying them to Paul's wrists. 'He's under arrest.'

'What are you doing?' Paul tried to pull away, but he was clamped.

'No one's going to stop *me* leading you away now, are they, honey?' Marty tapped his white tin hat. 'Not dressed like this.'

Paul handed Dot her case, murmuring into her ear, 'There are war brides, love, and war brides.'

To Violet, Marty said: 'Like I said, we've all got something in common – we're all flowers, by name, profession or inclination…'

'A Lilly, a Violet, a Snowdrop and a…' Violet started laughing.

'As they say in Olde England,' said Paul, waving his cuffs.

'Pansy!' said Marty and Paul in unison. 'Bye, all!'

Nancy pulled close to Dot.

'So far, so good…'

Dot's heart was thundering. Every step seemed fraught with threat.

'Brides for beyond New York, travelling by train, this way.' An official stood by a dividing rope, steering women either side.

'Here we go.' Nancy led Dot towards the roped-off area marked 'Train Only'. 'Onwards, girl.'

To one side, sporting her label on her ample bosom, Barbara climbed up onto the dais, children at her side, baby in arms.

'Caruso?' A man read Barbara's label and shouted to the room. 'Caruso?' Tony jumped up to join them. He picked up each child, kissed it, ran down the steps and placed it gently inside the hot dog stand. Once his arms were free, he grabbed Barbara and kissed her for a good minute, then they strolled out of the hall without looking back.

Dot waved, but Nancy pushed her forward.

'Hey! You! Nurse Gallagher, isn't it?' A man leaned over the ropes and grabbed hold of Dot's arm.

Gallagher! Her maiden name. Her number was up. This was it. She was to be returned to England, already considered single again. She put up her hands in surrender.

'I'm looking for my wife,' said the man. 'She didn't write ahead, but I heard y'all were arriving today, so…'

'I can't help, really.' Dot breathed again. 'If they're for New York, the wives' names get read out from the stage.'

'But I know you, nurse. You once put a bandage on my finger. She worked at Rainbow Corner too. Name of Liz Webb.'

'Oh no!' Dot stood stunned. 'I…'

'Come with me.' Nancy gently took the man's arm and led him aside. Dot watched her give him the terrible news, then point to a Red Cross van outside the hall.

The loudspeaker boomed.

'Buses for Penn Station for out-of-towners travelling by train are waiting, ready to board.'

'Poor man.' Nancy rushed back to Dot's side. 'What dreadful luck.'

'You'd think someone would have let him know.'

'Stop gossiping, you two,' screeched a woman pushing towards the open door. 'Or we'll miss the ruddy train.'

Dot pressed forward, dragged by the crowd.

'Hey,' said Violet, reaching them. 'I've lost June, Thelma and Peggy.'

'Probably having a last retch, for good luck,' said Nancy. 'Anyone got a fag?' She leaned into Dot to whisper, 'All going well. We're almost in the bus.'

An official stepped in front of them and held up one hand.

'Stop here!'

Dot could barely breathe.

'That bus is full. Wait for the next one to come round.'

The crowd stood still.

'Hi, girls!' Earl leaned over the rope barrier. 'Where's Pearl got to?'

'Over there, waiting for you,' yelled Violet, pointing back towards the dais. 'Go claim her.'

Pearl stood on the steps to the stage, arguing with an official. Earl pushed through. They watched him thrusting paper after paper up to the official's sour face.

'She cannot enter the USA.' Two guards were yelling, pushing Pearl through the door leading back to the ship. 'Her permit to enter is invalid.'

Pearl turned and shouted: 'Me or America, Earl?' before the official dragged her away, and slammed the door after her.

'Any reason I can't desert my own country?' Earl asked the official.

'We can stop her entering the USA but can't prevent you leaving.'

'Where's the ticket office? I'm off to buy me a passage to England.' Earl ran along the rope barrier, passing Dot, Nancy and Violet. 'Got no clothes, no nothing,' he said. 'Just what I'm standing in. You can buy clothes. You can't buy love.'

'Nancy Olsen, Violet King, June Pemberton, Peggy Jaeger-Smith, Thelma Johnson … this way.' A Red Cross woman called their names and ticked them off a list. 'Straight through and onto the bus. Where are Pemberton and the others?'

A scream from behind and the three women surged forward, holding their hands in the air to get the woman's attention.

'We're here! We're here!'

June, Peggy and Thelma passed through.

Dot took a step forward.

'Not you.'

Dot shot a look to Nancy. 'I knew it was too good to be true.'

Nancy asked the woman: 'What about her? Dot Hopkins should be on that list.'

The woman ran her bony finger down the list. 'Hopkins? Wrong line. She's wanted in the superintendent's office.'

The Red Cross woman unhooked the rope and pushed Dot to the other side.

Dot felt numb. Now that her fears were confirmed, what else was there to feel.

'Bye, everyone,' she said quietly. She had no tears to cry, just a sense of dull resignation.

'I need to go with her.' Nancy grabbed Dot's hand across the ropes.

You can't,' said the Red Cross woman. 'You're a train woman.'

'I am,' said Nancy.

'Then off you go to the train.'

'I want to accompany my friend.'

'She is a grown woman. I'm sure she can find her way.' Hands on hips, the woman rounded on Nancy. 'Your name has already been called, Mrs Olsen, to go forward to the bus.' The woman pointed to the open doorway, then pushed Dot back towards the sign which said: 'Embarkation'.

How could she have been mistaken in Howard? He had seemed so true and noble. Her hopes smashed, Dot walked slowly towards the same door through which Pearl had been pushed.

'Hurry along there, Hopkins.' Another woman pushed Dot to the door of the superintendent's office.

Dot entered.

'What now?' Sitting behind a desk stacked with mounds of papers in metal trays, the manager peered up over his steel-rimmed half-specs.

'The Hopkins woman for you.'

The man lay down his pen and leaned back in his chair. 'Trying to avoid us, Mrs Hopkins?'

'I wasn't aware I needed to come this way.'

The supervisor waved a hand at the Red Cross woman. 'Thank you, Miss Jones. You may go.'

She went.

'Mrs Hopkins. Were you not given a message on board the ship ordering you to come straight here?'

'No.'

'You can't slip past Miss Jones's beady eye, my dear. She's a veritable dragon.' He pulled open a drawer and rooted about in it. 'It's about your husband. He contacted us because…'

So it *was* true. Howard *had* sent the telegrams. He was making sure Dot went back. It was over.

'He didn't want you to get on the train…' The superintendent slammed the drawer shut.

'I know,' said Dot. 'He didn't want me to go any further…'

'Exactly!' The superintendent knelt down and pulled open the bottom drawer. 'It's in here somewhere…' He tilted the desk lamp over the edge to see better. 'We don't usually do things like this, but in the case of Colonel Hopkins … quite the war hero … we wouldn't want to disoblige him…'

'Do I go straight back to the ship or can I say goodbye to my friends first?'

'I have to give you this.' The man pulled out an envelope, sat back onto his chair and pushed it across the desk. She recognised Howard's bold, clear hand. She pulled at the flap to open it. 'You've no time to read it now, Mrs Hopkins. You have to get on the…'

'Ship?' said Dot.

At the same time, the superintendent said, 'Train.'

THIRTY-FIVE

SIX DAYS EARLIER

'A car will arrive shortly to take you to the railway station, Miss Deane.' The sergeant slapped a travel pass from Salisbury to Waterloo into Lilly's hand.

Earlier, feeling at once powerless and furious, Lilly had watched the other women being herded onto buses and driven away to the ship. Who had decided that the paperwork, planned so meticulously by Jack, was null and void? And why?

Lilly sat in the same bus shelter she had sat in with Dot and tried to piece it all together. She was certain this had to be linked with the trouble at Rainbow Corner. A last desperate attempt to keep her and Dot off the trail.

When the car arrived, Lilly jumped up and put her suitcase in the boot.

She opened the door to get in and saw that the driver was Gloria Fergusson.

'Good morning, Miss Deane,' Fergusson said loudly. 'Salisbury Station, I gather?'

Fergusson patted the front passenger seat, so Lilly climbed in next to her. Fergusson waved gaily at the guard on the gate and turned the car into the lane indicating Salisbury.

When Lilly tried to start conversation, Fergusson simply said, 'Not yet.' So they drove in silence for twenty minutes. As they came into Salisbury, Fergusson asked Lilly if she fancied being disobedient.

Worried this was a test, Lilly asked in what way, to which Fergusson replied: 'Check over your shoulder. Are there any army vehicles behind us?'

She could see only private cars.

'Then let's go!' said Fergusson, grinding the gears and driving past the slip road to the station. She skidded around the roundabout and turned onto the Southampton road.

'If only you had phoned earlier,' Fergusson said. 'Why didn't you?'

'I only knew yesterday evening and you had already left the office,' Lilly said. 'Are we heading for the *Queen Mary*?'

'Heading for it, yes,' replied Fergusson. 'But she sails at four.'

Lilly glanced at her watch. 'It's already half past three.'

'I am aware.'

Fergusson drove like Jehu. At twenty past four, the car hurtled through the dock gate and pulled up with screeching tyres.

But the Cunard quay was empty.

The *Queen Mary* had sailed.

Lilly's brief moment of hope died.

'Back to London?'

'Absolutely not,' replied Fergusson. 'I was supposed to be on board, myself. One of the guardians. I missed it, Miss Deane, because I made this detour to save you.'

'Sorry.'

'What are *you* sorry for?' asked Fergusson. 'You were stitched up. Having led us a merry dance, the person responsible is now happily on board. I am determined that we don't let them get away with it.'

'But how...?'

Lilly wondered whether Fergusson knew about Dot. She told her about the last-minute telegram from Oklahoma.

'Not genuine?'

'Don't think so. But I imagine the partner in crime must be in Oklahoma. And our woman has sailed to meet him. I suppose the Oklahoma partner has to be a "him".'

Fergusson nodded. 'Well deduced. So we have one person to find and they are merrily sailing away down the Solent without us.'

'I can't bear to let them get away with it.'

'Nor me. And that is why we have to find a way to get on board.' Fergusson grabbed her handbag from the floor of the car. 'Get the cases out of the boot. Hurry!'

Fergusson marched towards the harbour master's office.

Lilly waited at the water's edge, watching tugboats steaming up the water.

What was Fergusson planning? To row the Atlantic? To swim? Lilly doubted they'd get very far in a tug, or even the small white boat tied up near where she stood.

Then a man clad in a yellow sou'wester rushed out of the harbour master's office, and jumped over the narrow strip of water onto the white boat.

'On you go!' shouted Fergusson, following that man. 'Throw the cases on!'

Minutes later Lilly and Fergusson were huddled together in the wheelhouse of the pilot boat heading down the Solent towards the Nab Tower.

'Don't do this often: putting late passengers on board,' said the skipper from the wheel. 'You must have a lot of clout.'

'I do,' replied Gloria. 'But as you have to go out to the ship anyway to collect the pilot, I surmised there would be no problem.'

Ahead of them a tiny dot grew, until they recognised the grey outline of the *Queen Mary*. Soon the white boat was bumping alongside its hull.

A door low in the side of the ship opened. A man in oilskins stepped out and climbed down a short ladder onto the boat. Fergusson and Lilly gave him a curt 'good evening' before climbing up the same ladder and going aboard. The skipper threw their cases in after them.

'I'm afraid, Lilly dear, you only have me for company. All our meals will be brought to us in our cabins.'

'I can't go out and surprise my friends?'

'We're going to give them a much bigger surprise in Chicago. If the guilty party is heading for Oklahoma or nearby, they must be travelling on the connecting train. We're going to give them a massive surprise. Meanwhile, we're not here. We've been put in special cabins well away from the brides.'

During the voyage Lilly occasionally heard sounds of laughter through the open porthole; sometimes she heard women chatting as they swayed along the corridor outside her cabin. Fergusson gave her a newspaper. In her boredom Lilly read every word. It was on the last page that she saw a small article about some traitors who had been picked up and interned since the end of the war.

On the list was Sir Martin Luther Everard Bough of Brunswick Terrace, Brighton. Brunswick Terrace? Could that have been the destination of the packet Otis had delivered on Lilly's first day in London? She tore out the cutting to show Dot when they met.

As soon as the ship docked in New York, Fergusson and Lilly were taken off through the crew exit, bundled into a taxi and driven to Penn Station. There they boarded the *Broadway Limited* as paying passengers. At dinner Fergusson told Lilly that Pearl Young had been refused entry at New York immigration, due to information passed on by someone on board the *Queen Mary*.

'It's obvious to see the motivation,' Fergusson explained as they sat in the club car having an evening drink. 'Mixed marriage is something these types are violently opposed to.'

'Have you any idea who?'

'Have you?'

Lilly thought back to how she had suspected everyone, including Fergusson herself, and remained silent.

'I've laid traps, false information...' said Fergusson. 'Troop movements which weren't going to happen, faked-up names of high-ranked soldiers who were due to be leading non-existent units.'

'The carbon copies in the wastepaper?'

'Exactly. When we heard that that very information being transmitted as fact by Nazi sympathisers, we were certain there was a traitor in Rainbow Corner,' Fergusson explained. 'On the whole, we knew who those sympathisers were, and had people in adjacent apartments taping them – or else, with the rich ones, we planted girls in their homes as maids to fiddle with their equipment and relay back the names of anyone who attended their secret meetings.' Fergusson laughed. 'Nancy did it but had to be pulled out after a day because she got too flip with them.'

'I can't imagine Nancy fitting the bill as a maid.'

'No. But she has a very sharp memory so she did get us a long list of names.'

'Those people had radio equipment in their homes?'

'Oh yes. Many of them were quite well off, and exceedingly well connected. Some had knocked around with King Edward before the abdication.'

Lilly tried to imagine the types. Quite possibly she had encountered them with her parents.

'For a while I had wondered whether General Smith was involved, so I had him moved on, citing other more obvious reasons, of course. But after Jack was installed in the office it continued in much the same way, so my suspicions appeared unfounded.'

'How did you know it continued?' Lilly realised that exposing a mole was a tricky business.

'Half the time these despicable collaborators thought they were sending info to the Nazi military intelligence services, the Abwehr, but in fact they were radioing everything to our people in St James's. We knew about Brunswick Terrace and Onslow Square long before the owners were picked up.'

'Lieutenant Oakewood delivered a packet to Brunswick Terrace before meeting me on the train from Brighton.'

'Correct. And what he delivered was a whole package about US troops arriving at Rainbow Corner from the north, taken from my wastepaper basket.'

'And Onslow Square was the place Joe talked about to Dot.'

'That's right. When I realised that Dot knew about the business from an external source, I arranged for her to be away for a few weeks, so as not to muddy the waters. Unfortunately at that point, our Rainbow Corner suspects went to ground.'

'Will we ever discover them?'

'It's why we're on this journey.'

A whistle blew and the train pulled out of Penn Station.

*

Now that she had read Howard's loving letter, Dot was exhilarated by the train, which was nothing like the sleeper from Euston to Liverpool. This one had a long corridor of bunks, a café car, even a sitting room. Dot loved the mournful wail of the horn, the clanking bells and the melancholy feel of those sounds. The rhythm of the wheels was like a jazz beat counterpointed with the discordance of the whistle.

Tall buildings flashed by, neon signs flickering their wares. The city lights were replaced with rows of electric pylons and tall striped chimneys billowing out smoke, then gradually trees and wide open spaces. Sitting with the other women in the café car, sipping coffees, Dot told how her two telegrams had been a hoax. She watched them with a beady eye, wondering which among them was responsible.

She had tried a little test. As the telegrams had come from Oklahoma, she asked everyone where their beaux lived, but the answers were

Arizona, Texas, New Mexico, California ... so many states. No one said Oklahoma.

Howard had posted his chatty letter the same day as the second fake telegram arrived on board. He was going on location, he wrote, filming a Western. A small role but maybe he might jump the train somewhere along the line. He gave a hotel phone number where, if Dot had a minute when they were changing trains at Chicago tomorrow, she could call him. He also wrote over and over how he loved her and how he longed for them to be together again.

On the other side of the aisle, Maisie was again regaling everyone about her manly, handsome, wise doctor husband, Mike. Dot could barely wait for Harrisburg, Pennsylvania, so that they'd hear no more of him, and the ghost of Otis would leave the train with her.

Half an hour later: 'Next stop: Harrisburg. All passengers detraining please make your way to the doors. Don't forget your belongings. Don't want your gloves sailing on to Chicago, ladies. Baggage claim inside the station. Harrisburg! Harrisburg, next stop!'

Maisie pressed her face to the window trying to get a glimpse of Mike.

'You need to get down to the door, Maisie.' Nancy snatched up Maisie's valise. 'It's the other end. Hurry. Come on, Dot.'

Dot was reluctant to go, but Nancy gave her such a huge wink she followed anyway.

As they arrived in the vestibule, the guard pushed open the door. 'Wait there, ladies!'

He jumped down onto the platform and laid down a small set of steps.

'You two ladies alighting?'

'We're helping our friend,' said Nancy, marching down, suitcase in hand. 'Don't go without us.'

'Make sure to listen out for the whistle, girls.'

'Righto, sir.' Dot gave a mock salute.

Neon arc lights threw a ghostly hue on the few people waiting on the platform.

Further up the train, paying passengers climbed off. More were standing patiently ready to board.

Nancy peered either way. 'I see no handsome hunk.'

'Where's Maisie?' Dot looked back into the train. The vestibule was empty. 'Do you think she's changed her mind? Shall we bang on the window?'

The guard looked at his watch.

Suddenly a train standing on the adjacent track blew off a large amount of steam, fogging the platform. Dot and Nancy jumped, laughing in surprise.

'I'm going to look for her.' Dot ran alongside the train on tiptoe, yelling Maisie's name.

Seeing men inside, Dot realised she had run the wrong way. There was a woman who looked exactly like Gloria Fergusson! Then Lilly. But how? She waved but they weren't looking out. How could it be?

'Last call!' shouted the guard. '*Broadway Limited* to Chicago.'

Running back, Dot cupped her mouth with both hands, yelling at the top of her voice: 'MAISIE!'

A spectacled man ran towards her.

'Oh, my God!' Nancy grabbed Dot's arm. 'That's him. Tiny four-eyes with a squint.'

'Darling!' he shouted, running at Nancy, lifting his hat to reveal a bald pate. 'Maisie! You've changed your hair colour! It suits you.'

'No! No!' Nancy backed away. '*I'm* not Maisie. She's just…'

He flung his arms around Dot.

'No! Not me either. MAISIE!' Dot screamed.

Blinking, Mike halted for a moment, then ran past them, heading for the open door.

'Mike! Darling Mike!' Maisie, make-up perfect, hair neatly coiffed, stepped coyly down the three steps and ran in feminine baby steps towards Dr Mike Froncek.

'Darling!' she cried again, falling into his most unmanly arms.

The whistle blew. 'All aboard!'

'Each to his own,' muttered Nancy, grabbing Dot by the wrist and dragging her on board. 'Wow! What fun!'

Slowly the train moved off.

'Time for chow!' Nancy rolled her eyes as Norah emerged from her bunk, face once more smothered in her green face cream.

'Oh God!' laughed Norah. 'Better take it off again.'

Dot followed Nancy through the long aisle of bunk beds. Mothers sat on lower berths, tucking up their babies. Most bunks had their curtains drawn, their inhabitants already asleep.

'It's only just past eight o'clock,' whispered Nancy. 'What kind of lives do these people live?'

Dot followed Nancy into the café and sat with Thelma and June.

'I was just telling the others about my days in service.' Thelma took a bite of bread roll.

'I thought you were a nippy,' said June.

'Before that I was a domestic help. What a life those poor girls lead.'

'Is it like it is in Victorian novels?' Dot unfolded her napkin and took a bread roll. 'Did you get up in the dark and break the ice on the water you washed with?'

'Yes, actually, then we went downstairs to empty the chamber pots.' Thelma gazed up, remembering. 'The worst thing was they talked about me when I was in the room, saying "let the drudge get it!" and "the maid looks scruffy today". My mum would have said they had no manners.'

Norah arrived, slightly rouge from cream removal.

'Norah, can I try some of your face cream tomorrow?' Thelma asked. 'I want to look radiant too.'

'Bring me a jar, and I'll put a little in for tonight.'

Gales of laughter came from the next table as Nancy, performing for Peggy and Violet, embellished her description of hunky Dr Mike. 'Let's put it this way. He's so short-sighted he mistook *me* for Maisie!'

'The platform *was* kind of gloomy,' said Dot, leaning over. 'And the lights in the train so bright ... In fact, I could have sworn I saw Controller Fergusson on board this train with Lilly Deane!'

'Now there really *is* an example of a fertile imagination at work.' Nancy stretched her arm across the gangway and pressed her hand hard on Dot's thigh. 'In that shrimp in a trilby, Maisie saw Johnny Weissmuller. Now Dot sees people who can't be there. Did they fly over on Superman's back?'

Nancy squeezed again. Dot understood. They *were* there. Travelling separately.

'Mind you, I was convinced I saw Clark Gable waiting to board the train in New York too,' Dot added, to help. 'America has made us mad!'

Thelma was still talking about her life as a maid. 'There was this other girl, Rachel. A refugee, from Germany. They gave her hell.'

'Rachel is my middle name,' said Nancy. 'Nancy Rachel Olsen, née Newton. Originally Neuberger. Surname changed by my mother in the thirties ... for obvious reasons. Tell us more, Thelma.'

'I only stayed cos it was so easy to get there from my mum's place in Stepney.'

'I didn't know posh people lived in the East End?'

'It was Kensington. Right near the tube. Just off Old Brompton Road. Onslow—'

'You don't want to depress everyone, Thelma.' Peggy leaned across the aisle. 'Look what they're giving us for dessert!' She held up her menu, pointing at the words 'ice cream sundae'.

Dot knew that there was more behind this. But what? What did Thelma know? And why had Nancy suddenly admitted her changed surname? Obviously she must be Jewish and was comparing herself to Thelma's fellow maid. But why?

During the night Dot was aware of Nancy climbing out of her bunk and heading down the corridor.

She looked at her watch. One o'clock in the morning. She couldn't be suspecting everyone all the time. The poor woman obviously needed the lavatory.

Dot turned over and went back to sleep.

But a sudden jerk as the train crossed points, with clanging bell and mournful horn, woke her.

It was almost four now. Nancy was not back in her bunk. Dot didn't know whether to raise the alarm. She put on her dressing gown and went in search.

She reached the vestibule just as the train slowed down and stopped. The carriage door opened, sending in a gale of freezing air.

Nancy climbed aboard.

'What's going on?'

Nancy put a finger to her lips, drawing Dot away from the rows of bunks.

'That *was* Fergusson with Lilly,' she hissed. 'I saw them at Newark, too. They're joining us tomorrow on the *Super Chief*. We're to act surprised but not ask too many questions about how they did it. I know you're an ally, Dot. We have to smoke the bloody traitor out on this journey, or she'll get away with it. I don't know about you, but I couldn't bear that.'

Dot was relieved that Lilly had managed to make it across the Atlantic after all, and looked forward to catching up with her soon.

Nancy climbed onto her bunk and invited Dot to sit, then closed the curtains on them.

'The Old Brompton Road, near South Ken tube,' she whispered. 'I'd say remarkably near to Onslow Square.'

'She practically said it. That's where Joe saw the woman handing over papers and giving the Nazi salute,' said Dot. 'Do you think it was Thelma?'

'We need more proof.' Nancy sighed.

'One more thing.' Dot knew if she didn't ask now she never would. 'Why did you think that it wouldn't have worked with Edward Cornell? Was it because you're Jewish?'

Nancy nodded. 'I should have realised when he went on about his pal, Charles Lindbergh, a famous anti-Semite. Those elite families in New England may have money, but, despite what they think of themselves, they have no class. They'd have winkled the truth out of me and ... I dread to think. I'm an East Ender. Born in a little street just off Petticoat Lane. Father died when I was an infant. Mother was a cleaner.'

Dot looked at this super elegant woman, with her BBC accent and smart talk. Who would have known?

'Mum trailed me around with her at work. When I was about five, we moved down to the coast. I seemed always to be ill, and she thought I needed country air. So she took a job cleaning in a posh school in Sussex, and she helped with dinners too. Fergusson was a teacher there. She was the only person who treated us with any humanity. She invited us round for Christmas, took me in for private lessons.'

'Is that how you learned to talk so posh?' Dot found it impossible to imagine Nancy with any other accent. 'From Fergusson?'

'No, she taught me about books and art and all the important things. I picked up how to talk like this from those horrible girls and their parents. As they sneered and clicked their fingers at my mother, calling her "the skivvy" and "the plod", I drank in every nuance.'

'"The plod". How horrible,' said Dot, trying to imagine how she'd feel if someone tried this on her own mammy. 'Your poor mum.'

'I was determined to get revenge, then I realised the only way was to blend in with those vile people. I knew, even at that early age, that only if they mistook me for one of their own could I fight my mother's corner. No one was ever going to call me common.'

'That's what George said about me, Nancy. He told Lilly I sounded common, and he hoped it didn't rub off on her.'

Nancy nodded slightly.

'It's thanks to George's snobbery that I first realised Edward would end up looking down at me, hating me.'

Dot couldn't imagine anyone talking down to this sophisticated, startling woman.

'To this day I remain beady in their presence. And though I might pass for one of them, I do know I could never really be one.'

'Who'd want to?' Dot thought of her own parents, who, although they had nothing, always helped those worse off than themselves. 'I'm proud of where I came from.'

'Don't get me wrong, Dot. So am I. I'll be happy with Sydney cos he's a hick. He couldn't give two hoots about my background. Nor I his.'

'You should be an actress, Nancy. You certainly had me fooled.'

'Dear Dot.' Nancy briefly squeezed Dot's hand. 'You've got a good one in Howard. He's a true gent. For all my husband engineering, it was you, of all of us, who did best. What a catch! And you *really* deserve it. You're a great gal. Now let's get some sack time. Tomorrow could be a long day.'

PART SIX

The *Super Chief*

THIRTY-SIX

'DID YOU ENJOY YOUR hours in the Windy City?' Gloria Fergusson sipped a whisky in the brides' lounge compartment of the westbound *Super Chief*. 'My Rainbow Corner girls, together for the last time.'

Lilly had boarded the special war brides' carriage with Fergusson just before it pulled out of Chicago. While Fergusson talked to Nancy, Lilly had gone straight to Dot to whisper their plan in her ear.

'This train journey really gives you the idea of how immense this country is, doesn't it?' Fergusson cupped her drink with both hands to steady it as the train shuddered across points. 'Thirty-six hours till the end of the line.'

Having had a week to formulate their entrapment plan, Lilly couldn't believe that Gloria had decided to launch it so soon. She knew where the conversation was heading and did her part: watching faces carefully, searching for giveaway tics and uncontrollable indications, like blushes or jiggling feet.

'The longest journey I ever took was the Golden Arrow.' Nancy lit up a cigarette and took a long drag. 'London to Paris. You had to sleep on the train. Like this.'

'I went on that with my parents,' said Lilly.

'I always wanted to go on the Liverpool sleeper, but never did,' said Dot. 'This is my first.'

'I'm used to sleeping compartments,' said Peggy. 'I worked up in Scotland. We had to travel up each Christmas for hunting and again in August for the grouse season.'

'Sounds plush,' said Nancy. 'Someone very rich?'

'A duke.'

'And he paid for you to travel in the sleeper? That was kind.'

'Course not!' Peggy chuckled. 'I had to be there to make sure everything was perfect in the sleeper for his lordship. But I sat up, of course, in third class.'

'Which duke?' Fergusson asked.

'I forget. Name of some Scottish town: Crieff, Dunbar. Can't remember. Had a little castle about an hour's drive from the station.'

'A *little* castle?' Lilly cocked an eyebrow. 'I'd like to see one of those.'

'That's how *he* referred to it.'

Everyone laughed.

'He should have seen my old gaffe in the Aldwych,' said Violet. 'Posh people aren't the only ones who can lie about size. Enormous flat I had. Twelve bathrooms.'

'So *this* is where you all got to after dinner.' Norah stood at the door. 'Mind if I join you? I'm stifled by the pong of nappy changing back there.'

'Diaper changing!' the women yelled in unison.

Lilly sat back. Norah wasn't a Rainbow Corner woman, so their plan was to go on hold.

'Diaper/nappy, chips/crisps, bangs/fringe, vest/waistcoat, trunk/boot.' Norah flopped down in an empty seat. 'Why can't Americans just speak English?'

'How on earth can you possibly have caught this train, Lilly?' While Norah was taking her place, Thelma asked quietly, 'Did you fly across?'

Lilly was about to explain, when Fergusson dismissed the subject with a wave of her hand. 'Not interesting, Thelma,' she said. 'The question *I'd* be asking is why anyone wanted to *prevent* Lilly coming. Dot too. Why would anyone want to keep them away from their men?'

A steward had entered the car to pull down blinds and switch on small table lamps. Lilly was at a loss. She realised that when she and Fergusson had banged out this plan on the last train, they should have made provision for interruptions.

'I want to know about Tidworth.' Fergusson drank another swig of whisky. 'I hear there were a few episodes with prisoners of war.'

'I got into a fight with one,' said Dot.

'No, dear,' Violet interrupted. 'He got into a fight with you. I was there. I saw him. Vile sour Kraut.'

'I was referring to the lady...' Fergusson waited until the steward left the carriage, 'caught onstage with her knickers down.'

'Appalling,' said June.

'But what was *he* was up to? The prisoner of war?'

'The answer to that's pretty obvious.' Nancy took a handful of peanuts and tossed them into her mouth.

'Lilly says that Mrs Levinsky said that the POW had shown her packets of nylons and a lovely pair of high-heeled shoes. As you all know from the talks at Rainbow Corner, American women won't understand your clothing was rationed. And with your threadbare clothes and worn shoes they'll think you're ... below par. Mrs Levinsky was promised things which would make her more acceptable. Things which in England money can't buy at this time. A temptation hard to resist.'

'She didn't have to sink quite so low,' said June.

'I agree. But I was wondering how a POW could possess those items.'

'Must have brought them with him,' said Peggy.

'From the trenches?' Fergusson put her glass down. 'Highly unlikely. Presumably somebody lent them to him. I suspect that person still has them.'

Lilly noticed Peggy was anxiously twiddling her fingers. Then she started feeling around the edges of her seat. 'My wedding ring!' she cried. 'Please God, I left it in the washroom.'

She rushed out of the carriage.

'Jewish name, isn't it, Levinsky?' asked June.

'What difference does that make?' Nancy snapped.

'Perhaps the POW took against her because of it.'

'Perhaps, June, you should shut up.'

'Chicago was an interesting city, wasn't it?' said Dot, swerving an argument. 'We saw quite a lot from the bus when we changed stations, Controller Fergusson. Then while we were waiting in the station, we all phoned our husbands from booths.'

'Yes.' Nancy shot Dot a look, thanking her. 'Sydney told me there was going to be a big surprise along the route. I'm not to get off at Kansas but stay on till Albuquerque,' said Nancy. 'He said our gang's husbands will all be there. After that, everyone wanted to telephone to find out what was going on.'

'Jack's throwing a party on the platform at Albuquerque.' Lilly sipped her drink, wondering when Fergusson would get the plan going again.

'Albuquerque!' Violet sprawled back in her seat. 'What a name for a town! How would you spell that? Virgil's going to be there, I gather.'

'Howard called it a powwow,' added Dot. 'Is that an American thing?'

Peggy stood at the door, her face smeared with tears. 'My wedding ring!' she cried. 'And my little jewellery box with everything is gone from my case. I had it out just before dinner, wondering which brooch to wear.'

Everyone clasped their wrists, necks and fingers checking for their own jewellery.

'It's like one of those detective novels,' said Dot, feeling her own wedding ring with her thumb. 'A locked room.'

'Of course,' said Lilly. 'If anything was stolen on this train, it will still be here. We've not stopped.'

'Unless the thief chucked them out of the windows,' said Norah.

'What would be the point of stealing them?' Lilly shot Fergusson a glance and stood up. 'I am going to find them.'

'What business is it of yours?' June jumped to her feet. 'You can't go through our things!'

'Peggy?' Lilly strode towards the door. 'What would you suggest?'

'I want my things back,' said Peggy. 'Someone must have them.'

'Who's to say *you're* not the thief, Lilly,' said June. 'Rushing off to plant it on someone.'

'All right,' said Lilly. 'Let's find an independent witness. Should I ask a steward?'

'I'm not having no steward tootling about in my smalls,' said Violet.

'Why don't we *all* come with you, Lilly?' Nancy remained sitting. 'Safety in numbers.'

'Good idea,' said Peggy.

Everyone followed Lilly. She started by searching Peggy's bunk.

'I'm the victim,' said Peggy. 'You don't need to search my things.'

'Have to be sure, Peggy, in case you just mislaid them.'

Lilly moved on. Bride by bride, she went through the cases and beds of Dot, Nancy, Norah, then Violet before moving onto June's case.

'This is a lousy idea,' said June. 'It could be any of those mothers and children up the other end.'

'It has to be one of us,' said Peggy. 'They were at dinner. We were the *only* ones not in the dining car.'

At the next bunk Lilly unclicked the clasps on Thelma's case. After running her hands around the lining, she pulled out three pairs of nylons, still in their wrappers, followed by a pair of new high-heeled shoes.

'What are those?' Thelma gaped, open-mouthed. 'I've never seen them before.'

Lilly pulled a small pot from Thelma's washbag.

'That's the cream Norah lent me earlier.'

Lilly opened the lid. Green face cream. She inserted her finger, twirled it around and pulled out a ring.

'How did that get there?' Thelma looked at the ring, horrified. 'I didn't do it. I swear. Really!' She turned to face everyone. 'Why would I?'

'Wait a minute…' Lilly was about to close the pot when she saw something glinting. She took it out, wiped it clean and held up a Nazi lapel badge.

Dot took one look. 'Exactly the same as the one Tony found sewn into his uniform.'

Thelma was now shaking.

Lilly rooted in Thelma's bedclothes. Under the folds of a blanket lay a small box.

'My jewellery!' Peggy lurched forward and snatched it, opening to reveal a motley collection of costume jewellery.

'This has put rather a damper on the joyous evening,' said Fergusson, from the back of the gang. 'Thelma – I will need to talk to you.'

'This public shaming is enough.' Peggy stepped forward. 'I've got my things back now, Controller Fergusson. We don't need to humiliate the girl.' She looked at Thelma with scorn. 'I'm surprised and disappointed, Thelma. I took you under my wing.'

'It wasn't me, Peggy. I'm not a thief!'

'Aren't you?' Peggy looked Thelma in the eye. 'Remember, Thelma, I, of all people, know that you *are* a thief.'

Thelma looked at the floor.

'Enough.' Fergusson clapped her hands. 'No one's getting off the train overnight, so I think everyone should go to bed. We'll assemble over breakfast.'

*

Dot went to her bunk and sat there, fully clothed. This was not the end. She knew it.

'Knock, knock!' Her curtain pulled back. Lilly put her head through. 'Got a moment?'

'Come in, Lilly.' Dot was so happy to see her. 'At this rate I'll never sleep.'

Lilly climbed up and pulled the curtain across.

'Thelma!'

'I know. Understands German too. And, though she denies it, she has that connection with Brighton. And that place she was a maid – Onslow Square.'

'Hey, Dot, I almost forgot. I tore this from a newspaper to show you.' Lilly pulled out the clipping about the arrest of a traitor in Brighton and handed it to Dot. 'Weird name. Martin Luther Everard Bough, prominent member of the January Club. Brunswick Terrace, Brighton. Arrested for passing on info to the Germans. It has to be the same place.'

'Martin Luther Everard Bough, always known to friends by his initials, M. L. E.' Dot stared at the cutting. 'Do you think it's pronounced "buff" or "bow"?'

'Oh, "buff", I'd think,' said Lilly.

'M. L. E. Bough,' read Dot aloud. 'M. L. E.! Emily! Don't you get it, Lilly? M. L. E. Bough. M. L. E. Bough. Otis said the name M. L. E. Bough right in front of us that first day in Rainbow Corner. Thelma had given him some parcel she told him was for her sister, Emily, but a man took it and slammed the door in Otis's face. That was M. L. E. Emily! Being American, Otis pronounced Bough as "bow", like the bow of a ship or taking a bow at the end of a show.'

'Emily Bowe!' Lilly sat back, wide-eyed at the revelation. 'M. L. E. Bough!'

'We had the treacherous creature's name all along. M. L. E. Bough. Only we assumed it was a girl, because Otis did. And that envelope wasn't a simple gift for a sister in Brighton, it was more info from Rainbow Corner going to a different quisling after Lord Banff had been arrested. Oh, yes. Everything points to Thelma.' Lilly sat back, confident they had cracked it. 'The token, Onslow Square, German, Brighton, the shoes…'

'Yeah. The shoes.'

The shoes!

No!

Dot knew it couldn't be Thelma after all. Everything fell apart with the shoes.

'At Tidworth, Thelma *couldn't* have had the shoes.'

'I pulled them out of her case in front of you, Dot.'

'I helped her pack. No shoes nor nylons and not a chance in hell of fitting them in. There wasn't room for a handkerchief.' Dot tried to picture that first day in the canteen at Rainbow Corner when that name M. L. E. Bough had been mentioned. She felt sure Thelma wasn't there. 'You know, Lilly, it wasn't Thelma who was so worried that Otis said the name aloud…'

'Ssssshhhhhh!' Lilly put up her hand. 'What's that rustling?' They both fell silent, listening.

'The train's slowing down,' said Dot. 'What's the time?'

'Half past two,' said Lilly.

'Someone's trying to get off.' Dot inspected the schedule on the wall. 'Kansas City.'

The two women tiptoed along the corridor to the vestibule, the only exit.

Fully dressed, suitcase at her feet, hand on the handle, stood Thelma.

'Please don't try and stop me.' Thelma held up a gloved hand. 'I know I'm miles away from where I'm heading but I'll phone him to explain.'

'So, did you do it, Thelma?' asked Lilly. 'Otherwise, why run?'

'Those shoes aren't even my size. I've got the same clothing rations as everyone else. And how could I afford them on my pay? I'm a nippy, and a volunteer canteen assistant. I earned a pittance.'

With a clanging of bells and the screech of brakes, the train pulled to a stop.

Thelma picked up her case.

'Why did you ask Otis to go to Brighton?' Dot tried one last time. 'For Emily?'

'How many times? I have no sister called Emily or anything else. And I didn't have a packet to deliver. I don't even know anyone in Brighton. The terrible thing is that you can't prove you *didn't* do something, only that you did.'

The guard emerged from his cabin, yawning, pulling on his cap. 'I didn't think any of you young ladies were alighting at Kansas City!'

'She's not.' Dot grabbed Thelma's suitcase.

'I have to,' said Thelma.

'No, Thelma.' Lilly stepped forward. 'Please, sir, could we ask a favour? Might you allow her to sit next door in the main coach? Just till tomorrow morning, when we stop at La Junta?'

The guard looked dubious.

'There's been some spitefulness among the women. The poor girl is distressed. Please could you do this for me?'

Lilly palmed him a dollar note. He pocketed it, jumped off the train, then helped Thelma down. A minute or so later he was back, and the train pulled out.

'Mission accomplished,' he said. 'Now, ladies, *please* go back to bed.'

*

At dawn, Lilly was woken by chatter in the corridor.

'Thelma's gone.'

'She wasn't supposed to get off till Arizona!'

'Arizona?' Violet laughed. 'As though I know where Arizona or anywhere is. But I do have the timetable…'

'Schedule!'

'Schedule. And Arizona is any town ending Ay Zed…'

'Ay ZEE!'

'All right … and Ay Zee is hours away! It's even after Albuquerque.'

'It shows that Thelma was the thief though, doesn't it…' June lay in her bunk, leaning up on one elbow. 'That Nazi badge!' June shuddered. 'She seemed such a quiet little thing…'

'I really can't care one way or the other about the past, I'm afraid, girls.' Norah was slapping on green cream. 'It's the immediate future I'm concerned with – I need to look tip-top. In less than an hour, I'm meeting my in-laws for the first time. I'll be sad to see the back of you lot actually.' Norah spoke through a mouthful of hairgrips. 'It's been fun.' As the train jerked, Norah grabbed the bedframe, steadying herself. 'Oh, no! We're slowing down. We can't have arrived half an hour early…' She turned to the guard who was striding along towards the door. 'Tell me this isn't Lamar.'

'No, ma'am. This is Garden City. We've been whistle-stopped. Lamar in around thirty-five minutes.'

'Phew.' Norah bent down and started rearranging things in her case. 'Where's that pesky hairbrush?'

The train shuddered to a stop. A chill wind blew from the vestibule.

'Brrr!' cried Violet. 'Who opened a window?'

A gaggle of voices headed their way.

'Must be a mistake,' said the guard. 'This carriage is reserved for war brides only. Sorry, folks, you must've got into the wrong part of the train.'

'Where is she?' A man's voice.

Women in their nightgowns shrank back into their bunks as a burly man in a pin-striped suit, followed by a middle-aged couple, marched up the aisle.

The man looked down at Norah's backside.

'Norah? Is that you, dear?'

'John?' Norah remained bent over, green face hidden in her suitcase. 'Oh, darling. I'm not quite ready.'

'You'll have to scram, Norah.' John shut the case and snatched it up. Norah remained in the same position, bent over her bed.

'Norah! We have to get off. Can't hold up the train! Come on! Now!'

'Hurry along there, folks.' The guard came into the carriage, tapping his watch. 'Off you get. Need to be moving along.'

Very, very slowly, Norah straightened up, her curlers bumping the top bunk, her smile gleaming through the green face cream.

'John! Darling!'

She moved forward for a kiss.

John backed away. 'Don't get that stuff on my new suit.' He took a step to the side, revealing his parents in their Sunday best.

'Mom and Dad were so eager to see you…'

'So excited,' said John's mom. 'We simply couldn't wait.'

'So we drove back one station,' added John's dad. 'And jumped the train.'

'Mom! Dad! This is Norah.' John threw his arm around her. 'Isn't she just beautiful?'

Still lathered in green face cream, Norah smiled.

Once Norah had left the train, Dot and Lilly found a quiet spot in the lounge.

'We've arrived at the truth now, haven't we?' said Dot. 'It was staring us in the face.'

Lilly nodded. 'But how did they make space in Thelma's case?'

'Before we go any further,' said Dot, 'we'd better find out.'

The two women strolled back to the bunks. They stopped at Thelma's. Dot knelt down, peering underneath.

'What are you doing down there?' asked June, from the adjacent bed.

'Lost an earring,' said Dot.

'But your bunk's up there.'

'Train keeps jolting. Things roll away.'

As if on cue the train clacked over some points and rocked from side to side.

'There we go again.' Dot stretched her arm as far as she could under the bed and felt something soft. 'Lilly, pass me your shoe.'

Moments later Dot hooked something.

'Look!' Dot presented the bundle to Lilly. 'Aren't these Thelma's jumpers?'

'I think you mean Thelma's *sweaters*,' said June.

'Sweaters, then. Two of them, and a cardigan. Are we allowed to say cardigan?'

'She'll be bloody cold without them.' June pulled up the covers. 'It's bitter cold. In fact, this whole trip is endless and making me quite miserable.'

'La Junta, next station stop, ladies. Anyone for La Junta, you have twenty minutes to gather your things and make yourselves presentable. Don't want any surprises, like the last stop.'

'Excuse me,' Lilly asked the guard who was moving down the corridor. 'Have you seen Miss Fergusson?'

He pointed towards the back of the train. 'She's in the lounge.'

Standing and bundling the knitwear under her arm, Dot looked at Lilly. 'Ready?'

'Ready.'

THIRTY-SEVEN

Dot felt nervous as the steward announced the second sitting of lunch. Mothers and children always took the first, so now was the perfect time to bring back Thelma.

Dot led her in and they sat opposite Nancy and Fergusson.

June, Violet and Peggy were too busy studying the menu to notice. Thelma had spent the last three hours hiding in the end bed, vacated just before La Junta. The curtain remained drawn while first Dot and Lilly, then Fergusson, went to question her.

'I think I'll have the chicken,' said Thelma, moving over to the empty seat beside Peggy.

'I thought you had gone, Thelma.' Peggy nervously flicked the menu. 'I'm amazed you dare show your face.'

Thelma remained silent.

'Cat got your tongue, girl?'

Thelma ran a finger down the list. 'I heard one of the mothers say the chicken was lovely.'

The steward arrived, pencil and notepad in hand. When he had taken their orders, Dot started questioning.

'Tell us more about Onslow Square, Thelma. It was Onslow Square you were about to say yesterday, wasn't it?'

'I worked there just after King George V died, during the abdication crisis. I was about thirteen. My mum was taken ill around the same time. Lung trouble. So I left. Then the war started and that was that.'

'Why are we listening to this thief?' Peggy glared at Thelma. 'Why isn't she being brought to account?'

Dot spoke over Peggy. 'During your time at Onslow Square, the owner held meetings, didn't he?'

'The January Club. We had to stay below stairs those nights.' Thelma unfolded her napkin. 'Lords and ladies, they were. Sir Oswald Mosley, rich businessmen.'

'Who lived at Onslow Square, Thelma?' It was Fergusson's turn to ask. 'Could it be Lord Banff?'

Everyone looked to Peggy.

'I say,' said Dot, 'didn't he also own that "little castle" where you spent your idyllic summers?'

'I don't remember.'

'Where is Lord Banff now, Peggy? Do you know?'

Everyone saw the blush rising from Peggy's throat.

Dot looked to Gloria Fergusson.

'Pentonville Prison,' she said. 'Crimes against the state.'

'Rather like the crimes you committed, I suspect, Peggy,' added Lilly.

'I never ... It was Thelma. Everything was Thelma. You're going to take her word over mine? There's a laugh.' Peggy folded her arms and glared at Lilly then at Dot. 'We all know that Thelma sewed Nazi badges into the GIs' stripes. Anyway, wasn't Vi in charge of making and mending?'

'Don't you start accusing me again.' Violet turned round so violently that Peggy almost lost her balance. 'I was acquitted of all that. For starters, where would I have laid my hands on them badges?'

'The January Club wore swastika badges, discreetly pinned inside their lapels, I gather,' added Lilly, turning to Peggy. 'Perhaps Lord Banff gifted you a few.'

'Perhaps she just took 'em,' said Violet. 'More 'er style.'

'I don't know anything about the January Club. It wasn't me who worked at Onslow Square. I hadn't worked for Lord Banff for years. It was Thelma. Perhaps he gave those badges to her. Makes sense.'

'But you visited him.' Dot threw up her hands. 'One of my patients followed you. Heard your whole exchange.'

'Prove it. In the dark all cats are grey.'

'Who said anything about it being dark?'

'Can't a woman visit her old employer? Nothing wrong with that.'

The waiter laid their dishes down. Everyone remained silent till he had gone.

'Oh well.' Peggy neatly cut her potatoes into small squares and swirled them around in the gravy. 'Is he coming aboard to give testimony, this patient of yours?'

'Joe died in a frenzy of worry about it.'

'A dead witness? That's a good one.'

'But he saw you handing over papers, heard you say they were from Rainbow Corner...'

Lilly interrupted, 'And we know from when Lord Banff's house was searched, those papers were about troop activity, information you got from listening to the boys in the canteen and from filching anything you could scavenge from wastepaper baskets.'

Peggy pointed her fork towards Violet. 'She was the person caught taking carbons.'

Violet looked as though she was about to get up and start a fight. Fergusson put up a hand to stop her.

'How do you know it was carbons, Peggy?'

'When I emptied those bins, Miss Fergusson, I was only doing my job. If you left them full of state secrets, I would say the responsibility lies with you.'

'That's the thing, Peggy. Most of the information on those carbons was invented. Created especially for you to pass on to your Nazi chums.'

'Talking of those chums...' Lilly took her cue. 'There are discrepancies in your version of what happened in the shower at Tidworth. You were in the last cubicle, Peggy. There were two occupied cubicles, then me, then two empty ones before the last. After you screamed, I saw the POW run out. Later I realised you prearranged a meeting with him.'

'Why would I do that? The man tried to assault me.'

'I saw you come in. If you were in the end cubicle, which is where I found you weeping, you must have walked right past him!' Lilly grabbed her paper napkin and a pen. 'Here are the cubicles. If he was hiding, he could only have been in one of the two cubicles between mine and yours.'

'Why would I want to meet a POW in a public shower?'

'Everyone was up a lot earlier than you expected. It was easy in the washroom to pretend you were being attacked, taking attention away from what you were really doing.' Lilly spoke very quietly: 'Giving Gerd the shoes and nylons with which to entrap Mrs Levinsky.'

'That Jew?' said Peggy. 'She showed us why she had no right to a better life.'

'Because Gerd tempted her, using things which she couldn't possibly have afforded,' said Dot.

'What rubbish!' Peggy spun round and pointed a finger at Dot, sitting at the other table. 'Thelma had the shoes and nylons. We all know it was her. You found those shoes in her case.'

'They weren't.' Dot stood up. 'I helped Thelma pack her case that day.'

'Then she must have put them in later.'

'There wasn't room.'

'Everybody saw Lilly find them.'

'Only because you'd made space inside by taking out all her jumpers…'

'Sweaters!' corrected June.

'Her sweaters…' Dot carried on, 'and you threw those under Thelma's bed, where Lilly and I found them.'

Peggy shrugged. 'Fuss about nothing.'

'You cooked up some story about me,' said Lilly. 'Pearl too. Because her husband is black. But, despite you, love won through.'

Dot flung the final accusation: 'I presume your friend in Oklahoma sent me imaginary telegrams purporting to be from Howard, telling me not to come to the USA?'

'I don't have a friend in Oklahoma. My husband's in Texas.'

The steward arrived to clear the table. No one had eaten much.

'You ladies all on slimming diets?'

'It all looks lovely,' said June, trying to lighten the mood. 'We just need a little more time.'

The steward left.

'After Lord Banff was arrested, you wanted to continue.' Lilly took over the accusations. 'You got a stooge to take the papers down to another member of the January Club in Brighton. That stooge was Otis Oakewood. And the recipient was just picked up last week.'

'He did that for Thelma, not me. He wanted to go out with her. It was for her sister.'

'He did it for you, Peggy. And Emily was a man called Martin Luther Everard Bough. M. L. E. Bough, a member of the January Club, a great fan of Hitler and his cronies. We all understood M. L. E. to be Emily, like you intended us to.'

Peggy paused and smirked. 'Lieutenant Oakewood is dead. So, again, where's your proof? You have nothing on me, and you know it. Everything points at Thelma. Nothing at me. There's your criminal. Bang her up.'

Peggy continued calmly eating her dinner.

A short silence, then Thelma spoke, very quietly: 'All right. I confess.'

'Told you so!' Peggy tucked in as though she had not eaten for days. 'It was Thelma. You know it. I know it. Thelma.'

Flinging her napkin onto the table, Thelma stood.

'It *was* me who asked Otis to go to Brighton. But I did everything under pressure from you. I knew an awful lot about *you*, too, Peggy. I saw you with the carbon copies, I saw you making notes after those boys talked about planes and things. But you were safe cos you knew I could never report you. Because of what you knew I had done.'

Lilly and Dot exchanged a look. This was not how they were expecting things to go.

'I stole from Rainbow Corner. Not secrets. Food. If I'd got caught I'd have been sacked by you...' Thelma looked to Fergusson. 'And you would have felt duty-bound to tell Mr O'Kelly at the Corner House that I was stealing food and breaking rationing rules, and I'd have been sacked from there, too. I'd have been imprisoned for it, probably. And hated for taking from those Americans who were always so generous with us...' Thelma wiped away a tear. 'But you have to understand. My mother was sick. Dying, actually. She'd lie in bed all day, coughing and coughing. Thin as a rake, she was. She was all I had, my mum. And I was all she had. But I couldn't be with her, not the day nor the night, cos I had to work, otherwise who would pay our rent and, even worse, her doctor's bills. I couldn't bear watching her waste away. She was so thin. I really believed that if I brought home donuts and eggs, cheese, bread, bacon, all the things she couldn't get legally, she might get better.' Thelma flopped down and sobbed. 'But she died anyway. But at least in her last days she had a few little treats.' Holding back her tears, Thelma turned to Peggy. 'There you are, Peggy. All out now. You can't hold it over me anymore.' She reached a hand across the table to Dot and Lilly. 'I'm sorry I caused such trouble. But I was so scared I'd be arrested and my poor mum would have no one to be there to get her food and medicine and she'd have to die alone. I did anything Peggy asked me to. Anything. Yes – I gave the package to Otis to take to Brighton. Yes – I sewed on those horrible badges. Though I'd always cross myself because it seemed so unlucky and I didn't want anything horrible to happen to those lovely boys.'

Thelma turned to Dot.

'One last thing, Dot. That morning – the day after he'd gone down to Brighton – that was the day after I found out about him. Then later on I saw him flirting with you, in the canteen. I saw you back away. I was going to rush over and tell you how he was married, that he lived with her parents, that he wasn't this actor who lived in Hollywood, he was just a fake and a liar and a cadge. But Peggy stopped me.'

'I never.'

Thelma talked over her. 'Peggy stopped me, because she needed to keep Otis sweet, so he would go to Kent and Portsmouth and everywhere else because it was easier for a GI to go…'

'He came to visit me in Portsmouth. I was used as bait. Is that it?'

'He went on her instructions,' Thelma pointed at Peggy, 'delivering her packages of information to traitors. When Lord Banff got arrested, that put the wind up her. Cos it was Peggy who always went to Onslow Square. Once a week she went. Since she'd worked for him, he'd moved his London gaffe and she didn't know where. When I mentioned him, that I knew his address, she went to ingratiate herself with him.' Thelma looked at Fergusson, imploring. 'I know I should have told her to go to hell. But I couldn't go to prison, not with my poor old mum…' She burst into tears. Tentatively, June put her arm around her shoulder.

'End of melodrama.' Peggy stood up. 'If I'm not wrong, your culprit just confessed.' She threw down her napkin and squeezed out from the table. 'You can't get me, Miss Fergusson, nor you two, Miss Cleverclogs and Miss Innocence. Everyone told me how you were always sniffing around. Even sleuthing around at Tidworth, for God's sake. So I thought it best to scuttle you both. I even managed to persuade the immigration people to stop the brassy slut who married that Negro. Explained how the marriage was forbidden by his CO. Didn't think he'd turn out to be so enslaved to a blonde drummer that he'd give it all up and follow her.' Peggy slapped her hands together as though wiping them clean. 'But you'll never get me now. Not as a Nazi. Though I was one. Still am. Proudly so. He was a great man, Herr Hitler. The day he died I was devastated. I thought my world had come to an end. Couldn't stop crying. Nancy even made one of her snide remarks about it. But, the world is still turning and I'm still here. We can carry on cleaning the world of those impure races and there's nothing you can do about it. Nothing.'

Peggy stooped to get her handbag.

'The final piece of the jigsaw falls into place.' Dot felt that she would burst with anger. 'I will get you, Peggy. You almost ruined me. If I hadn't been supported by Lilly, those telegrams would have made me give up the best man anyone could meet. Everyone else might let you go, Peggy. But not me. There must be some anti-Nazi laws over here and I will move heaven and earth to make sure you end your days in prison.'

'Easiest piece of bait I ever put on a line.' Peggy walked calmly towards the door. 'You can't do anything, dear. Face it. Enjoy the rest of your lives, pathetic bitches. Couple of hours till I get off and then I'll never see any of you again. My husband will be waiting for me. And together, with all those of a like mind, we will win. Wait and see.'

After Peggy left the carriage, no one spoke or touched their food.

After a moment the steward came back in to clear the tables.

'What's going on? I've never seen English women turn down our wonderful food.'

'We've lost our appetites.' Nancy reached in her pocket for her compact and started tidying up her lipstick. 'Something in here started to stink.'

'Anything I can do about it?' The steward piled up the plates.

'Apart from chucking a certain person under the train, no.'

'I don't suppose you'll be wanting dessert?'

'Oh yes, we will.' Fergusson spoke for everyone. 'We need something sweet to take away the bitterness of the last half hour. Please, sir, bring more of your lovely food.'

They watched him hobble away, balancing the plates against the rocking of the train.

June piped up: 'Who is Peggy's husband anyhow? Anybody know?'

'Her label at Tidworth said "Peggy Jaeger-Smith",' said Violet.

'Not unlike my old moniker,' said June. 'Jagger.'

'Yes. Only it was spelled with an E in the middle. Does that make a difference to how it sounds?'

'Jagger rhymes with stagger, whereas Jaeger starts with a Y sound and rhymes with…' Nancy ran through the alphabet. 'Not much.'

'Jaeger is a German word,' said Thelma softly. 'It means hunter.'

'But that's her old name,' said Lilly. 'Peggy Hunter.'

'So the old cow's found a man with her own name, but in German.' Nancy picked up some crumbs left from the bread rolls and ate them. 'There lies madness.'

'Perhaps she made it up and she's not married at all…'

'So how did she pass the same interview which I failed?' asked Lilly.

The loudspeaker crackled.

'Message for Mrs Dorothy Hopkins. Mrs Dorothy Hopkins.'

'They're calling me!' Dot got up. 'Where do I go? What can it be about?'

'Please contact the steward. Mrs Dorothy Hopkins, please contact the steward, urgently.'

'Oh God. I hope everything's all right.' Dot crossed herself and ran out of the dining car.

'Vaguer.'

'What?'

'A word which rhymes with Jaeger. Where's that menu?' Nancy grabbed it and slid her finger down to desserts. 'I'm starving.'

'Do you think that Peggy has perhaps double-barrelled her name, and because she is already a Hunter or Jaeger…' Lilly wrote the words on the back of her napkin, 'her husband could be called Smith?'

'Not General Gropey Smith?' Violet winced. 'Actually, looking back, she was always chatting to him in a whispery kind of way. I thought she was reporting us for being late and things.'

'How grim!' Nancy clutched at an imaginary necklace. 'The fat cook and the old groper. Please don't put me off my pud.'

Lilly recalled her early days at Rainbow Corner. 'Peggy was often up there first thing in the morning, sometimes late in the day. Maybe…'

'Andrew Smith can't be a Nazi sympathiser.' June lay down her menu in thought. 'He was a decorated hero from the Great War.'

'So was Marshal Pétain,' Lilly replied. 'That didn't stop him signing away France to Hitler.'

'I had so many complaints against General Smith for groping the women at Rainbow Corner,' said Fergusson. 'I imagined he was going senile. Seems that was the least of our concerns.'

'Sodding Peggy and Handy Andy planning to take over the world. And the only thing I want is a slice of warm apple pie.' Nancy glanced around, hoping the steward was arriving to take their orders. But it was Dot standing in the doorway, beaming from ear to ear.

'Howard sent a message to the train. He's just finished filming. But he's had a flat tyre.'

'I hope he'll still make the party at Albuquerque.'

'He's at a petrol station...'

'Gas station!'

'Oh yes, a gas station, somewhere called Lamy, which is the next stop. He wants me to get off there so we can drive the rest of the way together in his car. I've got to pack. I don't have much time.'

THIRTY-EIGHT

As the train pulled in, the gang hovered in the vestibule to help Dot down.

'Excuse me!' Peggy, suitcase in hand, shoved through. 'I need to get off this train.'

'And good riddance.' Nancy stepped forward. Lilly had to restrain her from pushing Peggy down the three steps to the platform.

'Don't be late for the party.' Lilly gave Dot a hug. 'See you in Albuquerque in about an hour. Tell that man of yours to drive carefully. You're precious cargo.'

'What a bleak-looking place,' said June, leaning out, as Dot stepped down onto the platform. 'I don't think it's manned, is it? I hope Dot doesn't have long to wait.'

'All aboard!' The guard blew his whistle, jumped aboard and slammed the door. The women ran back to the nearest window and waved frantically at Dot, who stood waving back, suitcase at her feet.

'Look behind her.' Violet pointed. 'Must be what Sydney was always going on about. Big skies.' She held both arms up. 'Look at that! Biiiiiig!'

The red sun hung on the horizon, in front of it, the vast empty expanse of the desert, framing Dot, tiny and alone, waving back at the train.

She waved until the train disappeared, snaking into scrublands, then she walked out onto the forecourt. Several yards away Peggy stood, alone.

The station manager was locking up the single room which made up the station.

'Evening, ladies.' The station manager tipped his cap with his forefinger. 'No more trains today, you know. Last train, your own westbound *Super Chief*.'

He climbed onto a large motorbike, revved up and sped away through an empty plain, dotted with ankle-high bushes, edged with low hills.

One winding road ran through it.

There was thunder in the air. Puffy violet clouds crept across the sky from the north.

Dot eyed Peggy, the woman who supported the Nazis and used Otis and Thelma's weaknesses to Hitler's advantage.

Her stomach churned with revulsion.

'They should have put you in one of those horror camps, Peggy. See how you like it.'

Peggy laughed.

'Oh, that's all made up. A fairy story invented by Jews to get pity.'

'I've met some of the men who liberated Belsen, Peggy. Even a year on they still have nightmares. And they only saw it from the outside.'

'You're a fantasist, Dot. A pea-brain. Leave the world to the grown-ups, dear.'

Dot knew there was no argument, no words strong enough to shake Peggy out of her delusions.

But she couldn't leave it there.

'You do realise that despite everything you did, you're still at the bottom of the pile, Peggy. You can suck up to those posh people all you like, but none of them care a jot about you. Because to them you are nothing. That's all you've ever been and all you'll always be. A "plod". That's their name for you, Peggy. A nothing. A nobody.'

A hum in the air, then a big black car appeared some way along the road.

Please let this be Howard.

The car pulled into the forecourt. Tyres skidded to a halt. The driver's door opened.

But it wasn't him. It was, as they'd all assumed, General Andrew Smith, looking even more seedy in civvies than he had back in his uniformed Rainbow Corner days.

Dot had no desire to greet him.

She needn't have worried. Ignoring her, he fell into a lingering embrace with Peggy.

Dot felt they were putting it on for her benefit.

'If there's any bloody justice in this world, they will get you,' she shouted. 'They will put an end to you and your hideous crusade.'

'Gullible oaf!' Peggy pulled away from the general. 'So stupid, you'd fall for anything.' Peggy got into the car and wound down the window. 'At least my man loves me enough to turn up! Yours won't be coming.'

They drove off in a cloud of dust, leaving Dot alone.

Gullible. Another word for too trusting. Dot would rather be that than wicked, like them.

She looked at her watch.

Where was Howard?

In every direction, nothing. The entire vista was motionless but for the red tail-lights of General Smith's car, growing smaller and smaller.

Slowly the sun sank behind the distant hills, casting blue shadows across the land.

The train would soon be pulling in at Albuquerque.

Dot wandered around the station, hoping to find a phone. But who could she call?

Would she have to stay here until the station opened again to receive tomorrow's trains?

Howard couldn't have meant for Dot to wait so long in this bleak, inhospitable place. Had his car broken down? Was he stranded, with no way of contacting her?

What if he never arrived, like those husbands in New York who had believed that because their marriage took place in England, it wasn't real, just a toytown wedding? But then why had Howard sent that letter to New York, or spoken so warmly to her on the phone in Chicago, or messaged the train guard?

With darkness came cold. Rustling noises, wild creatures scurrying through the brush, all around her. Wolves or snakes, or worse?

A light rain started to fall.

Dot lay her suitcase against the station wall and pushed herself tight under the narrow awning.

There was no escaping the rain, which grew heavier.

Despair set in.

Then, on the horizon, a tiny light appeared.

It grew and split. Two yellowish white lights, eyes sparkling in the black.

A car.

Heading her way.

*

'Albuquerque, next station stop, ladies and gentlemen. May I remind you that Albuquerque is a long stop, twenty whole minutes. You are welcome to take some time on the platform to stretch your legs. But please make sure to stay in range of the train and listen out for those whistles. Albuquerque.'

Lilly didn't need telling. Long before the train started slowing, she and her case were in the vestibule, Violet and Nancy behind her.

'It's so exciting!' Violet whooped.

'Thanks, Lilly, for this invitation.' Nancy pulled on her hat. 'It's so much more fun to have a get-together before we go our own ways.'

'It was Jack's idea. The men will all be there.'

'I suppose they felt the same way as us.'

As the train slowly ran into the station, they could hear banging. Further down the platform, orange light flickered.

'The ruddy station hasn't caught fire, has it?' Violet put her hand to her head. 'Wouldn't that be our luck?'

Lilly flattened her face against the window. 'There *are* flames. It looks like torches on sticks, you know, like in films about the olden days.'

With a screech of metal, the train shuddered to a stop.

The guard squeezed past, hauled open the great metal door and jumped down.

'Off you get now, ladies. Looks like you've got a genuine local welcome.'

He took Lilly's case and laid it down on the platform, then reached in to grab Violet's and Nancy's.

'Mind if I join you, girls.' Fergusson squeezed into the vestibule.

'Of course, Controller.' Lilly smiled.

'Please call me Gloria. I must say bye-bye, see the boys again and, as the man said, stretch my legs.'

'We're coming too!' June and Thelma squeezed in behind.

As Lilly climbed down onto the platform, she saw something unimaginable.

On a bit of scrubland adjacent to the station stood fifty or so people in a great circle, some holding flambeaux, others beating a large drum. Before them stood Jack. He was taller than she remembered and more handsome. Over his long black hair, he wore an ornate feather headdress, which spilled down his back.

Standing beside him, their medals glinting in the light of the flames, Sydney and Virgil stood to attention, in dress uniform.

'Oh lawks, Lilly!' Violet stepped forward and took her arm. 'This is not at all what I was expecting.'

'Me neither.' Lilly walked up to face Jack.

He nodded and smiled, then tapped his chest twice, that old familiar gesture.

Someone touched her arm. She turned to find Elan, who guided her, Violet and Nancy to a line drawn on the ground.

'For the visitors.'

Lilly waved across to call Gloria, June and Thelma.

Elan addressed the women. 'This is the Navajo Hózhó ceremony. Welcoming soldiers back from the war. We welcome *you* also, you who fought alongside us. After violent upheavals, like battles and deaths, this ceremony is performed to restore balance and beauty with the universe.'

'How long does it last?'

'Around thirty minutes.'

Lilly called Gloria Fergusson. 'Please stay. Get another train tomorrow. You must see this...'

'I wouldn't miss it for the world. Jack's my friend too, remember. I'll hop on board and get my case. There must be a hotel nearby where I can rest my head.'

'Tell June and Thelma they're welcome too.'

Gloria strode off, beckoning the others.

The drums beat louder and louder; the rhythm picked up speed.

All the men closed in around Jack. Some started to sing a loud, wailing song; others, holding their torches high, danced to the beat of the drum. Beside them, in full dress uniform, their husbands' faces were lit by flickering orange light.

Nancy and Violet slid their arms around Lilly's waist.

'Don't they look splendid...' Nancy laughed. 'But yours, Lilly ... Wow!'

Lilly thought back to so many moments with Jack: the strange code, pressing his ear to the ground for distant wheels, his worry about the moon, and his wondering whether she might be put off by his life...

'All aboard the *Super Chief*! Last call. All aboard.'

The whistle blew, the doors slammed, adding dissonance to the drumbeats and song. Lilly caught sight of Thelma slowly climbing up the steps, and the great metal train, slipping away behind them, meandering along the westbound tracks, chasing the sun as it sank below the horizon.

Violet jabbed Lilly in the ribs. 'Look!'

Virgil and Sydney took torches from the dancing men so that they could mount horses, leaving the uniformed soldiers, Elan and the men Lilly remembered from Normandy to lead the way on foot.

Jack leapt onto the back of a large white horse. As the horse turned, almost dancing a whole circle, the drumbeats slowed. The music grew quieter and quieter until Lilly could hear nothing but the breathing of horses and the crackling of flambeaux.

Jack's horse pawed the earth.

The dancers gathered up the torches and one by one extinguished them, leaving everyone standing in the dim grey radiance which spilled from the station arc lights.

Ceremony over, Sydney and Virgil rushed forward to greet their wives.

As Lilly walked towards Jack, who was still up on his horse, Howard came forward and touched her elbow.

'Where's Dot?'

'Didn't you pick her up at Lamy?'

'No.'

'She got a message from you telling her to get off the train because your car had a flat.'

Howard shot Lilly a puzzled glance. 'I've been here all afternoon, with the other guys, rehearsing. Anyway, what car? I came up last night on the *Super Chief*, got here just in time to find out where we had to stand.'

'You didn't send a message to the train?'

'I did not.'

'Lilly?' Even in the gloaming, Lilly saw his face pale. 'Where is Dot?'

*

The headlights grew and grew until the car swept into the off-road bay of Lamy Station.

Dot bent to pick up her case.

She could barely see, the rain was beating down so hard.

But it wasn't Howard standing in the glare of the headlamps. It was General Smith.

'Why are you here?' Dot felt stupid asking the question. She knew why. It was to do her harm.

Andrew Smith lifted his arm and struck Dot across the face, knocking her to the ground.

'Troublemaker!'

She landed on the ground with a painful thud, her palms scratched, her mouth full of dust.

'My wife is *not* a nobody.'

Footsteps approaching.

'Bind her!' Peggy's voice.

Hands grabbed her feet, dragging her through the dirt. Dot kicked out, but Peggy threw herself down, landing on top of Dot, while Smith yanked Peggy's scarf from her shoulders. He used it to gag Dot.

Desperately attempting to free herself, Dot writhed and jerked. But while she fought off Peggy, Smith was busily tying her feet together. Then Peggy wrapped a rope around her wrists.

'All secure, like a hog to the spit,' shouted Peggy. 'One, two, three, lift!'

Next thing Dot was yanked off the ground, carried a few yards and thrown across the back seat of the car.

Slamming doors.

The choke pulled.

Dot lay face down, her face pressed into the polished dark leather. Her muddy clothing was soaked through.

The engine revved, then with a gentle sway, the car sped away.

*

Lilly sat in the front of the truck, Jack in the driving seat.

They were heading east. Elan sat in the open back, radioing to all the Navajo in the area to be on the lookout.

Lilly knew that Peggy was at the bottom of this. She must have got the guard to make the announcement which had lured Dot off the train.

'They live in Texas, you say?' Jack peered through the windscreen.

'Somewhere near Amarillo, called McLean.'

'I know the place. They must join the highway soon.'

From his paddy wagon, Virgil had phoned the Lamy police, telling them to head for the railway station and search for Dot. Within minutes they radioed back. Dot was not there. But they had located her suitcase. Track marks in the mud indicated that at least one car had recently driven up to the station, then turned south onto the highway in the direction of Clines Corners.

'They'll be on country roads. We might catch them before they hit this highway – Route 66. It runs from Albuquerque through to Amarillo and into Oklahoma.'

'Oklahoma!' said Lilly. 'Oh, my God.'

Jack interrupted her. 'Tell Elan: "Assemble Clines Corners. Follow any car which comes from the direction of Lamy."'

Lilly turned, kneeling on the seat to yell back at Elan, then she settled back, looking forward along the straight, dark highway. Occasional cars were coming their way. Ahead of them the red tail-lights of Virgil's paddy wagon.

Jack reached across but instead of handling the gear lever, he touched her thigh. 'It's wonderful to have you back, Lilly. We're a good team.'

'That we are, Chief.'

*

Dot had managed to edge herself around until she was face up. From the dim light thrown up by the dashboard, she could see that Peggy was driving, General Smith sitting in the passenger seat, in front of her head.

Slowly, silently, she manipulated her wrists, wriggling them, picking at the strands of rope with her fingernails.

Suddenly the car braked and Dot shot forward, landing in the footwell.

'What the hell are you doing?' yelled Peggy.

'A peccary ran in front of the damned car,' he shouted back. 'Didn't you see it?'

'What the hell is a peccary?'

'Are you simple, woman? It's a kind of hairy pig.'

Like you, thought Dot.

Then she remembered. They were in America. People drove on the other side.

Peggy was the passenger, not the driver.

'How's the prisoner?' asked General Smith, lurching the car forward.

'On the floor,' replied Peggy, glancing round.

'Where she deserves to be.' The general laughed. 'Like the dirt she is.'

The scarf around Dot's mouth was soaked from a mix of rain, spit and perspiration. It felt slightly looser. Perhaps the damp had expanded the fabric. Dot tried to work her jaws and chin, realigning the scarf.

When her eyes became accustomed to the dark, she searched the floor, looking for anything which might help.

But the well beneath the general's seat was bare.

*

'What's that?' Lilly could see a mass of light, like a ring of fire around the road.

'My men.' Jack gave Elan a thumbs up. 'They will track anything that moves.'

Jack pulled in near a lone service station and ran over to one of the waiting cars. Lilly watched him talking, pointing northwards, then he ran back.

'Elan! Join Payat and his men. Take them back towards Lamy.'

'The radio, Chief?'

'Lilly will use it. You go with Payat.'

Jack climbed back into the driver's seat, and Elan handed Lilly the radio.

'Now we head east, towards Texas. Other men are heading this way from Santa Rosa. Smith and Hunter have to be somewhere between us.'

Cradling the familiar radio box, Lilly prayed that Jack was right.

Dot had got off that train hours ago.

She prayed they were not too late.

THIRTY-NINE

THE GAG WAS NOW under Dot's chin. It was easier to breathe and hear. Being in the footwell was also an improvement. For one thing, the nauseating smell of leather was gone. There was a central hump on the floor, pressing hard against her stomach, but it gave her some traction. It was easier to control her movements on a carpeted surface than the slippery seat.

The odd light flashed by. Passing cars, thought Dot, service stations, road junctions.

She rubbed the ropes binding her hands against the carpet.

Her wrists felt freer.

'Where will we dump her?' The general's voice was raspy and deep. 'A ditch on the roadside?'

'I'll know the place when I see it.'

The general's sleeve crossed between the two seats.

'Keep your hands on the wheel.' Peggy's voice didn't sound welcoming.

'You can be real cold sometimes, woman, you know that?'

'And you can be a real pain in the arse.'

The general wiggled in his seat and started to wind down the window. 'I'm too hot.'

'Well, I'm too cold. So shut that window.'

The car swerved, throwing Dot back against the seat.

'What are you playing at?'

'Trying to take off this damned jacket.'

'Pull in and do it. I don't want you killing us.'

The car abruptly stopped, the engine still running.

Could Dot get out now? Flip like a fish and reach the handle with her feet? She tried but her legs were numb. And she couldn't reach.

The general's jacket fell onto the floor beneath his legs. His foot then slammed back onto the accelerator and the car sped off, throwing Dot back.

She let out a yelp.

Peggy turned. Dot thrust her head as far as she could under the general's seat.

'What's that?'

'What's what?'

'Ahead. Lights.'

'We don't own the roads, you know. You're so jumpy, woman.'

Peggy twisted around. 'There are lights out of the back too.'

'It's a damned highway, Peggy. There are other cars.'

'It doesn't feel right. What if there's been a crash and the police flag us down?'

'Perhaps you should have thought of that before deciding on this hare-brained scheme.'

'Pull off the road.'

'Stop again?'

'No. Turn off your lights and drive onto the scrub.'

'Are you mad?'

Peggy leaned over and grabbed the steering wheel, and at the same time, flicked the dashboard light-switch off.

'I can't see where I'm going.'

'That's the whole point.'

Dot was aware of the car rocking from side to side, the tyres crunching over small thorn bushes and the metal sides scraping boulders. Dot was flung up and down, smashing her knees against the hump, bashing her head against the car door.

The pain was excruciating.

*

'Radio Elan, Lilly. See what he has found.'

Lilly picked up the receiver. Once more she spoke in the old code.

'Nothing, Chief.'

'Then they must already be on 66.' Jack leaned towards the windscreen. 'Between us and those distant lights.'

The road ahead was higher. Like a bright string of pearls, thought Lilly, tiny white vehicle lights coming their way.

'That must be them!' Lilly pointed ahead at a lone pair of red tail-lights, far in the distance. But before Jack replied, the glowing rear lamps vanished.

'What happened? Did they go down into a dip?'

'They must have turned them off. Perhaps they pulled in. Radio Elan. Warn him to look out for a parked car with no lights. And to take to the plains from the west.'

For fifteen minutes Jack drove on, until they came face to face with the trucks from the other tribe on the far side of the highway.

Jack pulled up and jumped out.

The other men ran across to Jack. They huddled together talking.

Jack shouted to Lilly, 'We think they've driven off the road.'

Lilly surveyed the blackness either side of the highway.

'How will we ever find them?'

'There's a quarter moon, but the sky is all clouds. Our strength will be in numbers.'

Virgil's wagon pulled up beside them, then Sydney's old banger.

'They've gone onto the plains. We're going to encircle them on foot.'

'Why don't we all drive?' yelled Violet.

'Too dangerous,' replied Virgil. 'The tyres would blow, we'd rupture our gas pipes.'

'Also,' said Jack, 'if they've dumped Dot, we may well run her down and not even know it.'

'What can we do?' Howard stepped forward. 'I can't just stand here. That's Dot out there.'

'Look!' Jack raised his arms. The horizon was peppered with flickering lights. 'Those are my men.'

A large carrier drew up beside them. Elan wound down the window.

'I brought two, Chief.'

Jack ran round to the back of the van and pulled down the tailgate.

Two large horses clopped onto the road.

'One for me, one for Elan.'

'No!' Howard shouted. 'I must have one.'

'Can you ride?'

'Bareback, side-saddle, standing up, whatever you like. Yes, I can ride.'

Howard put his foot into the stirrup of the grey, and threw himself into the saddle, while Jack climbed onto the bay.

'You can't leave me here,' shouted Lilly, jumping up behind Jack. 'Elan, hand me a torch.'

Elan lit a flambeau and passed it to her.

Jack turned to the people assembled around Virgil's vehicle. 'Elan will guide you. Let's go.'

*

The car rumbled over the rough terrain, then braked suddenly. Items from the general's jacket pockets slid back, hitting Dot in the face.

She suppressed a cry.

Then she saw it, gleaming in the dark a few inches from her head. The blade of a hunting knife. At the end of the hilt a hook. Dot tried to grasp it with her teeth.

But another jolt of the car knocked it out of reach.

'Those lights over there have gone out.'

'Probably hunters.'

'What would they hunt in the dark? There isn't even a moon.'

'How in God's name do I know, woman? Coyotes? Bears? Peccary pigs?'

'There are more flickering lights behind us now.'

'So let's get back on the road where we know the damned lights are just oncoming cars.'

Dot had an idea. She raised her ribcage an inch off the floor. Next time the knife slid she would trap it.

Suddenly Peggy snatched the steering wheel and spun the car round. 'I don't like that row of lights. We need to drive away from them.'

As the car lurched, the knife skidded to a halt beneath Dot's coat.

She turned her body so that she could jam the knife up against the back seat, letting the blade touch the ropes holding her hands. Then, gingerly, she started to let the bumping of the car rub the blade, cutting the line which tied her.

*

Jack put out a hand, bringing Howard to a halt.

'My men are signalling to me that there is a car.' He pointed his hand towards a space in the darkness. 'They caught the reflection. We're closing in. Tread with care. Slowly goes it.'

Jack touched Howard's arm. 'We will find her.'

He called back to Lilly, 'Throw the torch to the ground. We'll use its light to navigate.'

Jack and Howard geed the horses and stepped forward into the dark.

Lilly could hear rustling all around her, then she heard another sound – the bashing of the car as it rolled over bushes and rocks, the low hum of its engine.

'It's coming right at us,' she whispered into Jack's ear.

'I see it.'

A low rumble of thunder in the distance.

Jack put his hand out to call Howard to a halt.

'Look.'

A flicker of lighting shimmered, creating a sudden splash of lilac sky.

The car was a hundred yards ahead.

Howard jumped down from his horse.

'Stop!' shouted Lilly.

'I *will* save her.' Howard bent low and sprinted forward.

Another flicker of light.

Then Lilly caught sight of Howard leaping onto the roof of the car.

*

A really loud thud caused the car to rock and Peggy to shriek, 'What the hell was that?'

'Felt like a bear jumped on the trunk.'

Dot looked up. The rear window of the car was covered.

'We're surrounded,' wailed Peggy. 'In the lightning you could see them everywhere. Why are they here?'

'It'll be those damned Navajos,' growled the general. 'Nothing to do with us. Perhaps we're on their burial grounds or something. I told you we should stick to the road.'

For the third time, Peggy took hold of the steering wheel, dragging it as far round as she could. The car swerved, and Dot's wrists were free.

A blinding web of lightning followed by a loud clap of thunder.

'Where is the road gone? Who are all those people?'

'I told you, woman. Local vermin. We'll just drive through them!'

The general pressed the accelerator. Dot used the drag to haul herself up onto the back seat. She rolled down the window.

'She's got up! And there's someone on the roof. Put your foot down, Andrew. He'll fall off.'

With a noise like a machine gun, the car suddenly lost traction.

Sparks lit the area around the hubcaps.

'We've got a flat,' shouted the general. 'I think they all went. We must have hit a cactus or something. We're not going to get far and my car will be ruined.'

Dot waved the scarf out of the window, shouting, 'I'm here.'

Ghostly figures approached from every side, then, lighting up one by one, a circle of flames surrounded them.

As the car limped to a halt, Peggy hauled open the passenger door. 'Run for it!'

The general clambered from the driver's seat and stumbled away across the rough ground.

Jack and Lilly caught him. He was too feeble to struggle.

'Good evening, General.' Gloria ran up with Violet. 'Disappointed that you were caught by people you consider your inferiors? Two mere women who'd been repulsed by your groping fingers, alongside Chief Kirk, a Navajo?'

Heading in the other direction, Peggy ran straight into Elan's group.

'Gotcha!' Sydney stepped forward and grabbed her.

She writhed in his grip.

'You're pathetic,' Peggy screamed. 'All of you. Pathetic.'

'Pathetic, perhaps,' Virgil emerged from the shadows, 'but I represent the law of this country.' Unhooking a pair of handcuffs from his belt, he slapped them around Peggy's wrists.

Nancy stepped forward and linked arms with Sydney. 'Sieg Heil, darling. You're nicked.'

'Now you walk with me to the paddy wagon.' Virgil pushed Peggy forward.

'I think you mean "goose-step", Virgil dear.'

Dot struggled on the back seat, grasping the door handle. She tried to get out, but her feet were still bound. She stretched her arms out of the window and pulled.

'I've got you, Dot.' A hand reached down from the roof, grasping Dot's fingers. 'You're safe. I've got you.'

'Howard!'

He slithered down, hauled open the car door and threw his arms around her.

He pulled Dot out and held her tight.

'Oh, my precious, darling girl.'

'Howard. Darling! Thank you.'

A gap in the clouds let through the moonlight.

'"And when the night is new,"' Howard sang softly into her ear. '"I'll be looking at the moon, but I'll be seeing you."'

Epilogue

FORTY

OCTOBER 1946
Havenhurst Drive
West Hollywood, CA

Dear Mammy and Pop,

A note to keep you up to date with the gossip from the other side of the pond. (That's what Americans say when they mean England. The Atlantic Ocean seems that small to them!)

Doesn't freedom seem a strange tonic after the exhilaration of war?

Vi, you remember, the big girl with the mass of red hair, just gave birth to twins. They've named them Vivien (after Vivien Leigh) and Victor (after Victor Mature). So there's a lot of Vs in that household. They sign their letters 'The Victory Vs!' Since the arrests Virgil made that night, he has been elected sheriff, which means he's a really important person in charge of jails, and not, like it sounds, a cowboy in a Western. I wonder if he wears a silver star. Vi still sews for a living. She's part-time with a local gent's outfitters and is about to start working at a new firm in Needles called Butterick. They make patterns for dresses that anyone can run up at home.

I can't remember whether I told you about June? She decided not to get off the train after all! She took one look at her husband, Art Pemberton, standing on the platform, peering over his specs, hat in hands, turned to Gloria Fergusson and said, 'I've made a terrible mistake. I never really loved him, it was just his donuts.' !!!! And Gloria had to get out and explain to poor Art, and almost missed getting back on the train.

June's back in England now, though it took her a long time till her divorce came through, and then she had to find a berth on a homeward-bound ship. While she was waiting in New York, she called in on

Tony and Barbara. They've decided to stop at just five children. Between you and me, I think when Barbara saw she was getting a hot dog stand, not a Broadway restaurant chain, she went on strike … if you know what I mean.

June also saw Paul. He sends his love to Liverpool and all Scousers. His friend Marty is a traffic cop and stands on an island in the middle of the road all day long waving his arms around. Lucky, in his pre-war days, he did all that wrestling!

Thelma wrote us long apologetic letters from Germany. Her husband, Teddy, is stationed in Ansbach, part of the US occupying army.

You're more likely to hear about Pearl and Earl than I am. They're part of a jazz combo. One of Earl's GI friends who defected to England is on saxophone, and two members of the all-girl band from Rainbow Corner on piano and guitar. They're called the Earl Young Quintet and perform all over England. Look out for them in the *Echo* in case they come to Liverpool. I think they're making a gramophone record. Perhaps you can bring a copy when you come.

I almost forgot to tell you about Nancy. You might remember, when I first arrived at Rainbow Corner, I found her quite intimidating. But when you get used to the wicked quips, she's rather fun and very understanding. Anyway, she took one look at Sydney's 'as far as the eye could see' farm and was all for divorcing him and going straight home. Sydney lives in a shack, she says, next to a tall metal windmill, which they need to pump the water from the well. Heat is provided by a stove, for which they have to go out and cut logs, and there aren't that many trees around the place. Sydney really did own everything as far as the eye could see, but it was just rough terrain ending abruptly at the highway. Good only, Nancy says, for grazing goats. So she's building a hotel. Over here they call that a 'motel' because it's on the main road, specially designed for people with motorcars. It's a prime site, she says, so they're going deluxe, with a swimming pool and all. She's also bringing in soil experts to see whether they can do anything to improve the land and grow something called sweetcorn. We get a lot of it here. It's bright yellow and tastes lovely. You might have seen the movie (that's American for film, flicks or the pictures) where Mickey Mouse and Donald Duck eat them as if they were typewriters.

Do you remember me talking about Lilly's ex, George, marrying a brassy lady from Des Moines? Well, he is doing what everyone expected of him and now teaches at Sandhurst Military Academy. But, despite enormous opposition from the locals, Lady Dolores, as she styles herself, is quite a wow at opening fetes, and makes often hilarious speeches, all of which seem to irritate George quite a lot. Dolores is also a leading light in the Cuckfield Amateur Dramatics Society. Apparently she made a stunning Lady Macbeth.

Gloria Fergusson, the posh boss of Rainbow Corner, is secretly a lady. I don't mean that I ever thought she was a man, but it turns out her father was a duke, so, if she hadn't hidden her rank, we should have been calling her Lady Gloria. But none of that stuff matters over here, and she says she prefers it that way. She stayed in California for a few weeks, then moved up to Chicago, where she has started a detective agency.

She asked Lilly to join, but Lilly is far too busy learning all about the Navajo, their customs and ceremonies. Now that she is married to Jack, who is one of their chiefs, she is determined to know everything. It's funny, isn't it, that his military rank was chief, but that all along he really was a chief in his own right.

Lilly loves the life, the countryside, the people, the horses, and of course adores Jack, to whom I owe my life. We plan to meet up very soon for a chinwag about the war.

The grisly Nazi couple who tried to do away with me have been jailed. Gloria Fergusson pointed out that, now the war is over, what they did seems so minor compared to the terrible war crimes and atrocities we read about in the horror camps. So in England their treachery probably would not even have led to a prison sentence. But, over here, by kidnapping me and tying me up, the Hunter-Smiths laid themselves at risk of a far stiffer sentence – twenty years in the state penitentiary (which is American for prison)!

I know I've already told you this, but I was never so happy to see anyone as I was to see Howard that night. He's doing fine, by the way, and sends tons of love. He gets offered more and more roles. In the last few months, he's played everything from gangsters to circus performers. I sneak into cinema sometimes just to see him in those fleeting scenes. He went up for a starring part last week, at Paramount Studios. If he gets that, it'll be a seven-year contract and his face will be on posters all over the world. But I won't need to pin them to my wall, because I can just turn around to look at him.

Most evenings, when Howard's not working, he plays the piano and I dance around the living room. And when the nights are warm (which is almost always out here), he puts on the record player and we lie in the garden together, holding hands, counting the stars.

We're both looking forward so much, Mammy and Pop, to you coming out. I hope you got the boat and train tickets Howard sent. First class, too! But that's Howard all the way. I'm very glad that you'll be here in time for Christmas. It really wouldn't be the same without you. Did you know that that Bing Crosby song 'White Christmas' is really about Christmas here in Hollywood? That's why he's *dreaming* of snow, which drops down in thick blankets over on the eastern coast of the US, but never happens in California.

Hopefully, by the time you arrive, Junior will have made his or her appearance. Boy or girl, the tiny new member of the Hopkins family is due early December, probably while you're on the *Queen Mary*, dancing the night away in the beautiful ballroom (which was our medical centre!).

Anyhow, my darlings, keep writing, and see you soon.

Life is good, isn't it?

Your loving daughter,
Dot xxxx

The Truth Behind *Meet Me at Rainbow Corner*
By Fidelis Morgan

RAINBOW CORNER

The American Red Cross Serviceman's Club, Rainbow Corner, was created from merging a Lyons' Corner House and Monico's Restaurant with the offices above them. The building, on the corner of Denman Street, at 23 Shaftesbury Avenue, stood five storeys high with a basement.

The club opened its doors on 11 November 1942 and officially closed on 9 January 1946. In February 1949, a bronze plaque was unveiled marking the site where Rainbow Corner had once stood. But that building was knocked down in the 1960s, and its replacement demolished a few years ago, and today nothing remains to mark the spot.

On the foggy opening day, the directors ceremoniously threw away the key to the front door, demonstrating that, while war continued, Rainbow Corner would never close its doors to US troops stationed in Britain.

Rather like an embassy, the Rainbow Corner American Red Cross Club was essentially a plot of America in central London. Once inside, the constraints of wartime Britain disappeared. There was no rationing. All luxuries were available, including food galore: a constant stream of donuts, chewing gum and cola.

Dinner – consisting of fish or meat, vegetables, potatoes, bread and gravy, followed by dessert made up of pie, pudding, waffles, and even maple syrup – cost 1/-, a shilling.

Unlike other Red Cross Clubs, Rainbow Corner did not provide accommodation, though there was a desk which helped GIs to find lodging with families or in commandeered hotels.

During the latter years of the war, Rainbow Corner operated twenty-four hours a day, seven days a week, providing restaurants and cafés, boxing matches, concerts, movies, tours of London, pinball machines, pool tables and jukeboxes laden with all the latest US hits which were changed weekly. There was also a huge dance hall. Classes were offered in everything from languages and shorthand dictation, through to art, swimming, golf and ballroom dancing. There were people to help you write letters home, and others to do minor bits of mending, including sewing on stripes for the newly promoted. One woman, Ma Irene, famously sewed farthing coins under stripes.

During the last years of WWII, hundreds of thousands of American troops passed through the doors of Rainbow Corner. On its first birthday, over 70,000 US servicemen were counted coming in.

Rainbow Corner was staffed by retired American military and British workers. All they needed for entry was a US uniform. British uniforms could only come in by personal invitation of an American serviceman, and the areas they could visit were limited.

While every transatlantic ship was carrying troops over for D-Day, bringing American women and civilians was near impossible. As a result, the club's staff was 80 per cent British.

A sample month, October 1943, saw 470 British workers paid for a usual working day in the club. British workers spent an average of twenty to forty hours a week there. That same month, 312 British volunteers worked 5,774 hours. Many of the staff divided their time between work in nursing or the WVS and volunteering at Rainbow Corner. To gain entry to the club, British workers were issued papers and an American Red Cross lapel pin.

Radio broadcasts were made from Rainbow Corner and beamed everywhere American troops were stationed.

Actors and musicians including James Stewart, Bette Davis, Bebe Daniels, Fred Astaire, Irving Berlin, George Raft, Kim Hunter, Glenn Miller and Artie Shaw visited or performed at the club, as did local child star, Petula Clark. Fred Astaire's dancing sister, Adele (by then, having married a British aristocrat, Lady Charles Cavendish) worked the occasional day on the front desk.

Eleanor Roosevelt came in, not only to talk to the American servicemen, but later to advise the British war brides. She was also there, along with John Winant (the American ambassador) and Anthony Eden, on the day Rainbow Corner closed. That day, all the volunteers got a personal letter from her with an enamel pin.

GIS

'Overpaid, oversexed and over here,' goes the saying. More than two million American servicemen passed through the United Kingdom to fight alongside the Allies in WWII. They were paid roughly five times the amount received by their British counterparts, which caused much resentment. They were also provided luxurious home comforts, like chewing gum, cola, donuts and hearty meals, while British servicemen subsisted on meagre rations. Free theatre tickets to West End shows and invitations to tour Parliament and other national buildings were doled out to them. For the first few years, hardly any GIs, save pilots, saw any military action, and many of them felt they had been called up under false pretences. But American soldiers, pilots, marines and sailors played a major role in the D-Day landings and the subsequent push to Berlin.

HOSTESSES AT RAINBOW CORNER

A voluntary job, part of the war effort, hostesses at Rainbow Corner were British girls, strictly vetted and chosen for looks and charm. They were expected to know all the regular ballroom dances as well as the latest crazes like the jive and jitterbug. Hostesses could be called on to dance five nights a week. Approximately seventy-five women worked as hostesses during the Rainbow Corner years.

BABY BLITZ

Also known as Operation Steinbock, the Baby Blitz of early 1944 was a German offensive aimed at London.

Though they frequently missed their targets, German planes dropped hundreds of bombs over London, Kent, Essex and Sussex.

London was first hit on the night of 21–22 January, when, after a long lull in bombing, two waves of bombers flew over central London, hitting the bell tower of Westminster and buildings in Whitehall and the Strand. A week later the London docks and Stoke Newington took the rap. A few days after that, Hackney and Wimbledon were badly hit. Between 18 and 21 February, Hampstead, Kensington, Putney,

Whitehall, Battersea, Chelsea, Lancaster Gate, Downing Street and Highgate suffered substantial damage. Then another calm descended, Operation Steinbock was over, and London once again had some respite from nightly bombings.

V-1S AND V-2S

After the humiliation of D-Day, Nazi Germany was spurred to revenge, and let loose a new terrifying weapon, the unmanned, self-propelled V-1, and later, the even more powerful V-2 bombs. V-1s were mini pilotless planes, known as buzz bombs or doodlebugs, which caused substantial damage and fear across London. Laden with 850 kg of high-grade explosive, they made a sound like a rickety motorbike. When the noise cut out, the bomb tumbled from the sky, destroying the area where it landed. V-2s carried more explosive and gave no warning sound. Dropping silently from the sky, they caused immediate devastation. During the few short months they were deployed, the V-1 and V-2 bombs killed 5,475 and seriously injured 16,000 more.

DONUT DOLLIES

Later in the war, American girls, nicknamed Donut Dollies, travelled across the Atlantic to join the war effort. As the Allied troops swept over Europe, American Red Cross Clubmobiles followed, staffed by the Donut Dollies, providing hot coffee, razors, toothbrushes and toothpaste and (of course) donuts to GIs behind the lines. (Donut Dollies were essentially a cheerier version of *Mother Courage*!)

VE DAY

After almost six years of terror, deaths, suffering and privation, when Churchill declared a national holiday of celebration with the words 'Advance, Britannia! Long live the cause of freedom', everyone in Britain was ready to celebrate.

The party started the night before and continued for around forty-eight hours, during which the streets of London were jammed with servicemen and -women, and civilians letting loose after years of fear and loss. Contrary to current popular belief, Union Jacks weren't the only flags strung over buildings and streets. In photos and movie reels you can clearly see a flurry of American, Norwegian, French, Czech, Polish, Australian, Scottish, Welsh and Soviet flags.

In the area around Rainbow Corner, where the crowds were most dense, bonfires were lit, and conga lines snaked through the crowds.

WAR BRIDES

During World War II, around 100,000 British women married American servicemen. From early 1946 they moved to the USA to join their husbands.

Due to transportation problems, GI brides were left in the UK for many months after the end of the war. Most of their husbands had departed early in 1945.

It was deemed essential to get the men home first, but, once that was achieved, their wives were all but forgotten.

Exceedingly frustrated at being left behind, many of them now with infants to look after, the wives loudly and successfully lobbied and, with the passing of the US War Brides Act of 28 December 1945, ships were finally commissioned to transport the wives and their children across the Atlantic.

Everything was done to warn the women not to get their hopes too high. In lectures, wives were advised that 'the clinging vine is wonderful now, but she has to be strong enough to take what is coming'.

Trains carrying the war brides to the British ports departed from Waterloo Station, where all farewells were to be made. After that, no friends or family members were allowed to make contact again until after the women arrived in the States.

Most of the stories used in this novel were taken from real accounts by war brides, while details of Dot's story were taken from the thousands of letters, notebooks and diaries written between my own mother and her American pals. Aged just under eighteen, she signed up as a Royal Navy VAD in Liverpool, subsequently serving on US troop ships in Mediterranean campaigns at Salerno and Anzio. She was three times engaged to GIs, all of whom were killed – one in 1942, the other two during the last few months of the war. It's startling to realise that, by the age of twenty-four, an entire generation came to think it quite usual to lose multiple fiancés, lovers and friends to sudden, frequently violent, death.

Unlike in film and TV dramatisations, the bad news usually didn't come via a knock on the door and a telegram boy or senior officer, but by one of their own letters coming back bleakly stamped 'Deceased – return to sender'.

My mother never did forget those wartime Yanks, though, and still talked fondly of them up to her own death in 2001, aged seventy-nine.

TIDWORTH CAMP

Immigration formalities for the GI brides were carried out in a disused army barracks at Tidworth Camp, just outside Salisbury. American soldiers presided, but the serving staff were German prisoners of war.

The GIs in charge were resentful of the women, feeling that they should have been repatriated first, knowing that they had been left behind expressly to supervise the exodus of the war brides.

Compulsory medical exams at Tidworth provoked much wrath among the women. One by one they were expected to turn up bare, but for a bathrobe. Then, before a gang of men, they had to drop the robe to the floor and stand naked while the men prodded and poked, shone torches into their private parts and generally manhandled them. If they tried it today, the US medical authorities would probably be done for assault!

Once the brides passed the dubious medical, provided the appropriate paperwork, had their passport stamped, handed over the cash allowance of £15 (which was converted into dollars) and turned in their ration books, they were bussed directly from the camp to waiting ships.

RMS *QUEEN MARY*

In 1940, luxury liners had been stripped down for use as troop carriers. Immediately after the war the ships plied back and forth across the Atlantic carrying those troops home again.

During the war Winston Churchill travelled to and from the USA by *Queen Mary*. He was always listed under the alias Colonel Warden. He later said that the ship 'shortened the war by a year'.

Having held the record for carrying the highest number of men to Europe and back, the *Grey Ghost* (as *Queen Mary* was dubbed during the war) conveyed more than 10,000 wives and 3,700 children on their journey to a new life in America.

But by the time the wives came on board, conditions on the ship were pretty bad. The *Queen Mary* was still painted grey (though early in 1946 the funnels wore the Cunard red livery again) and the internal fancy furniture had been stripped out. Graffiti covered the walls, ballrooms had been turned into hospitals or dormitories, the swimming pools boarded up.[1]

On top of the discomfort of the stripped-out ship, the wives' crossings encountered rough seas. Many women were terribly seasick for the whole voyage. There were no special provisions for babies' nappies, which had to be washed by hand and hung out to dry wherever space could be found.

RMS *Queen Mary* now stands (in a very sorry state) in dry dock at Long Beach, California. The displays on board concentrate little on the wonderful way the ship carried troops during the war, zigzagging and outrunning U-boats. Disgracefully, there is no evidence whatsoever on the sad old ship that she also transported black American stars like Ella Fitzgerald, Count Basie and Duke Ellington, who voyaged on *Queen Mary* to perform in England during and after the war. They all travelled first class, with no racial segregation, and wrote fondly about their experience on board.[2]

On the other hand, the current owners of the *Queen Mary* seem star-struck by those Hitler-supporting narcissists, Edward 'abdication' Windsor and his American wife, Wallis Simpson, whose photos are plastered all over the place.

Shame on *Queen Mary*'s owners of the last twenty years for letting the ship fall into such disrepair, and shame on them too for celebrating that treacherous ex-royal couple, rather than the true stars who came to boost a wilting country's morale in the time of its greatest hardship.

ARRIVAL IN NYC

The arrival of the GI brides became a major US newspaper story: 'Here Come the Brides', rang out the headlines.

[1]Renovations bringing the ship back into passenger service only started after the last wives were transported.

[2]Much more information about those passengers and their voyages on board *Queen Mary* can be found on illuminating placards on the lower decks of Cunard's *Queen Mary 2*.

At immigration (and throughout their passage), the women, many with children in tow, were obliged to wear name labels and were reclaimed in the same manner as at a cattle auction. A name was called, the woman stood forward, the man claimed you … or not.

Many women were left unspoken for by men who believed England was a toytown country, therefore their marriage was invalid. Some men, once home, had married American women, forgetting they had an English wife, while others had taken out one-sided divorces without even letting their British wives know.

One woman whose husband didn't turn up to the wife-claiming circus was questioned on live radio: 'Where's your husband?'

'God knows,' she replied, 'but wherever he is, I'd like to break his neck.'

His family heard the broadcast and never forgave her.

RECEPTION IN AMERICA

The brides had been warned in talks at Rainbow Corner that US citizens might not welcome immigrants, or understand that English women dressed like they did only because they had suffered years of clothes rationing and 'make do and mend'. Fashionable and stylish Americans regarded the incoming English women in their dowdy, patched clothing as bums – the American word for tramps.

Once in their new homes, many GI brides found it hard to adjust. No one had warned the women about certain things:

1. The sound of a New York fire brigade siren was exactly the same as a British air-raid warning;
2. phrases like 'please knock me up in the morning', 'give me a fag', and 'keep your pecker up' were immoral;
3. in certain households, playing music or the radio on a Sunday was forbidden;
4. saying grace before meals was often expected;
5. they might have a joint bank account with their husband, but were unable to access the money in it;
6. their children were automatically given pocket money but the wife always had to ask for any cash;
7. racial segregation was widespread (see below, 'Segregation in the USA');

8. though most English women were used to outside toilets, they weren't used to having to run through a field of turkeys to reach them.

In the USA, many familiar items were impossible to find, including self-raising flour, scones, crumpets, Capstan cigarettes, Rich Tea biscuits, Yardley and Pears soap, Ovaltine, Tizer, Devon toffees, fish and chips and pantomime.

Many brides were surprised by an American ritual: when a newly-wed couple arrived at the husband's parents' home, they were chased out of the house with a broom.

WAR BRIDES' TRAINS

Familiar through films like *Some Like It Hot*, American trains of the 1940s were glamorous affairs with names to match. But the brides, having been given free travel by the US government, were not put in the deluxe part of the train. They were transported in a separate carriage hooked on to the back of the scheduled services.[3]

East coast trains from New York took the brides north, south and as far west as Chicago, where they had to change to other services, spidering out from that great railway hub to cities on the West Coast, from Seattle in the north-west down to San Diego.

In this book, the two services used are Pennsylvania Railroad's the *Broadway Limited*, and Atchison, Topeka and Santa Fe's celebrated *Super Chief*.

The *Broadway Limited* left New York's Penn Station on track four at 5 p.m., arriving 907 miles away in Chicago Union Station at eight the following morning. Bedrooms with drawing rooms, a dining car and buffet-lounge-observation car were carried by diesel locomotive through Newark, NJ; Trenton, NJ; Philadelphia, PA; Harrisburg, PA; Pittsburgh, PA; Fort Wayne, IN and Gary, IN.

The Super Chief, dubbed the 'Train of the Stars' as it carried so many movie actors back and forth to Hollywood, left Chicago's Dearborn Station at 7.15 p.m., travelling 2,227.3 miles to arrive in Los Angeles

[3]These days you can still see the occasional private carriage linked to the back of normal Amtrak trains.

on the morning of the third day. Its locomotive was a slant-nosed, sleek diesel-electric train. Like the *Broadway Limited*, the *Super Chief* was deluxe, with facilities including bars, lounge and observation carriages, a barber shop, and cafeteria and dining cars, which served food on real china. They even provided valet and maid services including shoeshines and manicures.

The route included official station stops at Kansas City, MO; Newton, KS; Dodge City, KS; La Junta, CO; Raton, NM; Las Vegas, NM; Albuquerque, NM; Gallup, NM; Winslow, AZ; Seligman, AZ; Needles, CA; Barstow, CA; San Bernardino, CA; Pasadena, CA; and final stop, Union Station Los Angeles.

Similar original locomotives and carriages can be seen in all their splendour in the wonderful California Railroad Museum at Sacramento.

MI5

At the start of the war, the British Security Services operated from Wormwood Scrubs Prison. After September 1940, when the former prison was bombed, the main operation moved to Blenheim Palace. Sometime after that, the serious business, decoding et cetera, was centred in the now famous HQ at Bletchley Park.

But decoding wasn't everything.

Various officers stayed in London, working from the MGM film company's former offices in St James's Street. The building, disguised by dusty windows and a large 'TO LET' sign, provided the HQ for other activities: surveillance of suspected traitors and Nazi sympathisers, and working up misinformation. Information was deliberately leaked implying the invasion of Europe would start from the Kent coast, with Allied landings around the Pas-de-Calais. That particular exercise included constructing inflatable tanks and cardboard planes in Kent fields, so that enemy reconnaissance planes would believe that troops and weapons were being assembled in the south-east, ready to launch over that narrow stretch of the English Channel rather than from the south coast.

The London counterintelligence departments spent much of their time luring Nazi sympathisers into groups, recording and transcribing their conversations, tracking down those who were passing on information about troop movements, and searching for people who committed minor acts of sabotage, like cutting lines to phone boxes so that ARP wardens could not communicate.

Although the 1940 Treachery Act suggested the death penalty for such traitors and saboteurs, there were very few hangings. Usually, suspects were simply kept under observation. Where possible, the Security Service intercepted serious information leaks before they were transmitted to Germany or replaced them with misinformation.

In February 2014, almost sixty years after the end of WWII, a large batch of MI5 files detailing low-level spying cases were finally declassified and released to the public domain. It is believed that many more files remain classified, hidden away deep in the archives of MI5, perhaps never to be released.

The 2014 haul suggests that most of the spies targeted by British counter-espionage went unpunished. Some of the spies and Nazi sympathisers never even knew they had been rumbled, and died believing that they got away with it.

Many fifth columnists had links to the BUF and the January Club.

BRITISH FASCISTS AND THE JANUARY CLUB

Oswald Mosley and his British Union of Fascists is well known to followers of *Peaky Blinders*. Flourishing in the 1930s, the BUF was popular with certain right-wing supporters of the Nazis, attracting both the working class and aristocrats.

The January Club was an elite branch of Mosley's group. They wore enamel swastika pins hidden under their lapels.

In the 1930s, members held fundraising soirees at the Savoy Hotel. Their glamorous social events were covered by the *Tatler*. Once war was declared their activities went underground.

Prominent members of the January Club included lords, MPs from the Conservative, Unionist and Labour parties, the owner of the *Daily Mail*, the captain of the English cricket team, many directors of high-flying financial institutions, including the Bank of England, and the author Henry Williamson, famed for *Tarka the Otter*. (Tarka the Rotter!)

FRENCH RESISTANCE AND BERTRAM MILLS CIRCUS

Cyril Mills, the owner of the Bertram Mills Circus, always employed many French speakers. When France was invaded in 1940, the circus HQ at 1 Dorset Square, Marylebone, became the centre for the British Special Operations Executive RF (de Gaullist) Division, working closely with the French Resistance. From the circus HQ, Resistance leaders like Jean Moulin planned misinformation as well as the infiltration of France by resistance fighters.

'Life is a circus,' was their motto, 'you have to laugh.'

The renowned mime Marcel Marceau was a distinguished resistance fighter.

Today the Bertram Mills building in Dorset Square is the home of the excellent *Alliance Française*. Many photos, posters, uniforms and other artefacts relating both to the Bertram Mills and the house's role in WWII are on display.

FASCISM IN THE USA AND AMERICA FIRST

In the 1930s a movement with the name America First[4] attracted all kinds of Americans: anti-British, anti-Roosevelt, anti-New Deal, anti-Semites, supporters of Hitler, isolationists and racists of every variety.

One of the men who spurred on the members of America First was national hero, aviator Charles Lindbergh. In the 1930s, while studying aviation in Germany, Lindbergh flirted with the Nazis, sat in the box with Hitler at the 1936 Olympic Games and, in 1938, received a medal, the Service Cross of the Order of the Golden Eagle, from Hermann Göring himself.

After the attack on Pearl Harbor, Lindbergh's association with Nazism destroyed his reputation.

British intelligence services broke down supporters of America First into six groups:

1. Chicago big business (the most important),
2. Republicans and opposers of the New Deal,
3. Pacifists like Quakers, intellectuals and philosophers,
4. Extreme left-wing opposers to Roosevelt,

[4]Newly minted by Donald Trump.

5. Anti-Semitic fascists, particularly among retired generals and ex-servicemen,
6. 'Emotional mothers'.

This book includes a member of group 5, a retired general.

SEGREGATION IN THE USA

In 1940s America, segregation was widespread. When GI brides saw fountains and restrooms called 'Coloured' for the first time, they imagined they would issue coloured water or be painted in bright colours. Official segregation based on the colour of a person's skin was unknown in the UK.

British pub owners were furious when American commanding officers ordered them to make separate rooms or have different nights for Black and white soldiers. As a revolt, the publicans frequently put up signs that said 'Black GIs only'.

In the USA it was different, especially in the south where Black people were obliged to use separate hotels, bars, cinemas and lavatories.

In many areas of the US, including the north, realtors (estate agents) frequently had a clause in their contracts: 'The said lot may not be resold to a coloured person, a Polander, an Italian or a Jew,' while rental landlords forbade couples who had interracially married to inhabit their buildings.

And although in Britain mixed marriage could be a social problem, it was not illegal as it was in many areas of the USA.

NATIVE AMERICAN CODE TALKERS

Around 25,000 Native Americans, one in eight men, served in the military during WWII. Code talkers were an elite force who used their tribal languages to transmit messages live from battlefields and behind the lines. The codes worked up from native languages were never penetrated by enemy forces.

The most celebrated code talkers worked in the Pacific, but there were smaller groups who took part in the European theatre, D-Day landings and subsequent campaigns.

Records are slim, as their work was strictly verbal, and their deployment highly classified. In fact, the work of the Native American code talkers has been so badly overlooked that the *first* Congressional Medals weren't awarded until 2001.

After several failed attempts, a new museum dedicated to the code talkers is currently planned to be built on a 300-acre site on the New Mexico/Arizona border.

THE NAVAJO ENEMY WAY CEREMONY

The Navajo Enemy Way Ceremony, otherwise called the Squaw Dance, is still a ceremony performed for soldiers who have recently seen active service. The intention is to restore the soldiers to a state of balance and beauty within the universe (a state known as Hózhó).

The powwow is led by those who have been in any conflict, the chiefs wearing the traditional feather bonnet, behind them dancers and musicians. The American flag, the American Eagle Staff, the flags of their tribe and other banners are carried. Music is provided by members of the tribes beating on a large drum. The large powwow drums, usually made from a large cedar-wood base topped with stretched cow, buffalo, or deer hide, are at least 20 inches in diameter and played by several drummers at the same time, frequently simultaneously singing and chanting.

SOURCES

Below are some of the works consulted in the writing of *Meet Me at Rainbow Corner*, for further reading.

London ARC Light (weekly publication of the American Red Cross, various dates 1943–45)

The Story of Rainbow Corner – Verbon F. Gay

At His Side: The Story of the American Red Cross Overseas in World War II – George Korson

War Brides of World War II – Elfrieda Berthiaume Shukert & Barbara Smith Scibetta

Blackouts to Bright Lights – Barbara Ladouceur & Phyllis Spence

Promise You'll Take Care of My Daughter – Ben Wicks

Good-bye, Piccadilly: British War Brides in America – Jenel Virden

USA No. 10 – a handbook to help Brits understand America, foreword by Franklin Delano Roosevelt

Good Housekeeping – A War Bride's Guide to the USA, 1945

Illustrated London News, 1943–46

The Sketch, 1943–46

The Sphere, 1943–46

The Stars and Stripes Magazine, 1943–46

Red Cross Courier, 1944–46

Red Cross News, 1944–46

Over Here

Blighty Magazine, 1939–1945

Wives Aweigh, February 1946

Newspapers.com

Chronicling America – The Library of Congress Historic American Newspapers

British Newspaper Archive
Hitler's British Traitors – Tim Tate
Hitler's American Friends – Bradley W. Hart
Agent Jack: The True Story of MI5's Secret Nazi Hunter – Robert Hutton
The Battle of London 1939–45 – Jerry White
Citizens of London – Lynne Olson
The London County Council Bomb Damage Maps 1939–1945 – Laurence Ward
A to Z Atlas and Guide to London and Suburbs – Phyllis Pearsall
20th Century Day by Day – Sharon Lucas
Top Secret Files: World War II – Stephanie Bearce
V2 – Robert Harris
Native American Code Talker in World War II – Ed Gilbert
Native American Code Talkers – M. M. Eboch
The British Army 1939–41 – Martin Brayley, Osprey
US Army Air Force – Gordon L. Rottman, Osprey
The US Navy in World War II – Mark Henry, Osprey
The US Army 1941–45 – Philip Katcher, Osprey
Women at War 1939–45 – Jack Cassin-Scott, Osprey
World War II Allied Women's Services – Martin Brayley, Osprey
World War II Allied Nursing Services – Martin Brayley, Osprey
Baillière's Nurses' Complete Medical Dictionary – Hitch & Marshall, 1936
The Royal Naval Medical Service: Administration – Jack Leonard Sagar Coulter, 1954
'L'Esprit de Résistance' – *Le Monde*
Maritime Royalty: The Queen Mary *and the* Cunard Queens
Ships of Splendour – William H. Miller
100 Years of Cruise Ships – William H. Miller
Cunard the Golden Years in Colour – William H. Miller, Anton Logvinenko
Memories of Mary, RMS Queen Mary *in Pictures, IV & V Interiors* – Thomas Cornwall
RMS Queen Mary: Voices from Her Voyages – Nicole Strickland
Images of America, RMS Queen Mary – Arcadia Publishing
American-Rails.com
streamlinerschedules.com

THANK YOU TO:

The staff at the Imperial War Museum and Archive, particularly Debbie
Thomas McAnear at NARA, US National Archives
Staff at RMS *Queen Mary*, Long Beach, California
William H. Miller. Thanks, Bill!
Staff at Musée de la Résistance Azuréenne, Nice, France
Everyone at the Alliance Française London, Los Angeles and Nice
Everyone at the Institute de Français, Villefranche-sur-Mer
Staff at the California State Railroad Museum, Sacramento, CA
Staff at the Military Intelligence Museum, Bedfordshire

Cunard's Entertainment team and Robert Howie. When it was in service during the war, Cunard's ship *Queen Mary*, now out of service and moored at Long Beach, CA, was an integral part of the war effort, carrying GIs and war brides across the Atlantic

The two Joes in Hollywood, for giving us Dot's new home

Cyril, Raymond, JF and their équipes at Le Safari and La Civette du Cours, who always gave us a warm welcome at the end of the working day

Caroline Cointat who got me dancing again

Lina Vieira for being our angel guardienne

Paul O'Grady who sadly never made it to the denouement

Sally Lindsay, who spurred us on at the start

Lynda La Plante, always there with advice and encouragement

and

The much-missed Fidelis Morgan senior, without whose wartime letters and diaries this book would neither have captured our imaginations, nor been enriched with so many surprising details.

A NOTE ON THE AUTHOR

Celia Imrie is an actress, winner of an Olivier Award and nominated for a Screen Actors Guild Award. She is known for her roles in *The Best* (and *Second Best*) *Exotic Marigold Hotel, Calendar Girls, Nanny McPhee, Bridget Jones's Diary, Absolutely Fabulous, Finding Your Feet, Mamma Mia! Here We Go Again, Good Grief, Better Things* and *The Diplomat*. Along with the memoir *The Happy Hoofer*, she is the author of the top ten *Sunday Times* bestselling novels in the Nice Trilogy – *Not Quite Nice, Nice Work (If You Can Get It)* and *A Nice Cup of Tea* – *Sail Away* and *Orphans of the Storm*.

@CeliaImrie

A NOTE ON THE RESEARCHER

Fidelis Morgan is the historical researcher on Celia's novels. She is an actress, writer and director, and the author of several non-fiction books. She has lectured around the world from Stanford to the University of Utrecht and was Granada Artist-in-Residence at University of California. Her four historical mysteries have been translated into many languages.

www.fidelismorgan.com

A NOTE ON THE TYPE

The text of this book is set in Adobe Caslon, named after the English punch-cutter and type-founder William Caslon I (1692–1766). Caslon's rather old-fashioned types were modelled on seventeenth-century Dutch designs, but found wide acceptance throughout the English-speaking world for much of the eighteenth century until replaced by newer types towards the end of the century. Used in 1776 to print the Declaration of Independence, they were revived in the nineteenth century and have been popular ever since, particularly amongst fine printers. There are several digital versions, of which Carol Twombly's Adobe Caslon is one.